A NOVEL

Joseph Flynn

Stray Dog Press, Inc.
Springfield, IL
2013

PRAISE FOR JOSEPH FLYNN AND HIS NOVELS

"Flynn is an excellent storyteller." — *Booklist*

"Flynn propels his plot with potent but flexible force."
— *Publishers Weekly*

Digger
"A mystery cloaked as cleverly as (and perhaps better than) any John Grisham work." — *Denver Post*

"Surefooted, suspenseful and in its breathless final moments unexpectedly heartbreaking." — *Booklist*

The Next President
"*The Next President* bears favorable comparison to such classics as *The Best Man, Advise and Consent* and *The Manchurian Candidate*."
— *Booklist*

"A thriller fast enough to read in one sitting."
— *Rocky Mountain News*

The President's Henchman (A Jim McGill Novel)
"Marvelously entertaining." — *ForeWord Magazine*

ALSO BY JOSEPH FLYNN

The Concrete Inquisition
Digger
The Next President
Farewell Performance
Gasoline, Texas
Hot Type

The Jim McGill Series
The President's Henchman
The Hangman's Companion
The K Street Killer
Part 1: The Last Ballot Cast
Part 2: The Last Ballot Cast
The Devil on the Doorstep
Short Cases 1-3, Three McGill Short Stories

Round Robin
Pointy Teeth
Blood Street Punx
One False Step
Still Coming
Still Coming Expanded Edition
Tall Man in Ray-Bans, A John Tall Wolf Novel
Defiled, A Ron Ketchum Mystery
Hangman, A Western Novella

Published by Stray Dog Press, Inc.
Springfield, IL 62704, U.S.A.

Originally published as an eBook, November, 2011
First Stray Dog Press, Inc. Printing, August, 2013

Visit the author's web site: *www.josephflynn.com*

Flynn, Joseph
Nailed / Joseph Flynn
420 p.
ISBN 978-0-9837975-1-7
eBook ISBN 978-0-9830312-7-7

Printed in the United States of America

PUBLISHER'S NOTE
This is a work of fiction. Names, characters, places, and incidents are either the product of the author's imagination or are used fictitiously; any resemblance to actual persons, living or dead, events, or locales is entirely coincidental.

Book design by Aha! Designs

DEDICATION

This book is dedicated to my aunts
Mary Zydowsky, Pat Flynn and Judy Flynn,
and my uncle Tom Flynn

ACKNOWLEDGEMENTS

Doug Updike, Senior Wildlife Biologist, retired
California Department of Fish and Game

Sheila Stanton
Tahoe-Douglas Chamber of Commerce

NAILED

CAST OF CHARACTERS

Ron Ketchum, Police Chief, Goldstrike
Oliver Gosden, Deputy Police Chief, Goldstrike
Lauren Fells Gosden, wife of Deputy Chief Gosden
Daniel Gosden, only child of Oliver and Lauren Gosden
Reverend Issac Cardwell, homicide victim
Clay Steadman, Mayor of Goldstrike
Annie Stratton, Press Secretary to Mayor Steadman
Michael and Adeline Walsh, founders of Goldstrike, 1849
Casimir Stanley, Police Sergeant, Goldstrike
Mahalia Cardwell, mother of Reverend Issac Cardwell
Charmaine Cardwell, wife of Rev. Issac Cardwell
Jimmy Thunder [aka Jimmy Leverette], televangelist
Walt Ketchum, father of Ron Ketchum, retired LAPD
Leilani Ketchum, actress and ex-wife of Ron Ketchum
Marcus Martin, lawyer for Jimmy Thunder
Corrie Knox, Warden, California Department of Fish & Game
Tucker Marsden, Warden, California Department of Fish & Game
DiDi DuPree, ex-con compatriot of Rev. Thunder
Francis Horgan, Special Agent, head of San Francisco FBI

CHAPTER 1

Friday

The two cops, both ex-LAPD, cruised the California Sierra and talked about crime and race. Crime, in this case, consisted of public drunkenness outside a new bar, a floating poker game run by a professional gambler, and a small but disturbing spike in the number of burglary calls. Race consisted of black and white.

The early morning sky was a rain-scrubbed blue and the mountain scenery was some of the most magnificent in the United States, but they noticed it only in passing. They were looking for — but not expecting — breaches of the peace. Finding none, their conversation flowed without impediment.

"Skin color matters," Deputy Chief Oliver Gosden said from the passenger seat.

"Yeah," Chief Ron Ketchum agreed. "Mostly because people won't let it alone."

"Some people *can't* let it alone."

The chief wasn't about to get into that. Instead, he asked, "You know the ultimate proof of racial equality? Rednecks come in all colors."

"Maybe so. But you know one advantage of being a minority in this country? There are fewer assholes who look like me than look like you."

"You saying I look like an asshole?" the chief replied.

Ron Ketchum had once saved Oliver Gosden's life at the risk of his own. Gosden had once saved Ketchum's reputation at the cost of his job.

The chief was forty-eight years old, six-two, with a lean, hard frame. He had dark brown hair and hazel eyes. He was white. The deputy chief was thirty-seven years old, five-ten, and still had the densely muscular build of the heavyweight collegiate wrestler he'd been at the University of Iowa. He still carried himself like a jock, too. One who could pin the whole world to the mat, if need be. He was black.

"Nah, not an asshole," Oliver said. "White devil slave-master, maybe."

Ron gave him a look. "The shit I put up with."

As the sun climbed over the mountaintops that Friday in the second week of August, the two top law enforcement officers of the town of Goldstrike were on their weekly patrol. Serving and protecting. Keeping their jurisdiction safe. Their aggregate blood pressure was sixty points lower than it ever had been in Los Angeles.

Goldstrike was perched in an alpine valley six thousand feet up in the mountains the colonial Spaniards had named the Snowy Range. The centerpiece of the affluent resort town was Lake Adeline whose pristine waters ranged in color from sapphire to emerald. The setting for this liquid jewel was a twelve mile long shoreline gilded with a chain of manicured estates, four-star hotels, and immaculately kept public parks and beaches. The outskirts of town climbed high up the sea of majestic evergreens that covered the slopes of the mountains. A half-dozen ski resorts stood as sentinels above the town, their slopes descending through the conifers like the spokes of a wheel.

Nature had been lavish in bestowing its wonders on Goldstrike, and the real estate prices had been set accordingly. For the most part, those who lived there had either gotten in early or had made their bundles in high-tech, show biz or some other megabucks profession, and then retreated to "Eden on High," as the town's founder, Adeline Walsh, had described the area in 1849.

Ron said, "As important as color is to some people, it's going to take a back seat real soon to cultural questions."

"What do you mean?" Oliver asked.

"I mean the way the PC types have subverted the idea of assimilation, there's going to be a whole new set of worries to get people's attention."

"Such as?"

"Such as, who do you think the average white guy would rather see move in next door? A black guy who goes to work in the morning, takes his wife and kids to church on Sunday, and watches the NBA Finals? Or a blue-eyed Caucasian Afghan who's a former member of the Taliban and wants to shoot up the white guy's stereo system, not because he's playing it too loud, but because the new neighbor interprets the Koran as forbidding recorded music?"

The deputy chief snorted. "I think if *either* of those guys moves into a white neighborhood, 'For Sale' signs get posted on every lawn on the block."

Ron sighed. "Okay, let's try it this way. *You're* the black guy who goes to work every morning, takes your wife and son to church on Sunday, and, for some reason, follows NCAA wrestling." Which described Oliver to a T. "Now, another black family moves in next door. Only they practice Santerîa. Worships several gods. Believes in casting spells and conducting animal sacrifices. Right there in the yard next to yours." Out of the corner of his eye, Ron saw Oliver frown. "And lets say your boy, Danny, comes up to you one Sunday and says, 'Pop, I don't feel like singing in the church choir anymore. I want to go over to the neighbor's place and cut up a goat.' What do you think is going to matter to you, the new neighbor's color or his culture?"

"They're *both* important."

"Okay. But wouldn't you rather have another hard-working, church-going college wrestling fan next door even if he were — oh, my God — white?"

Oliver grimaced, conceding silently that Ron had a point.

He would have offered a rebuttal, but the chief had just guided their police department Ford Explorer onto the Tightrope, a narrow two lane isthmus of blacktop in a sea of blue sky. To their left was a spectacular view of Lake Adeline. To their right was a staggering vista of mountain wilderness. Neither view was obstructed by a guardrail. For the next quarter mile, only a steady hand kept them on the road. The fall-off on each side was steep enough to launch a hang glider. Which more than a few loons did. Illegally.

The speed limit on the Tightrope was ten miles per hour. The deputy chief thought it should be cut in half — if people had to use the damn thing at all.

Ron looked over at Oliver with a grin. "I thought you had something more on your mind."

"Keep your eyes on the road!" the deputy chief ordered. Oliver was tough-minded, fearless in most cases, but he was a devout flatlander who'd lived the majority of his life on the mostly level plane of the L.A. Basin. He'd moved to the mountains only because he'd needed the job Ron Ketchum had offered him, and he saw it as the stepping-stone to his own chief's spot someday.

Ron gave his deputy chief a mock salute, and did as he was told.

"I haven't run off this road yet, Oliver," he said. "Haven't asked you to drive it, either. But someday, most likely, you will have to make the trip on your own. Maybe at night. In the rain or snow. Maybe with a big truck in the oncoming lane. What are you going to do then?"

Ron completed the crossing, and Oliver heaved a sigh of relief as the comforting bulk of a mountainside loomed to his right. Ron grinned again. Oliver gave him a look that had put many a wrestling opponent at an immediate disadvantage.

The two men might have pulled each other's ass out of the fire once upon a time, but there were definitely times when each felt stuck with the other.

"I'll tell you what I'll do," the deputy chief said. "I'll aim straight down the middle of that sucker, turn on my lights and siren, and everybody else better pull the hell over."

The chief laughed. "Toss 'em over the side, huh?"

"Bet your ass."

"Maybe I'll just keep driving then." Ron gave it a beat and then picked up the main thread of the conversation. "It's your in-laws, isn't it? Didn't they just leave town?"

"Yeah, it's them," Oliver said glumly. "And, thank God, they're gone."

"Did Warren and Loretta finally do something unfortunate? Tip you for bringing them a drink or something."

"You're a funny man," the deputy chief said dryly. "You ever retire from police work, you could do stand-up comedy."

Neither rank nor race kept either man from speaking freely when they were alone. Protocol was strictly for public situations. You laid your life or your livelihood on the line for the other guy, that was how it went.

"Come on, Oliver. I know you're not a cracker. Can it really be that bad having a white mother-in-law and father-in-law? They must have done a pretty terrific job raising Lauren, back there in Iowa, the way you love her."

Lauren Fells Gosden was the deputy chief's beautiful and adored black wife. She'd been abandoned as an infant by her fourteen-year-old birth mother and given a home by Warren and Loretta Fells, shortly before such adoptions had been labeled "cultural genocide" by black social workers.

"They're fine people," the deputy chief said of the Fells, "I know that. And I know what'd happen to me if I ever said one bad word about Lauren's parents in front of her." A small shudder passed through Oliver at the thought, and he fell silent. But his jaw muscles kept working. Finally, he said, "They told Daniel last night that skin color doesn't matter. Warren sat my boy right up on his lap, looked him in the eye, and said skin color just does *not* matter. What counts is who you are inside."

Ron started to speak, but Oliver cut him off. "And don't go

telling me he was only paraphrasing Dr. King."

The chief shook his head. "I was just wondering if Danny maybe had asked his grandpa why the two of them are different colors. A six year old might think of something like that."

The sharp look Oliver shot Ron told him he'd scored a bull's-eye. Content that he understood the situation, the chief didn't push it. Just kept his eyes on the road as the Explorer entered a series of descending S-curves.

Undaunted by this road feature, the deputy chief continued to speak his mind. "That's not the only thing," he said.

"What else?" Ron asked.

"Lauren came out with a new button."

The deputy chief's wife, a surgical nurse, liked to express herself in epigrams that she put onto buttons. She'd pin a given button to her blouse or her blue scrubs until she decided the message had been seen and digested by a large enough audience. It was a low-key method of preaching, a part of Lauren's charm.

"What's this one say?" Ron asked.

"It's one of her cheerleader series."

"Yeah?"

"It says: *2-4-6-8, I don't want to hyphenate.*"

"She doesn't want to be a writer-director?" asked the former L.A. cop.

The deputy chief ignored the gibe. "She doesn't want to be called an African-American. The bottom of the button says: *Just call me an American.*"

Ron thought about it for a moment and nodded.

"Ask her if she's got one for me, will you?"

Oliver turned to Ron and said, "This is serious shi—"

The deputy chief suddenly had to throw his hands against the dashboard as Ron braked sharply. A rush of icy fear filled Oliver as he felt sure they were about to skid over a precipice and plunge to their deaths. When he looked up he saw death, all right. Not the prospect of his own, but still horrifying.

"Jesus Christ," Ron Ketchum whispered.

"Got that right," Oliver agreed.

There, just ahead of them, adjacent to the last curve in the road, was the body of a nearly naked black man. He was stretched out against the charred trunk of a lightning-struck tree, a big incense cedar. He'd been nailed to it.

Crucified.

CHAPTER 2

Mary Kay Mallory breathed deeply but easily, one part of her large, luminous mind measuring her footfalls against her heart rate, another part doing quick scans of her muscles, from the toes to scalp, for any sign of cramping. When you ran alone at 6,000 feet elevation, you had to be aware of how oxygen deprivation could affect your body. It wouldn't do at all to have her quads or calves knot up unexpectedly and leave her writhing in the roadway, just as a group of happy campers from Marin County came barreling around a curve in their Cadillac Escalade.

No, no, no. She had too much to live for.

At thirty-five, Mary Kay was the owner and chief designer of HeraSoft, the fastest rising computer game company for girls and young women in the country. She was worth twenty million dollars already, and could add hundreds of millions more if she decided to take her company public. But she didn't think she would do an IPO. Not any time soon. The money wasn't worth the meddling outsiders that came with it.

If she sold out, she'd probably have to leave Goldstrike and move the company back to San Francisco, or even set up shop in — yuck! — Silicon Valley. Most of the guys in the valley made Bill Gates look like George Clooney. And if a lot of them were rich and getting richer, so what? So was she. San Francisco was still a great town, her hometown in fact, but … she'd been stalked there.

A guy she'd hired as a sales rep and then declined to date

— because you had to be nuts to be anything but polite and professional with a co-worker these days — had refused to take no for an answer. When she'd given him, "You're fired," for an answer, he got weird on her. So weird he followed her everywhere, and one night she came home and found him naked in her bed. Pointing a gun at her. He told her she had to have sex with him. Just once. Then they'd get married. But she could have an uncontested divorce once they'd been together long enough to establish his community property rights. Not terribly romantic, the creep admitted, but she would either go along with his plan or he'd kill her.

Mary Kay had managed to hit the light switch and run screaming from the darkened bedroom, sped on by a hail of gunfire. The guy followed Mary Kay right out of her house. *Naked.* But by this time his gun was empty, and a responsive neighbor broke the maniac's right leg with a baseball bat. The larcenous stalker had been sent away for twelve years for trespassing and attempted murder, but he was appealing both convictions on a number of legal technicalities. With the way the so-called justice system worked these days, you never knew what might happen.

No, she wasn't going back to San Francisco. She was staying right here in these glorious mountains. Where she could run along this empty road in the morning, watch the sun poke through the trees, fill her lungs with the thin but bracing air, and experience the joy of gliding along as her muscles gathered and stretched with fluid ease.

Her buoyant mood was helped by the fact that in the past month she'd met two new men, and had dared to allow each of them to buy her a drink — the first time she'd permitted anything like that in over a year. And, wonder of wonders, neither of them had gone psycho on her. Just the opposite. Each of them was charming, each in his way.

Brad and Carter were both good looking. Neither was pushy, thank God. Brad was about her age; Carter was ten years older. Brad was in the first flush of professional success — not on her scale, of course, but he wouldn't be moving back in with mom and dad any time soon; Carter was starting over after a ruinous divorce, but seemed determined to rebuild his life and not be permanently embittered. Brad was maybe a touch too taken with himself; Carter was a trifle gun-shy.

How to choose, Mary Kay wondered. Or whether to choose at all.

Rounding a curve in the road, she had the uneasy feeling that she was no longer running alone. She looked over both shoulders, but saw no one behind her, and the trees off to either side of the road were too thick for a pursuer to negotiate easily. She listened for the sound of an oncoming runner approaching from beyond the next curve. Nothing. Only the soft whisper of the breeze stirring the trees.

She chided herself for being paranoid. Her stalker was still in prison. He didn't know where she was; and she'd been told she would be notified in advance of any decision to let him out early. Still, for the first time since she'd come to the mountains, she had that old gut-wrenching feeling: she was being followed.

Another survey of her surroundings, however, produced the same negative results. She didn't see a soul. As she approached the upcoming curve, though, her hand went to the canister of pepper spray clipped to the waistband of her running shorts. By leaving San Francisco and moving to Goldstrike, she'd fled as far as she ever intended to flee; she had made a vow that anybody who fucked with her from now on was going to have a fight on his hands. Rounding the curve, she saw no one coming uphill.

Mary Kay took her hand off the pepper spray, and forced herself to relax. Her breathing fell back in synch with her stride. She wondered if she'd ever be able to *really* trust a man again.

That was when the idea for the game hit her: *Sorting 'Em Out.*

She would collect the experiences of hundreds — no, thousands — of bright, successful women. Listen to all the smart moves they'd made with men. All the disastrous ones, too. Define the categories of men available to date. List their pros and cons. Start with a first date. Program male moves. Female countermoves. Add some humor, music, and cool graphics. Offer the chance to commit to, or bail out of, the relationship at any point. Then show the likely results of the choice.

What a great game for young women! All women, really.

Pretty big market.

Might even be a movie if sales—

The bolt of fear struck Mary Kay like an axe between her shoulder blades. There *was* a stalker behind her. She felt it. He was closing in fast. Her throat went dry with fear. She could imagine being dragged into the trees.

She started to sprint, and her right hand closed on the canister of pepper spray.

Then, only two strides into her burst, she heard a deep, guttural grunt. Something stunningly strong hit her, a cluster of razor sharp blades slashed her left shoulder and the back of her neck. The force of the blow spun her around and knocked her off her feet. She came to rest on her bottom and her bloodied elbows.

And there looking down at her, above huge, gleaming fangs, close enough to feel and smell its heated, putrid breath, were the feral yellow eyes of a mountain lion.

The cat snarled and raised a claws-out paw, but it didn't strike. It paused as if unsure as to how it should dispatch prey that met its fearsome gaze and refused to look away.

In that instant of hesitation, it was the woman who struck.

She blasted the beast's eyes, nose and mouth with her pepper spray. The lion howled and backed off, raking her abdomen and thighs as it went. But it didn't run away. It stood not five feet from her shaking its head frantically, trying to rid itself of the effects of the spray.

Mary Kay scrambled to her knees and leaning in as far as she dared emptied the canister in the big cat's face. The animal shrieked with pain, and swiped at her, but partially blinded now, it missed.

Still, the mountain lion didn't run away. It lay flat on its belly and ran its forelegs over its eyes and nose trying to relieve the terrible pain and clear its vision. Mary Kay knew if the cat succeeded it would kill her for sure. But she was out of spray.

So she did the only thing she could think of. She got to her feet, held the canister out at arm's length and hissed to mimic the sound of the stinging spray being released.

That was enough for the mountain lion.

If fled clumsily into the trees from which it had stalked her.

Terrified, bleeding and stiff, Mary Kay Mallory began to run haltingly in the direction from which she'd come. She knew it was a little better than a mile to the scenic overlook where she'd parked her car. She had to make it back there before the cat's senses cleared, before it could regain her scent, before it came for her again.

CHAPTER 3

Ron Ketchum was lucky that Route 99 had a turnout at the point opposite the crucifixion. He moved the Explorer off the road so nobody would come around the curve and rear end them. Oliver called for back-up: cops to keep the traffic moving; Officer Benny Marx, the department's crime scene specialist and Dr. George Ryman, a retired internist, who served *pro bono* as the town's medical examiner. Ron also told the deputy chief to have somebody scrounge up some kind of screen to shield the victim from public view. The sight had jolted two cops with almost thirty-five years of experience between them. If the motoring public came around the bend and saw that corpse, the result might be anything from a vehicular accident to a heart attack to ... well, nightmares were a pretty good bet for anybody who saw this particular body.

Ron got out of the car and noticed the tire marks on the pavement. Somebody else had pulled into the turnout recently, and then taken off fast enough that a fair amount of rubber had been left behind. Ron saw that Oliver had noticed the tire marks, too.

"Killer or just a coincidence?" the chief asked.

"Never met a coincidence in my life," the deputy chief replied. He leaned back into the Explorer and came out with a digital camera. He started taking pictures of the tire marks from several angles. He dropped into a squat and eyeballed the black streaks.

"Nice wide tires. Probably expensive. Kind you find on some

fancy foreign car."

Ron gave Oliver a bleak look as the deputy chief stood up.

"Yeah, I know," Oliver said. "Fat lotta good that'll do us around here."

Goldstrike didn't have the Rolls-Royce density of Beverly Hills, but there were more than enough Range Rovers to make up the difference. And any car that ever raced down a mountain road in a James Bond movie could be found in somebody's garage in town. Unlike Oliver, there were plenty of people in the Sierra who liked to drive fast right out there on the edge of eternity.

"Tell Benny when he gets here to take some samples of that rubber and make some measurements and impressions anyway," Ron said. "Even if the marks are from tires found on something common like a Beemer, it's good to be thorough. You never know when you'll get lucky."

"Right," Oliver agreed, making a note of the instruction.

Then Ron dictated the time they'd found the body, and the weather conditions. Oliver wrote it all down. Back in the City of Angels, the chief had been the homicide detective, the deputy chief had been the street cop.

They crossed the road and saw the two sets of footprints in the rain-softened earth. Both sets had the toes pointing toward the road. Both sets appeared to have been made by the same shoes or boots. But one set of footprints was outlined by a pair of grooves. The chief interpreted the signs.

"The killer dragged the victim to the tree walking backward. Means the poor sonofabitch was was at least incapacitated before he got nailed up. We'll need Benny to make molds of these footprints."

Oliver wrote it down.

"You see any sign anybody else was up here?" Ron asked.

The deputy chief took a long look around. The charred tree rose from a shelf of bare earth that was approximately fifteen feet wide. Just behind it, the land dropped away. Not a cliff exactly, but a steep slope covered with fir trees. Oliver didn't think anyone involved in the crime had arrived or departed that way.

"No," he answered.

"Okay, photograph the footprints from here." After Oliver had taken several exposures, Ron added, "Follow behind me so we disturb the area as little as possible."

The two cops walked over to the corpse, paying careful attention not to step on any possible evidence. Ron saw no signs of blood spatter. If there'd been any, the rain must have washed it away.

The victim was a very dark skinned man. His head rested on his right shoulder. He appeared to be in his mid-to-late twenties. The flesh above the left brow had been laid open to the bone. His arms had been stretched upward with his elbows bent and his wrists twisted to accommodate the curvature of the tree. One nail had been driven through each of his palms. The victim's knees were bent and the sole of his left foot had been place over the instep of his right. A nail had been driven through both feet and into the tree. The victim's toes touched the soil at the base of the dead tree.

The only article of clothing on the body was a pair of pale blue boxer shorts that were stained with urine. A smell of feces indicated that the bowels had also vented. Maybe post-mortem, maybe while the man was still alive.

The victim had been roughly Deputy Chief Gosden's height, but his lean build was more like Ron Ketchum's. There were indentations on either side of the nose, as if the victim had been a long-time wearer of eyeglasses.

Oliver, looking over the chief's shoulder, nodded at the blow to the forehead. "You think the poor sonofabitch was dead before he got stuck to this tree?"

Ron, having a better vantage point, noticed there was a second gash at the crown of the victim's skull. "Looks like he caught another whack up here."

"So, what do you think? The one in back to knock him out, then nail him up, then the one in front to keep him from screaming too loud?"

Ron looked around. The road behind them was the only sign of the twenty-first century. Otherwise, it was a wilderness. He asked, "Who'd hear him scream out here?"

Oliver took an old Zippo lighter out of his pocket and started flicking the top open and shut. A former smoker, he had finally managed to quit last month, with considerable persuasion from his wife and additional coaxing from Ron. Now, the deputy chief played with his lighter whenever he wanted a cigarette.

Ron intended to indulge the nervous tic for another week or two. Then he'd tell Oliver to knock it the hell off; it was driving him crazy.

"You look at his face," Ron said, reconsidering the victim, "it seems there's just too much pain there for him not to know what was happening to him. He might have been dazed, but I think he was alive and aware when he got nailed up."

"Yeah, me too." Oliver snapped the lighter shut sharply, trying to control his rage.

"Can't have happened too long ago. The hands would start to give way; he'd be sagging more. And the coyotes would have started in on him." Ron glanced at Oliver. "You recognize him?"

"No."

"Neither do I."

"Motherfucker," the deputy chief cursed, jamming the lighter back in his pocket.

"Oliver," Ron said, "this doesn't have to be a racial killing."

"It doesn't?" Oliver asked in open disbelief.

"Could have been one black guy killing another."

They'd both seen plenty of that in L.A. But neither had seen a crucifixion before.

The deputy chief was in no mood to debate. He just asked, "You want me to call the mayor now?"

"Oh, yeah," Ron said. "Mayor for Life Steadman won't want to miss this one."

Clay Steadman, a movie icon for forty years, billionaire real estate developer, the town's largest property owner, and the fifth-term mayor of Goldstrike, arrived in his gleaming black Land Rover shortly after Dr. Ryman and the detail of back-up cops had appeared. Nobody, as of the moment, had yet to find a way to screen the corpse from public view, and Officer Benny Marx advised against it regardless, not wanting to take a chance of displacing some subtle piece of evidence.

The chief noted the mayor's arrival and escorted him to the victim along the now well trampled path that everyone had used. The two men arrived at the victim just as Dr. Ryman was making an incision in the man's abdomen, not terribly far, anatomically, from where the Roman soldier's spear had pierced the side of Christ.

"What the hell are you doing, George?" the mayor demanded of the doctor.

Dr. Ryman answered mildly, "Taking his liver temperature to fix the time of death. Problem is, with the rain last night cooling him down, that could be a little tricky."

The physician inserted a probe with a thermometer through the incision he'd just made. The mayor grimaced and looked over his shoulder. He wasn't being squeamish, Ron knew, he was just making sure no townsfolk were approaching to witness the ghastly proceedings. Townsfolk or reporters. But it was still early, and the only witnesses were those who had a professional interest.

The mayor fixed his chief of police with a steely stare known to moviegoers around the world and instructed him in an equally familiar glacial whisper, "I want the bastard who did this."

"Now, there's an idea," Ron responded blandly.

Clay Steadman had hired Ron Ketchum personally, and the chief respected the mayor. But unlike most people, Ron never really cared for Clay's movies, or the way the mayor sometimes lapsed into dialogue from the silver screen.

The mayor's ball-bearing gaze bore down on his chief of police, but he knew if there was one man in town — or anywhere else — he couldn't stare down, it was Ron Ketchum.

"Let me know when you have something," Clay told Ron.

"Yes, sir."

"Nobody's going to do this in my town and get away with it."

More movie dialogue, Ron thought. But he agreed with the sentiment completely. Goldstrike was his town, too.

CHAPTER 4

In January, 1848, a carpenter named James Marshall, originally from New Jersey, was building a millrace for his partner, John Sutter, in California's Coloma Valley when a gleaming pebble approximately half the size of a pea caught his eye. He stooped to pick it up. It was gold. By the fall of that year, gold was being sought and found in California from Tuolumne in the south to the Trinity River in the north — a distance of four hundred miles.

By 1849, word of the discovery of gold in California had spread across the United States and around the world, and the rush was on. In just that first year of the gold rush, more than ninety thousand people heard the news, imagined themselves wealthy, and abandoned their homes and former lives with scarcely a second thought or a backward glance.

And that was just the Americans. Additional thousands poured in from Canada, Mexico, Central and South America, Europe and even Australia.

Most of the gold seekers were the young, adventurous and desperate; an estimated 98% of them were male. A cottage industry of publishing guidebooks on how a traveler might find his way west sprang up. One such publication indicated an overland route from New Orleans to the Sierra that could be traversed in only thirty-six days — when the actual travel time was *two hundred and sixteen days.* Another suggested a southern route through Mexico that crossed "thickly settled country." Instead, it passed through a killing desert and the territory of hostile Apaches. Of the ninety thousand who headed west in 1849, only forty thousand made it to the gold fields. Of those who did make it, 99% didn't find enough gold to cover their expenses. All the best claims had been staked in 1848.

Still, the gold rush, far more than earlier agrarian migrations, was largely responsible for the development of the American West. It was the primary reason for the founding of the city of Denver. It was responsible for the direct admission of California to the Union in 1850, having been ceded to the United States by Mexico in 1848, just after the Sutter's Mill find, but before the word got out. Congress didn't bother with the usual requirement of California becoming a recognized territory first.

Besides finding gold, the other impetus to head west was the opportunity to "mine the miners." At a time when the prevailing wage for a laborer was a dollar a day, jobs digging gold on someone else's claim were being offered at a pay scale of ten to fifteen dollars per day. Simple labor had become a way to strike it at least moderately rich.

A not dissimilar thought occurred to a young man in Chicago when in early 1849 he first heard the news of gold being found. Michael Walsh was, fittingly enough, a journeyman brewer. At the time, Walsh was chafing under the stern direction of his mentor and father-in-law, master brewer Hans Koenig. True, Hans had taught him the marvelous craft of making beer. And Hans had allowed the young man to marry his only daughter, the tall and comely Adeline. And the old *braumeister* had even built a home for his daughter and son-in-law when the first of their three children had been born.

But Michael Walsh and Hans Koenig could not agree on their beer.

Herr Koenig insisted that beer be brewed only one way — the way he had learned. The way German law had decreed beer should be brewed since medieval times. Michael Walsh had no objection to brewing his father-in-law's way. It made a grand beer, right enough. But he, too, came from a country with a proud tradition of brewing and distilling, and anytime Michael tried to brew some fine dark stout, even in his own house, Hans would fly into a rage about "Irish swill," throw all of Michael's wonderful elixir into the street, and threaten to take back his daughter, his grandchildren and the house in which Michael lived.

All of which led Michael Walsh, at age thirty-one, to sell the house his father-in-law had fortuitously put in his name, buy two wagons, four oxen, brewing equipment and all the supplies Adeline insisted upon, bid the bitter Hans farewell and set off for California with his family to brew Irish stout for all those miners, many of them his countrymen, making ten to fifteen dollars a day.

He was sure they were thirsty. He was sure his fortune would soon be made.

The early part of the Walsh's journey was relatively easy. They drove their wagons, in caravan with those of four other families leaving Chicago, across the blessedly flat and relatively settled prairies of Illinois to St. Louis. From there, they enjoyed the comparative comfort of a steamboat ride to Independence, Missouri.

But once in Independence, the place where large parties of migrants formed for the westward push across the vast wilderness, life became a great deal more precarious. The plague of cholera struck. The disease was debilitating at the very least, producing bouts of diarrhea, projectile vomiting of blood and, most commonly, death.

Michael and Adeline were fearful for their family: nearly panicked on the one hand that they would die and leave their children orphans, stranded hundreds of miles from their Chicago home; filled with dread on the other hand that their children would die, leaving them with broken hearts.

To ward off the possibility of disease, the Walshes hit on two strategies. Adeline made sure that each of them was meticulously clean, right down to scraping the dirt from under their fingernails. She'd noticed, growing up, that those people most susceptible to disease and death were invariably the ones who went the longest between baths. Michael's contribution was to soak bandannas in a barrel of his stout that he'd brought along, and then cover the faces of his family with them.

The Walshes' masked countenances soon drew public notice, as did the fact that they remained healthy. Others emulated them, though not many chose to bathe, and Michael even allowed them to dip their bandannas — once they'd been well laundered, at Adeline's insistence — into his barrel of stout. In short order, a party was formed to head west on the Overland Trail, and escape the pestilence of the staging area. The Walshes were among them. Many in the party came by the Walshes' wagons to dip their face masks in the stout again, until they were sure that the danger of contracting cholera was well past.

Not a single migrant in the Masked Man Party, as it came to be called, came down with the dread disease.

Neither did a single migrant come to consider Michael Walsh's stout anything but medicine. It worked just fine for that, thank God. But drink it for pleasure? A substitute for real beer?

"Mister, don't make me laugh," one and all told Michael Walsh.

The gold seekers pushed on through present day Nebraska. Even though the greatest hardships lay ahead, the long journey was beginning to take its toll on the Walsh children, the oldest of whom, Wilhelmine, was only six. Rory and Erik were four and three, respectively.

Adeline did not want to see her children die of exhaustion or depletion of their spirits, not after she'd kept them safe from the cholera. At every trading post along the way, she asked her husband if they might not establish their home there, if he might not make a success of his business there. After all, so many others had set up their businesses and were prospering from selling to the flood of immigrants.

But Michael Walsh was determined to make it to California. He said that's where the greatest concentration of riches lay, and that's where they would go. Unspoken, even to his wife, was his fear that if he didn't find a large gathering of fellow Irishmen with gold in their pockets, he'd never be able to sell the stout he wanted to brew.

So, they pushed on through the treacherous mountain passes of the Rockies and the great, deadly deserts of the West. In Nevada, the sun was so fierce they had to travel at night by torchlight. One morning as the migrant party stopped to rest in the shade of an outcropping of rock, Michael Walsh found his three children with his wife's fingers in their mouths. Their parched little mouths were red. They were suckling on Adeline's blood.

It was moisture, she said. She'd pricked her fingers and was giving her children their mother's strength.

Others in the wagon train sought a less drastic way to slake their thirst and preserve their meager stores of water. They finally came to Michael Walsh for small measures of his stout. But even dying of thirst, they developed no taste for the stuff. This filled Walsh with a dread almost as great as the thought of death.

Finally, eighteen grueling weeks after leaving Independence, Missouri, the Masked Man Party reached the Sierra Nevada, only to find inclines so steep that their wagons had to be broken down and hauled over jagged ridges. But now, even this backbreaking work could not dampen the enthusiasm of the gold seekers. They knew they were near their destination. Just the other side of these mountains was the green, fertile Sacramento Valley where gold lay waiting to be found. They would dig their fortunes — their dreams — right out of the earth.

The Walshes never made it that far.

They were stopped by the epiphany Adeline Walsh experienced when the sparkling majesty of the lake that would later bear her name first filled her eyes. She drew a deep breath, clasped her hands to her heart, and turned to her husband. The words she spoke to him that day were later recorded for posterity.

"Michael, we have found Eden on high." Her next words were less poetic but had far more immediate impact. "This is where we will stay."

Assuming his wife meant where they would rest, fill their

barrels with the crystalline water from the lake, and gather their energies for the final push, Michael did not argue. But by the very next morning he understood clearly that if he were to continue the journey, he would do so alone. On foot.

Adeline felt certain that it was her destiny to live out her days in this place. Michael argued that it was already September, and that if they didn't leave soon, they would be snowbound and no doubt die there. Adeline's response was that she better start felling some trees then, build a cabin and lay in some food.

Michael Walsh was galled to have come so far and be stopped just short of his goal. But try as he might — and try he did — he couldn't imagine going on and leaving his wife and children behind. He was sure he'd be consigning them to their deaths, and even if they were to survive somehow, he'd miss them sorely. Taking pity on her husband without losing a bit of her resolve, Adeline comforted Michael. Then she cajoled him into making a further concession, even more vexing than the last. She talked him into brewing beer her father's way.

Adeline was sure that once word spread about the lake, anyone traveling through these mountains would stop there to replenish their water supplies. Doubtless, many of those who did would like something stronger to drink. She was sure that Michael could brew and sell the beer her father had taught him to make.

With great gentleness, she reminded him that her father's beer was a very good brew.

"And everyone thinks mine is snake oil," Michael Walsh said bitterly.

Hurt to his soul, but still wanting to make his fortune, he reluctantly agreed.

When the remainder of the Masked Man Party was told of the Walshes's decision, they viewed it with suspicion. To a man, they were sure that Michael Walsh had somehow stumbled on to gold. The Miner's Commandment said: *Thou shall not tell any false tales of good diggings.* Meaning don't send your fellow gold-seeker off on a wild goose chase to your own advantage, lest you taste his vengeance.

But Michael Walsh hadn't done that.

Rather, he'd said he was staying because his wife wanted him to stay. With one exception, the other twenty-three gold seekers of the Masked Man Party were bachelors — but even the married man couldn't imagine having come so far, enduring so many hardships, and then stopping just short of your goal solely for the sake of a woman.

In the early days of the gold rush, one of the most alluring tales pulling migrants westward was that of Goldstrike Lake. Legend had it that a prospector had found a beautiful mountain lake where gold was strewn on the shores just waiting to be picked up. Unfortunately, the prospector had died, been killed, some said, before he could file his claim and reveal the lake's whereabouts.

The common suspicion in the Masked Man Party was that Michael Walsh had found those legendary golden shores. So in the name of gratitude for the aid the Walshes had given in the face of the cholera outbreak, the party delayed its departure to help the family fell trees and erect a rough log cabin. Of course, they really stayed to make a collective effort to find the gold that tight-mouthed, want-it-all-for-himself, papist bastard Walsh had blundered upon.

The problem was, the lakeshore was twelve miles long. And with all of the shoreline's inlets and points, there had to be twenty-five miles of ground to explore. More daunting than that, some parts of the shoreline could be reached only by descending sheer cliffs. That or paddling in by canoe. Many a gold seeker in the Masked Man Party tried to worm the secret out of Michael Walsh, but the brewer never let on. Not a word. Just pretended like he didn't know what the hell any of them was hinting at.

The cunning Mick.

Several men took to following Michael Walsh around when he wasn't busy working on his cabin. They watched him fish and hunt. But they couldn't catch him out. He didn't drop the smallest clue as to where he'd made his strike. When he wasn't engaged in providing for his family, he spent most of his free time filling his bucket in the little springs that fed the lake, and then he toted the water home.

Pretty soon, some of the men wanted to beat his secret out of him.

If he hadn't had his wife and children with him, they might have tried.

But as October approached all but one of the party finally decided they had to push on before they became snowbound. As a farewell gift, Michael Walsh gave them a barrel of his new beer — the kind Hans Koenig had taught him to make. The Masked Man Party was delighted with the brew, said it was the best beer they'd ever tasted. Then they rebuked Michael Walsh for not making it earlier. Such good beer certainly would have made crossing the desert less painful.

The Masked Man Party departed drunk, singing and promising to return. They'd be back to have some more beer, and see if Walsh hadn't had a little luck prospecting the area.

Michael Walsh never did. It had never been his intention to prospect. But Timothy Johnson, the gold-seeker who had stayed behind, became a legend.

In the dead of winter, in the middle of a howling blizzard, when the Walshes hadn't set foot outside their cabin for weeks, except to fetch snow to melt for water, and after they'd had to butcher one of their oxen for food, Johnson banged on their cabin door. He'd gone off into the mountains by himself shortly after the others had left, and now he returned covered with snow and in the company of a short Indian woman with a solemn face.

He also had with him a dozen nuggets of gold.

Ranging in size from a raspberry to a baby's fist.

"She led me right to these," Johnson told the wide-eyed Walshes. "She's teaching me her language, and I just know when I understand it better, she's going to take me straight to the mother lode."

The Indian woman said nothing. She didn't speak a word in the four days that she and Timothy Johnson sheltered in the Walshes's cabin.

Before they left, when the blizzard had finally blown out, Johnson grandly traded his twelve nuggets of gold for all the beef and beer he and his female companion could carry. As the two made ready to leave, Johnson thanked the Walshes for their hospitality.

"The next time you see me," he said with a farewell smile, "I'll be a rich man."

But that was the last any white person ever saw of Timothy Johnson or the short Indian woman. The only trace left of him was the gold he'd given Michael Walsh.

Which was more than enough.

In the spring of 1850, several of the Masked Man Party who'd failed to find gold further west returned. Along with them they brought others who'd been similarly unlucky in their search for riches. All of them thought to make one last stab at wealth by prospecting the mountain lake.

Michael Walsh told them he'd named the lake in honor of his wife, Adeline. Nobody was about to debate the point with the man who made the best beer west of St. Louis. They accepted Walsh's decision and the name stuck.

Then Walsh told them the tale of Timothy Johnson. And he showed them the nuggets of gold to prove he was telling the truth. He did the same for the newcomers heading west who were among the tens of thousands caught up in the second year of the rush.

He said he had no idea of where Johnson and the Indian woman had gone or where they'd found the gold. The mystery didn't deter the gold seekers; it fired their imaginations. Just as staring at the twelve nuggets of gold renewed their lust for riches.

The prospectors speculated aloud about what they knew of Tim Johnson, then made whispered plans with favored partners, and then stared some more at the golden nuggets, all while drinking Michael Walsh's wonderful new beer.

By the fall of that year, three hundred men and fourteen women lived in the vicinity of Lake Adeline. Michael Walsh prospered on their thirst. He built a large addition to the original cabin. He established a trading post that sold durable goods hauled in from San Francisco.

Years later, for his own consumption and that of his sons, he brewed Walsh's Private Reserve. The dark stout nobody else would drink.

One hundred and twenty-three years later, a former Navy chief petty officer, trying to make a go of it in civilian life as a bill collector decided to take an acting class in Los Angeles. He didn't aspire to a movie career. He just wanted to improve and diversify his collection technique. Jack up his take-home pay as much as he could.

His name was Clay Steadman.

Steadman had been knocked off his intended career path as a navy lifer after he'd beaten a lieutenant commander to a pulp. He took this drastic action when he caught the officer screwing the wife of one of his men. The sailor had been the first to catch his spouse and his superior in the sack, but had been intimidated by the officer into not filing charges. Instead, the sailor had complained to his chief.

Clay Steadman had never liked the brass in general, and that particular officer was a pustule he'd wanted to squeeze for a long time. In short order, he managed to ambush the officer, timing his entrance to the San Diego motel room to catch the officer and the cheating wife in mid-stroke.

He said to the illicit lovers, "Naughty, naughty."

The woman screamed. After stealing a pillow from her to cover his flagging member, the lieutenant commander promised to court martial the chief petty officer. He ordered Clay Steadman to leave the room immediately, and to confine himself to his quarters.

Chief Steadman considered the situation. "You're fucking the wife of one of my men. When he objects, you threaten to court martial him. Now, I catch you at it, and you threaten to court martial me. Have I got all this right?"

The officer arrogantly assured him he had.

"Well, if you're going to court martial me," Clay Steadman said, yanking the man upright by his hair, "let's make it for something worthwhile."

The court martial never took place. CPO Steadman let the base commander know that if he was charged with assaulting an officer — breaking the man's nose, jaw, and six ribs — he would file an adultery complaint against that officer. A deal was struck: the adultery charge would go away, and so would Steadman. He was given an honorable discharge.

In the civilian work force for the first time, Clay joined the EZ Does It Collection Agency in North Hollywood. The policy of his new employer was not to browbeat their deadbeats, but to speak to them in tones of such cold, quiet menace they'd think if they didn't pay up immediately, someone from EZ would creep through their bedroom window that night and repossess all their vital organs. Clay Steadman was a natural.

But after a couple months on the job, he began to feel his delivery was getting stale. He thought that, as a collection technique, quiet menace was so … expected. The only thing more obvious would have been giggling-lunatic menace. The Richard Widmark bit that had been done to death. What Clay thought might be interesting was *woeful* menace. Tell the deadbeat assholes *his* sad story, imply how it would truly pain him to work them over with a baseball bat, but he had bills to pay, too, or people would be coming after *him.*

The thing was, he didn't know if he could bring it off, be believable enough that the freeloaders wouldn't laugh at him. Still, he wanted to try, so he signed up for acting lessons.

He'd had all of six lessons, at a workshop in the Valley, for God's sake, when he landed the second-lead role in his first movie. His acting coach, who knew greatness when he saw it, had a cousin who knew the movie's casting director from high school. The coach sent Clay to the casting director on a flier, after explaining to his student that while most actors did in fact starve, the ones who got lucky made somewhat more money than people collecting on unpaid toaster ovens.

The casting director said Clay's reading just about made him cream his pants — and he was straight. Clay was given the second-lead, the part of the arson investigator in *The Fire Within.*

The lead was supposed to be Terry O'Dare, who played the giggling lunatic arsonist. All the reviews said O'Dare gave a fine, nuanced performance … given the limitations of his cliché-ridden part. But the actor who stole the show was newcomer Clay Steadman, whose dogged investigator pursued the villain with a sense of menace that was made human by his almost palpable melancholy.

Nobody had ever seen a good guy bare his soul to the bad guy before, explaining how things had been tough for *him.* And when the arsonist laughed at the good guy's vulnerability, as the bad guy's character dictated he must, that made it all the more satisfying when Clay pitched him into a blast furnace for the finale.

From the very first screening, the buzz was about Clay Steadman. He was the guy who got the word of mouth. He was the one people came to see in droves. He was the one who got the best supporting actor nomination.

He was on his way.

As part of his compensation for *The Fire Within,* Clay was given five net points of the profit. A novice, he didn't know that a studio's job was to keep a movie from ever showing a profit, no matter how many millions of dollars it took in at the box office. He learned.

When the studio asked the picture's producer and director to take Clay on a deep-sea fishing trip off Baja California, in the hopes of getting him to sign a multi-picture deal, Clay was only too happy to accept. The trip lasted only one day, and nobody caught any fish. But when the three sportsmen returned to port in Cabo San Lucas, Clay Steadman's five net points in *The Fire Within* had been miraculously converted to five *gross* points. Starting from the first dollar of box office receipts.

The gross points came equally out of the director's and producer's pockets, and nobody ever revealed the reasoning — or threat — that Clay used to bring about such unprecedented generosity. But in Hollywood circles, it conferred an immediate sense of awe upon the new actor that only helped his legend grow over the years.

The other thing that day at sea conferred upon Clay Steadman was a taste for a brand of stout he'd never had, or even heard of, before. Walsh's Private Reserve.

The producer told him he had the stuff flown in from a little place up in the Sierra.

A town called Goldstrike.

CHAPTER 5

After the body had been taken down and the crime scene taped off, Ron and Oliver drove back to police headquarters.

"This is the first homicide in my two years here," Oliver said. "I thought I was leaving this shit behind in L.A. Come to think of it, I can recall just about any kind of killing you can name in L.A. *except* a crucifixion."

Ron replied, "It's my second homicide here in three years. The other was a domestic."

"A *domestic?*" Oliver asked incredulously. "What the hell would anyone have to fight about up here? Somebody serve the wrong wine with dinner?"

Ron shook his head. "Wounded pride. Can happen anywhere."

"Somebody steppin' out on somebody else? Hanky panky?"

"In a manner of speaking. He was a director and she was an editor. He had the contractual final cut on a film they'd both worked on, but she went back in on the sly and did a little more cutting and splicing. He found out and went ape. They yelled and screamed, and he summed up his argument by hitting her over the head with his DGA award. She died the next day."

"Why do I think this SOB's not on death row?"

"He copped to manslaughter. He's at a medium security facility teaching theater arts."

Oliver Gosden shook his head. "People are fucked."

"Must be why the courts are, too," Ron opined.

"I want in on this one," the deputy chief told his boss bluntly.

The chief looked at his second-in-command with an air of assessment.

Oliver Gosden's interest in the case might have been purely professional, a desire to expand his base of experience. Or his feelings could be a lot more personal than that. You didn't have to be Joe Friday to see the anger in those dark brown eyes. In either case, Ron knew he'd have to trust him.

"I didn't bring you up here to ride the bench," he said.

"Good."

"But insofar as possible, Oliver, you've got to keep an open mind about the case. You prejudge things, you might step on your dick."

The deputy chief chose to remain silent.

The two men pulled into the police garage at the Municipal Services Complex. The Muni was the mall for governmental services in Goldstrike. One stop shopping. Located in a campus setting on the shore of Lake Adeline, the police and fire departments anchored the ends of the complex. The mayor's office, the town council chamber, and the municipal court formed the centerpiece. The health department, building department, parks and recreation, and street maintenance all had offices there. The public library and the center for the performing arts had the best views of the lake. The mayor and town council were considering the addition of an outdoor ice skating rink.

All of the buildings were connected by tree-shaded paths and an underground complex which included spaces leased from the town for private restaurants and shops.

The whole idea — Clay Steadman's idea — was to make town government as accessible and welcoming as possible. His philosophy of governance was to make sure the people who paid the taxes got the biggest bang for their buck. The motto for all municipal employees was: *Be citizen friendly.* The *Or else* was clearly implied.

Police headquarters was carpeted, furnished in gleaming oak, provided with all the latest communications and computer technology, and nearly as quiet as the town library. The chief's office had a view of the lake, and if the ice skating rink went in, he'd be able to watch the skaters, too. Rumor had it that the striking shade of blue of the tailored police uniforms was the result of the designer matching the color of the mayor's eyes. There were six holding cells that smelled of fresh, unmarked paint rather than urine, vomit and despair. Prisoners were rare commodities.

When Ron first took Oliver on a tour of the facility, the police officer who had worked inner-city L.A. was agog. "Man, Disneyland don't have a cop-shop this nice," he said.

Now, as Ron and Oliver entered the chief's office, it was time to see if a twenty-four officer police department that worked in such genteel surroundings, in such a gilded community, had the smarts, stomach and will to solve a truly vicious murder. Probably the town's first since local prospectors stopped settling claim disputes with pickaxes.

Ron took a seat behind his desk, buzzed his secretary, and asked her to send in Sergeant Stanley. The door opened immediately and Stanley walked in like he'd been standing there all along, just waiting for his cue like some kind of comedy gag.

Casimir "Caz" Stanley was fifty years old. He was the longest-serving officer in the department, a man entirely sure of himself, and not about to be bothered by two younger outsiders being brought in to fill the two top slots.

But then, while Ron and Oliver set policy and made command decisions, Sergeant Stanley was the one who ran the department on a day-to-day basis, and the boys from the LAPD were smart enough to let him do it. He nodded politely and greeted his superiors.

"I was just on my way in to see you, Chief."

"You heard?" Ron asked.

The sergeant's reputation for omniscience, regarding both the department and the town, was the stuff of legends. Clay Steadman had once told Ron that Caz and God drank at the same bar. Caz bought the drinks and God dished the dirt.

But Stanley was smart enough to admit the occasional development that slipped past him. "I have big news, Chief. But I've got the feeling you have some of your own."

"We had a homicide, Sarge," Oliver said. He plugged the digital camera into Ron's computer and brought up a full-body shot of the crucifixion victim.

Sergeant Stanley blinked once as he absorbed the gruesome image. Then he nodded briefly to himself. "I recognize that tree. It's on Highway 99, about a mile down from the Tightrope. Got hit by lightning last summer, went up like a torch. Only reason it didn't char half the mountainside is because rain swept in right behind the lightning. Came down in buckets."

Oliver clicked his way through several more images of the victim. He stopped on a close-up of the victim's face. "Use this one?" he asked the chief.

Ron nodded, and Oliver started the image printing out. The deputy chief handed the first sheet to Sergeant Stanley and he looked at it.

"You recognize him, Sarge?" Ron asked.

"No, sir."

"Can you think of anyone in town who might do this?"

Sergeant Stanley rubbed his hand across his face and thought. Then he shook his head. "The thing that bothers me — other than that poor sonofabitch getting killed — is that a guy twisted enough to kill someone like this should stand out like he's wearing a neon hat. But I can't think of anybody. And I know just about everybody."

"Are there any hate groups in town?" Oliver asked.

The sergeant gave his superior a tight grin. "Come on, Deputy Chief. An *organized* hate group? That shows its face? You really think the mayor or the chief — or I — would stand for that?"

"Even racists have constitutional rights."

"The thing about rights is how they're interpreted," the sergeant shrugged. "I can tell you for a fact, though, there are no known hate groups in town. Never have been. Never will be as long as

Clay Steadman is mayor." The sergeant gave the chief an inquiring look, and Ron nodded. "Now, I can't say there aren't some people who don't like it that Goldstrike isn't as lily white as it once was, and maybe they'd like to see it that way again, but if people want to be assholes in the privacy of their own homes, so to speak, *that* is their right."

"Sarge, how many of our people are out sick," Ron asked, "and who's on vacation?"

"Nobody's sick. Hopkins, Mulroy, Barzov and Tall Elk are on vacation. Per our contract with the sheriff's department, four deputies are available to cover for vacationing personnel at the agreed upon per diem, should the need arise."

"Skip the sheriff's people for now. Leave four officers on patrol. Everyone else, have them here within the hour. The mayor says he wants the bastard who nailed this man to that cedar tree."

"I bet he does."

"So do the deputy chief and I. Patrol function goes on skeleton staff until further notice. The homicide gets top priority."

Ron saw unexpected hesitation in Sergeant Stanley's eyes. "Something wrong, Caz?"

"Remember I said I had news, too, Chief?"

Ron nodded. "It's important enough to bring up now?"

"Yes, sir. This morning, a woman by the name of Mary Kaye Mallory was jogging out on Highway 38, about two miles northwest of town, when she was attacked by a mountain lion."

Ron knew that only five years ago a female runner had been killed by a lion in the foothills of the Sierra. That death had frayed a lot of nerves in the nearby resort communities. And, now, the idea that there might be *two* fatalities in his town on the same morning stunned the chief.

"Is she dead?"

"No, sir. She fought off the attack. I was at Community Hospital with her. Maybe that's why I didn't hear about the homicide."

"A woman fought off a mountain lion?" Oliver Gosden asked

in disbelief.

"Pepper sprayed it, Deputy Chief. But the cat slashed her belly and legs pretty bad. The wounds aren't life-threatening, but … " The sergeant looked at his watch. "She's due to be airlifted out to San Francisco in thirty minutes. The docs at Community said her best chance for scar revision is to get her to the specialists right away. I thought you might want to talk with her before she left, Chief."

"I do. But I still want everybody here within an hour. I'll be back. Oliver, you get the troops organized as they come in. Sarge, walk out with me."

Ron and Caz Stanley walked quickly toward the police garage.

"Do we have anybody in the department with hunting skills, Sarge?"

"Barzov says he hunted wolves in Siberia as a kid, but Barzov says a lot of things."

"Is he vacationing close by?"

"Tahiti."

"Due back when?"

"Not for 10 days, Chief."

"And there's nobody else?"

"Maybe forty years ago you'd have had a chance of finding a hunter or outdoorsman in the department. Nowadays, leisure time activities for our personnel run more to mountain biking and snowboarding, depending on the season. Weightlifting and tanning are year 'round."

"Anything to catch the eye of a passing producer, huh?" Ron asked.

The sergeant just grinned.

Ron said, "Okay. We have to report the incident to the state fish and game people, anyway. Tell them the mayor and I would appreciate it if they could send out one of their best people right away."

Sergeant Stanley saluted and left the chief at the doorway to the parking structure.

Clay Steadman was going to love this, Ron thought as he got into his Explorer. A mountain lion attack on top of a crucifixion. He tried not to wonder how things could get worse. Then he snorted to himself as he nosed the patrol unit onto the street.

One way he could have made things worse would have been to voice the idea that had immediately occurred to him back at his office. A mountain lion attack? Call Tall Elk back from vacation. Who could track a wild animal better than an Indian? Except he remembered Donald Tall Elk was only half Native American and would probably do better tracking a stock fraud than a mountain lion.

Oh, what grief Oliver would have given Ron had he opened his mouth.

A little more than four years ago, a lawyer Ron had hired to defend him in a wrongful death suit had described then-Lieutenant Ketchum of the LAPD as a "recovering bigot."

The label had shocked Ron the first time he'd heard it. Then he came to realize the characterization had a grain or two of truth to it. Possibly several grains of truth. And at moments like this, he wondered just how far his recovery had progressed. But he didn't have time for introspection right now.

He had to talk to the woman who was 1-0 versus a mountain lion.

CHAPTER 6

Mary Kaye Mallory lay on a gurney in a curtained-off corner of the Community Hospital emergency room, clad in a hospital gown from which the sterile dressings on her legs protruded. Her ginger-colored hair stood on end as if from fright, and she had a large gauze pad taped to each of her elbows. But she hadn't withdrawn behind a wall of shock. Her green eyes gleamed, and she was speaking to the ER physician with animation in her voice when Ron stepped into the enclosure.

A smile lit her face when Ron first entered, and then slipped back into an grin of self-satisfaction, the corners of her mouth turning up just enough to be noticed.

"Ms. Mallory, I'm Chief Ketchum, Goldstrike PD," Ron said with a nod of greeting. "Sorry if I'm not who you were expecting."

"I just thought someone might come see me before I left," she answered. "But I'm not sure if he even heard what happened."

"If there's someone you'd like me to contact …"

The thing was, Mary Kaye wasn't sure if she wanted Brad or Carter to rush to her side. And how would they even know what had happened to her? And why would she want either of them to see her looking the way she did? Then it occurred to her that maybe a brush with death was something of an aphrodisiac. But she wasn't about to say so.

"No thank you, Chief. I'm sure you have better things to do."

The ever-efficient Sergeant Stanley had radioed Ron on his

way to the hospital and gave him a brief sketch of Mary Kaye Mallory's background. A millionaire businesswoman, she could have played the prima donna. But she looked like the kid sister who early on always wanted to play ball with the guys, and later on you warned your no-account buddies to stay away from if they knew what was good for them.

Ron liked her immediately.

"If you feel up to it, Ms. Mallory, I have a few questions."

The ER doc smiled and told Ron, "Oh, she's up to it, and it's a helluva story." Then he excused himself.

"I got that sonofabitch good," Mary Kaye said with a hard smile, as if she'd just humbled the neighborhood bully. "I only wish I'd had sulfuric acid in my canister."

She then proceeded to describe in detail the events of that morning.

"How are you able to recall so precisely where the attack occurred?" Ron wanted to know.

"I parked my car at the scenic overlook at Alpine Glen, the way I always do. I run a seven and a half minute mile. When the cat ran back into the woods and I started back to my car, I looked at my watch. Ten minutes had passed since I'd started out. Ergo I'd run about a mile and a third, minus a little for the time the actual confrontation lasted."

She grinned and added again, "I really kicked his ass."

"What was the animal's coloration, Ms. Mallory? And did you notice any unusual markings or features?"

Mary Kaye looked inward, remembering. A slight trembling started in both of her feet that she didn't seem to notice: the subconscious urge of the body to flee from the power of the memory. The first sign of a chink in her bravado. Ron decided to ask again at the end of the interview if there was anyone he could contact for her.

"He was the usual tawny brown color. The eyes, I remember the eyes — I don't think I'll ever forget them — were a malignant yellow." She furrowed her brow in concentration. "And above the

... the left eye he had a jagged scar."

The tremor in her feet started working its way up her body. Ron knew he had to ask the rest of his questions before she got too upset.

"Can you estimate the lion's size?" He realized he was asking the same questions he'd ask if the assailant had been human, but that was what he knew.

Mary Kaye Mallory's teeth started to chatter as she considered the question, and that was when she became aware of the dread that had slipped past the drawbridge of her conscious mind. It was also when Ron saw just how strong this woman was. She might actually have been somebody's kid sister, but she needed no one to watch out for her. The look of determination that came into her eyes was so fierce that he had no problem understanding her professional success. She made a tooth-grinding effort to master her fear. A long moment and several controlled breaths later her trembling stopped.

Then she exhaled deeply and said, "It's just a guess, but I'd have to say he was about a hundred and forty pounds. Average for males of his species, from what I've read."

Ron said, "You keep referring to the animal in masculine terms. Did you actually notice its ... gender?"

Now, Mary Kaye Mallory grinned. "No, I didn't. It just helps me to think of the bastard as male. Does such sexism offend you, Chief Ketchum?"

Ron shook his head.

"You've probably got it right, Ms. Mallory."

At that moment, a man of about Ron's age poked his head into the enclosure. "I called your office and heard what happened," he said to Mary Kaye. "May I come in? The nurse told me you're leaving for San Francisco soon. If you like, I can accompany you."

A repeat of the smile she'd mistakenly given Ron was all the answer he needed. He stepped to the side of the bed and took Mary Kaye's hand. She squeezed his in return.

Apparently, Ms. Mallory had the good sense to recognize that not all males were bastards.

Ron slipped away unnoticed.

As Ron entered the roll call room at police headquarters, the sixteen available officers of Goldstrike's finest snapped to attention at Oliver Gosden's crisp command. They held the rigid posture as the chief stepped behind the lectern where Sergeant Stanley usually stood. He regarded his ten men and six women individually and then put them at ease.

There was no need to ask whether Oliver had briefed them and handed out copies of the victim's likeness, so he started right in.

"A man was killed in our town last night. He died very badly. If the killer hasn't fled our jurisdiction, we are going to catch him. We are going to work smart and hard and for as long as it takes. We are going to catch him.

"As you can imagine, the mayor feels very strongly about this situation. As do the deputy chief and I. As, undoubtedly, do all of you. Every decent person abhors a killing. But, in my view, a murder offends a police officer more grievously than anyone else. A homicide *mocks* our pledge to protect the public. It *violates* our very sense of who we are.

"It doesn't take a lot of imagination to know that this killing has enormous potential for being sensationalized. Once that happens, it will become a media event and quite likely a political football. There will be great pressure on this department to solve the case quickly. So that the story will have a neat ending. So that the politics of the situation can be distilled and peddled to the voters."

Ron spoke here from personal experience, and again he paused to look at each and every one of his officers.

"None of this is your concern. Any and all questions from anyone outside this department are to be referred to my office. This is not to cover anyone's ass, it's to free you from any distraction to doing your police work. I'll remind you again. If the killer is still in our town, we *will* catch him

"The first order of business is to identify the victim. If he was a resident, someone will know him. If he was a visitor, he had to have a means of transportation and probably a place to stay. I want the man's picture shown at every hotel, motel, and campground in town. I want it shown at every eating-place, from four-star to fast food. I want it shown at every grocery store and convenience store. I want it shown at every single place of business where this man might conceivably have walked in off the street.

"And I want this done as quickly as possible without sacrificing due diligence. Because if we can't identify him this way, we will go door-to-door to every residence in town. Sergeant Stanley will detail each officer's initial assignment."

Ron laid the weight of one last stare from the chief on his cops.

"As of now, you're all working continuous shifts until we know who the victim is."

That Friday evening, Mayor Clay Steadman made Ron Ketchum's job both easier and much more difficult. Since Goldstrike was in many ways the mayor's town, that was his prerogative. He used the forum of the Clay Steadman Show to spread his message.

Whenever the mayor was in town, not off making a movie, he appeared on the government access cable TV channel each weekday at 6:45 PM. Sometimes he discussed municipal ballot propositions on which the electorate would vote; sometimes he did movie reviews on upcoming films he'd seen at industry screenings; sometimes he just read the weather report and wished everyone a pleasant evening.

It was his way of staying in touch, as broadly as possible, with his constituency.

And his constituency watched faithfully, loving the fact that they alone got to see the only TV program that Clay Steadman would ever do. In homes, public places and even on electronics store displays, if a TV in Goldstrike was on at 6:45 PM, it was tuned to the Clay Steadman Show.

That included the TV in Ron Ketchum's office. As soon as the chief saw the look on the mayor's face, he knew what Clay was going to do. It was all Ron could do to watch. But he knew he'd better, so he did.

"I have something shocking to show you tonight, something horrible to talk about. So right now I'd like to give you parents out there a few seconds to shoo the kids out of the room. Any of you more impressionable adults might just want to turn off your sets, too."

Then the mayor simply focused his cold, blue, unblinking eyes on the camera. Ron counted to himself. Clay Steadman gave his audience ten seconds to follow his advice — a good deal longer than the three count he was famous for giving movie villains.

Then the mayor held up a photograph and the TV camera zoomed in close on it. It was a full-length picture of the crucifixion victim, one of the shots Oliver had taken. Ron hadn't known the mayor had requested it, but he couldn't have stopped him from getting it in any event.

"This man was killed in our town this morning," Clay said in voice-over as the gruesome image continued to fill the screen. "He was crucified."

Ron said a silent prayer that the mayor wouldn't give away *all* the details of the killing. That'd he'd leave the police something to distinguish any real tips they might get from the flood of crackpot calls that would soon inundate the department's phone lines.

The angry face of the mayor came back on the screen.

"To say that this is the work of a sick, twisted sonofabitch belabors the obvious. To understand why it happened here is not so simple."

Oliver Gosden came into Ron's office and took a seat on the corner of his desk to watch the mayor speak.

"You look at what was done to this man ..." Ron was glad that Clay chose not to show the crucifixion picture again. "... and you know that someone wanted to achieve more than the taking of his life. Someone wanted to send a grotesque message."

Clay Steadman let his audience think about that while he took a sip of water.

"The first conclusion you might reach is that this killing is racially motivated. Somebody hated this man for the color of his skin. Our country's history is tragically filled with such outrages. And why else would anyone go to the trouble of staging such a vile, sacrilegious execution?"

Oliver exchanged a glance with Ron.

"The answer is we don't know. But that's exactly what we have to find out. Was this man killed for what he looked like ... or was he killed for who he was ... or for something he did? Only when we know the answer to those questions will we be able to pursue his killer."

The mayor paused for another sip of water.

Oliver asked Ron, "You think he's gonna—"

"Yeah," Ron answered, not needing to hear the rest of the question.

"The first thing our police department needs to know is this man's identity," Clay said. "Please take a good look at him. See if you know him."

Sergeant Stanley stepped into Ron's office as a headshot of the victim filled the TV screen. The sergeant stood next to the deputy chief.

"Please call the number on your screen if you know who this man is," Clay narrated as the telephone number for police headquarters appeared on the screen below the victim's face. "Do *not* call 911. Leave that line open for emergencies."

All three cops listened for the sound of their main phone line starting to ring. The first call came within five seconds.

"At least we won't have to do a house to house canvas now," Sergeant Stanley said. "I'll get additional clerical help to cover the phones."

The mayor came back on the screen. "I know everybody in town wants to catch this bastard as badly as I do. And I know this murder couldn't have been committed without somebody in Goldstrike having some information that will help our police catch the killer. But I'm also aware that in a situation like this people can sometimes be afraid to come forward. So I am offering a reward …

"You were right," Oliver told Ron.

"… I will pay $100,000 from my own pocket for information leading to the arrest and conviction of whoever killed this man."

The victim's face reappeared on the screen, as did the police phone number.

Sergeant Stanley left to find the clerical help he'd need.

"You think our boy's packing his bags right about now?" Oliver asked.

Ron knew the question was more than just rhetorical, and he nodded.

"Might not be a bad idea, at that, to have a few units out watching for anybody leaving town and looking spooked," Ron answered.

There were only four roads out of town that hooked up with the interstate system. It was just another of Goldstrike's natural advantages, as far as the police were concerned.

"I'll get Stanley on it right away," Oliver said, heading for the door.

"You think we could get that lucky?" Ron asked.

The deputy chief just snorted and kept going.

Another member of the Clay Steadman Show's viewing audience was Perk Lawler, the local stringer for the Associated Press. She videotaped every episode. She also had an urgent reaction to the mayor's announcement. Perk picked up her phone and called her boss in Los Angeles. Did she have a story for him.

And by Saturday morning, so did every newspaper in the country.

Hours later, news of the murder in Goldstrike and Clay Steadman's reward offer was in worldwide circulation.

CHAPTER 7

Saturday

About the same time on Saturday morning that the rest of the country was learning about the horrific killing in the Sierra Nevada resort town, two tired and cranky patrol officers Santo Alighieri and Divine Babson, made a discovery. At the far corner of the parking lot of the Evergreen Supermarket on Timberline Road sat an old dark blue Ford Taurus. There was an acre of available parking between the car and the store.

Officer Babson, the mother of three, gave her partner a fish-eyed look.

"Santo," she asked, "you ever feel the urge to carry a bag of groceries one step farther than you absolutely had to?"

"Beautiful car like that, maybe the owner just don't want to get it dinged," he responded deadpan, but he drove slowly over to the isolated car.

As they got close, Divine said, "Something wrong here. I feel it. You feel it?"

"Yeah. Either there's a body in that trunk or we're the lucky cops about to get a commendation."

Officer Babson radioed the dispatcher that she and her partner were about to investigate a suspicious vehicle and gave their location. The dispatcher acknowledged their message.

Approaching the car from the rear, Alighieri said, "The plate's current."

"I'll call it in," Babson replied "See what we can see."

"Hey, Divine," Alighieri interrupted as he moved to the front of the car. "Come on over here and look at this."

She joined her partner and looked in the direction of his nod. The driver's side sun visor hung down. On it was a label: *Clergy.*

Officer Babson just shook her head. "A man gets himself crucified, and we find a minister's car parked all lonely over here? Makes me want to go home and hold my babies."

Alighieri, a bachelor, took the practical point of view.

"Let's call the chief in on this. Maybe he'll let you."

Ron came and so did Oliver, who'd been about to leave for breakfast at home. They brought Officer Benny Marx, the department's crime scene man, with them. By the time they arrived at the supermarket parking lot Officers Babson and Alighieri had a name for them.

"DMV says this car's registered to a Reverend Isaac Cardwell," Babson said.

"A black male," Alighieri added.

A number of early morning shoppers noticed the police presence, but the cops didn't seem to be doing more than talking, and they were too far away for anyone to casually rubberneck.

"You guys touch anything?" Benny Marx asked.

Both cops shook their heads.

"Eyeballed it is all," Babson explained.

Alighieri added, "Divine spotted the car over here, wondered why anyone would park so far from the store. When we got within ten feet of it, we knew something was wrong."

Oliver looked up from glancing at the Clergy label. "The DMV sent you the reverend's driver's license photo, right?"

Babson held up her department-issued BlackBerry. Isaac Cardwell's photographic likeness looked out at the assembly of cops.

Ron nodded. "Good work, officers. You two have been working all night?"

Alighieri said, "Yes, sir."

The chief told the two cops, "Okay, go home and get some rest. Come back for second shift. See if you can find another lead for us."

Divine Babson and Santo Alighieri smiled, saluted and left.

The deputy chief had Cardwell's photo up on his smart phone now.

"That's him," Oliver said.

Ron and Benny Marx agreed.

They'd identified the victim. Reverend Isaac Cardwell of Echo Avenue, Oakland, California. In the DMV photo, though, Reverend Cardwell wore wire frame glasses; his license mandated corrective lenses when he drove. Ron remembered the indentations on the victim's nose. So what had happened to the man's glasses?

"Benny," Ron asked, "you find any eyeglasses in the area where the victim was found?"

"No, Chief."

"Look for a pair when you go over that car. Oliver, go talk to the supermarket manager and his staff. See if their security cameras cover the spot where the reverend's car is parked. If not, ask if anyone noticed when Cardwell's car was left here. See if anybody remembers seeing him in the store; if so, was anyone was with him? If the store personnel are no help, ask them for the names of regular customers who came in the past few days. There have to be times this parking lot gets a lot more filled up than it is now. Somebody might have seen something. Ask the manager when his slow times are, when it's least likely anyone would notice a car being dumped here. If we don't get anything else, that might give us a time frame to work with."

Oliver and Benny knew Ron was saving the heavy lifting for himself.

The chief said, "I'll notify the next of kin — and the mayor."

***

Ron went to see the mayor first. He'd been to Clay Steadman's house a dozen times in the three years he'd been Goldstrike's chief of police. Every time he visited, he had the same thought. It was perfectly sited for the man who governed — *ruled*, Ron often thought — the town.

The house sat alone on a rise that looked directly down on the center of town and the sparkling waters of the lake. If the mayor were so inclined, he could step out his front door and, with a pair of good binoculars, peer into half of the windows in the Muni Complex. And since Clay Steadman had everyone who worked for the town out to his place twice a year, for a Fourth of July picnic and a Christmas party, every municipal employee on the inland side of the Muni knew that the boss might be watching at any time.

On the other hand, nobody was going to get the drop on Clay Steadman. His grounds were high enough above the adjacent road that he felt no need to enclose the property behind a wall. A private lane was the only way in. It cut through a grand sweep of lawns, terraced flowerbeds, ornamental trees and a recirculating stream that featured a small waterfall and a large pond. All of the features of the landscaping fit together like a masterfully composed oil painting — and all of them allowed for a clear view from the house to the property line. Out back were a simple lap pool and an austere tennis court. Just beyond these amenities, the sheer face of a cliff rose over two hundred feet.

The house itself was a single story rambling structure of redwood weathered to a handsome silver with a pitched roof and tinted Thermopane windows. It was big but seemed exceedingly unpretentious for a man who'd made a billion or so dollars in entertainment and real estate. When you stepped inside, there were understated furnishings that cost more than most people made in a lifetime, paintings by Winslow Homer and three generations of Wyeths and Remington bronzes. Everything had been arranged by somebody whose sense of interior design was probably genetic.

For all the room in the house, Clay was the only one who lived there. His only ex-wife didn't like snow and lived, elegantly, in the

Arizona desert. He had no children. He drove his own cars. The cook and the cleaning people were ferried back and forth, and the groundskeeper came and went in his own truck.

It was only when the mayor had an occasional lady friend over or threw one of his rare parties for his Hollywood associates, that anyone else spent a night under his roof.

The sense of isolation and asceticism Clay had cultivated in his home was intentional. During the shooting of his tenth film, aptly named *Criminal Mischief,* he'd encountered the one foe he couldn't overcome: cocaine addiction.

By the time he made *Criminal Mischief,* most of Clay's movies were being produced by his own company. But this effort was a co-production deal because another company owned the script. Ironically, the picture had an anti-drug theme.

Not that you'd know it from looking at most of the cast. The only reason Clay didn't kick their asses the first time he'd seen drugs being passed around was that these people still got their jobs done, and did them damn well.

At the wrap party, Clay was struck by a life changing temptation. He thought if his fellow actors could handle coke without suffering, he ought to at least know what all the shouting was about. It was the worst mistake of his life.

What he discovered was that he *loved* cocaine.

Worse, he had all the money he needed to indulge his new love to death. Which he just about did one day when he was pushing his Ford Cobra through the mountain roads so fast he thought it might be fun to see if the car could actually *fly.* So he pointed it straight at an unprotected curve and flattened the accelerator.

He would have killed himself that day if his path hadn't taken him past a scenic overlook and he hadn't registered the looks of utter shock on a family of tourists who thought they were witnessing a madman committing suicide. The horrified concern of complete strangers brought Clay back into last-second contact with reality.

Clay had publicly told the story of this epiphany many times. But he'd never once been able to explain how he'd managed to keep his car on the road and make that curve at the speed he'd been traveling.

The next day, Clay resigned as mayor — he was serving his second term — and checked himself into rehab. When he successfully completed his course of therapy and returned to Goldstrike, he found that his resignation had been declined by the town council. He was told if he could stay clean Goldstrike still wanted him as its mayor.

After maintaining his sobriety and winning his third term, the town council gave him a plaque for his office that said: *Clay Steadman, Mayor for Life.*

He put things in perspective with a new nameplate for his mayoral desk: *Clay Steadman, Recovering Drug Addict.*

He didn't believe in sugarcoating anything, especially his own weaknesses. He knew his demons were close at hand, and always would be. That's why he tried to live his personal life in a style he called tastefully monastic.

As Ron pulled up to the mayor's front door, Clay stepped out with a cup of coffee in each hand. Further proof the mayor saw all. He gave one cup to the chief and invited him in.

They sat in the breakfast nook off the kitchen. The public rooms in the house faced the town. The bedrooms and Clay's home office were guarded by the cliff.

"*Reverend* Isaac Cardwell?" the mayor asked.

"That's the way the DMV has him."

"So the killing could be a racial thing or it could be a religious thing."

"Or it could be purely personal," the chief said.

"Just as painful for him, but a lot easier for us." Ron didn't doubt that Clay Steadman was just as angry as he had been yesterday. But by now he'd had the time to consider the situation as the town's mayor. Clay asked, "Too soon to know if the reverend lived here or was just visiting?"

Ron told Clay that Isaac Cardwell had lived in Oakland.

"So was he was here on vacation. Or he'd come to meet someone."

"We don't know why he was here. Or if he was killed somewhere else and left here."

The mayor gave the chief a level gaze. Ron met his stare without blinking or looking away. It was one of the things Clay liked about him.

"Someone wants to cause trouble for us?" the mayor asked. He thought about that. "Sure, why not?" Then the mayor asked. "You pissed about the reward I offered?"

"I'd have liked to know about it beforehand. It probably will save some legwork, and cause some headaches with scammers trying to cash in. On balance … yeah, I'm pissed."

Clay nodded, not taking offense.

"I'll let you know first, next time. You can state your case. But I'm going to do what I think is right."

"Me too," Ron said.

The mayor had the grace and self-assurance to smile at the remark.

The chief said thanks for the coffee and got up to go.

"You want me to notify the next of kin?" Clay offered.

Ron shook his head. "I want to check out Reverend Cardwell with the Oakland PD before I call them."

It was only when Clay walked him to the door that Ron remembered to give the mayor the other piece of news concerning his happy little mountain kingdom.

"Oh, yeah," the chief said. "Before I forget again, you should know that a woman running on Route 38 yesterday was attacked by a mountain lion."

"Thanks. I already heard, "the mayor replied. "Flowers and wishes for a speedy recovery should be reaching Ms. Mallory in San Francisco right about now."

CHAPTER 8

By the time Ron got back to the Muni Complex, he was surprised to find a contingent of reporters waiting for him. Sergeant Stanley had them efficiently tucked away in a conference room, but the room had a glass wall and the newsies all leapt to their feet when they saw the chief arrive.

They sat back down, however, when the sergeant pointed a stern finger at them. He'd given them strict and simple ground rules: Good manners would get every bit of cooperation the department could reasonably give; rude, disruptive behavior that distracted the department from its important work would meet with instant ejection.

"Who's here?" Ron asked.

"The town paper and both local radio stations, the *L.A. Times,* the *San Francisco Chronicle, The Sacramento Bee,* and two network TV affiliates, one from San Jose, the other from Reno."

"So, it's just regional right now."

"Planes are landing as we speak, Chief. Won't be an empty hotel room by evening."

Ron sighed. "I better go give them something."

"Before you do," the sergeant said, "I have to tell you they're not the only unwelcome visitors this morning."

The chief gave the sergeant an inquiring look.

"You've got feds in your office. I had to put them there because I'd already put the press in the conference room."

"FBI? Trying to big-foot the case?"

Sergeant Stanley nodded. "I've got Annie coming in, so at least you won't have to spend much time with the media."

"Thanks." Ron started for the conference room, then stopped. "Sarge, you didn't tell the feds we've ID'd the victim?"

Caz Stanley felt he was well within his rights to give his boss a disdainful look.

"Sorry. Just wanted to be sure I can piss them off by telling the media first."

Sergeant Stanley grinned his approval.

Ron stepped into the conference room to meet the press.

"Chief, Chief, Chief!" Every voice in the room shouted, demanding attention. They were all on their feet again, leaning forward as if to rip him apart and study his entrails for his every secret. Not even the formidable Sergeant Stanley could potty train the press completely.

"Please," Ron said, holding up his hands, calling for order. "Please take your seats and I'll give you my statement."

The reporters sat down reluctantly. The two refugees from grunge bands behind the videocams stayed on their feet and cast their harsh light on Ron.

"Yesterday morning at 6:30 AM, Deputy Chief Oliver Gosden and I were on routine patrol and —"

"It's routine for the chief and deputy chief to patrol the town?" the *Chronicle* interrupted.

"Every Friday morning. We like to stay in touch with the patrol officer's point of view and discuss department business without distractions. As I was saying, we were on patrol when we found the body of a man nailed to a tree adjacent to Highway 99."

"A *black* man," added the *Times* reporter, an African-American.

"That's correct. For the past twenty-four hours the department has made every effort to identify this man."

"Isn't it true," the San Jose TV reporter asked, drawing the attention of both videocams, "that if the police don't *catch* the killer in the first twenty-four hours, they most likely never will? And you're still trying to identify the victim."

The cameras swung back to Ron.

He took a moment to compose himself.

"Homicide investigations, unless closed by an immediate and credible confession, are never easy. And it's true the passage of time makes the task ever more difficult. But the idea that a murder must be solved within the span of a single day or it never will be solved is absolute *garbage.* If it weren't, it would be reasonable for police departments to conserve their resources and stop looking for killers after the twenty-four hours. How do you think the public would respond if we did that?"

Ron focused his question on the TV reporter who'd implicitly insulted him, and now the cameras were back on the reporter. He turned red and groped for an answer, one that wouldn't make him sound like a complete jerk.

As much as Ron enjoyed roasting reporters, he didn't have the time.

"I can also tell you that we have identified the victim." He held up his hand to forestall the obvious question as the cameras pounced on him again. "I can't reveal that identity right now as I've yet to identify the next of kin. I was on my way to do that when Sergeant Stanley pointed out that the media had arrived."

"Chief," *The Sacramento Bee* said, "you spoke about resources just now. Do you think you have the manpower for this kind of investigation?"

The *Times* quickly added, "More to the point, do you think *you're* the man to investigate the killing of an African-American?"

Annie Stratton slipped into the room in time to hear that last question. She was Clay Steadman's press secretary. A former journalist herself, she'd gone over to the other side when the mainstream press started picking up stories broken by supermarket tabloids. She'd figured the moral climate couldn't be any worse working for

Clay, and the money was a whole lot better.

She came as naturally by her red hair as she did her incendiary temper. She raised an eyebrow at Ron, silently inquiring whether he'd like her to ream the asshole who had asked the insulting question.

Ron gave a small shake of his head.

"Answering your questions in order," he said. "Yes, I believe we have both the personnel and other resources we need within the Goldstrike Police Department to successfully complete this investigation. And more to the point, *I'm* the man who's going to catch this killer."

He left the room, letting Annie take it from there.

Now, he'd have the pleasure of dealing with the feds.

Two young FBI agents sat in Ron's guest chairs and their boss, a pugnacious looking guy in his late forties, had helped himself to Ron's seat behind his desk. It was a calculated affront, and the grin he gave Ron was both an insult and a further provocation. He wanted to see what kind of rise he could get out of the chief.

Ron regarded him silently for a moment, and then called out through the open door behind him. "Dinah," he asked his secretary, "has the deputy chief returned yet?"

"Just this minute, Chief."

"Would you ask him to step in here, please?"

"Right away, Chief."

"Get Sergeant Stanley, too."

"Yes, sir."

Ron didn't have to wait ten seconds for his subordinates to join him at the threshold of his office. The feds held their positions silently as the opposition evened the numbers.

"Sarge," Ron asked, "are these gentlemen from the federal government sitting in the same places where you left them?"

"No, sir. I left them seated at your planning table." He indicated a teak table, across the room from Ron's desk, with six empty chairs around it. Three of the places at the table had coffee cups in front of them. Stanley continued, "I offered the agents refreshment and told them they should buzz Dinah or call for me if they needed anything else."

The two agents in the guest chairs had to turn sideways to keep an eye on the cops. Their boss still hadn't given the least indication that he was willing to budge from Ron's chair, the seat of power in the room. But he was no longer smiling. He was doing his best to look intimidating.

"Then you didn't invite that gentleman to sit behind my desk?"

"No, sir. I most definitely did not."

The chief turned to his deputy chief.

"Are we clear on the situation here?"

"Yes, Chief. We are."

"You think that fed was poking through my desk?"

"Hey!" shouted one of the junior agents. He might have said more but he caught sight of the frown on his boss's face.

"It wouldn't surprise me at all if he went through your desk, Chief. Might even have photographed everything in it with a smart phone."

Ron considered this possibility, then he turned to the sergeant. "Let's get Officer Marx in here to dust my desk."

That finally got a rise out of the guy in Ron's seat.

"You can't do that! Do you know who I am?"

Ron continued, "And have that man fingerprinted so we can see if there's a match."

Now the fed was on his feet, and his subordinates quickly joined him. "I'm Francis Horgan, special agent in charge of the FBI's San Francisco office."

Ron ignored the man. "If you get a match, Sarge, we'll have to consider the possibility the deputy chief mentioned about them photographing my papers, so seize their phones."

"Like hell you will!" Horgan shouted, stepping out from behind Ron's desk.

Now Ron looked at the man, looked him square in the eyes.

"If they try to escape or go for their guns, Sarge ..."

"Yes, sir?"

"Shoot them."

Several more cops appeared in the doorway behind their superiors, and the FBI agents felt they were in a very bad spot. One in which there would be no explaining whatever happened next.

What happened next was the phone rang.

Sergeant Stanley said, "I believe that's for you, Mr. Horgan. Probably Mayor Steadman wanting to have a little talk with you and your colleagues."

As usual, Sergeant Stanley had it exactly right.

The meeting reconvened thirty minutes later in the mayor's office when Clay Steadman arrived at the Muni Complex. There was no question at all who would sit behind his desk. Ron was the only member of the Goldstrike PD in the room. With Clay also present, the odds were stacked decidedly in the town's favor. Especially after Ron told the mayor his suspicion regarding the federal agent.

"Did you rifle Chief Ketchum's desk, Agent Horgan?"

The fed couldn't hold the mayor's glare, and he evaded the question.

"I came here to advise the chief that the bureau will be taking over the investigation of the homicide that occurred in Goldstrike yesterday."

"Is that right?"

The amount of contempt and sarcasm Clay packed into three innocuous words made the FBI men shrivel. It was the best delivery Ron had ever heard from the mayor. But then he wasn't acting.

"A hate crime like this, a racial killing, comes under federal jurisdiction."

"Well, it's plain to see that there were some very hard feelings involved in this killing. But I'd like to know how the FBI has determined from its offices in San Francisco that the nature of that animosity was racial, when our police department, working around the clock right here, has yet to determine a motive."

Horgan found the nerve to sneer at Ron and, implicitly, the Goldstrike Police Department. Then he turned to Clay and said, "Mr. Mayor, you, yourself, said on television last night that race was the first thing you thought of when you saw the body."

Clay agreed. "I did say that. But I also said we needed to learn more before we reached any conclusion. And I said only then could we hope to find the killer. Right now, Chief Ketchum's department is investigating to find out just what happened."

"With all due respect to your town's department," Horgan said in a tone devoid of any respect, "I think the bureau is better equipped both to make a determination of motive and apprehend the person or persons responsible for this killing."

"You're entitled to your opinion, Mr. Horgan." Clay paused until he had the fed looking at him again. "But unless you have *proof* that this crime was racially motivated, you have no jurisdiction, and you will *not* involve yourself or your agents in Chief Ketchum's investigation within the town limits of Goldstrike."

Even with the weight of Clay's stare upon him, Horgan managed to bristle. He was a senior federal officer. He wasn't about to take marching orders from any small town mayor, no matter how many movies the drug-snorting sonofabitch had made, no matter how much money the asshole had.

Through clenched teeth, Horgan said, "With all due re—

The mayor cut him off, keying his intercom. "Jenny, has my call to Washington been placed yet?"

"I just reached your party, Mr. Mayor," his secretary responded. "Line one."

Clay picked up his phone, said hello and made small talk for a moment. The three FBI men watched in tense anticipation as the mayor said, "We have a little situation here."

Ron had a hard time not smiling, wondering if the president was actually on the other end of the line. Everybody knew that guy had a thing for rubbing elbows in Hollywood. But it wasn't the president. Almost as good, though.

Clay extended the phone to Horgan. "The attorney general of the United States."

The fed's face became a death mask as he pressed the phone to his ear and announced himself. As he listened, the lines in his face deepened dramatically. It took a truly heroic effort for him to choke out the words, "Very well," and hand the phone back to Clay.

"Are we clear now where we all stand, Agent Horgan?" the mayor asked.

"Yes, sir."

"Chief Ketchum will investigate locally. If he determines that the killer has fled town, he will advise your office and provide you with any relevant information in his possession."

Horgan and his underlings rose to leave, but Clay wasn't finished.

"You never did answer my question about rifling the chief's desk. Ron, you see if there is any evidence of an illegal search. We don't have to worry about taking Agent Horgan's fingerprints now. The bureau will have them on record."

Clay looked at the special agent in charge, and his message was perfectly clear: Your ass is mine, pal, and you damn well better play ball.

"Chief," the mayor continued, "I think you can escort these people back to their car now. Have a safe trip back to San Francisco, gentlemen."

Ron walked the feds through the Muni Complex to their car. To that point, not a word was exchanged. But when the FBI men got inside their vehicle, Ron said, "Say hi to all my friends in your L.A. office, guys."

When Ron turned to go, he pretended not to hear Horgan calling him an asshole.

The mayor was waiting for Ron in the chief's office when he got back.

"You have anything important in your desk?" Clay asked.

"No. Anything important goes in my safe."

Clay nodded and said, "I came down on those jerks about as

hard as I could … but Horgan, he's one of those sonsabitches who relishes the idea of revenge. He gets back to San Francisco, he'll devote himself to finding a way to screw you. Don't let him."

"I won't."

"Do your best to get this bastard soon. I wasn't kidding yesterday. I want him."

"Yes, sir."

"And play it straight. If you find the bastard has run, call Horgan immediately."

"I will … but I don't think he's left town. I've got the feeling he's still right here."

Clay agreed. "So do I."

CHAPTER 9

Ron's call to the Oakland PD was routed to a Captain Walter Nance, the officer in charge of community relations. The captain's tone wasn't unfriendly, but it was guarded.

"Chief Ketchum, I'm told you're calling regarding the death of an Oakland resident in your jurisdiction. Have I got that right?"

"That's right, Captain. Have you seen the morning paper or the television news today?"

The captain said he hadn't, so Ron filled him in on what had happened.

"Crucified?" The revulsion in Nance's voice was clear.

"Yes. We just learned the victim's identity an hour ago. His name was Isaac Cardwell."

"Oh my God!"

Ron was surprised by the depth of emotion in Nance's voice. It wasn't the reaction he expected from a cop, at least not one who'd likely worked the streets, at some point in his career, in a tough town like Oakland.

"Did you know him?" Ron asked.

"You are talking about *Reverend* Isaac Cardwell?"

"Yes."

"He's the pastor of Mount Olive AME Church. My church. My wife sings in the choir."

"I'm sorry," Ron said. He waited a moment for Nance to collect himself and then went on. "The reason I called, before I notify his family, is I wondered if you know anything about the man. Something that might help with my investigation."

"Are you asking me if Reverend Cardwell had a criminal record?" Now Ron had the Oakland cop pissed.

"No, I know he doesn't. I already checked him for that."

"You sonofabitch! You're white, aren't you? Wait, a minute, where'd you say you're calling from?"

Ron knew what was coming, but he didn't hesitate with his reply.

"I didn't. But I'm the chief in Goldstrike. Up in the Sierra."

"Yeah, I know you. You're Ron Ketchum from L.A."

"That was a while ago, Captain."

Nance snorted contemptuously.

"Captain, I don't know what you're experience is, but mine is that people are capable of redemption."

"You talking about yourself?"

"No. Not right now. I was wondering if perhaps Reverend Cardwell had a troubled youth and then turned himself around. I was wondering if maybe he had a past that caught up with him yesterday. I'm trying to cover all the bases to find his killer."

"Yeah, I bet you are."

Ron was reaching the end of his patience — it had already been a very long morning — but he maintained a civil tone. "You want to help me, Captain, or should I speak directly to your chief? I think you know I'll find a way to do that if have to."

"What do you want, Chief?" Nance's snarl made chief sound like motherfucker, but Ron had heard it before.

"I'd like you to tell me whatever you know about Reverend Cardwell."

"I know that he was a *fine* man, and before that he was a fine young man. The reason you didn't find any criminal record on him is because he wouldn't have *dreamed* of committing a crime. He was raised by his grandmother, and she brought him up right. She made sure no street trash ever got near him when he was a boy. He graduated high school with honors. He went to San Francisco

State on full scholarship. He was ordained a minister. He believed his special mission was serving the poor." The way Nance rattled off the details of Isaac Cardwell's life told Ron that the man had to be a close friend of long standing. As further proof, the anger in his voice finally yielded to a catch of sorrow. "He ... he married his childhood sweetheart and they have a three year old son. He was probably the most effective community partner this department had in our fight against kids using drugs."

Captain Walter Nance's voice was too choked with emotion to continue.

Ron wondered if maybe Reverend Isaac Cardwell had been too effective in Oakland's fight against drugs. Drug dealers made bad enemies. But if that were the case, why wouldn't they just kill him at home? Maybe include his family to really make their point. But if drug thugs were behind the killing, how did Cardwell wind up nailed to a tree two hundred miles from home?

Ron didn't think he should ask Nance.

He only said, "Thank you for your cooperation, Captain. I'm sorry for your loss."

Ron called the Cardwell residence and spoke to a woman who identified herself as Charmaine Cardwell and said she was Isaac Cardwell's wife. When she asked what this was all about, Ron knew she'd yet to see her husband's picture in the media, but the way such images were endlessly repeated, he knew this was but a fleeting dispensation of grace. She'd soon see the likeness of the man she loved, the father of her child, nailed to a tree.

As it was, when Ron broke the bad news to her that her husband was dead, she responded with a sharp gasp and a shriek. He heard the phone drop and then a small child's frightened voice joined in sympathetic lamentations. Somewhere further in the distance came an elderly female voice, this one filled with urgency, but definitely in control.

The older woman asked what was wrong and got another shriek in response. Apparently, she understood because Ron clearly heard her say, "Save us, sweet Jesus!"

He was in the awful spot of having to eavesdrop on the family's grief. He had to ask if they wanted a local funeral home to bring the body to Oakland, once the autopsy was completed. And he wanted to ask how Reverend Cardwell came to be in Goldstrike in the first place. But he expected that someone would finally notice the phone on the floor and hang it up.

He was wrong. The older woman managed to comfort both Mrs. Cardwell and the child to the point where Ron could no longer hear them. Then she came on the line. Under control.

"This is Mahalia Cardwell," she said. "I am Isaac Cardwell's grandmother. To whom am I speaking?"

Ron remembered Nance telling him Cardwell had been raised by his grandmother — and that she'd been tough enough to keep the gangs at bay. Hearing her now, Ron believed it.

"This is Chief of Police Ronald Ketchum of Goldstrike, California. I'm sorry for your loss, Mrs. Cardwell."

"Did my grandson die in your town?" she asked brusquely.

"It's where his body was found, ma'am. Most likely, it's also where he was killed."

"Somebody shot Isaac?"

"No, ma'am." Details hadn't been necessary to ruin Charmaine Cardwell's life, but it was clear that this woman would want them, and there was no point trying to spare her. She'd see the pictures, too. "He suffered two blows to the head, and then he was nailed to a tree."

Ron thought he'd hear the sounds of another heart torn asunder, but all he got was silence. Again, he expected to hear the phone hung up. But a minute later the woman came back on the line, her voice, if anything, colder than before.

"You know who killed my grandson?"

Mahalia Cardwell's tone made the question sound almost rhetorical, as if she knew who did it. But Ron didn't feel certain enough that he'd read her right to push it. He could always come back to it later.

"No, I don't."

"You will *find* who killed my grandson?"

Ron knew better than to make promises, but he said, "Yes, ma'am, I will."

She seemed to accept that, and replied, "We'll leave to come get Isaac as soon as I can get Charmaine ready to drive."

"Mrs. Cardwell, that's not necessary. We can have your grandson returned to you."

"We're coming, Mr. Chief of Police," she said vehemently.

"Very well," Ron conceded. "Let me give you directions."

"We know how to get there."

She knew how to get there? *He* hadn't known how to get to Goldstrke the first time he'd had to make the trip. So, how would a grandmother from inner city Oakland know how to reach a small resort town in the Sierra? He was about to ask when Mahalia Cardwell interrupted his thoughts.

"Do not give my grandson's body to anyone else before I arrive," she commanded.

Who'd want it, Ron wondered.

Before he could ask any of his questions, the phone was hung up.

CHAPTER 10

Ron found out who else would want the body ten minutes later when Sergeant Stanley knocked on his door and stepped inside. In a quiet voice, the sergeant said, "Chief, there's someone here regarding the Cardwell case. I think you should see him."

"Is there a reason you're whispering, Sarge?"

"The media crowd's gotten bigger. Annie's taking them over to the civic auditorium. I want to give her a minute to get them out of our hair before you talk to this gentleman. I thought a little discretion might be in order. I've got him talking with the deputy chief in his office at the moment."

"Okay," Ron said, "bring him in when you're ready."

The sergeant slipped back out before Ron could ask who the mystery man was. So he mentally sorted through the possibilities. Goldstrike had any number of celebrity residents, though many of them were seasonal, from entertainment people to business magnates to politicians. He thought it had to be somebody with a high profile or what would be the need for the sergeant's subterfuge?

And who among the Goldstrike *glitterati* would know anything about a man of the cloth who ministered to the poor in Oakland?

Sergeant Stanley returned with the man who answered the chief's questions: the Reverend Jimmy Thunder, the most famous black televangelist in the country. His dark, handsome face, proud bearing and deep, booming voice were known to millions.

Including, as the sergeant knew, the media pack that had just been shuffled off to another part of the Muni.

This morning, Thunder looked nothing like the image he projected on his weekly television show. Oh, he wore his usual conservative blue custom made suit and his hand-tooled shoes. But his hair wasn't its usual perfect closely cropped white halo around his head. The normally taut skin of his face was deeply creased, his flashing eyes were muddied and red, and his athlete's shoulders were slumped. Jimmy Thunder looked like he'd spent the last several hours lost in deep despair.

Deputy Chief Gosden had accompanied the reverend and Sergeant Stanley into the chief's office. He gave Ron an inquiring look as to whether he should stay. Ron nodded.

Ron stood and said, "Thank you, Sergeant," dismissing Stanley. He extended his hand to the televangelist. "What can I do for you, Reverend Thunder?"

"I've come for my son's body."

The implications of those six simple words hit Ron like a pile driver. If Isaac Cardwell were Jimmy Thunder's son, the press would really go crazy. A black man is murdered — crucified — and he turns out to be the son of one of the most prominent African-American religious figures in the country. Ron remembered the words he'd heard just minutes ago from Mahalia Cardwell: Sweet Jesus, save us. Then he remembered the old lady's injunction against releasing the body to anyone but her. If there were going to be a grotesque family squabble over the remains of Isaac Cardwell, the situation would be an even worse circus.

On the other hand, Ron thought perversely, where there was family strife, a cop could often find a reason for violence and even homicide.

Ron made sure he kept all such thoughts off his face.

He gestured to a guest chair. "Please, Reverend. Have a seat."

Thunder and Oliver sat down, as did Ron.

"Tell me, Reverend Thunder," Ron said, "did you know your son was in town?"

"Yes. He'd been staying with me."

Ron nodded. "Why don't we start at the beginning?"

In the beginning, as anyone who'd read his autobiography knew, the Reverend Jimmy Thunder had been born Jimmy Leverette in East Texas. His father had abandoned his mother, his two sisters and him to run off to Shreveport with a Louisiana whore who needed a new pimp. That experience soured his mother on life in general and men in particular, including her young son, Jimmy, who bore a strong resemblance to his departed father.

Deloris Leverette raised her son to obey her every command, and her daughters to be life long virgins. Discipline was enforced with a thump to the back of the head with the family Bible. Mrs. Leverette called this "driving out the devil." Fortunately for the children, all the family could afford was a vinyl-bound copy of the Scriptures.

Deloris also read from the Bible, and made her children read it to each other. Passages about children who didn't honor their mother burning in hell were her particular favorites. And nobody dared tell Mama that wasn't quite what the words on the pages said.

For all the physical and emotional battering he took, Jimmy Thunder said his childhood prepared him perfectly to excel as a football player. He was literate, tough and not afraid in the least of being hit by an opponent or yelled at by a coach.

Jimmy was also aided by a farseeing Texas high school football coach who, only twenty some years after Jackie Robinson broke the major league color barrier, figured out that he might have an advantage over the other schools on his schedule if he let a few talented colored boys play for his team. Jimmy's coach had told the local paper he knew young Leverette was a natural athlete, just watching him walk down the school corridors. "He moves so smooth, it's like he has roller skates on the ends of his legs instead of feet."

Jimmy was so clearly the best athlete on his team that the

coach at first wanted him to play quarterback, even at the risk of alienating the local folks who might grudgingly accept a colored boy or two on the team, but surely were not ready to have one lead the school to glory. But the coach's new star spared him that potential problem.

He didn't want to play quarterback, running back or receiver. He wanted to play defense. He wanted to *hit* somebody, as hard and often as possible. The coach knew the team's fans could get behind that idea: having their own tough nigger keeping the opposition's white boys from scoring. He acceded to Jimmy's wishes.

The team never won a championship, but it did have a winning record all three years Jimmy played varsity ball, and Jimmy took all-state honors as a defensive back who hit like a linebacker. He was given a full scholarship to Southwest Texas State.

Jimmy graduated with a degree in television arts and sciences. More important, at the time, he was drafted in the first round by the Dallas Gunslingers. He made all-pro five times, and became known as the most devastating tackler in the league. On eight separate occasions, he knocked opposing players out cold and sent them to hospitals with concussions. Two of the eight players he'd separated from their senses, with clean hits, had to retire due to the severity of their injuries.

For years, Jimmy was the toast of the town. The team paid him a small fortune, and the high rollers he met were happy to supply him with all the women, booze and cocaine he could consume. His lifestyle led to frequent run-ins with the police, but team officials and lawyers always smoothed things over before indictments could be returned. But even the team's dedicated PR staff couldn't keep the stories of Jimmy's notorious behavior out of the papers and off TV.

Jimmy didn't mind. He'd clip the newspaper stories and send them to his mother. Let's see her drive that ol' devil out now, he'd tell his friends with a laugh.

But Jimmy didn't have the last laugh. Time and riotous living took their inevitable toll. In his tenth year in the league, the number of touchdown passes he gave up increased by 50% over the previous year. The next season his number of tackles fell dramatically. The year after that he'd barely made the cut from training camp.

And in the first game of his final season a rookie halfback from Chicago flat ran over him. A picture in one of the Dallas papers showed the sonofabitch actually stepping on Jimmy's helmet as he broke free to score the winning touchdown. The caption under the picture read: *Fallen Hero.*

The talk at the Gunslingers' practice facility the week after the Chicago game was that Jimmy Leverette better show that he had *something* left when New York came to town next Sunday or he was gone.

Jimmy wrote frankly in his autobiography that at that time he'd never known a greater fear. In addition to the anabolic steroids that he swallowed like sugar pills, Jimmy amped himself up that week with both coke and speed. He practically lived in the team's weight room after practice. In a scrimmage the Friday before the New York game, Jimmy knocked out both a receiver and an offensive lineman with colossal hits. He was such a madman that the coaches had to send him off the field, conceding, okay, maybe he still could play.

When Jimmy got to the locker room, he started pissing blood. He didn't give it a second thought. Tonight was when New York got to town. Jimmy knew the hotel where the visiting team stayed, the bar where they drank, and he had plans.

He went home, put on black leather pants, a gunmetal gray silk shirt, a black leather jacket and his best Tony Lama boots. He did four lines of coke, a hit of crystal meth and chased it all with a double shot of Swedish vodka. He checked himself out in a full-length mirror, smiled and decided he looked bad enough to take on the devil and spot him six points.

Jimmy walked into the bar at the MetroPlex Medallion Hotel at 8:30 that night and as he'd hoped a dozen or more players from

New York were there. He wasn't sure of the exact number because he couldn't focus long enough to keep count. But there was a sufficient number for his purposes.

He announced himself by shouting at the top of his voice. "I just want all y'all to know that New Yorkers are PUSSIES!"

The declaration got everyone's attention. The bar manager recognized him — as a renowned troublemaker — and quickly picked up the phone to summon the police. Several members of an optometrists' convention started edging toward the exits. But the football players from New York, who were as big or bigger than Jimmy Leverette, were completely unimpressed. One of them turned his back on Jimmy, and loudly passed gas in his direction.

"Motherfucker!" Jimmy yelled. Then he giggled insanely and said, "That's about the only thing you cocksuckers will ever get past me. That's why I came down here. To *warn* you. Stay away from Jimmy Leverette on Sunday — or your ass is *mine!*"

A tight end for New York named Bergman snorted and said to the huge lineman next to him at the bar, "Hey, Pete, which side of this idiot's head did that guy from Chicago step on? Maybe we can do the other side Sunday and even him out a little."

The New York players roared.

Being ridiculed was not how Jimmy Leverette had seen things going. He'd seen them regarding him as someone to be feared. Someone to stay the hell away from. Not as a fool. Not the butt of their jokes. That wasn't how it was supposed to go at all.

Just then Jimmy spotted New York's hot-shit rookie quarterback, Roger Braddock. Guy was the number one pick in the whole draft last spring. Now, he was just standing at the bar with a tall glass in his hand looking at Jimmy. Not laughing like all the others, just looking at Jimmy. Like he was a bug that flew in through a hole in a window screen or something.

Jimmy zipped right over to him, taking the New York players by surprise.

"What the fuck you looking at?" Jimmy demanded. "You drinking ginger ale or something there, you pussy? You best stay away from my side of the field Sunday. You don't, I'll —"

A pair of huge arms encircled Jimmy from behind.

"That's enough, asshole. Time for you to hit the road. Face first, if that's the way you want it."

It was obvious that Braddock's teammates weren't going to let Jimmy threaten their new star player. Jimmy was lifted off his feet and carried backward, but he kept his eyes on the young quarterback who'd yet to say a word to him.

"You think these limp dicks gonna save you?" he asked Braddock. "That what you think?"

For some reason even Jimmy would never be able to understand, all of his fear and rage found a focal point in the young quarterback who merely stood and watched him, probably wanting nothing more than for him to go away. But Jimmy didn't go away. He pushed up on the two clasped hands that held him and bit down on the man's thumb as hard as he could. Jimmy's captor howled and immediately let him go.

What happened next moved too fast for anyone to stop.

Jimmy hit the ground running. He yelled, "Blitz!" and hit Roger Braddock in the head with his right forearm as hard as he could. The young man's glass flew from his hand, and he dropped like he'd been shot. His fall was interrupted only when his head smashed into the bar rail.

The coroner's report said, upon its release, that Roger Braddock was dead before his body came to rest on the floor.

Jimmy nearly died himself that night from the beating he received from Braddock's teammates. Only the arrival of the police saved him, and the officers involved later admitted that had they known what Jimmy Leverette had done, they wouldn't have interfered.

This time the Gunslingers made no effort to help Jimmy, legally or financially. In fact, they cut him from the team, and to help in the suit which the New York team was bringing against them, they started a PR campaign outlining how they'd tried to help "reform" Jimmy Leverette over the years, but he'd proved perversely incorrigible.

Jimmy was held in jail without bond on a charge of second-degree homicide, and had a public defender for a lawyer. His defense was that he was deranged by steroids and other drugs at the time he struck Roger Braddock, and that the Gunslingers were culpable as Jimmy had received all of his drugs from the team trainer, and that the team physician was aware that players were encouraged to use steroids without warning them that such substances had serious side-effects, including uncontrollable fits of rage.

In a nutshell, Jimmy copped a temporary insanity plea and placed the blame elsewhere.

The team trainer and physician vehemently denied Jimmy's allegations, and since no other player or any of the coaches would corroborate the charges, the district attorney declined to prosecute the two team officials. Lab reports on blood samples taken from Jimmy just after the incident did, however, show levels of drugs that should have killed him, much less impair his judgment.

For that reason, the judge reduced the charge against Jimmy to manslaughter, and when a guilty verdict was returned, after the jury deliberated for all of eight minutes, sentenced him to twelve years in the state prison at Huntsville.

He served every last day of his sentence, as the parole board consistently rejected any plea for early release. When he got out, Jimmy was 46 years old, had a hundred and seventeen dollars in his pockets, and no hope of ever again finding a job having anything remotely to do with pro football. As far as the big-time sports establishment was concerned, Jimmy Leverette had been given a life sentence.

Adding to his misfortune, just as he got out, the Braddock family released to the media a highlight video of their late son's life, to remind everyone of just what a fine young man had been killed, who was responsible for his death and that the killer was now free.

Ironically, it was in response to that video that Jimmy Leverette reinvented himself. When a Dallas TV crew caught up with him at a local flophouse and asked if he now had any remorse for what he'd done, he let loose with a rant: His father had abandoned him. His mother had beaten him. He'd been dirt poor. All the schools he'd attended wanted him only for his athletic ability. The Gunslingers had shot him full of steroids. All his life he'd been somebody's nigger. And that's what those Braddock people wanted him to stay. Well, he might be stone broke, he might be the most hated man in America, but he was nobody's nigger now.

And he never would be again.

To Jimmy's amazement, just days after his tirade aired, unsolicited letters found their way to him. Some of it was hate mail, but a far greater part praised him for what he'd said. And enclosed in many of the letters was money. Most came with only a few dollars, but one envelope from a lady in Alabama contained a hundred dollar bill. She wrote that his voice rang with the Lord's righteous thunder.

That was the moment of Jimmy's epiphany, and he never looked back. He legally changed his last name to Thunder. He found a bleeding-heart ghostwriter to tell his life story: *Nobody's Nigger.* He printed a hundred copies of the book with the money that continued to trickle in. He took those first copies to black churches around Dallas to sell from the trunk of a twenty year old Cadillac. He used the proceeds to print more copies and started selling them all over the South. Then a Boston publisher picked up the book — nobody in New York would touch it — and it became a best-seller.

From there, Jimmy acquired a mail-order divinity degree and backstopped it with his childhood readings of the Bible. He parlayed that with his college education in television arts and sciences and the money from his book to become a televangelist. His message was simple and compelling: Have faith in God, live a good, clean life, and no black person in America would ever have to be anybody's nigger again.

The Reverend Jimmy Thunder never asked directly for money.

At the end of each show, a simple message came on the screen that the preceding program was furnished by a publicly supported ministry. It would continue to be presented as funds permitted.

The soft sell worked. Dollars rolled in by the millions.

After hearing from a woman in his audience one day that he spoke as if he stood on a high mountaintop with Jesus and could see the whole world, Jimmy decided to find some nice place at the right altitude so he could back up that perception with a degree of reality.

Let the flock see how he had risen to the heights. Tell them they could climb the mountain, too. Jimmy moved to a fenced-in lakeshore estate in Goldstrike, California, and built his new TV studio on the property.

Now, four years after his release from prison, at age fifty, he stood in front of Ron Ketchum and told the chief he'd come for the body of his son.

"I didn't know you had a son," Ron told Reverend Thunder. "I don't recall reading about him in your book."

Ron kept his tone civil, but like most cops he wasn't well disposed to ex-cons, especially one who'd killed somebody and then didn't have the decency to die behind bars. Jimmy Thunder was familiar with the chief's attitude, though he hadn't encountered it anytime recently. Still, he kept from lashing out. Didn't say a word.

"Maybe you mentioned him in a later edition," Ron surmised.

"I'm here for my son's body," Thunder said, holding his temper. "Are you going to let me give him a Christian burial or not?"

"I'm afraid I can't. I haven't received word that his autopsy is complete … and Reverend Cardwell's widow has first claim on his body. She and Mrs. Mahalia Cardwell are on their way to town as we speak."

Now, the Reverend Thunder's eyes flashed with an anger that would have done credit to a wrathful God. He leaned toward Ron and said portentously, "I know who you are."

"We know each other, Reverend," Ron replied evenly.

Jimmy Thunder glared at the chief a moment longer, then he got to his feet and left the chief's office with a seeming sense of purpose in his step.

"Ten to one the man finds all those reporters swarming around here," Oliver Gosden offered.

"No bet."

"A hundred to one he pours poison in their ears about our racist chief of police."

"Maybe I should write a book," Ron responded. *"Nobody's Cracker."*

Annie Stratton saw Jimmy Thunder striding toward the stage, looking like his namesake storm front. Of greater importance, the swelling media mob saw and recognized him, too. The reporters had grown restless with her explanations of why the police couldn't tell them anything yet, not even the victim's identity. She'd had to tongue-lash several of them back into their seats when they'd gotten snotty with her, and the mood in the room was foul. Now, though, the newsies grew excited. They could feel a story was about to fall in their laps like manna from heaven.

They moved to the edges of their seats and gathered their legs under them, ready to leap to their feet and bellow the first question that popped into their heads. It was feeding time at the zoo.

Annie fleetingly considered the possibility of cutting the power to the microphone on the lectern. But that would do no good. Reverend Thunder came by his adopted name honestly. He could project his voice to the back row of the auditorium without breaking a sweat or dropping a consonant.

For an instant, she even considered throwing the fire alarm to clear the room. But that would give her only a short respite, and would make things look worse in the end. So, whatever Jimmy Thunder had to say, and she knew she wouldn't like it, she'd have to yield the stage to him and simply let him say it.

Annie smiled to literally put the best face on things, stepped back and gestured to Jimmy Thunder to take her place. If she *really* didn't like what the sonofabitch had to say, she could always tackle him from behind.

Jimmy got right to it. "I believe y'all know me, and I think many of you know I live in this town. Undoubtedly, you're all here because you heard that yesterday a black man was found crucified to a tree."

The Reverend Thunder enunciated his next statement with exquisite precision. "That man was my *son.*"

The auditorium was hushed. Not even Annie Stratton had expected this.

Jimmy Thunder continued before his audience could collect their wits or catch their breath. "His name was Isaac Cardwell. He was my only child."

Now, the media regained their footing, figuratively and literally. They shouted a babble of questions at Jimmy Thunder. He couldn't have understood them even if he wanted to, but he was interested only in making his statement, not answering questions. His voice boomed out, overwhelming theirs.

"This heinous crime happened in Mayor Clay Steadman's town. It happened in the town where the chief of police is Ronald Ketchum. He's the man responsible for catching my son's killer. But when I asked him just now to release my son's body to me, he refused."

Jimmy Thunder's anger was so intense his voice quivered.

"He would *not* give me my son!"

The reverend hung his head and not even the crassest reporter in the room would intrude on the man's grief. After a long moment, Jimmy Thunder looked up and addressed the crowd.

"Do all of you remember who Ron Ketchum is?" he asked.

With the possible exception of the newly arrived foreign press, they all did.

But Jimmy Thunder told them anyway.

"That's right. He was Lieutenant Ronald Ketchum of the LAPD. The man who's supposed to catch my son's killer was once on trial himself for killing a black man."

CHAPTER 11

The media knew a big story when they heard one. Every paper, TV network and news website in the country would have as the lead for their next news cycle the fact that the man nailed to the tree in Goldstrike, California turned out to be the son of the Reverend Jimmy Thunder, and that the man responsible for catching Isaac Cardwell's killer had a reputation among African-Americans that was questionable at best.

Then, as was their wont, the ladies and gentlemen of the press would dredge up the story of Ron Ketchum for the edification of their audiences. Just in case anyone had missed it the umpteen times it had been told four years earlier.

In his twenty years with the LAPD, both as a patrol officer and a homicide detective, Ron Ketchum had never had to fire his weapon in the line of duty. But two times, when he was off duty, he'd had to shoot criminals. In each case, the man he'd shot was black.

The first time, Ron had been shooting baskets by himself at night in a park in Beverly Hills. He'd been busy concentrating on trying to sink one hundred free throws in a row when a carjacked Porsche came careening off of La Cienega Boulevard and into the park. He had to leap out of the way just to avoid getting splattered. An LAPD patrol unit, lights blazing and siren screaming, barreled into the park not five seconds behind the stolen car.

Ron ran to his car to get his weapon out of the trunk

By the time he had his Beretta in hand, the carjacker had stopped the Porsche and was crouched behind it opening up on the patrol unit with an Uzi. Ron saw the officer behind the wheel killed outright. The dead man's partner managed to dive out through the passenger side door, but he was shot in the leg as the carjacker kept firing.

Ron ran toward the shooter. The carjacker exhausted his clip just as Ron put his gun on him and announced himself as a police officer. The carjacker responded by reaching for a handgun sticking out of his pants. Ron shot him in the chest five times.

He ran to the shooter, pulled the gun out of his pants, flung it aside and made sure the man wouldn't be able to resume firing. As far as Ron could tell from his cursory examination, the guy was dead. Good, he thought to himself. One fewer asshole on the streets.

He then went to the aid of the wounded officer. His name tag said Gosden. Ron used the T-shirt off his back as a tourniquet to stop the bleeding from the wounded cop's femoral artery. Then ignoring the blood and brain matter splashed about the interior of the patrol car, he called in a Code 30 on the unit's radio: Officer needs help, emergency.

He hurried back to Gosden. It seemed like blood was still leaking from the wounded man's leg. He pulled on his T-shirt as hard as he could, making the tourniquet as tight as possible. Gosden moaned, but Ron could see there was already a large pool of blood under the man's leg. And, worse, his eyes were starting to glaze over.

Ron knew somehow that if he let this man go into shock, there'd be no bringing him back. He cradled Gosden's head in his lap and started talking to him, demanding his attention, that he stay with him.

"My name's Lieutenant Ronald Ketchum," he told the wounded officer. "Help is on the way, and the perp is down."

The words seemed to penetrate the fog of Gosden's terrible pain. He blinked several times, trying to bring Ron into focus.

Finally, he groaned, "Bauer?"

Gosden was asking about his partner, Ron knew.

"He's gone. But you're not. You hang on just a minute and the ambulance will be here." But Ron saw Gosden's eyes begin to swim again. So he yelled, "Hang on, goddamnit! You gonna let that sonofabitch kill both of you?"

Ron could hear the approaching sirens. He was desperate not to let this man die before medical help could arrive.

"Listen to me, Officer Gosden. You have a family? Tell me about your family."

Ron Ketchum knew he'd never be able to explain it clearly to anyone, but he felt with those words he'd extended his hand across a great void to a man who was just about to turn his back on life — and Gosden reached out and took the hand he offered.

"Wi-ife," the wounded officer whispered. "Ba...baby boy. Danny."

"Don't leave your wife, man," Ron urged. "Don't you let your son grow up without you."

"Lauren . . . s-so beautiful." Gosden swallowed hard. "Da-anny . . . sleep just like ... angel."

Then Officer Gosden's eyes closed, and Ron thought he'd lost him. But he saw the wounded man's chest rise and fall as he continued to breathe. And he noticed there was a peaceful smile on his face.

Help arrived in time.

The carjacker, Dantrell Weems, was resuscitated and he lived, too. That stunned Ron, because he was sure he'd killed Weems. The news of the carjacker's survival left Ron uncertain how he felt. Should he be relieved that he didn't have a man's life on his conscience? Or should he feel annoyed that he'd have to go through all the hassle of testifying against a cop-killer at his trial?

For the most part, he felt more annoyed than relieved.

But Ron's aggravation was only beginning. It was about to take a quantum leap forward in the form of Marcus Martin. Martin, an African American, had been Ron's nemesis since he was a teenager. As high school athletes at rival schools, Martin had once put Ron in the hospital by undercutting him during a basketball game. Ron had repaid Martin by spiking him viciously when baseball season rolled around.

Now, Marcus Martin was a big time lawyer and a man who loved the limelight. While Dantrell Weems was still unconscious in the prison ward at County Hospital, Martin gave a news conference in which he appeared with Weems' mother and his common-law wife. Martin announced plans to sue the city and Lieutenant Ronald Ketchum on behalf of Dantrell Weems, at the behest of his family.

The charge would be abuse of authority. Martin claimed that Ron should have arrested Weems instead of shooting him. He said that even a cursory reading of the police report on the incident revealed that by his own words Lieutenant Ketchum admitted that the automatic weapon in Weems possession had run out of ammunition, and that the only other weapon, a handgun, that Lieutenant Ketchum *claimed* Weems possessed had been found twenty feet from his client's body. Martin insinuated that the handgun found at the scene had been dropped by the lieutenant after the fact as an excuse for shooting Weems. He suggested that the judgment against the city would run into the millions.

He also urged the district attorney to look into filing charges against Lieutenant Ketchum, and hinted darkly that the man was a known racist.

Marcus Martin's plans were undercut by responses from two quarters.

The family of Officer Oliver Gosden held a bedside press conference in the hospital room where the wounded cop lay recovering.

Speaking for her family, Lauren Gosden said, "Lieutenant Ronald Ketchum saved my husband's life. He kept me from becoming a widow, and my son from never knowing his father. We will be grateful to him for as long as we live. As to the charges that Lieutenant Ketchum is a racist, well, as he held my husband's head in his lap and kept him talking about Danny and me until the paramedics arrived, I really think he must have noticed that Oliver is black. And he probably guessed my son and I are, too."

But what really wrecked Marcus Martin's case was what Dantrell Weems said when he regained consciousness.

"I been to the other side," Weems told his mother. "I know what's waiting. I got to get right or there ain't no hope for me at all."

Neither Weems nor his mother would pursue the case Marcus Martin wanted to file. The common-law wife still wanted to go after the money. Dantrell was going to prison, damnit. What good would he be to her in there? But Martin knew that without at least the mother, he couldn't even get away with pleading that Dantrell had been brain damaged by the shooting, and was incompetent to plea for himself in either a criminal trial or a civil action.

But Dantrell Weems did plea for himself: He pled guilty to the murder of Officer Conrad Bauer. He pled for forgiveness from the slain cop's family. And when he was sentenced to die he pled to God to have mercy upon his soul.

The second incident occurred shortly before Ron had put in his twenty years with the department and was considering retirement. He was at a gas station near his Westchester home filling the tank of his personal car. He heard a toot from a car horn and looked up. He saw Jeff Woodridge, the son of his next door neighbors, drive past. The boy waved from behind the wheel of his new car, a used but immaculate BMW 325i.

Ron had known the Woodridge boy since he was six years old, and since that time, Jeff had been telling Ron and his wife, Leilani, and any other neighbor who'd listen, how he was saving to buy his first car. Now, at age eighteen, the day had finally arrived for Jeff. Ron smiled. But not for long.

He noticed another car with two black guys in it who seemed to be following Jeff. The city had been experiencing a large number of follow-home robberies in the past month, and Ron didn't like the feeling he got off these two guys. He got in his car and tailed them — which he had to do anyway since he was going home and they were following Jeff to the house next door.

Ron's heart raced when he saw the two guys following Jeff pull stocking caps over their heads. He used the radio in his car to call for assistance and laid his gun on the seat next to him.

The bad guys' car sped up just as Jeff pulled into his driveway. Ron hit the gas, too.

Jeff had just stepped clear of his prized new set of wheels when the bad guys slammed into his rear bumper. The boy looked around at the sound of the crash. He couldn't believe what had just happened to his new car. Redfaced with anger, he started to stomp toward the driver of the offending vehicle. Then he saw something that made him turn and run for his house. He was trying to open the front door when his father pulled it open from inside.

At that point, the bad guys got out of their car. Each of them had a gun in his hand. The weapons were immediately pointed at the Woodridges. The driver yelled, "Leave that door open, motherfuckers! Y'all got company."

Before either bad guy could take a step, though, they heard a screech of tires and then another voice of command: "Drop your weapons! Police!"

When the driver turned toward Ron with his gun still in his hand, Ron shot him. Just once. The other bad guy started to run. Ron called for him to halt, and fired a warning shot into the ground. As Ron raised his weapon, not intending to let this sonofabitch get away, but dreading what the consequences of shooting him in the back would be, the guy skidded to a stop. He dropped his weapon, and put his hands in the air. He tensed his shoulders, too, as if bracing himself for the shot he expected to be fired.

That was when Ron realized how much he'd like to oblige the little shit.

But he didn't. Instead, he came up from behind and swept the guy's feet out from under him. He quickly cuffed him, and told him to stay flat on his face or he would be shot. Then he ran back to the first asshole to make sure he wasn't getting ready to run. Or to shoot him from behind.

He wasn't.

The Woodridges had kicked the guy's gun away from his body, and stood between it and the robber. George Woodridge, Jeff's father, looked at Ron and said with an approving nod, "I think you killed this one."

Ron had.

There'd be no reviving sixteen year old Qadry Carter.

Neither would there be any stopping Marcus Martin this time. Sharrod Carter, the late Qadry's accomplice and surviving twin brother, claimed Ron had never given him or his brother any warning before he'd gunned down Qadry. And when he'd chased Sharrod, he'd yelled, "Get down, nigger, or I'll kill you, too!" Then he'd shot at Sharrod.

Jeff and George Woodridge refuted these accusations. The LAPD found the bullet from the warning shot Ron had fired into his neighbor's lawn, and the department recovered ninety-seven items of property missing from other follow-home robberies in the crawlspace of the garage behind the Carter boys parents' house.

Teddy and Mavis Carter claimed to have no knowledge of the stolen goods found on their property, and didn't condone what their sons had done. But they believed Sharrod's story and said that white racist cop had no business killing Qadry, who'd been only a sixteen year old boy, after all. The Carters were happy to have Mr. Marcus Martin protect their interests.

The DA, however, found those interests to be less compelling. He accepted the Woodridge's testimony to be credible; he knew that the Carter boys had a history of juvenile offenses dating back to when they were nine years old; and he liked the idea of prosecuting Sharrod for multiple home invasions a lot better than trying to nail a police lieutenant for protecting his neighbors.

The county of Los Angeles declined to institute any criminal proceedings against Lieutenant Ronald Ketchum. And because the DA was savvy enough to notify the police department in advance of making his decision public, there was no immediate outbreak of civil disorder.

Marcus Martin railed publicly against the system, saying there was no hope for justice for the black man in America. Within hours of his outburst, the Korean owner of a car stereo shop on Vermont Avenue exchanged gunfire with an irate African American customer who claimed the man had sold him a defective iPod dock. Both combatants died at the scene. Only a swift and massive deployment of police, who were already on alert, kept the town from exploding.

The fallen customer's girlfriend told a radio reporter that her boyfriend had heard Marcus Martin's comments about the lack of justice for blacks and had picked up his gun, told her where he was going and said, "I'm gonna to get me some justice right now."

At that point, the federal government decided to enter the picture. The U.S. Attorney for Southern California said he would look into filing charges against Ronald Ketchum for violating the civil rights of Qadry Carter. The FBI would be investigating Lieutenant Ketchum, and would report to him on their findings.

The response from the district attorney who was genuinely pissed at this action by the feds, which was a none too subtle slap at his decision on the matter — and who saw the chance to curry favor with the cops — promptly brought charges against Marcus Martin for incitement to riot, and said he would be looking into the lawyer's culpability in the deaths of Noh Ree Kim and Lester DeChance.

That was the situation for a month. Each investigation proceeded apace. The FBI pored over every aspect of Ron's life with the implicit presumption of guilt. Cops working with the DA made Marcus Martin's life equally miserable. Accusations were hurled back and forth. The DA and the U.S. Attorney held daily press conference. Marcus Martin never passed up a single microphone without getting in a barbed sound bite.

Only Ron Ketchum refused to comment. He was concentrating on his retirement plans, and wondering if there was any way to save his marriage, which was not holding up well under all the stress. Things got to the point where Ron thought a divorce would be the least of his worries.

In the end, a deal was struck. In separate press conferences, held at precisely the same time, the DA and the U.S. Attorney announced that all charges were being dropped against each man. Both prosecutors had concluded there wasn't enough evidence to go forward.

But a tie wasn't good enough for Marcus Martin. Not this time.

He filed a wrongful death suit against Lieutenant Ronald Ketchum on behalf of Teddy and Mavis Carter. Ron Ketchum, he said, had shot two black men, killing one of them. He was a homicidal, racist cop and he had to pay. Marcus Martin would make him pay.

By the time the trial started, Ron and Leilani Ketchum had decided to call it quits. He'd been after her for years about having kids, and she'd been refusing, pleading the need to maintain her figure for an acting career that had amounted to nothing more than a handful of walk-ons over a period of twenty years. Their dreams, both personally and as a couple, seemed about to expire of natural causes, and once they'd gotten past a final shouting match, they'd decided to be decent to each other in honor of the love they'd once had. They would divorce amicably.

In the meantime, Leilani decided she would bear up under the ordeal of the civil action and would support Ron and escort him to court every day. Make it that much more difficult for that bastard Marcus Martin to say a man with a Polynesian Japanese English Swedish American wife was a racist. She would make a silent, favorable impression upon the jury for Ron, and there would be nothing Marcus Martin could do about it.

Ron and his lawyer, Jack Hobart, knew that Martin was going to paint Ron as the worst bigot since Nathan Bedford Forrest started dressing people in white sheets. They planned their defense accordingly and with more than a little irony. They were going to be pre-emptive. After the O.J. Simpson debacle, L.A. cops knew better than to pretend they were angels, or even boy scouts. So, Ron's defense was going to be a new twist on a classic theme: He was the victim of his childhood.

When Marcus Martin called Ron to the stand for direct examination, he asked Ron if he had shouted at Sharrod Carter, "Get down, nigger, or I'll kill you, too."

"No," Ron replied simply.

"You neither threatened Sharrod Carter nor referred to him as a nigger?"

Jack Hobart didn't object to the question that had already been asked and answered.

"I did neither."

"Did you refer to Sharrod Carter as a nigger at any time?"

"No."

"Did you refer to Qadry Carder as a nigger before you killed him?"

"Objection! Prejudicial!" Jack Hobart roared. The defense lawyer didn't want Martin to realize they were laying in wait for him. He would have smelled a rat if Hobart had let that one slide by.

"Your Honor," Martin boomed, "prejudice is at the very heart of this case. The prejudice of the defendant, who has a history of —"

"That'll be enough, Mr. Martin," the judge interrupted. "Objection sustained. Rephrase your question if you wish."

Martin gathered his dignity with a deep breath. "Did you call Qadry Carter a nigger at any time?"

"No."

"You called neither of the Carters a nigger at any time?"

Ron knew that a large part of Martin's game was to say nigger as many times as he could while Ron was on the stand. The plaintiff's lawyer wanted the jury to see the word written across Ron's forehead any time they thought of him.

"No, I did not." Then Ron added, "If I don't like a suspect, I call him an asshole."

The jury laughed, and the judge admonished Ron, but only mildly. He was suppressing a grin himself.

The reaction didn't please Marcus Martin. Bigots weren't supposed to be funny. It humanized them too much. So he decided it was time to go straight for the jugular.

"Are we to believe then, Lieutenant Ketchum, that at no time in your life have you ever referred to a black person as a nigger?"

That was when Ron's defensive strategy kicked in.

"No, it would be untrue to say that. As a child, I routinely called black people niggers. It was what I had been taught. In fact, growing up, I didn't consider black people to *be* people."

The five African Americans on the jury sat up straight at this brutally candid admission; the expressions on their faces were not particularly sympathetic. Ron seemed to have won no absolution by his extraordinary public confession.

But Marcus Martin was smart enough to know he'd just been thrown a curve. An affirmative response, much less one so bluntly forthcoming, had been the last thing he'd expected his question to elicit. He'd been ready to mock and destroy Ron's denial. So now he had to proceed with great care.

"Are you admitting to this court, Lieutenant Ketchum," he asked softly, "that you are the worst kind of racist, one who would deny even the basic humanity of your fellow man simply because the color of his skin is different from your own?"

Ron looked straight at Martin so he would not suggest even the slightest hint of dishonesty.

"No, Mr. Martin, I am not. What I'm saying is, that was the kind of man I was raised to be."

Marcus Martin took a sip of water, and glanced at the jury out of the corner of his eye. All twelve jurors were paying rapt attention now. Worse for him, the black members of the panel seemed visibly less hostile than only a moment ago.

But Ron Ketchum had just given him a denial. It wasn't as sweeping as the one for which he'd originally hoped, but it was still something to attack. It was still an opportunity to destroy the prick's credibility. Brand him a liar as well as a racist.

Martin had disliked Ron from the very first moment the lawyer had stepped onto the basketball court at Agnus Dei High School for pre-game warm-ups and saw Ron's face among the members of the opposing team. Ketchum had been a short, skinny kid in those days. But as absurd as he looked compared to his bigger, far more physically mature black teammates, Ketchum had this look on his face like he was tough. Bad. And when Marcus Martin, six inches taller and forty pounds heavier than Ketchum then, had stared at him, Ketchum stared right back.

It was ridiculous. Ketchum trying to stare down Marcus Martin. He was so small. So skinny. So *white.* It still made Martin burn with shame every time he admitted to himself that he'd looked away first.

The thing was, the little shit had been cat quick, and put up an outside shot that those skinny wrists never should have been able to launch, much less hit with such frightening regularity. So, one time when Ketchum faked that jump shot, the guy defending him left his feet. Ketchum then thought he had a clear lane to the basket, and Marcus Martin let him have it. But as Ketchum was up in the air making his lay-up, Martin cut his legs out from under him, and the white boy landed on the floor head first.

Now, after all the intervening years, they were still going at it. Martin asked, "Are you saying, then, that your parents failed to raise you in the way they considered right? Or should I say white?"

Ron didn't take the bait.

"What I'm saying is that my father is a bigot who comes from a long line of bigots, and he expected me to carry on in the family tradition. But I'm a disappointment to him."

"So now you *love* black people, when you aren't shooting them, is that it?"

"Objection, Your Honor!" Jack Hobart shouted. "Prejudicial. Counsel is attacking the witness."

"Sustained," the judge ruled emphatically. "The jury will disregard, Mr. Martin's last remark. Mr. Martin, you may represent your client's case vigorously, but if you make another such blatantly inflammatory remark, I will declare a mistrial and hold you in contempt of court."

"Yes, Your Honor," Martin said with false humility. He knew he'd walked right to the edge on that one, but he was worried now. He'd had to make the point that this unflappable bastard was still a lying racist who'd shot two black men.

"Lieutenant Ketchum," Martin resumed, "you testified that you used the word nigger routinely as a child. Did you ever use it in the course of your duties as a police officer?"

"No."

Martin let the sneering look of disbelief linger on his face for the jury to see. He asked his next question only when he sensed the judge was becoming restive.

"You must have undergone quite a change of heart then. Can you tell us what it was?"

This was it, Martin knew. Ron Ketchum would have to come across with a story right now that was so persuasive and substantive that Martin couldn't destroy it with either ridicule or logic. And Martin didn't believe Ron had such a story.

Ron began, "I made a friend when I was twelve years old. His name was DeWayne Michaels. He was a little guy like me, so when he came up to me one day when I was shooting baskets in the park and asked if I wanted to play some one on one, I agreed. I still regarded black people as niggers at that time, but I didn't think of DeWayne as black. He didn't look any darker than I was when I had a tan, and he had green eyes. So, by the values my father taught me, I didn't see anything wrong in playing ball with him. And we had great games. We were very evenly matched, and we both played our hearts out.

"After a couple weeks of playing every day, DeWayne asked me if I wanted to come over to his house. I said sure, but on the way I started getting nervous because we were going a long way and heading toward a neighborhood where my father, who was a police officer, had told me never to go. I asked DeWayne if he lived around there, and he said yes. I asked why, and he said that's where black folks like him lived. I couldn't have been more shocked if he'd told me he was from Mars."

"Can we skip ahead to the good part, Lieutenant?" Martin asked sarcastically.

The judge castigated Martin without prompting from the defense. "You asked the question, Counselor. The witness is answering it. Remain silent until he finishes."

Martin nodded mutely. He was pissed. The judge had lectured him as if he were some little snot nosed law student who didn't know how to behave in a courtroom. He only hoped that the jury took into account that the judge was white, too.

Ron continued, "DeWayne introduced me to his mother and father and sister. His dad was plainly black; anyone could see that. But his mother looked as white as my mom. When I asked DeWayne, in the softest whisper I could manage, if she was white he said no. She was from New Orleans, the kind of person they called an octoroon down there. In the South, he told me, one drop of black blood made a person black. That was very hard for me to comprehend. I also had difficulty understanding the fact that both of DeWayne's parents had jobs and their house was as neat and clean as my own. I'd been told that black people were either thieves or welfare bums and lived in rat-infested tenements. When it came time to leave, DeWayne's dad insisted on driving me home. He said the neighborhood got a little dangerous at night.

"I was glad to have the ride, but I was very anxious about my father seeing that it was a black man and his son bringing me home. What was really bad was that I could tell DeWayne wanted to see my house after he'd shown me his. But there was no way I could bring him in. I mean, maybe I could have tried to fool my dad into thinking DeWayne was white, but what was I supposed to tell him, 'Sorry, DeWayne, but your father has to wait outside in the car.' Luckily for me, Mr. Michaels seemed to understand my problem, and didn't let on to DeWayne. He just said he was sorry they couldn't stop in and say hello to my family, but they had to get right home.

"I was still terribly embarrassed. I was also angry and confused that my father had lied to me. Most of all, I was fearful that De-

Wayne's father had told him what was what after I got out of the car, and he'd never be my friend again."

Now, Ron asked for a drink of water. Dredging up these memories was clearly painful for him, and the jury could see that he was not putting on an act for their benefit.

"DeWayne stayed my friend. We kept playing one on one at the park; sometimes we'd team up and play two on two against other guys. I kept waiting for him to ask to come to my house, but he never did. I figured his father must have told him something, but he wasn't holding it against me.

"One day, toward the end of the summer, my mom told me I needed new shoes for school, and she'd take me before she went to work that day. So when I didn't show up at the park to play basketball at the usual time, that was the day DeWayne decided he'd drop by my house to pick me up." Ron took a pause to finish his glass of water. "The only person home when he got there was my dad. He was sleeping after working a night shift and then having a few drinks at an after-hours place with some friends. That morning, DeWayne made the mistake of ringing my doorbell.

"The next thing he knows my dad yanks the door open and starts beating him over the head with his baton. My dad is six-two and weighs over two hundred pounds. DeWayne was a foot shorter and not much more than a hundred pounds. And all of a sudden he has this madman beating the hell out of him, probably going to kill him right then and there, for the crime of coming to pick up his friend to play basketball.

"I saw all this as I was coming home with my new shoes. My father was beating DeWayne on his kidneys with his baton. I threw myself at my dad, trying to tackle him, to get him to stop. But I was no bigger than DeWayne. I bounced off. So I ran in the house and got my father's gun."

Ron took a deep breath and rubbed his hand over his face.

"When I got back outside, my father was still hitting DeWayne. Now, he was working over the backs of his legs. I fired a shot into the air. That finally broke the spell for my dad. He looked around, saw I had his gun and that it was pointed up, and he jumped on me. I thought he was going to start beating me, but I was wrong. He was shielding me. He yelled at me that when you fired a bullet up into the air it had to come back down, and when it did it could kill you. So he'd thrown his body over mine to take the bullet I'd fired if he had to.

"I couldn't make heads or tails out of the man. Willing to die for his son, but lying to him about how he should think about other people. Where was the sense? With tears running down my face, I scrambled down to hold DeWayne, who was unconscious and bleeding from several places on his face and head. I demanded to know why my father had tried to kill my friend.

"I'll never forget the look of genuine surprise, and disgust, on my father's face. He said, 'Your *friend?* I thought he was just some nigger casing the house so he could break in.'"

Ron turned to look directly at the jury.

"DeWayne recovered. And he didn't even hold it against me for what my father had done to him. We went on to play basketball together for four years in high school. I've never addressed a black person as 'nigger' since the day my father nearly killed my best friend."

Now, Ron directed his attention at Marcus Martin.

"You might remember DeWayne Michaels, Counselor. You recall that time you cheap-shotted me when our frosh-soph teams played that basketball game? You sent me to the hospital. DeWayne Michaels was the guy who said he'd take care of you if you ever tried it again."

Martin could have objected to the personal reference as hearsay, but he knew it would be pointless. His case was lost. There was no way to attack *that* story.

Just to make sure the case was well in hand, Jack Hobart called Walter Ketchum, Ron's father, to corroborate his son's story. The old ex-cop dispassionately admitted he didn't like blacks and that he thought they were responsible for most of society's problems. He said he'd beaten DeWayne Michaels as his son had stated, and he'd honestly thought the boy had been about to burgle his house. Walter agreed that he, too, had learned his attitudes from his father, and if you went back far enough, you'd find a Ketchum who'd owned slaves in Texas, and had tried to keep them even after the Confederacy had lost the war.

Chantelle Michaels, DeWayne's sister, also was called as a defense witness. She told of Ron's friendship with her brother. She said that informing Ron her brother had been killed in an accident while serving in the army was one of the hardest things she'd ever done.

Sergeant Oliver Gosden testified for Ron. He insisted on testifying even after Ron had told him it probably wasn't necessary as the case looked to be won. Coming to the aid of a white officer — even one who'd saved his life — was sure to cause resentment among Gosden's fellow black officers on the LAPD, the force was so riven by racial and gender animosities. But Oliver decided he had a moral obligation, and he fulfilled it.

In his closing statement, Jack Hobart painted Ron not just as a good man but a noble one. He was the police officer who had literally served and protected his neighbors. He was the police officer who risked his own life to save that of his fellow officer. But more than that, he was the kind of man who overcame an insidious legacy of hate which could have made him a racist like his father and grandfather and who knew how many other of his forebears before that. Make no mistake, Jack Hobart told the jury, Ron Ketchum, too, was exposed to this awful virus of hatred. It was bred into him as soon as he was first taught to say the word nigger. But he overcame those malignant lessons by hard experience and great effort. To coin a phrase, Hobart said, the man you see before you was a recovering bigot. He fought every day against the potential for hatred within him, and every day since he saw his father beat his best friend, he had won that fight.

The jury took less than two hours to return a verdict in Ron's favor. But the media knew a sound bite when they heard one. They seized upon Jack Hobart's description of Ron and affixed it to him forever in the public consciousness: Ron Ketchum, recovering bigot. The label would be his epitaph.

Especially since he never publicly disputed it.

There were those, of course, who would have liked to see him stripped of the fig leaf that the adjective *recovering* provided. Marcus Martin was the foremost among them, suffering not only the injury of losing his case against Ron but also the insult of being ordered to pay Ron's legal fees.

Leilani Ketchum's last act of solidarity with her husband was rewarded when a TV producer who'd attended each session of the trial was struck by her exotic beauty and cast her in a highly-rated police drama, *Plainclothes,* giving her, at long last, her big break.

Walter Ketchum suffered a stroke four days after testifying, and after his hospitalization had his home care provided by Esther Gadwell, an African American LPN, the only person who would put up with him.

And Ron Ketchum pulled the pin on his badge and retired from the LAPD.

That was where most of the media coverage had left off with Ron. Now that he was being run through the news cycle again, he was sure there would be an update added. The press was nothing if not complete in its invasions of a person's privacy.

After his retirement and divorce, alone in a home he'd once hoped to fill with his children, still vital at 45, he tried to figure out what the hell he was going to do with himself. He hadn't the slightest idea. But he suspected whatever it was would have to be done elsewhere. He was too controversial to stay in L.A.

For three months, he divided his time between fishing and fixing up his house for the day when he'd eventually put it on the market. Then one Monday morning the phone rang and a woman with a high-tone British accent asked him if he might be free that day to take lunch with Mr. Clay Steadman. Yes, he was told, *that* Mr. Clay Steadman. Ron thought this was all part of a joke Leilani was playing on him, and since he'd missed her badly, he agreed.

Much to his surprise when he showed up at the appointed

place and time, he met Clay Steadman. Far more shocking, Mayor Steadman of the town of Goldstrike, had a job offer for him: He wanted Ron to be his new chief of police. The movie star mayor admitted that he'd had Ron thoroughly checked out, and he liked what he'd heard. He said the chief's job came with a good salary and benefits, and the town would provide a fully modern six room cabin for his use. What did Ron think?

Ron asked if the mayor really wanted a recovering bigot to head his police department. Clay asked if Ron would have a problem working for a recovering drug addict. The two men suited each other. Once Ron made certain he could run the department with a large degree of autonomy, he accepted, packed his bags, turned his house over to a broker and headed north.

He'd been happy in Goldstrike, high up in his mountain retreat, the past three years. But now he knew you could keep the world and its troubles at bay only so long.

Then some shit-head would come along and nail a minister to a tree.

CHAPTER 12

Annie Stratton had tired of hosting the ever growing media mob, and kicked them out of the Muni Complex so she could go have a quick dinner. The newsies didn't go far, however. They set up camp on the grassy area near the wishing fountain just outside police headquarters. They called in or emailed their stories about the victim's identity, the conflict between the victim's father and the chief of police, and the chief's history. It was a warm, pleasant evening; the press was happy with their pickings so far; they were content to chat amongst themselves in the Muni's genial environs and await further developments.

The senior people would leave when darkness fell and retire to dinner, drinks and their hotel rooms. The junior staffers would remain all night lest anyone in authority try to sneak something past the people's watchful messengers.

Shortly before dusk, the head of the public works department appeared and started taking a census of the media. Unused to *answering* questions, the reporters demanded to know why the man wanted their names and those of their employers. Was this some form of harassment? The man from public works said with a smile that he just wanted to know whom he should bill to have the Muni's lawn resodded, and whom he should hold responsible if there were any other damage to public property.

The media were in such a huff over this affront to the First Amendment that they almost missed the arrival of the victim's family. But Charmaine, Japhet, and Mahalia Cardwell looked too much like the three tired, grief stricken out of towners they were to go unnoticed. Their race, their obvious emotional distress and their stiffly formal dark clothing led the newsies to the unerring conclusion that these people had to be the victim's family.

Only the timely arrival of Annie Stratton, returning from her brief evening meal, kept the media from descending on the Cardwells like ravenous scavengers. The press secretary lashed the mob back with threats that they would be expelled from the Muni Complex entirely if they didn't behave civilly. Such unreasonable demands brought loud cries of complaint. But Annie held her ground while a police officer responding to the uproar escorted the Cardwells into the mayor's office.

Clay Steadman personally seated the bereaved family on a sofa in his office. Ron Ketchum and Oliver Gosden, also present, offered their condolences. The mayor assured the Cardwells that the town of Goldstrike grieved with them over their loss.

Charmaine Cardwell nodded her acceptance and fought back tears. Mahalia Cardwell only glared in silence. But four year old Japhet spoke up.

"Can I see my daddy now?" the boy asked.

The question was more than his mother could bear. She took her son in her arms and began to sob. Ron nodded to Oliver. He summoned a female police officer, and she took Charmaine and Japhet from the room.

That left Mahalia Cardwell. She stood and stuck her jaw out at the three men. She looked to be in her seventies, a tall, unbowed, rawboned woman with strength in her body and fury in her eyes.

"Charmaine lost her husband," she said, "and my great-grandson lost his daddy. But I ..." She looked as if she wanted to lash out, spend her rage rending flesh and crushing bones. "I raised Isaac since he was Japhet's age, since his mama died. I lost my baby."

"Mrs. Cardwell," Clay said, understanding her perfectly, "if I could hand your grandson's killer over to you right now, to dispose of as you please, I'd do it. But all I can tell you is, this town will spare no effort to see that justice is done."

Mahalia Cardwell nodded as if she'd expected no lesser promise.

"You catch the man who killed Isaac," she told the municipal authorities arrayed before her. "You catch him or heaven help you."

Just as when he'd spoken to her on the phone, Ron felt this woman knew who the killer was. And she had known that Jimmy Thunder would try to claim Isaac Cardwell's body. He wanted to question her, but he knew he'd do better to wait until tomorrow.

The mayor said, "Mrs. Cardwell, I've reserved a suite at the Hyatt for you and your family at my expense. I've also arranged to have your grandson's body returned to Oakland in the morning. If there's anything else I can do for any of you, just call. My staff will put you through to me at any hour. I'll have Chief Ketchum take you and Mrs. Cardwell and Japhet out the back way so you won't be bothered by the reporters."

"No!" the old lady said so fiercely she surprised all three men. "You can take Charmaine and Japhet out back, but I want to talk to those people. I have something to say. And I want the whole world to hear it."

"As you like," Clay conceded.

Ron took Mahalia Cardwell out the front door of police headquarters. They were hit by TV lights immediately. The old woman squinted in their glare, but her step did not falter.

Whatever it was she had to say, Ron Ketchum wanted to hear it.

Addressing the press, now packed five deep, Mahalia Cardwell said, "I want all you people to know what a good man my grandson, Isaac, was. I want you to know he was kind and gentle. He never had a mean thought or word for anybody. He loved crackheads and whores just like he loved his own wife and baby, because he believed we are all Jesus' children." For just a moment, the old woman's fierce eyes softened, allowing her own deep sorrow to be revealed. "And that's the only reason I can think the Lord took him so soon: He could no longer bear not having Isaac at his side in heaven."

Then her rage returned, more fierce than ever.

"But the last thing I want you all to know is … God will *curse* this town, this place where my grandson was killed … He will curse it until Isaac's killer is delivered to justice."

Having spoken her piece, Mahalia Cardwell did not deign to take any of the questions shouted at her. Ron escorted her to a waiting police car. He opened the front passenger door for her and got her seated.

"This officer will take you to your hotel, Mrs. Cardwell. If you don't mind, I'd like to talk with you at your convenience in the morning."

She looked at Ron with a penetrating stare.

"Walter Nance told me all about you," she said, mentioning the Oakland police captain Ron had called that morning. "I remember reading about you in the newspaper, too. What you did down there in Los Angeles. Shooting those colored boys."

She nodded to herself. "You might be just the man I need."

A considerably younger woman stepped out from behind the media crowd to approach Ron as he headed back to his office. The chief saw one of his men intercept her, but she said something to the officer, who nodded and let her pass. Ron kept walking, but he watched her as she drew near.

She was tall, about five nine, he thought, sizing her up instinctively. Medium build but she had broad shoulders, and the little bounce in her step indicated good muscle tone. So he put her weight at one forty, maybe one forty-five. Her hair was light brown with blonde highlights, and cut short. The practical appearance of her hairstyle made him think her color was natural rather than a salon's attempt at being artful.

She was wearing some kind of uniform: a khaki shirt with a badge over the left breast pocket. The nametag over the right pocket said KNOX. There was a patch on her left shoulder that featured a grizzly bear. Her pants were green, and her belt and shoes were black.

"Chief Ketchum," she said, falling into step with Ron, "I'm Cordelia Knox, California Department of Fish and Game." She had a faint New England accent.

Ron reached the front door of police headquarters and held it open for her. Standing close to her now, he thought Cordelia Knox looked young enough to be a kid going to a costume party. She seemed to recognize his appraisal, but didn't let it bother her.

"I'm a game warden and a wildlife biologist," she said in a matter of fact tone, entering the building. Once inside, out of range of the media's pointed ears and microphones, she added. "I'm also a tracker and a hunter. And I was told you had a mountain lion attack on a female jogger yesterday morning."

Ron led the way to his office and offered her a guest chair. He took his own seat and considered her briefly again. He didn't doubt that she'd told him the truth about her credentials, but she still looked like a kid to him. He knew he'd better not let any criticism of her youth carry in his voice or show in manner. People might accuse him of being ageist as well as racist.

"Thank you for coming, Warden Knox. I'm glad you're here." Ron opened a desk drawer, took out a file, and handed it to his visitor. "Here's our report on the Mary Kaye Mallory attack. You can read it here or I can have a copy made for you to take with you."

"I'll do both, if you don't mind," she said with a smile.

Okay, he thought, she's a *good looking* kid, and he was starting to feel like a dirty old man. In the light of his office, he could see that her hair color was definitely natural and she had matching amber-brown eyes.

When she looked up from her reading there was a measure of concern in those eyes that made him think for the first time Cordelia Knox was a real grown-up, and a serious one at that.

"Chief, I think I have some bad news for you."

"What's that?" he asked evenly.

"When I heard of the attack on Ms. Mallory, it made me think of a cat I've been tracking for a month now."

"You've been after a mountain lion for a month, and haven't been able to catch it? Isn't that unusual?"

She shrugged, taking no offense.

"It can happen. A mountain lion has a pretty big range, up to a hundred square miles. But most times, when we want a big cat badly enough, we'll contract with a houndsman and, with the help of his dogs, run down our prey pretty quickly. But this animal … this one's different."

Ron frowned. "How's that?"

"Well," she said, "when we went after it with the hounds, it crippled two of them and killed a third. Damn near got the houndsman, too. It did all that damage, and still managed to get away before I could shoot it. And I'm a crack shot. But the really bad news is, this cat, in my opinion, is already responsible for the death of another person."

Ron didn't have any trouble reading between the lines. "Are you saying the mountain lion you've been tracking is the same one that attacked Mary Kaye Mallory?"

"Well, that's the puzzle. Because the location of the attack near Goldstrike would put it outside the normal range of the animal I've been hunting."

"But?" Ron asked.

"But your Ms. Mallory, who must be one tough woman, noticed this distinguishing mark." Cordelia Knox turned the report around for Ron and pointed out a particular notation. "This scar above the cat's left eye. The cat I want has the same feature."

"I have an occupational contempt for coincidence, Warden Knox," Ron said, "but *could* it be just a coincidence?"

"Could be," she conceded. "Mountain lions feed mainly on deer. Lots of cats get gored and gouged by antlers. It's a *possibility* we could have two of them with similar scars."

"But you don't think so."

Cordelia Knox shook her head.

"In my own way, I'm a cop, too. I hate coincidences as much as you do. But there may be something I can find that will pin it down for us."

"Like what?" Ron wanted to know.

"If I can find the tracks of the animal that attacked Ms. Mallory, I can compare them to those on record for the animal I want."

Ron had to laugh. "You're going to run a mountain lion for fingerprints?"

She smiled again, once more tapping into a wellspring of lechery whose existence Ron had heretofore never suspected. He forced a cough before he blushed for the first time since … well, he couldn't remember the last time.

"Not quite fingerprints," she said, "but it's the same idea. You find the animal's tracks, then you look for distinguishing features: a short toe; a missing toe; one foot turned in. You measure the size of the tracks. Maybe you even work out a ratio of the width of the front footpads to the width of the rear footpads. Things like that."

Ron found the calm, off-hand expertise of her explanation reassuring.

"So, you find out it's the same animal, the way we both think now, and then you send for some more dogs?"

His reassurance disappeared when she shook her head.

"Afraid not, Chief. We're clean out of hounds. At least the kind you use to go after mountain lions."

"You're kidding." Ron couldn't imagine a scarcity of anything in consumption obsessed California, except rain in drought years and prison space perennially.

She shook her head. "Sorry. Your basic houndsman come in two varieties these days. Traditional and commercial. The traditional guy is usually Southern or has his roots down south. His kind is getting fewer and farther between. The commercial guy will charge some two thousand to five thousand dollars to tree a lion or corner a bear for you."

"If it's a matter of money, don't worry," Ron said. "The town will make up any shortfall in your budget."

This time the game warden's smile was wry.

"Working for rich folks has its advantages, huh?"

"Some," Ron allowed.

"Well, money's not the only problem here. I don't like the commercial outfitters on principle, and even swallowing my pride for a situation like this, there's only a handful of them I'd trust. This being August, though, all those fine fellows are on vacation. They're off in Hawaii hunting wild boar or in Africa looking for really big game or just taking it easy on a beach somewhere. Believe me, Chief, I've been looking for a houndsman. The man I used last time says it'll take him six months to train new dogs."

"So, what'll you do?"

"I'll track the cat. My partner will be here on Monday. We'll get this animal."

"If there's any help my department can offer just let me know."

"Thanks," Cordelia Knox said. "The one problem I do have at the moment is I can't find a place to stay. I tried three hotels and each one told me every room in town has been taken."

Goddamn media invasion, Ron thought.

He took out his house keys, pulled one of the ring and extended it to her. "Use my place. I'm working a murder investigation —"

"The black guy nailed to the tree?"

"Yeah. So, I'll pretty much be living out of this office anyway."

"Your place has a spare bedroom?" Cordelia Knox asked, taking the key.

"Yeah."

"Then don't worry about me. I'm clean and quiet. You won't even know I'm around."

Ron doubted that seriously. He started to give her directions, wondering just how selfless this act of generosity was, and then he decided he'd better show her the way.

Ron had intended to stay only for a minute, just to show his guest where everything was, when the phone rang. Much to his surprise, it was his wife — ex-wife, he reminded himself — Leilani.

Divorced or not, he still smiled every time she called unexpectedly. Having her voice catch him by surprise always took him right back to the days when he was a young MP and she was the local girl on Sandy Beach, Oahu, watching all the pale *haoles* trying to body surf without breaking their necks on the sandbar none of the tourist guides mentioned. Ron had been the one she'd called out to, warning him about the hazard. She said he had too cute an *okole* to park it in a wheel chair where no *wahine* would ever get to see it again.

A week or two of remarks like that had led to Ron and Leilani's romance and eventual marriage — as well as Ron's fistfight with Leilani's former local boyfriend.

"Hey, Lei. It's good to hear from you."

"Aloha, *kane.* Those news bastards starting in on you again?"

The former Mrs. Ketchum shared a dismal view of the media with her ex, and apparently had seen coverage of events in Goldstrike.

"It's a dirty job, but there are always dirty people willing to do it," Ron said.

"I'd send my publicist to help you out, but I know you wouldn't want that. Clay Steadman has people way better than mine anyway."

Just then, Cordelia Knox stepped out of the guest bedroom. She had her socks and shoes off. Ron had never had a thing for women's feet, but looking at hers he thought this might be yet another area where he wasn't being sufficiently open minded. He asked Leilani to hold on a minute, and gestured to Cordelia to say what was on her mind.

"Is it all right if I take a shower?" she wanted to know. The cabin had only one bathroom.

"Go right ahead. Towels are in the cabinet."

"Thanks."

His guest went into the bathroom, and Ron took the phone into his bedroom and closed the door.

"Okay, I'm back," he told Leilani.

"Ronald Ketchum," his former mate teased, "do you have a

woman with you?"

"Yeah. Her name is Warden Knox."

"Is she good looking?"

"She's with the state department of fish and game."

"You didn't answer my question."

"She's here to shoot a mountain lion that's misbehaving."

Leilani chuckled.

"So she is good looking. Is she young?"

"Impossibly young."

Leilani whispered a soft string of Hawaiian through the phone and into his ear. The first time she did that — the first time they'd made love — he asked her what it meant. She refused to tell him, and after that he decided it was sexier not knowing. He didn't want to know now, either.

"And how's your love life?" he asked.

Now, her laughter had a rueful tone.

"You know better than anyone how badly I wanted to break into show biz. Well, bro, mo' bettah you be careful what you wish for. Now, I've got all the work I didn't get those first twenty years. I don't have *time* for a love life. I've got a five o'clock call tomorrow, and I should be sleeping right now."

The mere mention of sleep sent a wave of fatigue crashing over Ron. He'd been up for the past forty hours dealing with all sorts of unpleasant reality. Sitting on his bed, listening to Leilani's soft, musical voice, he felt his grip on consciousness failing rapidly.

"Yeah, me too," he replied.

"You stay well, *kane.* Anybody mess with you, I get my *kahuna* make their peckers fall off *wiki-wiki.*"

"I bet you would."

"Oh, and in case you forgot, we're not married anymore. You want to give your Warden Knox *wahine* a romp, it's okay with me."

"Gee, thanks."

"You want to give her a romp and think of me while you're doing it, that's okay, too."

"*Aloha,* Leilani."

CHAPTER 13

Sunday

Ron was pleased that he awoke at sunrise, refreshed. Okay, he conceded maybe he didn't look or smell too good, having slept in his clothes, shoes and all. But he felt good after not a lot of sleep, and that brightened his spirits considerably.

He'd been worried that maybe he was turning into some kind of nasty old creep, thinking the way he had about that young girl. But now in the day's first light he realized that he'd simply neglected a very basic need for a very long time. Christ, talking to Leilani last night made him realize that she was the last woman he'd made love to. And that farewell hula, just before their divorce, had been well over three years ago.

Hell, he was still vital. His body was telling him to find someone.

Someone his own age.

Or at least in the neighborhood.

He shucked his clothes and dropped them in the laundry hamper. He was on his way to the bathroom when he stopped short. It occurred to him that for the time being he could no longer walk around his house naked. He didn't think his guest would be awake yet, but he couldn't take any chances. What if she'd gotten up to pee or something and he blithely walked in wearing his birthday suit. Wouldn't look good at all.

Not that his body was anything to be ashamed of.

Ron slipped on a pair of gym shorts and knocked softly on the bathroom door. No response. He slipped inside and locked the door. The room was immaculate. No hair in the tub or sink or on the floor. No damp towels left around. No soap puddles or shampoo trickles anywhere. Warden Knox hadn't been kidding. She was very clean. And quiet. He couldn't hear a sound anywhere in the house.

He took his shower, shaved and for the first time in months weighed himself. Hadn't gained a pound. Looking in the mirror, he was pleased that his hairline was still firmly anchored in place, his teeth were still white, and his gums didn't seem to be receding. He wasn't so old, after all.

He got dressed and went quietly to the kitchen.

He needn't have worried about disturbing his guest. She was already up and out. She'd left a note for him on the kitchen table.

Chief —

Mountain lions are crepuscular, they hunt at sunrise and twilight . So I had to get an early start. I knocked on your door a couple times to see if you wanted to come with, but you didn't wake up. Wish me luck. Maybe I can bag the sucker this morning and get out of your hair.

Corrie Knox.

There was nothing in her note that was impolite or incorrect. In fact, it was considerate of her — professional, really — to advise him of her actions. And she'd offered him her implicit friendship by signing her name in a familiar manner.

But seeing that she'd gotten the jump on him ticked him off.

She'd knocked on his door and he'd been so dead to the world he hadn't heard it. Damnit, it wasn't that long ago he could have worked seventy-two hours straight and then gone out to play pickup basketball for several more. And he certainly wouldn't have let any schoolboy infatuation distract him from a murder case. Especially not one this big.

Surly and feeling a great deal older than he had only moments ago, he skipped his usual morning coffee for orange juice. The

English muffin was replaced with oat bran, a banana, and skim milk. He brushed his teeth with extra vigor. Then he strode briskly out his front door telling himself that he hadn't been one-upped.

He was the one hunting the biggest game of all.

Oliver Gosden was almost as cranky as Ron when he walked into the chief's office that morning. He said a terse good morning. Then his eyes kept darting around, and he scowled more or less continuously.

"What the hell are you looking for?" Ron asked.

"An ashtray."

"You don't smoke anymore, and you couldn't smoke in here if you did."

Oliver scowled again.

"Had a pleasant night at home, did you?" Ron asked

"First night I'm home after Lauren's parents leave and I was looking for a little company with my wife, if you know what I mean. And you know what happened?"

"What?"

"I fell asleep."

Ron's mood brightened immediately. Oliver was eleven years younger than him.

The deputy chief continued, "Then I think maybe I can make up for my lapse this morning. I'm snuggling in close to Lauren … and Danny comes in the room. He's carrying a broom. Lauren and I told him we'd give him a quarter every day he keeps his room clean. He's so excited about earning a living, he decides this morning to bump his income by cleaning our room, too."

The chief laughed.

"It isn't funny, Ron. I yelled at him. Poor little six year old kid is only trying to do the right thing and I send him away in tears. Felt like a prize shit, and Lauren let me know I was entirely correct in my judgment. Anyway, we got it all straightened out before I left, but even so I'd really like to wrack someone's ass this morning."

Ron nodded, his focus returning to business.

"The state sent in a game warden to kill that mountain lion."

"Yeah?"

Oliver took out his Zippo lighter.

"Yeah. She thinks it might be the same cat that she suspects already killed someone."

"Just what we need," the deputy chief said, flicking his lighter open and shut.

Ron had a hard time not telling him to knock it off.

"I want you to go talk to Mahalia Cardwell this morning. I have a real strong feeling that she knows something about her grandson's killing."

Oliver snapped his lighter shut and put it in his pocket.

"How come you want me to talk to her?"

"You said you wanted in on this case. And she's expecting me, so I thought we'd cross her up and see what you can get out of her. Don't let the Cardwells leave town before you're sure you have whatever she knows."

"Lock 'em up, if they make a break for it?"

"Use your considerable charm to get what you're after, Deputy Chief."

Oliver snorted. "And what are you going to be doing?"

Ron got up and started for the door.

"I'm going to have a few words this fine Sabbath day with my good friend the Reverend Jimmy Thunder."

Before leaving police headquarters, Ron checked in with Sergeant Stanley to see if there had been any Saturday night arrests. The town averaged a dozen drunk-and-disorderlies a month, most of them coming on the weekends. Not bad for a resort town. The chief liked to talk to his prisoners personally before they were released and carefully explain to them their obligations as either residents of or visitors to the town.

He never threatened anyone with physical harm, but his cops always let anyone they busted know — if they didn't know already — that the chief was from L.A., and everybody knew what kind of cops they had down there.

Ron had always resented the negative press the bad cops in the LAPD had given the whole department, but now he made it work for him. You use the tools you had, he thought.

"Three guys got in a fight in that new bar on Coldstream, and they took it outside to the sidewalk."

"What, two against one?" Ron asked.

The sergeant shook his head. "Every man for himself."

"Locals?"

"Yeah. Twenty somethings."

"Over a woman?"

"Unh-uh."

"Sports?"

"Politics. A Democrat, a Republican and a Libertarian."

"*Politics*," Ron repeated in disgust. "What's this country coming to?" Then he had another thought. "How many tips have we had trying to cash in on the mayor's reward offer?"

"Close to eight hundred, last count. About forty percent from out of town."

"Anything worth looking at?"

Sergeant Stanley shook his head.

"In that case, send the tips from the out of town scammers along to the FBI. Let the feds know we're cooperating fully."

The sergeant grinned and saluted smartly.

CHAPTER 14

As Ron pulled out of the police parking structure, an SUV started to follow him. It was a 4x4, but, unlike his all-business police Ford Explorer, this one was a gleaming black Range Rover. Complete with a rhino guard. For a second, Ron thought it might be the mayor behind him. He had a Rover like that, except the chief didn't remember the mayor worrying about rhinos. Then Ron noticed that the plates weren't the mayor's.

Clay Steadman's vanity plates read MFL — Mayor for Life.

Maybe the Rover behind him just happened to be going the same way he was. There were lots of fancy cars in town, and the guy was so blatantly obvious, hanging in there twenty feet off the chief's rear bumper, he couldn't be trying to fool anyone. But after two turns, the second of which caused the Rover to run a red, Ron decided the sonofabitch *was* following him. He just didn't care if Ron knew about it.

The chief took out his sidearm and laid it on the passenger seat. He took another look at the Rover's plate and called it in. When he got his response, he pulled over to the curb. The Rover nosed in a car length behind him.

Ron got out of his unit re-holstering his weapon and walked back to the fancy import. The tinted window went down with an electric hum. The driver was a wide-eyed white kid with beads of sweat on his downy upper lip. He was probably right out of journalism school, maybe even a summer intern.

"What are you doing?" Ron asked mildly.

"Driving," the kid replied, a picture of innocence.

"He's doing his job, Chief. Which is whatever I tell him to do."

This came from the black man sitting in the passenger seat. He had salt and pepper hair and a matching beard. He wore a khaki safari jacket, although the morning was already too warm for such clothing. But it did go nicely with the Rover, Ron thought, and it would look good on television.

The man's name was Ben Dexter. Ron recognized him from the tube. He'd been an anchor on one of the network news magazines. Now he was an independent producer-reporter. He liked to go after stories with racial angles. He sold them to whomever he thought would let him slant the story his way. He did a lot of things on PBS and the cable news channels, but he still turned up back at his old network stomping grounds once in a while.

He thought he was tough.

There was a guy with a videocam, and a soundman in the back seat. The camera operator looked like he was itching to start shooting video, but he hadn't been given his cue yet. Ron knew the camera guy would act on his own initiative, however, if he got rough with these bozos.

The chief knew Dexter would like nothing better than to have Ron muscle him.

White racist police chief harasses crusading black journalist.

Ron stepped around the Rover to Mr. Big. Dexter lowered his window. The camera operator had his lens pointed Ron's way, even though the camera was still off. The sound guy, however, had his recorder on and his mike pointed at the chief.

Ron crouched and leaned in close to Dexter, making it just about impossible for the camera operator to get a shot at him without his boss's head getting in the way. Maybe it would mess up the sound-man's levels, too.

"And did you tell your driver to follow me, Mr. Dexter?"

"Yes, I did."

The TV reporter kept his face nose to nose with Ron's, made

the chief sorry he'd brushed his teeth so thoroughly that morning. Dexter evidently hadn't.

"If you'd like an interview, why don't you call my secretary?"

"We're not looking for an interview. At the moment."

"So you're just following me?"

"That's right." The 'What are you going to do about it, motherfucker?' was implied.

"I'm conducting official business now."

"That's what we want to see. *How* you conduct official business."

"If I told you that your presence might hinder a murder investigation, what would your response be?"

"A free press comes at a price."

"Nice irony," Ron commented. He pushed off the Rover and stood up.

"Okay," he said. "You want to see how I work? Keep your eyes open. But I don't think it will make very good TV."

The camera operator exercised independent judgment on that point, hitting Ron with his bright light. But he didn't catch the chief punching out Dexter or breaking the Rover's windshield, or even kicking dents in the door. All he taped was Ron calmly walking back to his unit, making a call on his radio, and waiting there without moving.

Ten minutes later two cars arrived, one blocking the Rover in front, the other in back. But they weren't police units. There weren't cops inside. There would be no tape of Dexter being led away in handcuffs. Not in Goldstrike, thank you. Ron had called the district attorney's office and the town's corporation counsel. The two lawyers who had responded would explain to the intrepid reporter the criminal and civil penalties that could ensue for interfering with a police officer in the performance of his duties.

If the sonofabitch could make a TV show out of that legal boilerplate, more power to him. On the other hand, since Dexter was a member of the bar himself, he'd understand clearly that if he kept fucking around, there would be consequences.

Ron drove off, having shed his tail.

He felt there were times when it was very tiring to be a nationally known recovering bigot. People kept coming after him. Hoping with all their might to set him off.

Of course, sometimes, like right now, Ron felt a greater than usual empathy with his father, the unrepentant bigot. Times like these, he'd like nothing better than to ring his baton off some people's heads. Whatever their color was.

But he maintained control and worked on his problem.

One day at a time.

Just like recovering alcoholics and drug addicts.

CHAPTER 15

The guy who spoke to Ron over the intercom at the gates to Jimmy Thunder's estate was another candidate ripe for police brutality.

"I'd like to see the reverend, please," Ron said evenly.

"He ain't seein' nobody. He's in mournin'."

"I'm afraid this isn't a social call."

The guy on the other end of the intercom apparently had exhausted his gift for conversation and the gates remained closed. Ron leaned on the call button.

"Did I mention that I'm Chief of Police Ketchum? And that if I have to, I'll come back with a warrant. Now, how would that look to the neighbors?"

After several more seconds of silence, during which Ron thought he might actually have to follow through on his threat, the gates swung open. The chief idled his car onto the Thunder estate at five miles per hour. The better to eyeball the grounds.

A white man in a short-sleeved blue work shirt and matching pants was carefully maneuvering a riding mower around ornamental trees on an expanse of emerald grass the size of a football field. The man wore a Baltimore Orioles baseball cap, and though Ron couldn't see his face something seemed familiar about him.

If the man on the mower was the guy responsible for the grounds, he did a heckuva job. All the plantings the chief could see were meticulously kept. Flowerbeds featured colorful arrays of petunias, pansies and marigolds. Evergreens shrubs were set among well-placed granite boulders. Quaking aspens, mountain alders, and willows lent their grace and shade to the setting.

For a moment, Ron wondered why the man was working on Sunday. Then he thought that he himself would rather be in this park-like setting smelling newly mown grass than stuck in a church wearing a coat and tie. Or maybe the guy was Jewish. Or an atheist. Or he worshipped plant life. In California anything was possible — and usually encouraged.

Thunder's mansion was a large, imposing structure of cream-colored brick. Its graceful lines were disfigured by the functional cube of a TV studio appended to the far end. That and the adjacent parking area that had to be large enough for the chartered buses that brought in Jimmy Thunder's studio audiences. A row of willows only partially obscured this financial engine that both blighted and supported the rest of the property.

Ron got out of his Explorer directly in front of the mansion's entrance. He climbed the four shallow steps and rang the bell set in the shining brass fitting next to the gleaming oak doors. He waited long enough to consider leaning on the doorbell, but finally a scowling black man opened the door.

The man was six inches shorter than Ron, but he had the shoulders, chest, arms and muscle tone of a middleweight boxer ready for a championship bout. His hair was clipped as short and neat as the lawns behind Ron. He wore a white linen suit and an open at the throat French vanilla silk shirt. Pinned to the shirt's right collar point was a small golden cross.

"I'd like to see Reverend Thunder," Ron said again.

"He's busy with his TV show. It's Sunday morning."

"He tapes his show on Thursday afternoon," Ron countered patiently. "What kind of police chief would I be if I didn't notice when busloads of believers arrived in my town?"

"He likes to *watch* the show on Sundays. See how it plays."

"Then he's done with the mourning you talked about when I was at the gate?"

The man started to close the door but he thought better of it when Ron shook his head in stern disapproval.

"Do that," the chief said, "and I'll arrest you for fucking with me, also known as interfering with a police officer in the performance of his duties." There was a time to call in the lawyers, Ron knew, and there was a time to assert naked police authority. Besides, he had taken all the crap he intended to take for one morning. He continued, "Now, that'd be a chump charge for a tough guy … but for a man of the cloth, it'd be something he'd rather not face."

Let this guy define himself, Ron thought.

The man stepped back and opened the door to let Ron enter.

"What's your name?" he asked the middleweight as he moved into the mansion.

"Deacon Meeker."

"Deacon? Is that your name, or your position with the reverend?"

"Both. Reverend Thunder ain't gonna be happy to see you."

"So few are," Ron conceded.

In the woods adjacent to Highway 38, near the point where Mary Kaye Mallory was attacked, Corrie Knox found the tracks she was looking for. Mountain lion, no doubt about it. At a glance, the tracks appeared to belong to the same animal she'd been hunting for the past month. Corrie looked around, and then she looked up. Cats climbed, ate in and slept in trees. They also liked to pounce from them.

But people hardly ever looked up. Good for mountain lions. Bad for hikers who didn't aspire to become kibble.

Mountain lions almost always used sneak attacks. They struck from behind and crushed the base of the skull and the spine with one massive bite. Just in case the first bite didn't do it, they wrapped all four legs around their prey and held it helpless until they got the job done.

Pound for pound, mountain lions were the strongest and most

lethal of the big cats.

They also saw you a long time before you saw them. But even a tenderfoot, unless lost in the raptures of nature or otherwise distracted, often got the feeling that something was not quite right when a big cat was nearby. The police report on Mary Kaye Mallory stated that she'd felt, with complete accuracy, that she was being stalked.

Corrie Knox was no tenderfoot. Her father, a wildlife illustrator who held no illusions about the need to carry a rifle, had begun taking her into the woods as soon as she could walk. He'd started teaching her to shoot when she was five. She cradled her 30-30 Winchester 94 carbine as naturally as most women her age would hold a baby. She also had the strength to handle the .45 caliber pistol she wore on her hip.

But looking around, and up, once more, sniffing the air and extending her consciousness as far as she could, she couldn't feel the presence of any predator. Dropping into a squat, with her rifle across her legs, she shrugged out of her backpack. She took out a measuring tape, a sketchpad and a pencil. She flipped the pad open and started taking the measurements of the lion's tracks. First she wrote down the numbers and then she sketched the tracks. The daughter of an illustrator, she'd also received art lessons. Her drawings were highly accurate. But she also photographed the tracks.

When this work was accomplished, and not before, she looked at the images and dimensions of the tracks she'd previously recorded for the cat she'd been hunting. She didn't want to look at them earlier and have them subconsciously influence her present work.

She needn't have worried. The deformed toe on the animal's right rear foot and the dimensions of all four feet matched. You added that to the reported scar above the left eye and there was no doubt that the animal that attacked Mary Kaye Mallory was the same one that she felt certain had killed a hiker already.

Officially, Gary Jenkins, age eighteen, was a missing person. He'd gone alone into the Sierra, eighty miles south of Goldstrike, one weekend at the beginning of July to camp and test the wilderness skills he'd learned in an Outward Bound course. When he hadn't returned home as planned the following Monday, his parents alerted the police. Corrie had been called in when a park ranger found Gary Jenkins' campsite.

Everything was in perfect order. His tent was neatly pitched near a stream. His sleeping bag and all his other supplies were accounted for, as far as his parents had been able to tell officials. Even his wallet, with cash and a credit card still inside, was found in the tent.

But Gary Jenkins was gone.

His shirt was found hanging on a bush near the stream, and the ranger who'd summoned Corrie showed her the tracks he'd found nearby. Mountain lion. For Corrie, it had been easy to imagine what had happened. The young man had gotten up early on the last morning of his life, went down to the stream to wash up, bent over to splash water on his face, and the cat had pounced on him. Killed him. Dragged him off and ate him.

Gary Jenkins had been a small fellow. Five feet six, one thirty. Two or three good meals for a big cat. There might literally be nothing of him left.

Well, that wasn't entirely true. Corrie and the houndsman had tracked the mountain lion who'd left the tracks by the stream. The first pile of its dung they'd found had been thick with porcupine quills. The next pile had contained something equally unappetizing: blue denim. According to Gary's father, his son had worn his favorite pair of Levi's to go camping.

The powers that be still listed Gary Jenkins as missing, and wouldn't rule out the possibility of foul play at the hands of another person. Corrie, of course, had heard her share of grisly true-crime stories, even tales of psychotic cannibals, but she'd never heard of anyone who ate people while they were still in their blue jeans.

No, a lion had claimed the unfortunate young man. And if there were any remains that hadn't passed through the animal's digestive tract, they would be skeletal at best. Skeletal and tucked up in the branches of a tree or the recesses of some rocky den.

She stood up and wondered why the cat hadn't kept to its home range. In the Sierra, a given area of a hundred square miles usually provided enough game to keep half a dozen mountain lions well fed. Maybe this particular animal's area had gotten overpopulated, and he was the odd man out. Or maybe he was infected with some feline disease that made him behave out of character. Or …

Or maybe, as intelligent as these big cats could be, it had simply discovered that humans were very easy prey. They didn't have gouging antlers like deer, and they didn't run nearly as fast. And maybe, from the lion's point of view, people were a delicacy, too.

Corrie Knox smiled mirthlessly. Wouldn't that notion delight Chief Ketchum?

She repacked her materials, stood up and surveyed her surroundings again. No sign of the fucker. No sense that she was being hunted, either. Maybe her prey had travel plans to keep right on moving north. Felis concolor, the cat of one color, could be found anywhere from Canada to South America.

It'd make her job a helluva lot easier if the beast stayed nearby. Not that the chief would like to hear that, either.

Charmaine Cardwell ushered Oliver Gosden into the suite at the Hyatt that Clay Steadman had arranged for the Cardwell family. She seated him on a sofa and asked if she might call for coffee for him. The deputy chief politely declined.

Little Japhet Cardwell dressed in black slacks and a white shirt peeked out from behind the folds of his mother's black dress.

"Are you a policeman?" the four year old asked seriously.

"Yes, I am."

"You gonna catch the bad man who killed my daddy?"

The question pierced Oliver's heart like an arrow. This boy was two years younger than his own son. And he'd already lost his father. Glancing up at Charmaine, Oliver saw that she, too, was interested in how he answered the question.

"If he's in our town," the deputy chief told them, "we will catch him. If he's run away … then the FBI will have to catch him."

"What's gonna happen when you catch him?"

"He'll go to trial and when he's found guilty he'll have to pay the price."

"You mean if he's found guilty, don't you?"

Oliver looked up to see that Mahalia Cardwell, also dressed in black, had entered the room.

"Lots of folks get away with murder these days, don't they?" she asked.

"Grandma, please," Charmaine said. "You'll upset Japhet."

Tears were forming in the boy's eyes as his mother picked him up. He'd understood what his great-grandmother had said. He brushed his tears away with the back of a hand and turned his huge liquid brown eyes on Oliver.

"Don't let the bad man get away," the boy pleaded fearfully.

"We won't," Oliver said, and meant it. "I promise."

As Charmaine Cardwell carried her son from the room, her look said that she hoped Oliver wouldn't disappoint either of them.

"Where's that white boy?" Mahalia Cardwell asked, drawing Oliver's attention back to her. "He sent you to do his dirty work?"

The old woman had remained standing. Oliver got to his feet so she wouldn't be able to look down on him.

"I'm the deputy chief of police in this town, ma'am. I don't tote dat barge for anyone around here."

Mahalia Cardwell was unimpressed. "You don't come from around here, either, do you?"

"No, ma'am."

"The chief of police, he bring you in from Los Angeles, too?"

"Yes, ma'am."

"So you're his house nigger."

Oliver took a deep breath to maintain his cool. "I don't use that word, ma'am. I have a son not much older than Japhet, and he's not going to hear it from me or anyone else in my presence."

"Not even the chief of police? You're going tell your boss to watch his mouth?"

"The chief doesn't use that word, either."

"Oh, that's right. I forgot. He's a reformed white man, or somethin'."

Oliver didn't want to spend one minute more than necessary in this woman's company, so he decided it was time to get down to business.

"Mrs. Cardwell, I'd like to ask you some questions about your grandson now, if you don't mind. You might have some information that will help me keep my promise to Japhet."

"Oh, you bet I do. I know who killed my Isaac."

"And who would that be?" Oliver asked carefully.

"His no-good daddy, that's who," the old lady said. "That lying, thieving, whoring, murdering charlatan that calls himself Jimmy Thunder. That's who killed my baby. May he burn in hell!"

CHAPTER 16

As predicted, the Reverend Jimmy Thunder was not happy to see Ron Ketchum. But he had experience in the inevitability of talking to the police when they insisted on talking to you. He knew his current status could postpone the time when he'd have to talk to them, and in other circumstances he might have enjoyed making the bastards cool their heels. Right now, though, he just wanted to get it over with.

He received Ron in his sunroom.

"Nice view of the lake," the chief said, looking around.

Thunder was sitting, but he didn't offer Ron a chair. So the chief contented himself to stand.

"You come to get my alibi?"

Until that very moment, Ron hadn't considered the possibility that the man might have killed his son. He had to laugh inwardly, thinking all the clean mountain air he'd been breathing the past three years must have been responsible for that omission. Back in L.A., he'd never let a little thing like paternity excuse somebody from the suspicion of homicide.

"Do you need an alibi, Reverend?"

"I was playing cards all night. Until I went to bed."

"Solitaire?"

"Poker. With Texas Jack Telford."

Even in a town lousy with celebrities, Texas Jack stood out as one of the more colorful characters. A five time world poker champion, he'd retired on top. But now Jimmy Thunder had told the chief he had Texas Jack over to the house for a friendly little game.

"Guess I don't need to ask who won," Ron said.

As Jimmy Thunder had told Ron in his office, he repeated, "I know about you. Marcus Martin is a friend of mine … and one of my lawyers."

Ron kept his face blank, but he wondered if Marcus Martin was his personal curse in life, and if he'd ever be free of the prick.

The chief repeated his words to Thunder, "We know about each other, Reverend."

"Meaning to you I'm just another nigger and ex-con. Well, you think what you want. Deacon Meeker was here with Jack and me, too. He can back me up."

Ron smiled. "I'm sure he will. He likes to play cards, too?"

"He didn't play. He was just here. Reading his Bible."

The chief looked at Meeker. Fancy clothes and little gold cross or not, the guy was a graduate of a state pen, not the Yale Divinity School.

"Devout," Ron said. Then turned back to Thunder. "But what I came to ask you about is your son. How long was he in town? And did he stay with you?"

Thunder nodded. "He was with me here six days. I think he was at a hotel a night before that, but I don't know which one."

Jimmy Thunder picked up a fat manila folder from the table next to him, stood up, and handed it to Ron.

"What's this?"

"Hate mail. What came just last month. You want more, we got boxes of the stuff in storage. The top ones, the ones clipped together there, they were mailed locally."

"You think someone could have killed your son to get back at you? Are there letters in here that threaten him specifically?"

Reverend Thunder shook his head. "Weren't many people who knew Isaac was my son. So, no, nobody mentioned him by name. But you look at all that filth, then you tell me what people would do to hurt me."

Ron hefted the file in his hand. "I will. I'll read every piece of it myself."

"Like I said, you want more, just call. Now, can I do anything else for you?"

"I'd like to talk with the rest of your household staff. Without the deacon in the room. If that's all right with you."

Clearly, it wasn't. But Thunder knew this, too, was inevitable. He grunted his assent and walked out on Ron.

CHAPTER 17

Oliver Gosden was back on the sofa in the Cardwell's suite at the Hyatt. The old lady sat opposite him in an armchair. Her eyes were focused on the past, and the lack of movement in her face as she spoke would have done credit to a ventriloquist.

"Jimmy Leverette was black trash who lived at the end of our block in Baytown, Texas. The family moved in from somewhere out in the piney woods. Story was the daddy ran off with some whore. His mama, she was always spouting the Bible, but she was rattlesnake mean."

The deputy chief half expected a challenging look from the old lady, daring him to make a comparison, but the irony was lost on her and she continued with her deadpan reminiscence.

"The two Leverette girls, Dorothy and Marjean, they were quieter than whipped dogs. But Jimmy, his mama couldn't beat him down. He was a high school football hero, and in Texas that made you important, even if you were black. Jimmy strutted back and forth in front of my house in his football jacket. I knew what that boy was after. He wanted my baby girl, Natalie."

"Natalie is your daughter?" Oliver asked.

A moment of anger animated the old woman's face. "She was my daughter. The way I figure it, Jimmy Leverette killed her, too."

The deputy chief wanted to hear about that, but he knew better than to interrupt someone who was speaking freely. He'd let Mahalia Cardwell tell her story her own way. He would hold his questions until she was finished.

"Natalie was smart and pretty," Mahalia said, looking inward once again. "But she was too gentle for her own good. My late husband, Ernest, and I worked five jobs between us to see that our baby could go to college and amount to something in life. So, I wasn't too worried about Jimmy Leverette. Natalie would go off to college, and that would be the last she'd see of that piece of trash.

"I didn't know for a whole year that Jimmy Leverette had followed my baby girl. He had a scholarship offer from the University of Texas, but he chose West Texas State to run after Natalie. I didn't find out until my daughter came home pregnant after her freshman year and announced she was marrying Jimmy."

Mahalia Cardwell closed her eyes and put a hand flat on her chest. A minute passed before she could go on.

"I think that was what sent my Ernest to an early grave, so maybe that's another Cardwell the high-and-mighty Jimmy Thunder has on his conscience." The old woman snorted. "If he has a conscience.

"After Natalie got married, I wanted to visit her. Help her through those early days of pregnancy. She was a small girl, not like me. I worried about how carrying a baby might wear on her. But she kept putting me off. Said she didn't want to trouble me, make me travel all the way across Texas to El Paso. But the more she put me off, the more she worried her daddy and me. It wasn't like our baby not to take help from us.

"Then, one day, I got a call from the refinery. Ernest had a heart attack, the man told me. He was alive, but just only. I better get to the hospital right away, the man said. I did. My husband was unconscious, and he never would wake up and see me again. My heart broke just looking at him, but I didn't know what real sorrow was right then.

"I called Natalie to come quick and see her daddy before he passed on. She told me she'd come as soon as she could. But she didn't arrive until the day I put my Ernest in the ground. She turned up at the cemetery, and that was when I saw Jimmy Leverette had been beating my daughter. His pregnant wife.

"I took Natalie home and dragged the whole story out of her. Jimmy had been taking drugs, seeing other women, gambling, and spending the money the football boosters gave him on the high life instead of taking care of Natalie and her baby. It wasn't Natalie's nature to speak up or complain, but when she finally did, Jimmy started beating on her. Pretty soon, she didn't have to say a word to get a beating. Just look at him funny was all.

"She didn't come home to see her daddy before he died because Jimmy didn't want her to go, and she was far enough along in her pregnancy she thought another beating would kill her baby. Finally, she couldn't stand the thought of not seeing her daddy again and she borrowed bus money secretly from a neighbor. And right then, in her mama's house, as she was telling me all this, she was shaking with fear that her husband would come after her and kill her."

A smile of grim satisfaction crossed Mahalia Cardwell's face, and she nodded her head.

"He did come, too. That no-good nigger walked right up to my front door with all the nerve in the world and rang my doorbell. He didn't know I was expecting him; he didn't know I was ready for him. I had been hoping and praying he'd come. I yanked open that door and I had my rolling pin held high in my right hand. I smacked him alongside his head with all the strength God gave me. I don't recall just how many times it was I hit him. But when I got tired of swinging my arm, I finally dragged him off my porch and out to the gutter. I went back in my house and called the sanitation department to come haul him away."

"What did you do when the police came?" Oliver asked.

"I told them what Jimmy Leverette had done to my daughter. I showed them the teeth he'd knocked out of her head. I showed them the scars he left on her. I told them how she feared for her life if he got his hands on her again. Those policemen, they had children. They understood. One of them took me aside and told me if I hadn't laid such a good whipping on Jimmy Leverette, he would have. And he told me don't worry about Jimmy no more."

The old woman shook her head several times slowly, as if in deep regret.

"Jimmy went away, all right, but he never bothered about no divorce. In the end, that didn't matter, though. He broke something inside my Natalie, something I never could fix. Lord, how I tried. Gentling her, taking care of Isaac when he was born. Then I tried to make her mad at me, urged her to put up a fight. I knew if I could get her good and mad just once, I could turn her around and show her where to aim her anger. But I never could do it.

Mahalia Cardwell focused her eyes on Oliver.

"You ever hear of people who die of a broken heart?"

"Yes, ma'am."

"That's what my baby Natalie did. She gave her love, her heart and her body to Jimmy Leverette and he stomped her flat. She died when she was twenty-four. Doctors couldn't find a single reason why. But I knew she was fixing to go one night when she took my wrist with more strength than I ever knew she had and told me to take good care of Isaac."

"That's how Jimmy killed her?" the deputy chief asked.

Mahalia Cardwell nodded.

"I raised Isaac to be a fine man. I used his daddy as an example of everything he shouldn't be, and when Jimmy Leverette killed that poor white boy from New York, he proved me exactly right. Isaac grew up fine and righteous. Only thing I worried about was he had his mother's gentle nature. So, I helped him to learn to be strong. He took to it, too. Wouldn't back down from any man, but would never strike a blow, either. He went to the university and theological school out here in California — he was a real minister, not a charlatan like his father — and when he married Charmaine, they brought me out to live with them."

"How did Isaac come to be in Goldstrike, Mrs. Cardwell?"

"A man came to our house about two weeks ago, an Englishman name of Colin Ring. You ever hear of him?"

"No, ma'am," Oliver said, but he wrote the name down.

"He's a writer. Writes books about famous people. Only he tells folks the real story about what the high and mighty get up to when they think nobody's looking. He wanted to know if I could help him learn about the real Jimmy Thunder."

Oliver had to repress a grin. He'd bet his badge this old lady had practically dragged the man into her house. "You talked to him?"

"Of course, I did."

"Did you ever think he could be a scammer, a blackmailer?"

"I wouldn't have cared. But he had one of his books with him to show me. About some celebrity woman who was awful to her children. Said he'd done others, too. Believe me, I've never been so happy to meet a white man before in all my seventy-seven years."

"Do you remember the book's title?"

"No. But he said all his books were in the library, if I wanted to see the others."

Oliver noted that, too.

"Isaac came home while I was still talking to the Englishman, and heard what was going on. He got real quiet for a minute. Then he said he had an idea. He'd never met his father before. Why didn't they go see him now? After all, Jimmy didn't live much more than two hundred miles away. I didn't like the idea, not one bit, but Colin Ring he got so excited I thought he might soil his britches. He said the confrontation would be wonderful. It would reveal just what kind of man Jimmy Thunder was when it came to his own family. I didn't mind the world knowing that, not at all. So I didn't speak up, and the next day Isaac and the Englishman set off."

The deputy chief leaned forward.

"Colin Ring came to Goldstrike with your grandson?"

"Rode in the same car. That's what I'm telling you."

"Do you know if he's still here?"

"I can't say for sure, but I know he called me from here. He said Isaac would be staying at his daddy's house the next few days, and that was wonderful because then he'd have the chance to get the dirt on Jimmy from right under his own roof. Then he asked me if I had anything else to tell him, but I'd already told him everything I knew."

The old lady saw the light she'd turned on in the deputy chief's eyes.

"You see what I'm getting at, don't you?"

Oliver nodded.

"Jimmy wronged Isaac from before the time he was born. Now, if he figured his boy was going to pay him back …

Pay him back and help bring down Jimmy Thunder's empire, Oliver thought. That could be a reason for murder. Lots of other people had been killed for far less.

He told Mahalia Cardwell, "I'm sorry for your loss, Mrs. Cardwell, and I'm sorry if I've delayed your return home."

The old lady shook her head.

"Charmaine and Japhet are going home. But I'm staying right here. Stayin' until you and your chief of police give me justice."

CHAPTER 18

Deacon Meeker brought the four members of Jimmy Thunder's household staff to the sunroom where Ron waited. The houseman and the cook were African American: the chauffeur and the personal secretary were Korean American. Ron wondered if Thunder was trying to make a statement. Was he trying to prove traditional antagonists could get along if you paid them all enough money?

The deacon didn't issue any words of warning to the others about talking to Ron, at least not in his presence. Instead, he gave them a badass look — the kind of intimidating expression he might have learned in the yard at San Quentin. Ron stepped between him and his audience.

"Indigestion?" the chief asked the deacon neutrally. But he was giving the deacon his hard look, and Meeker was the one to turn away.

Ron turned to see if the others appreciated the fact that he would be there for them, if anyone tried muscling them. The houseman wore an amused little grin: he'd seen this kind of thing before. The cook looked like she had a brisket burning, she was so nervous. The chauffeur and the secretary were impassive.

Ron started with the houseman. He asked the others to seat themselves at a rectangular table where the chief could imagine the reverend taking breakfast on sunny mornings. He wondered if Isaac Cardwell had sat at the table with his father, and what they might have said. A bleak smile forced its way onto Ron's face when he saw the Koreans sit on the opposite side of the table from the cook. Maybe even money couldn't buy racial harmony.

Ron and the houseman sat in lounge chairs next to a small recirculating pond in the far corner of the room. At that distance, with the burbling of the water, they were out of earshot of the others.

"What's your name?" Ron asked.

"Leroi." The guy had another grin for Ron. The chief figured Leroi to be somewhere around his own age. The man wore a neat goatee that was flecked with gray. He looked quite natty in his work coat and slacks, as if they'd been custom tailored for him. And, working for Jimmy Thunder, maybe they had.

Ron smiled back. "You spell your name with a y or an i?"

"You're sharp." The houseman nodded in approval. "With an i. Leroi Grand is what my mama named me. Told me it means 'The Great King.' How 'bout that for a name?"

"Not bad."

"'Course I like yours, too."

"You do?"

"Sure. A cop named Ketchum." Leroi Grand chuckled. "How many times did you hear: 'Did you catch'em, Ketchum?'"

"A few," Ron admitted. "Mostly before I made rank. So, Great King, where'd you do your time?"

"Did three years at Joliet. Eighteen months at Pontiac."

Ron knew of the two Illinois institutions. He asked, "Chicagoan?"

"Mm-hmm."

"What did you do?"

"Little ghetto capitalism, is all."

"Not drugs, or you'd have been in a lot longer than that."

"Never did like drugs. Never took 'em, never sold 'em. Drugs make everybody too crazy. No, all I did was buy and sell things. Used to be an open-air market in Chicago on Maxwell Street for 'bout a hundred years worked like that. Vendors set up their displays right out on the sidewalk. Nobody asks where anybody got their merchandise. People come for the bargains. And the cops don't bother anyone. Even with the police station at the end of the block. Was one dude had a table set up sellin' blue Mars lights, like they come right off a police cruiser. Nobody says a word. Then urban renewal come through, and the market's gone. I make the mistake of tryin' to revive it at a new location. Bam, I'm busted for receivin' stolen goods. All of sudden, people lost all respect for tradition."

"Life's hard," Ron commiserated.

"Tell me. Anyway, this boy, just before I got sent away the second time, sold me just about a whole library of books, cheap. And, would you believe, I got hooked on reading. Never would pick up a book in school. Now, I got my nose in one every spare minute."

"That's wonderful. Where'd the books come from?"

"The boy said his grandma. In fact, everything I bought came from somebody's grandma. I called my business 'Grandma's Market.'"

"I bet that boy was lying," Ron said.

"Sad truth was," Leroi Grand lamented, "he killed a man whose house he was robbin'. Only reason he stole the books, they had fancy bindings that caught his eye. Which was the only reason I bought them, too. And the only reason I started reading them. When the police busted me, they told me the books were rare first editions. The little library I bought for two hundred dollars was worth more than ten keys of coke. Opened my eyes wide, that information. Books could give you pleasure, make you smart, and be worth a shitload of money. I went straight after I got out. Found work where I'd get a room and meals so I could spend all my money reading and hunting up first editions."

"The Chicago cops didn't like you as an accomplice to the murder of the original book owner?"

"Sure, they did. But I didn't have nothin' to do with it. And when I fingered the boy who sold me the books, I got my eighteen months for receivin' stolen property."

Ron nodded.

He asked, "Did you see Isaac Cardwell when he was here?"

"Course I did. I'm the one who keeps this place runnin'."

"How did he get along with his father?"

Leroi Grand rubbed his chin. "It was hard on both of 'em at first. All that time apart, a boy's gonna want to know why his daddy run out on him. And there ain't never a good enough answer for doin' that."

"Did they argue about it?" Ron asked.

"No. Isaac Cardwell … all I can say about him is, we all had ministers like him, you cops wouldn't have near as much work. I knock on the door to his room one night, and when I don't get an answer, I go in. He's down on his knees prayin' so hard he didn't even hear me. When's the last time you saw a grown man prayin' on his knees all by himself?"

"I don't think I ever have," Ron answered. "Jimmy Thunder doesn't do it, does he?"

The houseman shrugged. "I don't know. His door, I don't open unless the man say, 'Come on in.'"

"So there were no hard feelings at all between Cardwell and Thunder, despite the reverend abandoning his son?"

"Was this one time," Leroi said.

"What happened?" Ron asked.

"The reverend had another visitor at the house part of the time his boy was here. Isaac, he didn't like his daddy associatin' with this gentleman."

"Why not?"

"That, I honestly can't say. Some folks you just naturally give a little more breathin' room than others. This particular gentleman, I respected his privacy real good."

"Do you know his name?"

"Didi DuPree." Leroi spelled it for him.

"And was there something about him that warned you away?"

Leroi Grand smiled ruefully. "The way you made me for an ex con?"

"Yeah."

"I made Mr. DuPree the same way. Only I bet he was in for somethin' a lot worse than I was."

"You know that for a fact?"

"You look at the man yourself sometime and tell me what you know."

Ron had one last question for the man. "How come you're talking to me so freely?"

"Well, first off I learned to stop hating cops, and most everyone else, quite a while ago. Funny how a man's attitude changes once he starts makin' an honest dollar. Second, I promised myself I ain't never goin' back to prison — not even for a job as good as this one. And I know, a fella with my record, I don't cooperate, what you cops gonna think? That I'm in the middle of things, that's what." Leroi Grand shook his head. "No, sir, I ain't goin' back in. You wouldn't believe how bad prison libraries are."

Ron couldn't remember the last time anyone had told him he'd learned to stop hating, and never when the subject was cops.

"You're okay, Leroi. You let me know if anyone around here gives you any grief. I'll get the mayor to find you a job."

The houseman left with another of his trademark grins.

The two Koreans had their routines down pat.

The personal secretary answered every question with the same response: "I'm sorry. I regret I can't help you with that."

The chauffeur simply answered every question, "No." From the blank look on the man's face, Ron wasn't sure that the driver even understood English. But the chief highly doubted Jimmy Thunder had picked up a working knowledge of Korean anywhere in his travels. Not even enough to give his driver directions.

So just to see if he could get any kind of rise out of the little man with the rigid jaw, Ron asked jokingly, "Does your employer know you once worked for the Korean CIA?"

"No." Then there was a reptilian flicker behind the man's previously opaque brown eyes as he wondered if his standard denial was a sufficient answer. "I did not," he added tersely, and stomped from the room.

Ron was tempted to call him back, but by this time the cook was squirming in her chair like a small child waiting to use the bathroom. Which was just how Ron wanted her.

"What's your name?" Ron asked, when he had her seated next to him.

"Marvella McRay."

"Are you nervous about something, Marvella?"

"Today is my last day."

"I beg your pardon?"

"I'm leavin' this place," the woman elaborated.

"Why?"

"Why?" the woman echoed in disbelief. "You're the chief of police, and you don't know?"

"I don't know why you're leaving your job."

"Because that fine young man who was stayin' here got himself murdered so terrible bad. It's a sin against Jesus killin' someone that way — mockin' our sweet Lord like that. And then you ain't heard his grandmother callin' down the wrath of God on this town? I ain't stayin' here, no sir!"

"What are you going to do?" Ron asked.

"My boy's comin' from Reno to get me any minute now. I'll find work someplace else. I was packin' when Deacon Meeker said the police wanted to see me right away."

The woman was genuinely terrified and Ron didn't keep her long.

Just long enough for Marvella McCray to tell him that Reverend Thunder sent away his two lady friends while his son was in the house.

She gave Ron their names and told him where they were staying.

By the time Ron got back outside, the man on the riding mower was gone. The chief made a mental note to get the grounds-keeper's name and talk to him soon.

CHAPTER 19

Sitting at his desk in police headquarters, Ron read through the stack of hate mail Jimmy Thunder had given him. Attached to each letter was a photocopy of the envelope in which it had arrived. None of the envelope copies had a return address on it. The chief started his reading with the locally postmarked sewage:

"You call yourself a man of God?! Niggers ain't God's creatures! The goddamn devil made niggers, singed 'em up in the fires of Hell good and black, and set 'em loose in the world to torment white folks. That's the way I read my Bible, mister!"

"Reverend Thunder, huh? Hah! You sound more like a dry fart to me. Your allways up there yappin' on television, tellin' coons how to act right. What do you think they are, white? Even your average city-nigger knows better'n that. They'll take up against there own kind, if they try to act white. All niggers want is there wellfare checks, there crank cocain, and to be left alone in there getto jungles to shoot one another from cars. You know it and I do two."

"First we had the Jews, and they were Christ-killers. Now we got niggers like you, and you're Christ-stealers. You think we're going to let you get away with that? Your kind might mug us on dark streets and take all our money. But you'll never steal our God. You think I'm wrong? Just look around. See how many nigger churches are burning. Your turn is coming."

That was the first specific threat. Ron looked at the photocopy of the envelope. It was addressed to the P.O. box of Thunder's ministry, not his home address. But there was a Goldstrike postmark on the envelope, and it wasn't much of stretch to think a local could find out where Jimmy Thunder lived. It would be a better trick to get past Thunder's gate and Deacon Meeker to burn down the reverend's "church." But why wouldn't Thunder pass on such a threat to the police as a matter of course? Why wait until his son had been killed?

He'd have to talk to the reverend about that, and any other direct threat he found.

Ron was about to wade back into the postal cesspool when his phone rang. It was Leroi Grand. He wanted to know if the chief would like the name of the cleaning company he had come out to the house twice a week.

Ron said he would, and thanked Leroi for his cooperation.

Then he asked, "What's the name of the guy who does the lawns?"

"Man does more than cut the grass," Leroi said. "He's the one responsible for the place lookin' like Adam 'n' Eve might pop out from behind the next bush. His name's Art Gilbert."

"He have his own company?" Ron asked.

"Yeah." Leroi gave him the name.

"What kind of guy is he?"

"Quiet. But he's all right. Pretty much keeps to his work. Guess that's what an artist is like."

Having seen the landscaping at Jimmy Thunder's estate, Ron wouldn't argue that Gilbert was indeed an artist. "Thanks again, Leroi. Let me know if I can do anything for you."

Before he got back to the hate mail, Ron decided to stretch his legs and he buttonholed Sergeant Stanley.

"Run a name for me, Sarge. Query the state and NCIC data bases."

"Sure. What's the name?"

"Didi DuPree." Ron spelled it for him. "Let's see if there are any arrest warrants out for Mr. DuPree. Take a look at his criminal history. If he's done any serious time, see what you can find out about that. And if there are mug-shots available, I'll want those, too."

The sergeant nodded and did a quick first scan through the impressive database between his ears. "Don't know him, personally. If I find out Mr. DuPree is not your model citizen, you want me to take any further action?"

"I want to know if he's still in town. He was a guest at Jimmy Thunder's estate at least part of the time Isaac Cardwell was there. But don't start looking for him until I know what kind of sheet he has."

The sergeant nodded and went to perform his task.

"Hey, Sarge," Ron said, stopping him. "Add another name to that computer search: Deacon Meeker."

The chief returned to his office and looked at the stack of hate mail waiting for him. It put him in a sour mood. He went to his windows and looked out at the lake.

He'd been surprised and appalled by the racist crap that had been locally mailed to Thunder. He hadn't thought that kind of cretin could afford the rarefied precincts of Goldstrike. Sure, not everybody in town was rich, well educated and recently arrived. Somebody had to do oil changes, wait tables, ring up resort wear, and clean hotel rooms. But any resident who so desired could swim in the lake and ski the mountains just like all the millionaires. The town's recreation programs saw to that. And to Ron's certain knowledge, there were no desperate poor or career criminals living in town. The people of Goldstrike had always seemed a decent sort to him. So who was spewing their bile to Thunder? Living in a place of such surpassing beauty, what the hell did they have to complain about? What right did they have to hold a grudge against anybody?

Maybe they'd never had a chance to meet their DeWayne Michaels, he thought acidly. That notion was enough to bring the chief up short. If he hadn't met DeWayne, might he be just as twisted as the haters who had bared their deformed souls to

Jimmy Thunder?

Regardless of how his personal demons made him feel, he'd have to keep his ear close to the ground. If there were anything worse than having assholes in his jurisdiction, it would be letting them get organized. He wouldn't stand for that.

Then there was the matter of Mr. Didi DuPree, the seriously bad ex con, according to Leroi Grand. Ron didn't doubt the canny houseman's appraisal was accurate. It wouldn't do to have someone like DuPree on hand, sliding in and out of the shadows. Not at any time. But especially not now when Isaac Cardwell's killer was still looking to have his nametag filled in. A prompt sit down with DuPree would be imperative.

Ron let out a deep sigh.

A voice said, "The burdens of high office getting to be too much for you? Let me know if I should make my pitch to the mayor."

The chief turned to see that Oliver had entered his office.

"You keep telling me you're not going to spend another winter here," Ron said.

"My wife and son keep telling me they won't live anywhere else."

"We've all got our —" Ron stopped himself. "I was going to say crosses to bear. But in light of recent events I don't think that's a very happy metaphor."

"Not hardly," Oliver said, taking a seat.

Ron sat down behind his desk.

"Why don't you tell me about your day, and I'll tell you about mine?"

The two cops spent the next ten minutes sharing information, and they examined how some of the pieces of what they'd learned might fit together.

"The reverend has himself two girlfriends?" Oliver asked. "And they both live under his roof? That's not exactly living the fine, upstanding lifestyle he preaches, is it?"

Jimmy Thunder's ministry was predicated on the simple idea that if you followed the Ten Commandments, you were beyond reproof. If anyone hurled an epithet, racial or otherwise, at you while you lived a righteous life, they were only revealing their own flawed and sinful natures.

A moral, upright life was an invincible shield, the reverend preached. In time, even the wicked would tire of trying to attack it. Or they would be driven off by the multitudes of the godly. Whose numbers would surely increase if Jimmy Thunder's show remained on TV.

"Yeah," Ron responded. "And then there's his friend and houseguest, Didi DuPree, and whatever sins he makes his life's work. In the middle of all this, Isaac Cardwell arrives unexpectedly on Daddy's doorstep, with a Brit sleaze merchant in tow."

"You think the old lady's got it right? Jimmy Thunder did his son?"

"He says he was playing cards with Texas Jack."

"Gambling being another thing that surely wouldn't help his image."

"Besides which," Ron added, "Thunder could have hired it done, and never had to leave the card table."

A reflective look crossed the deputy chief's face.

"Killing your own son. Man, you can't get any colder than that."

Ron knew Oliver was thinking about his own beloved child.

"It's not like they really knew each other," the chief said. "From what you told me, Mahalia Cardwell drove Thunder off before Isaac Cardwell was even born."

"Yeah. And the good reverend never made an attempt to see his boy after that. So maybe he didn't care that Isaac was his own flesh and blood. Maybe all he cared about was saving his own sweet scam, and hired the killing done like you said."

Ron decided to play the devil's advocate for a moment.

"I thought you liked a white guy with a red neck for the murder."

"Maybe that's who Thunder hired," Oliver said.

"Or maybe he just had his boy nailed to that tree like that to throw us off."

"Yeah, shit. It could be like that," the deputy chief admitted.

"You think Isaac Cardwell was actually spying on his father for this Colin Ring scumbag?"

"Mrs. Cardwell paints a halo 'round Isaac's head. On the other hand, even Jesus had his moment of weakness. Maybe Reverend Cardwell was hitting back at Reverend Thunder for being such a miserable fucking excuse for a father."

Oliver shook his head several times.

Then he asked, "We get any word on physical evidence from the crime scene? "

"Such as it is," Ron answered. "Dr. Ryman estimates Isaac Cardwell's time of death as approximately three a.m. Friday morning. He says the rain that was falling off and on that night undoubtedly affected the body's temperature, but to what degree he can't say. So three in the morning is his best guess. Benny Marx tells me those footprints come from a size nine and a half E work boot, manufactured in South Korea and sold under various labels at department and discount stores around the country. The impressions indicate a man five nine to six feet, weighing between one fifty and two hundred pounds. Again, precision was made more difficult by the rain, by the fact that the killer was burdened by Isaac Cardwell's weight on the way to the tree, and the fact that slippery footing likely caused him to alter the length of his normal stride on the way out."

"No chance of getting anything of the killer's to do a DNA test on? "

Ron shook his head. "No tissue was found under Isaac Cardwell's fingernails. No strands of hair were found. No blood was found. "

Oliver Gosden's jaw was tight with frustration. Then he sighed as loudly as Ron had moments earlier. "You know, I wouldn't mind letting my family see their daddy part of this Sunday. That all right with you?"

"Sure, go ahead. Give my love to Lauren, and tell Danny his Uncle Ron says hello."

Oliver snorted. "Uncle Ron, huh? You think that's funny,

don't you?"

"A sense of humor is sanity's life preserver," Ron said with a grin.

"Yeah, I'll give you that. You going home, too?"

The smile fell off the chief's face.

"No. Not yet. I've got a lot of hate mail to read."

CHAPTER 20

Late afternoon had arrived by the time Ron had slogged through the last of the letters telling Jimmy Thunder he was a subhuman monster who fucked his mother when he wasn't out raping white women, conning the liberal dupe media and generally polluting a country that would otherwise be the Garden of Eden. The hate mail came from both near, and far, thirty-eight states including Alaska and Hawaii, and three foreign countries.

Ron hadn't known Thunder's show was broadcast internationally. And maybe it wasn't. These days, people overseas could be relying on their satellite dishes to pick up TV signals of someone they could hate.

The hard thing for the chief was not to hate them right back. It wasn't different skin colors that made the world a charnel house so often. It was the tribal mindset — fear the outsider — that the human race just could not seem to evolve past.

But if you hated the haters, you fell into the same trap.

The idea of hating the sin, but loving the sinner, well, maybe just giving him a kick in the ass, seemed to be about the only answer Ron could agree with. But look where that philosophy got its originator.

Crucified. Just like Isaac Cardwell.

The chief locked the file containing the hate mail in his office safe, all except the one mentioning the church burnings and the threat against Jimmy Thunder. The FBI had a legitimate interest in that one. Ron had Sergeant Stanley fax it to Special Agent Horgan in San Francisco.

Then he went to the Muni's rec center to shoot some hoops. It was closed at that hour on Sunday, but he had a key. It was one of the perks of his job, and the only one he'd had to request specifically of Clay Steadman.

Some cops, when they got wrung out by the job, went home and regained their sanity in the comfort of their families. Others went to bars and tried to forget the madness by drinking themselves into stupors. Ron went to the gym and lost himself in the familiar rhythms of basketball.

He went to the men's locker room and changed into his shorts and sneakers. He carried his T-shirt into the gym with him but didn't bother putting it on since he had the place to himself. He tossed the shirt onto a rack filled with basketballs.

He jogged five easy laps of the gym to get his muscles warmed up and then he stretched and did ten reps of abdominal crunches. He maintained an athlete's discipline not because he feared growing old — age didn't scare him — but because he relished the childlike joy of unrestrained physical movement, and he wanted to hang on to it as long as he could.

When he felt ready, he took a ball off a rack and dribbled it rapidly several times with each hand, then switched it deftly from hand to hand, behind his back, and back and forth between his legs. Not Pistol Pete Maravich, but not bad.

Then, holding the ball to his chest, he twisted his torso gently from side to side, and did a couple of light squats and toe raises. Still had some spring left in the old wheels, he felt. But how much? Only one way to tell

He stepped to the top of the key and fixed his eyes on the basket. In a sudden burst, he charged toward the hoop. The ball left his hand just once, hit the floor and bounced back to him as he jumped from the dotted arc below the free throw line. Ron held the ball high in his right hand, his arm extended as far as it could go. He measured the distance to the rim as he reached the top of his jump. It was going to be close and … BANG!

Slam dunk — but just barely.

Not that any dunk by a 48 year old guy was anything to be ashamed of. Heck, he'd never been able to do it when he was a kid in high school with fresh knees. But after he'd joined the army and finally hit a late growth spurt, and his hands got big enough to palm the ball, he'd discovered to his profound delight that he could jam the ball through the hole. This impressed the hell out of just about every black soldier he'd ever played ball with. It was his goal to still be able to dunk when he hit fifty.

That was going to take a lot of increased strength work for his legs, he knew. But what the hell else did he have in his life besides his job?

After the dunk, Ron started casually hitting jumpers from all over the court. He still had his shooter's eye. There was no problem with vision, thank God. He then stepped to the free throw line to finish up. One hundred free throws in a row before he could go home. Sometimes he wimped out and gave himself a pass if he knocked down eighty or more. Other times he stayed until he hit all one hundred consecutively.

He'd rung up seventy-eight in a row when the door to the gym opened and Corrie Knox stepped in, breaking his concentration and making him miss. The ball clanked off the front of the rim and Ron had to retrieve it on the second bounce

"Sorry if I'm interrupting," she said. "Sergeant Stanley said I might find you here."

Ron felt mildly embarrassed, as if she'd caught him shaving in his underwear. He stepped over to the ball rack and picked up his T-shirt.

"Don't bother on my account," Corrie said. "When I heard where I might find you, I was hoping I might shoot a few hoops myself."

"You like basketball?" Ron asked.

"Sure. Muggsy Bogues is my favorite player."

"He is?"

"Yeah. Everybody always talks about LeBron, D-Wade and Kobe. They're all great. But for my money, a guy who was five-three and played in the NBA, that's someone to really admire."

Corrie Knox sat down on the hardwood floor and took off her shoes and socks. Ron saw that she wore hiking shorts, and that her legs were very long and very tan. She stood up and pulled her shirt tails out of her shorts.

She bent from her waist, casually pressed her forehead to her knees and held it there. Turning her head but holding her position, she saw Ron looking at her. "Gotta stretch out those hammies, huh?"

Then she straightened, popped the ball out of Ron's hands, dribbled a few steps and drilled a twenty foot jumper.

She turned and looked at him. "So what'll it be? HORSE, 21, or some one on one?"

"One on one with what rules?"

She said, "You never stop the game to call a carrying violation, and you have to take more than three steps before it's traveling. You make it, you take it."

Ron laughed. Then he said, "Let's play HORSE or 21. I don't know you well enough to knock you down and sweat all over you."

Warden Knox replied. "Don't worry about me. I'm not exactly fragile. And I've been known to work up a pretty good lather myself."

Still, they started with HORSE. Ron had greater range and quickly had his opponent down by four letters, but when he missed his next long-range bomb, Corrie started canning fifteen to twenty foot jumpers, with her off hand. She completed the comeback for the win.

When they switched to 21, Ron's long years of Zen-like concentration on free throws gave him the edge. He went first and made fifty in a row before pleading the need for a drink of water and turning the ball over to Corrie. He'd almost quit too soon. She made forty-four consecutively before missing.

"So," she said with fine beads of perspiration on her brow, "it's one win apiece. A quick game of one-on-one to ten, gotta win by a deuce, to settle things?"

Ron regarded her, with her cockeyed smile, challenging him. Then he looked at her bare feet, wincing inwardly at how his own feet, not to mention his knees, would feel if he didn't wear shoes with shock absorbing soles.

"No, I don't think so. We need you around here. I'd feel terrible if I came down on one of those bare feet and broke several of your toes."

"Sounds like an excuse to me," Corrie said bluntly.

"Yeah, sure. You've got me scared."

"Thought so."

"Or maybe you could get yourself a pair of shoes. Then we'll see."

"I'll do that. I think playing you could be a lot of fun."

Now the grin on her face had enough mischief in it to make him uncomfortable. This time, he popped the ball out of her hands and put it back on the rack. He slipped his T-shirt on.

"If you're in town long enough, maybe we'll get around to it."

"Oh, I'm going to be here. For a while, anyway. That was the main reason I came to see you."

Ron understood immediately. "The mountain lion? You got a match?"

"I got a match. If he sticks around, so do I."

"Well, hell," the chief said. Then he sighed and suggested, "Why don't you clean up at my place, and I'll shower here. Then we can go somewhere and talk about it."

"That's the other thing I have to tell you."

"What?"

"I found a hotel room."

"Oh."

"A little motel that was redecorating opened up a room since the market's so tight."

"That's good."

"It's not as nice as your place, but this way people won't get the wrong idea."

"No, they won't."

"I mean I wouldn't want anyone thinking something's going on when you won't even play basketball with me," she said with a straight face.

"Get a pair of shoes."

"Count on it," Corrie Knox replied.

Oliver Gosden and his wife Lauren sat on the front porch glider at their home on Highwood Street. The six room house was well constructed, but all of the rooms were fairly small. Snug and cozy, Lauren liked to call them. The living room, dining room and kitchen occupied the right half of the floor plan. Three bedrooms filled the left half. There was access to the bedroom wing from the living room and the kitchen. The single bathroom was opposite the middle bedroom, and had a door that opened on the bedroom wing and another on an alcove between the dining room and kitchen. The house was situated one block from a pine forest that marked the eastern boundary of the town. Close to nature and hiking, the real estate lady had put it.

"Close to black bears and coyotes," was Oliver's point of view.

He definitely would have preferred a larger house in the middle of town, as close to the lake as possible. But prices for those places were way out of reach.

Not that the Gosdens were poor. Far from it. Their combined incomes nudged them north of one hundred and fifty thousand dollars that year, a new personal high for them. But after taxes, day care and putting money aside for when a second child filled their third bedroom, the Gosdens would not be moving lakeside anytime soon.

Lauren Gosden rubbed the tight muscles in her husband's neck to make him feel better about his lot in life. He was still complaining about the move to Goldstrike two years after they'd left L.A., when they both knew it was the best decision they could have made.

"I've been thinking about Arizona," the deputy chief told his wife.

"For what, a winter vacation? Fine with me."

"The chief of police in Sedona is coming up on retirement in another year."

"I don't want to live in a sandbox, Oliver. Not one that gets that hot. Might as well live in San Bernadino."

"Hey, now. Sedona's a nice town. Got a reputation for being artistic."

"That's going to do a lot for us. You're a cop, and I'm a nurse."

"I was thinking about Danny."

Both parents turned to look at their six year old son. He sat on the grass in their small front yard and was working his way through *Dr. Seuss's Foot Book* with a smile on his face. Every so often, he'd ask for help sounding out a word. Not too often, though. They'd been reading to him since he was born, and he'd started reading for himself at age four. In a few weeks, he'd be starting first grade.

"You find out if there are going to be any other black kids in Danny's class?" Oliver asked his wife.

"Two," she responded. "And one Asian child and three Hispanics."

"All God's children, huh? For up here, that's real diversity."

"Lots of middle class black folks in Sedona, I suppose"

"At least it's warm in the winter."

"And hot enough to broil your brain in the summer."

Lauren Gosden took her husband's hand and squeezed it affectionately.

"Are you really so unhappy here?"

"I … I feel out of place more than anything. This town is too rich. It's too high. And it's too damn white."

Danny, who'd been listening without his father noticing, asked, "Are Grandma and Grandpa Fells too damn white?"

Lauren Fells Gosden gave her husband a look, telling him he'd put his foot in it this time, and he better figure a way out fast.

"Not in the summer, son," Oliver said glibly. "Your grandparents tan up real nice."

Danny giggled and parlayed the joke, "Except for Grandpa's head where the hair's all gone — that gets red."

Even Lauren was laughing by now.

"Hey, Dad?"

"What?"

"I cleaned up my room today."

"You fishing for a quarter."

"Yep." The boy nodded his head emphatically.

Oliver took a coin out of his pocket and, feeling contrite as he remembered that he'd yelled at his son that morning, said, "I think I'll give you a bonus for all your good work. How about I take you and your mom out for some ice cream?"

"Yeah!" Danny grabbed the quarter and raced off for the family car, the Dr. Seuss book under his arm.

Oliver stood up and offered his arm to his wife. She rose and took it.

"So life around here isn't all bad?"

"It has its moments," the deputy chief conceded.

Then he kissed her. Deeply. He knew what his favorite sweet was.

CHAPTER 21

Less than two miles away, five-year-old Trent Derby sat playing with his toy fire truck on the deck in back of his home. The Derby house, unlike the Gosden residence, had no buffer between it and the forest. It was built flush against the wilderness, and the setting sun cast long shadows across the backyard.

The little boy called out, "Ding, ding, ding, ding, ding!" Moving onto his hands and knees, he raced his toy truck over to a planter box that he transformed in his mind into a burning building. Nearby, the family's seventy pound Akita, Sumo, lay drowsing in the warmth of the day's last light. The dog's eyelids twitched when Trent's voice squeaked into an uncomfortably high register.

Just inside the sliding screen door to the kitchen, Paula Derby, the little boy's mother, prepared stir-fry chicken on the stovetop. Every minute or so, she'd glance out at the deck to make sure her son wasn't getting into mischief. The yard was enclosed by a six foot high redwood fence. Electronic sensors would be turning on the floodlights soon. There was no cause for concern, but Paula was cautious by nature, and all the more so when it came to her son.

Trent was perfectly capable of trying to dig his way to the bottom of the planter he was kneeling next to, convinced that some imaginary treasure lay buried there. That or finding a bug he might catch and try to stick into poor Sumo's ear.

But Trent was still playing fireman when she glanced at him. Whooshing out illusory flames with make believe torrents of water. Paula tasted the stir-fry she was preparing and thought it could use a little more ginger. She turned to her cutting board to chop a bit more of the spice and missed seeing Sumo's head suddenly snap up.

The dog looked toward the fence. He sniffed the air, and the fur on the back of his neck rose. A low, rumbling growl began deep in his chest.

Playing only five feet away, the little boy failed to notice the activity of the family pet.

But Paula, more finely attuned to her surroundings, turned to see what was going on. She had a six inch kitchen knife in her hand as she moved to the sliding door. She saw Sumo was on his feet. His back was stiff and he neck was arched. The growl coming from the dog was continuous now: a low rumble filled with menace.

Paula couldn't see what was agitating Sumo. Trent wasn't bothering the dog. He was still busy with his fire truck, not even paying attention to Sumo. She slid the screen door open and took a more careful look around. She wondered if some small animal had burrowed under the fence and excited the dog. But at twilight with the sun almost gone and the floodlights not yet on she saw nothing unusual.

"Lie down, boy," she told the dog. "Go back to slee —"

The dog began to bark furiously, and Paula looked up just in time to see a mountain lion leap her fence and land soundlessly, not ten feet from where her son was just now lifting his head. Trent and his mother both saw the predator fix its gaze on him.

Paula screamed. Sumo growled. The dog's fur stood on end, puffing him up to twice his normal size. Trent looked around and saw his mother's fear and the flashing teeth of the dog. Panic welled up in his young heart. He screamed and started to scramble to his feet.

The cat made a lunge for the boy. But Sumo charged forward and snapped at the mountain lion. The dog's headlong rush sent the youngster crashing to the deck. Now, Sumo was between Trent and the big cat. The predator backed off, but only momentarily, and only to assess the situation.

The lion tried to circle the barking dog, but when it saw Paula scoop up Trent, stealing its intended prey, it leaped directly at both of them. Sumo launched himself without hesitation and met a predator that was twice his size in mid-air.

The two animals crashed to the deck hard enough to jolt the boards under Paula's feet. With Trent's head clasped firmly to her shoulder, cold sweat running down her spine, and a horrible cacophony of growls, barks and yelps ringing in her ears, she darted into the kitchen and slammed the sliding glass door to the deck shut, and locked it.

Shielding her son's eyes with her body, she looked out at the fight. Sumo and the mountain lion rolled and scrambled over one another in a maelstrom of teeth, fur, and limbs barely five feet from where she stood. Sumo brought his jaws together on one of the lion's ears, bringing a hideous howl of pain. Then the animals rolled into a patch of deep shadow. Paula lost sight of them but she still heard quite clearly the deep thud of a body being slammed to the deck. Almost immediately after that came a sickening crunch, a sound she would remember the rest of her life.

At that moment, the floodlights came on. There before Paula's horrified eyes, the mountain lion straddled Sumo, its fearsome jaws still busy crushing the neck of the family pet.

The dog's body shook in a death spasm and lay still. The mountain lion turned to look at the woman and the boy, its fangs dripping blood. Paula didn't know if the cat would try to break through the glass, but she realized she still had her kitchen knife in her hand. Baring her teeth, she brandished it at the cat. Before she knew it, she was growling.

The mountain lion rose to its feet, flashed its savage teeth, and snarled in return.

But then it dropped its head and took the dog's neck in its jaws once more. A wave of nausea swept through Paula as she thought the predator might devour Sumo right there on her deck. Instead, continuing to maintain a hold with its teeth, the cat flipped the dog's seventy pound carcass up onto its back. It crossed the deck, leaving a trail of blood, and leaped the six foot fence, leaving as soundlessly as it had arrived.

Paula Derby put the knife down and leaned against a counter before her knees gave way. She comforted the sobbing Trent as best she could, praying he hadn't peeked and seen the carnage. She tried to put her son down, but he clung to her with both arms and legs.

So, continuing to hold him, she picked up the phone and called 911.

"What I was thinking," Corrie Knox said, "was maybe the town should put up some signs, distribute some fliers, have your department generally notify the public that the cat might still be around. I suppose you'd want to work out the details with your famous mayor."

"Yeah," Ron agreed. "He likes to be involved in these things."

They were having grilled fish on the patio of Rainbow Traut's, a lakeside restaurant.

The chief raised another point, "You do know why you had such a hard time finding a room, don't you?"

"Sure. You've got a ton of reporters in town because of that murder."

"Right. So, the idea of informing the town with fliers is, what, a little quaint? I think the ladies and gentlemen of the press might just give some play to the story of a killer mountain lion."

"Yeah, I guess so. Sorry. I spend most of my time in the woods or a lab. I don't have any experience with the media."

"Lucky you." Just then a very unpleasant thought crossed Ron's mind, and apparently registered on his face.

"What's wrong?" Corrie wanted to know.

"Have you heard about Mahalia Cardwell, and what she had to say about her grandson's murder?"

"No."

Ron told her about the old lady's statement to the media: God would punish Goldstrike until Isaac Cardwell's killer was caught.

"What, she cursed the town? I can't believe you'd believe that."

"Not me," Ron said. "I don't see God as anybody's hitman. But a woman I talked to today, Jimmy Thunder's cook, in fact, quit her job and left town because she believes it. Now, this mountain lion shows up. It doesn't take much imagination to see the press making a connection."

Warden Cordelia Knox, wildlife biologist, frowned at the notion.

"Whatever is driving this cat is biological or environmental, not supernatural."

"Yeah. You know that as a scientist. I know that from common sense. But which would make a better story? The dry toast of science or the red meat of divine vengeance?"

"I see your point. Well, let's hope the cat has moved on then."

Corrie's words were no sooner spoken than Ron's BlackBerry chimed.

A silver BMW 525i and a patrol unit were parked in front of the Derby house when Ron and Corrie pulled up in his Explorer. Clay Steadman arrived practically on the chief's rear bumper. The mayor hadn't stopped by to say hello. He rang the front doorbell, and when the door was opened by a uniformed officer, the three officials filed inside.

The Goldstrike cop who'd come to the door, Hal Brookings, gave the new arrivals a quick, whispered summary of where things stood. He and his partner, Sally Waters, had received a call about a mountain lion attack and responded immediately. The man of the house, Edward Derby, a local stockbroker, had come home just ahead of the two cops. Derby had been playing golf all afternoon and drinking all evening. He got more than a little upset when he heard what had happened.

Brookings looked like he wanted to say more, and he might

have except he didn't know the woman with the mayor and the chief. Opting for discretion, he led them to the family room where his partner was gently trying to take a statement from Paula Derby.

Her husband, the young financial executive with the sunburned face and glazed eyes, started nodding vigorously when he recognized two of the three new visitors to his home.

"It's about time. About goddamn time somebody who knows what he's doing got here," Derby said. He rose unsteadily from the sofa where he'd sat next to his wife and son. "I told these two cops to get out there. Get out there and hunt that goddamn animal down. But they just stayed right here making my wife rehash the whole goddamn thing, upsetting her and my little boy all over again. What the hell took you people so long?"

Clay understood the man had a reason to be upset, but as the mayor he had to balance the interests of the town's citizens with that of the town's employees.

"Officer Brookings, what was your response time?" the mayor asked.

"Officer Waters and I received the call from the dispatcher at 19:30 hours, Mr. Mayor, and we arrived on the scene at 19:33 hours. When Mrs. Derby told us what happened we immediately called for the chief."

The mayor looked at his watch. "It's 7:42 now, Mr. Derby. You had a police response within three minutes, and the chief and I were here within twelve minutes."

"With Warden Knox from the state department of fish and game," Ron added, since the mayor had yet to be introduced to Corrie.

"They *didn't* go after the goddamn mountain lion," Derby persisted.

"Nor should they have," Corrie replied. "Do you officers have any rifles in your patrol unit?"

"No, ma'am," Brookings responded.

"All long-barrel weapons are kept under lock and key in an armory at headquarters," Ron added. "They're carried in patrol units only in extreme cases."

"And what the hell is this?" Derby yelled.

"Your wife and son are alive and well, Mr. Derby," Clay said. "That would make this your lucky day."

Corrie added, "And you don't hunt a dangerous animal in the dark. Not when he can see you and you can't see him. It's just not smart."

Derby was about to open his yap again, but the mayor put his arm around the man's shoulders, tight enough to make him wince, and walked him out of the room. As he left, he nodded to Ron that now was the time to question Mrs. Derby.

Ron asked Officers Brookings and Waters to take young Trent to his room, commend him for his bravery, and tell him all the things he'd have to know when the chief gave him his new badge as an honorary Goldstrike police officer next week.

The prospect of getting his own police badge enticed the boy out of the room.

Without the distractions of husband and son, Ron and Corrie were able to get a fairly clear picture from Paula Derby of what had happened. Corrie sat down next to Paula and asked if she could give a physical description of the mountain lion. She complied, though the likeness she outlined was limited to generalities.

Regardless, Corrie sketched the animal on a pad she'd brought with her. Despite a lack of detail, the resulting drawing was close enough to reality to make Mrs. Derby shudder.

"Yes," she said. "That's just what it looked like." She started to say something else, bit her tongue and took a peek over her shoulder. Looking back at Ron and Corrie, she went on, "I apologize for my husband. He's a little drunk, and nobody knows better than me how that can make him a pain in the ass … but I look at that drawing and I get just as mad he got. If you saw the way that animal looked at Trent and what it did to poor Sumo … I wish I could kill it!"

Corrie held the distraught woman's hand for a moment to comfort her. "I'm going to ask you to do something now that may be hard for you. I'm going to draw a sketch of a typical mountain lion's face. I'd like you to look at it, if you can, and tell me if there was anything different about the one you saw in your backyard. Can you do that?"

Ron added, "It could help us catch the animal."

Paula Derby nodded, a tear running down her cheek but her jaw firm.

Corrie sketched a lion's face on a fresh sheet of paper. When she was done she handed the pad and pencil to Paula Derby. The woman looked at the image intently.

"I had a knife in my hand."

"Pardon me?" the chief asked.

Paula didn't look up; she kept her eyes on the drawing.

"When I got Trent inside and closed the door … and saw that it had killed Sumo. I had a knife in my hand. I didn't know if it would try to break through the glass and get us, too. So, I held the knife up. I … I think I was growling at it. It had reduced me to its level, but I was ready to fight for my son's life. Ready to fight for mine."

Paula Derby used the pencil she held to sketch a jagged scar over the cat's left eye.

"There. That's what it looks like."

She gave the drawing materials back to Corrie. The game warden and the chief of police glanced at each other. No question. It was the same cat.

"Please find it," Paula said. "Find it and kill it. Before it takes somebody's kid, not just their pet."

CHAPTER 22

Monday

Clay Steadman, staying completely in character, decided to go pre-emptive. He called a news conference that morning at the civic auditorium. He did not have to say pretty please to draw a capacity crowd.

When Annie Stratton signaled that the media mob was ready, the mayor made his entrance. He strode to the lectern at center stage and took a sip from a glass of water that had been left there for him. He calmly looked out at his audience until they were as quiet and attentive as a classroom of parochial school kids.

"I have a statement to make," the mayor said. "Afterwards, I'll take your questions. Yesterday evening, a mountain lion entered the backyard of a residence in Goldstrike. A young boy was playing on the rear deck of the house at the time, but he was not hurt. His mother quickly took him indoors. However, the lion killed the family's dog and made off with it.

"This was the second attack by a lion within a span of three days. This past Friday, a female jogger was attacked while running on Route 38 two miles northwest of town. Fortunately, she also survived. After the initial attack, we had no reason to think the incident was anything but an aberration. Still, the chief of police had called for assistance from the state department of fish and game. The state responded by sending us Game Warden Cordelia

Knox, who is also a wildlife biologist.

"Through Warden Knox's efforts, we have determined that the same animal was involved in both attacks. Warden Knox is now hunting the animal. We hope, but cannot guarantee, that the animal will be killed quickly."

Several members of the media throng were desperate at this point to start shouting out questions. But they knew better than to interrupt Clay Steadman when he was speaking as the mayor of his town. He'd simply have them thrown out and make no apology about it. Still, if he didn't finish soon, there was a danger any number of reporters might spontaneously combust.

"That is why I'm using the good offices of all those present today to alert the public in Goldstrike about how dangerous this mountain lion has proven to be. I couldn't wait until I go on the air this evening to issue the warning. Warden Knox advises me that children are especially vulnerable to such predators, so I urge all parents and day care providers to be extremely careful.

"I also urge all of you in the media to report this story responsibly."

The mayor gave the crowd his best cold-blooded killer stare to emphasize his next point.

"I will be *very* unhappy with anyone who sensationalizes this story or causes undue public fear with scare mongering approaches to it."

Of course, not even Clay Steadman could completely inhibit the media from its love of the prurient, and he knew it. He just wanted to put them on notice, maybe give them pause before they went off the deep end entirely.

"I'll take your questions now," the mayor said.

There were the usual several seconds of competing babble until Annie Stratton pointed to a reporter and loudly called out his name.

"Mr. Mayor, will you tell us the name of the family that was attacked so we can interview them?"

"No. Their privacy is to be respected. If they wish to contact you, that's their call."

From their grumbling, this clearly was not an attitude the press appreciated or would want to see encouraged. Annie called out another reporter's name before the complaining could get too loud.

"Mr. Mayor, in your opinion, should the state have sent more than just one game warden to help hunt down this animal?"

"Warden Knox was joined by a colleague from the fish and game department this morning. I believe his name is …" The mayor turned to Annie Stratton for help.

"Tucker Marsden," the press secretary supplied.

"Tucker Marsden. But the thing you have to keep in mind is that the government's resources are as limited as the people's tolerance for taxes. That's the first lesson anyone who holds office learns. However, if it becomes clear to me that more help is needed, we'll ask for it. Or we'll find funds of our own to pay for it."

Before Annie could call on the next questioner, a wise guy at the back of the room called out, "Are you going to put a hundred thousand dollars on the lion's head, too, Mr. Mayor?"

There was no laughter. The room grew deathly still. With Clay Steadman, there was always the real possibility he might come down into the audience and punch out any loudmouth he didn't like. When the mayor and his ex-wife had come out of the courthouse in Santa Monica after receiving their divorce decree, he'd done just that to a photographer who jumped into their path to get a last picture of the Steadmans together. But the mayor didn't follow such a bare knuckle course at the moment.

"No," he said. "What I might do, though, is tie you up and cover you with steak sauce. When the lion comes for you, we can either shoot it or let the poor bastard die of food poisoning."

Now a ripple of laughter ran through the auditorium, but it was of the nervous variety. The media weren't entirely sure the mayor was kidding. Annie called on Ben Dexter next.

"Frivolous questions aside, Mayor Steadman, do you think this situation with the mountain lion will neither distract your police department nor strain its resources in its efforts to find the killer of Isaac Cardwell?"

"No."

"Then it's still your position that the FBI shouldn't be called in to assist with the case?"

"Chief Ketchum has been forwarding to the FBI any material he thinks they should have. He will continue to do so."

"One final question, sir. Are you struck by the timing of the attacks by this mountain lion, coming as they do after Mrs. Mahalia Cardwell said God would punish this town until her grandson's killer was caught?"

"Do you believe in curses, Mr. Dexter?"

"I'm just a reporter, sir. What matters is your opinion, and those of the townspeople."

"In that case, you can have my opinion. Goldstrike has always been a lucky town. And anyone who lives here pretty much has to consider himself lucky, too. But right now our luck has turned a bit sour. That happens to everyone. Things will right themselves soon enough. And that's my opinion. But the fact is, the first attack by the mountain lion happened *before* Mrs. Cardwell offered her opinion of what actions the Almighty might take."

"Yes, sir," Dexter conceded. "But you said the first attack happened this past Friday. Which, if I have my timeline right, was just *after* Isaac Cardwell was killed. Maybe that's the more important fact."

Deputy Chief Oliver Gosden didn't like Colin Ring from the moment he set eyes on him. The man had a big square pink face with piggy little blue eyes, a snub nose, and a lipless mouth. He had dark brown hair, going gray, cut short in a Caesar fashion that was a little too precious for someone as big as him. On the other hand, he seemed at ease in the olive drab short sleeve shirt with epaulettes, and matching o.d. slacks. And the thin white scar that ran down his right cheek to the dimple in his chin looked just right.

If Oliver had seen him in a line-up, he'd have said the man

was a stone-cold killer. Even coming across Ring for the first time in Teddy's diner, plowing through a plate of grilled hot dogs and scrambled eggs, the whole mess covered with ketchup, gave the deputy chief no reason to change his opinion.

Ring looked up at Oliver while chewing a forkful of his revolting breakfast with an open mouth. He washed the food down with a slug of buttermilk. He punctuated his gross mastication with a self-satisfied belch and a contemptuous grin.

Putting on a broad cockney accent, Ring asked, "'Aven't come to nick me for me criminal table manners, 'ave ye, guv?"

"Are you Colin Ring?" Oliver asked, unimpressed.

"At your bloody service," the man replied, returning his attention to his food.

The chief had called Oliver at home last night to tell him about the mountain lion attack. He'd also told the deputy chief to find Ring this morning. Question him about his relationships with Isaac and Mahalia Cardwell. Then the chief had apologized to Oliver for having to disturb him at home.

But the call had turned out not to be a disturbance at all. Oliver and Lauren had already tucked Danny into bed in the afterglow of ice cream and bedtime stories. Hearing how a young boy had been endangered and delivered from danger, they'd felt that much more grateful for the security and wellbeing of their own family. They'd made the sweetest love since … since the first time after Oliver had almost died four years ago.

Both of the Gosdens had sworn that the conception of their next child would be planned, but Oliver dearly hoped a baby — a girl this time — had been conceived last night. Someone they would protect fiercely from mountain lions or any other menace the world might spawn. Afterwards, they'd fallen asleep in each other's arms, and Oliver woke up feeling better than anytime he could remember.

The good feeling lasted only until he caught up with Colin Ring. The man hadn't been hard to find. He was registered under his own name at the Gasthaus Heidi, a hotel with a Swiss alpine motif and a staff fluent in German, French, Italian and the queen's English. It catered to European tourists but was owned by a Japanese conglomerate.

Ring hadn't been in his room when Oliver arrived, but the hotel manager made inquiries and told the deputy chief that English writer had asked the concierge to recommend a "greasy spoon" with a distinctly local flavor for his morning meal. So chances were good he could be found at Teddy's.

"Did Reverend Isaac Cardwell stay at the hotel with Mr. Ring?"

The hotel manager checked his computer. "Yes. That is, he checked in the same night as Mr. Ring. Of course, each gentleman had his own room."

"Of course," Oliver mimicked. "And you heard about Reverend Cardwell's murder?"

The manager nodded. "Shocking."

"But you didn't think to mention the fact that the victim had been a guest at your hotel to the police department?"

Now, the man looked truly shocked. "But what would his stay with us have to do with what befell the poor man?" The manager looked at his computer again. "He was here only one night."

The man's German accent became thicker the more defensive he got. It reminded Oliver that the Swiss were tight with their secrets. Didn't like to be embarrassed about little things like murdered hotel guests — or being bankers for the Nazis. The deputy chief was tempted to ask to see the concierge's green card.

Instead, he inquired, "How much did the reverend's room cost for that one night?"

The man was hesitant to reply, but he was astute enough to read the body language of the policeman standing in front of him. "Four hundred and twenty-four dollars and twelve cents."

"Did the reverend pay the tab himself?"

This really challenged the manager's native reticence, but finally he said, "No. Mr. Ring put both rooms on his credit card."

"Did you speak to Reverend Cardwell at all yourself?"

"Yes. Just once. The gentleman asked if there was a church

nearby. I told him he might find St. Mark's Episcopal a congenial place."

"That was it?"

The concierge nodded emphatically. "If you have any further questions, I'm most certain you can find Mr. Ring at Teddy's."

Most eating places in town had a view of the mountains, the lake, or both. Teddy's was at the end of an alley off Fremont Street and looked out on the loading dock of a Michelin tire store. The diner had a hand painted sign that didn't bother to include its name. Rather it showed a coffee cup with a lipstick stain on it, an accompanying saucer with a cigarette butt, and a pair of horn-rimmed sunglasses with a cracked right lens. The owner, Teddy Kapp, figured this iconography would clearly communicate the nature of his business to anyone he cared to see come through his door.

Apparently, it worked for Colin Ring.

Oliver sat down and asked the Brit, "How long did you know Isaac Cardwell?"

"All too briefly, I'm afraid." He looked up at the deputy chief. "I feel with a bit more prompting he could have been a bloody marvelous source for my book."

"How did you find him in the first place?"

"Indirectly. Didn't even know the bugger existed a few weeks ago. It was his granny I went to see. Then up he popped. Bloody miracle, I thought at the time. Unknown son of the bugger I'm doing my book on. Thought he'd have it in for his bloody old man."

"Did he?"

Oliver saw Ring's piggy eyes become reflective. "Truly hard to say, mate. He was eager enough to help me or so it seemed. But he never actually said a harsh word about Jimmy Bloody Thunder in front of me."

"What's your interest in Reverend Thunder in the first place?"

Ring snorted. "He's the subject of my bloody book, isn't he?"

"Yeah, I understand that. What I want to know is why you

picked him?"

Ring's lipless smile was lupine. "I'm fascinated by the idea of redemption, mate. Mainly because I don't believe it bloody exists. You look at your Jimmy Thunder, and what do you see? A poor fellow from a broken family, his mum beats him about his bloody head with the family Bible. He overcomes all that to become one of your gridiron football stars. Then after an unfortunate loss of composure in which an opponent accidentally dies, he's packed off to prison. But our lad's not done. After he comes out, he finds God and the telly. He ministers to millions and undoubtedly makes millions more for his own accounts. It's bloody marvelous, isn't it?"

Oliver chose not to offer an opinion.

"Except you know as well as me, mate, it's all a bloody *fraud!* Jimmy Leverette was a brute who beat his wife, abandoned his son, and bloody *murdered* a poor sod named Roger Braddock who was doing nothing more than having a beer with his mates. Thunder goes to prison but not death row — and I was surprised about that, a black killing a white in Texas and not getting the death penalty. Shows what they think of their gridiron heroes down there, doesn't it? Anyway, out he comes, not the least repentant, changes his name, says he's nobody's nigger, and he's off to the bloody races, isn't he?"

Ring brought his fork down on his plate hard enough to chip the rim. Not that the blemish would be enough to keep the plate from being used again at Teddy's. The Brit momentarily regarded his breakfast. The grease from the hot dogs and the eggs had congealed with the ketchup.

"Now, look what you've made me do, mate. Distracting me and all, my bloody breakfast has gone cold."

Oliver was notably lacking in sympathy. "So, the only regret you have about Isaac Cardwell's death is that a potential source on Jimmy Thunder has been lost?"

Ring shrugged. "Well, I hardly knew the bloke well enough to play darts with. As for the source part, that's true enough. But I'll tell you what, that old granny, Mahalia, she's a bloody brilliant source of bile when it comes to her son-in-law. I'll make out right well with her."

Oliver asked, "What were you doing last Thursday night and early Friday morning?"

Ring affected a look of wide-eyed surprise, as wide as his piggy little eyes would go. "You think I'd kill my own source? That wouldn't make me a very bright chap, would it?"

"What were you doing?" Oliver repeated.

"Working on my manuscript in my hotel room. Writers have bloody deadlines, you know."

"You were alone?"

"It's solitary labor, writing is. But as I like to work at night, I need a little help at one a.m. or so keeping my energy up. I called room service for a plate of bangers 'n' mash and a pint of whatever was cold. So check with the bloody hotel, if you don't believe me."

"I will," Oliver said. "You have any research notes on Thunder or the Cardwells, something that might help our investigation?"

"I've got notes, all right," Ring said. "But the only way you or any other bleedin' peeler will see them is with a court order."

Oliver stood and looked down on the Brit. "Man, the fucking people we let in this country."

Ring only laughed.

"Tell you what, mate," he said with a grin, "I'll give you this much. I couldn't have imagined a better ending for my book, if it turns out Thunder killed his own son. Be bloody Shakespearean, wouldn't it?"

CHAPTER 23

Ben Dexter was used to doing formal, sit-down interviews with heads of state, royalty and the elites of the entertainment and sports worlds. But when he had to, he could feign the common touch and revisit the long gone days when he'd had to pay his dues. He could go right down to sidewalk level and interview the man on the street.

That was just what he and his crew were doing after Mayor Steadman declined to speak for his constituents.

Dexter's questions were simple and direct: Given the recent mountain lion attacks, following the death of Isaac Cardwell, do you believe an actual curse has been placed upon your town? And if so, how do you feel about that?

"It's a bunch of malarkey, and you must be a horse's ass for even asking," asserted a robust gray haired man coming out of a health club.

The response jolted Dexter, not that he let it show. He was rustier at this journalistic stop-and-frisk than he'd thought. He certainly wasn't going to use that guy's sound bite. He tried to remember how he used to do it.

He seemed to recall that young mothers with small kids tended to give the answers they thought you wanted to hear. The Social Security set could usually be counted on, as well, to spout enough crap that you could edit out something useful. And if he could get lucky enough to find some yahoo actually showing signs he was a serious churchgoer, that'd be a slam dunk.

On the other hand, people coming out of a health club, they were likely to be pumped up and thinking they were world-beaters. What the hell was wrong with him? He'd forgotten that using this line of inquiry was just like selling real estate: Everything was location, location, location.

"Let's go," Dexter told his crew. "We're looking for a shopping mall near a church."

They found it, too. The Crossroads Center at Aspen and Glen Brae. Just two blocks up the street from St. Andrew's R.C.

"I don't know if the town's cursed," answered their first mom with kids. "Not anymore than the rest of the world, anyway. But I am keeping a close eye on my girls. No playing outside unless we go to the beach. Mountain lions don't swim, do they?"

An old gent out shopping with his wife offered, "I don't know about curses, but I have lived long enough to see some things strange enough that I couldn't explain them. So, I suppose. Maybe. But what I think that lady, Mrs. Cardwell, was doing was just showing how angry she was about her grandson being killed."

By now, a crowd was gathering. People shopping and others going to the mall's restaurants for lunch were curious to see what was going on. They were forming a semi-circle around Dexter. Without exception, they were white and polite. Very understanding about a difficult situation. That wasn't at all what Dexter wanted.

But off to one side, sitting on a planter, watching the whole show was a good-looking black woman with a very serious expression on her face. She was well dressed in a light summer suit, and she had some kind of button on her lapel. Dexter couldn't read it from where he stood, but he headed over her way. Maybe she'd have something interesting to say.

The woman stood as the news crew approached. Now Dexter could read the button. *2-4-6-8, I don't want to hyphenate. Just call me an American.* Uh-oh. The winner of two Emmies and a Peabody Award, Dexter just could not believe his luck in this town. Still, he couldn't simply back away from this woman, not with the crowd that had followed him watching. What was he going to say? Sorry, lady, you're not my kind of black woman.

So, Ben Dexter introduced himself and asked his questions.

"No, I don't believe in curses," Lauren Gosden replied. "Not the kind you mean. The kind I believe in is people who stir up trouble for their own gain. There's *far* too much of that kind of curse."

Dexter politely thanked her, and turned around. The woman's response had made all the others gathered nearby look at the reporter and crew in a new light. Dexter would later tell friends in New York and L.A. that just for a moment there he knew exactly how Custer felt at the Little Big Horn.

"I think we'll wrap it up here for now, guys," he told his crew.

The lunchtime crowd let them pass without a comment. But almost as they reached their Rover, Dexter felt a tug at his sleeve. It was enough to make him jump. There standing next to him was a small man past the crest of middle age with oily black hair done in a bad comb-over.

"I believe," he hissed at the reporter. "There is a curse on this town. Probably only the first of many to come." He nodded to himself as if he had private knowledge of what the others might be.

"What do you do for a living, friend?" Ben Dexter asked.

"Why do you have to know that?" the man asked, immediately suspicious.

"I guess I don't. Never mind. Thanks for sharing your views."

"Don't you want to put me on TV?"

"No."

Not even if the guy worked from a script Dexter wrote himself. He was too obviously loony. Too downscale. Not telegenic at all.

The thing that Ben Dexter failed to realize at the time was that he'd planted seeds. The relative handful of people he'd talked to that day all went back to work, home or out to eat and talked about him and his questions with their families and friends.

Was the town cursed? How did they feel about that?

In a small town, it didn't take long for such questions to become topics of common debate. And the dialogue was a lot more serious and candid without a TV crew around.

Ron Ketchum spent the morning talking with Jimmy Thunder's two exiled lady friends. They were sharing a suite at the Hilton. The chief interrupted their breakfast, and he was fortunate to catch them at all because they had their bags packed and were ready to leave town. They had first class tickets on the noon Reno Air flight to L.A.

Their names were Ashanti Royce and DaChelle Chenier. Each said she was twenty-eight. Both claimed to hold master's degrees from UCLA. Ms. Royce's area of study was demographics. Ms. Chenier's major, interestingly, was criminology. The women were so well spoken that Ron was hard pressed to doubt their educational accomplishments.

That was despite the fact that both of them could have worked any *haute couture* runway in Paris. Well, there was nothing to say women couldn't be tall, thin, beautiful *and* brilliant. And if he thought that seemed a rather unfair distribution of good fortune, maybe it was just another of his latent biases making itself known.

"Why are you leaving Goldstrike?" Ron asked.

"Our work here is finished, Chief," Ms. Royce responded without cracking a grin.

"And what exactly was your work?"

"We assisted Reverend Thunder."

Ron said, "Isn't that what Ms. Janet Pak does?"

"She's *clerical,*" Ms. Chenier sneered.

"And your duties were?"

"Professional."

"In what sense of the word?"

Now both women shared a smile.

"My, my, my, Chief Ketchum, are we having naughty thoughts?" Ms. Royce inquired.

"Not me," Ron replied. "I wouldn't even stray near one. Not with a criminologist in the room. What I was wondering, what kind of *work* did you do for the reverend?"

"I helped him understand his audience," Ms. Royce explained. "Reverend Thunder always shapes his own message, but by helping him identify just who he's talking to, he can better understand which words he should choose to couch his message."

"You worked together closely, then?"

"Every day."

"And you, Ms. Chenier, why would Reverend Thunder need a criminologist?"

"After his unfortunate experience with the law, and having his lawyer of the time fail him, he felt the need to have someone near to reassure him that he wouldn't attract any unfair attention from the authorities. He's told both of us on many occasions how unpleasant prison life is. He wants to be very careful that he doesn't give the police even the appearance of being responsible for a misdeed."

"Does he think we suspect him of killing his son?"

"Do you?" Ms. Chenier asked without blinking.

"I'm afraid I have to ask the questions. Is Reverend Thunder worried?"

"He hasn't said so. At least not to me." Ms. Chenier turned to her colleague.

"He hasn't said so to me, either," Ms.Royce added.

"Ladies, at the risk of being indelicate, how about we stop all the bullshitting?"

Neither Ashanti Royce nor DaChelle Chenier swooned. They laughed. Moderately.

"You doubt us, Chief?" Ms. Royce inquired.

"Or do you want to know if we're just fancy whores?" Ms. Chenier asked.

"What I want to know is why are you leaving town now? Why did Reverend Thunder kick you out of his house? Was it because he didn't want his son to think you are fancy whores his daddy was humping? And how did Reverend Thunder get along with Reverend Cardwell?"

The two women looked at each other for a five count, during which, Ron was sure, several gigabytes of data were silently exchanged.

Ms. Royce began: "We're leaving town because Jimmy can no longer afford us."

"In terms of public relations?"

Ms. Chenier picked up the baton. "Quite possibly that way, too. But it's more fundamental than that. The poor man is having a cash crisis."

"The collection plate is coming back empty?" Ron asked, surprised.

"No, not empty," Ms. Chenier elaborated, "but not nearly so full as it once did."

"Jimmy has a core of believers who would not abandon him even if he … well, even if he did kill his son," Ms. Royce said. "But that group of loyalists is not large enough to support either his broadcast operation or his lifestyle in the manner he prefers."

"So, exeunt Ms. Royce and Ms. Chenier stage left?"

"*Exeunt!*" Ms. Chenier smiled with delight. "Aren't you the surprise for a cop?"

"I went to UCLA, too. Twelve years part time while I was on the LAPD. Now, tell me, was it just a coincidence Reverend Thunder turned up strapped for cash when his son arrived unexpectedly? Do you mean to tell me Reverend Cardwell's presence had nothing to do with the two of you leaving the estate?"

"The timing was something of a coincidence," Ms. Royce agreed, nodding her head. "We'd seen that the situation was in decline for some time, of course, but Junior showing up right then, that was an anomaly."

"Junior?"

"We called Jimmy's boy that," Ms. Chenier informed Ron.

"Because?"

"Because he was too good to be an actual adult. He was like a little kid who doesn't know enough to be greedy or venial, hasn't been touched by temptation or corruption. But the way he acted so quietly righteous, not even bothered by the near occasion of sin, as the Catholics like to say, we could not believe he was for real," Ms. Chenier asserted.

"You couldn't find a handle on him, in other words."

"Not a one," Ms. Royce conceded.

"How did Reverend Thunder get along with his son?"

"I think Junior shamed his daddy," Ms. Royce said.

Ms. Chenier nodded. "Junior did his hitch in real divinity school. Jimmy is a mail-order kind of guy with enough Bible reading and natural gloss to smooth over the rough edges."

"You think the reverend could have nailed his son to that tree?"

The two women did another mute exchange of information.

Ms. Royce delivered the verdict. "Possibly. But don't bet your investment portfolio."

Ron looked at them, sighed and stood up.

"Thank you, ladies. I appreciate your help."

He started to leave, but Ms. Royce called out to him.

"You didn't ask if Jimmy was having sex with us."

"I don't think that's relevant to the case."

"You're not personally curious?" Ms. Chenier asked. "Like maybe did all three of us get it on together?"

"I have too great a respect for privacy to even wonder," Ron answered. "But there is one question you can answer for me, if you don't mind."

"What's that?" the women asked in unison.

"You ladies didn't need affirmative action to get into UCLA, did you?"

Ashanti Royce and DaChelle Chenier collapsed in gales of laughter.

"I didn't think so," Ron said, leaving.

CHAPTER 24

Corrie Knox and Tucker Marsden found the remains of the Derby family's heroic dog at the base of a sugar pine. Tuck squatted and looked at the little that was left of Sumo; the dog's bones had been picked clean.

"Too bad that lion was so hungry," Tucker said. "If he'd left some meat on the carcass, he might have cached it. Then we'd have a big advantage."

"Sure. We could have set out traps for when he came back for the leftovers."

Tucker stood up and stretched. His lean six foot four inch frame reached toward the sky. He had sandy blonde hair and crystal blue eyes. He looked like he should have been modeling or playing pro beach volleyball. But Tucker Marsden loved the wilderness and all the creatures in it.

Except when they got out of hand. Not that there weren't plenty of jerkwad campers who shouldn't be scoured from the earth by the savage fang and claw. That would be sound environmental management. But when a big cat started running down innocent joggers and bounding into people's backyards looking for kids to snack on, then steps had to be taken.

"How big was this poor pooch?" he asked Corrie.

"The owners say around seventy pounds."

"That ought to keep the beast sated for, what, a couple days?"

"Maybe," Corrie said.

"You don't sound too sure."

"I'm not. This cat's behavior is just plain weird."

"There's a highly scientific explanation," Tucker said with a grin.

Corrie rolled her eyes. "This animal is not following any kind of a normal travel-way, then, okay? His hunting path is totally idiosyncratic. He has to be violating the home ranges of other mountain lions. It's just as likely that one of his own kind will kill him, in a territorial dispute, as we will."

Tucker shook his head. "Things never work out that neatly. So, what do you think is behind this strange behavior?"

"If I had to make a guess right now, I think it's old age more than anything. He's not exactly up to going after a bull elk anymore."

"From what you tell me, he jumped a six foot fence with Rover here in his jaws. That's still pretty strong."

"Not compared to what we both know an animal like this can do in his prime."

Tucker's smile was rueful this time. "True. Did you hear that story out of Colorado? Mountain lion kills a *six hundred pound* heifer, drags it a *quarter mile* up a mountainside to eat."

"That's what I mean. This cat, if he's healthy, should be going after four-legged prey. But he's going after humans. I think what happened was, he got his first taste of people with poor Gary Jenkins. After that, from a predatory standpoint, he worked it out that two-legged creatures are easy pickings. "

"Fast food," Tucker said deadpan. "Maybe he even likes the way we taste."

"I thought of that, too. But I wasn't going to say anything. People in this town are tense enough as it is."

"Understandable," Tucker agreed.

But Corrie said he didn't know the half of it, and told him about the "curse."

"That's crazy!" Tucker protested.

"Maybe. Or maybe it's just being scared. Either way, I want to get this animal quickly."

"If it's old, like you say, it might just kick off on its own soon."

"Now, who's talking about neat endings? Besides, I wouldn't like the possible consequences if that happened," Corrie told him.

"What do you mean?"

"Look. If we can't find this cat and kill it and bring it in, what are people going to think?"

"I don't know."

"They're going to think we can't find it because it's got supernatural powers."

"That's really crazy."

"Yeah, but if you believe in a curse, it's *consistent.* Don't you see?"

Tucker nodded grudgingly. "Yeah, I guess I do."

"But do you think the people around here will be content to just hunker down forever, while they imagine some magical man-killer is stalking their town?"

"No." Now, Tucker saw where Corrie was heading. "They'd go after it."

"Just like the villagers went after Frankenstein's monster."

"Uh-huh. And you get people scared enough, and they don't exactly have a command of the facts … they'll kill any cat they come across. Won't matter a bit to them if it's some completely innocent animal."

"They won't be stopped by any state law saying please don't shoot the wildlife, either. So let's get this bastard fast, okay?"

"Yeah."

"Because for all we know he's already hungry again."

CHAPTER 25

Sergeant Stanley knocked twice on the doorframe of Ron's office, stepped inside, and closed the door behind him. In his hand, he had a half-dozen pages of computer printout held together by a bulldog clip. He gave the material to the chief.

"Two for two on those names you wanted checked," the sergeant said.

"Mr. Meeker and Mr. DuPree have been bad boys?"

"No outstanding arrest warrants unfortunately, but otherwise, yeah. Deacon Meeker's just average bad; Didier DuPree, he's real bad."

Ron looked at Deacon Meeker's sheet first. Convictions for assault, robbery and extortion. All strong-arm stuff. By today's standards, small beer. Didier DuPree, on the other hand, had only one conviction, but it was for involuntary manslaughter. He literally threw a man under a bus in Houston.

Not that his lawyer phrased what occurred that way. That distinguished member of the Texas bar had insisted that at worst his client "assisted in the fall" of the decedent in front of "a mass transit vehicle" that was undoubtedly exceeding the posted speed limit.

On the hot summer night in question, the story went, Didi DuPree was at a sidewalk party where alcohol was served. A fellow who had proposed marriage to a young woman and had been awaiting her answer for a week became upset when he saw Didi talking to her. He ran at Didi and tried to shove him away from the young lady. Didi, having the advantage of being a teetotaler and sober, sidestepped the angry young man's advance, and would have been home free if he hadn't helped the victim's momentum along with a hand to the small of his back. More than a dozen witnesses affirmed that Didi had acted in self-defense, but one of them let slip the detail about Didi giving his would-be assailant a helping hand.

As Didier DuPree had been arrested on suspicion of seventeen murders, but had never been brought to trial due to insufficient evidence, the D.A. considered the witness's slip of the tongue a gift from the gods. His only regrets, he said publicly, were that they couldn't prove Didi had seen the bus coming and the sentence was only six years.

"Yeah, this DuPree asshole is major league, all right," Ron agreed. "And now we've got him enjoying Jimmy Thunder's hospitality."

"Maybe they struck up their friendship in Huntsville," Sergeant Stanley suggested. "I did some additional checking with the authorities in Texas and found out they were both graduates of that institution."

"Were they there at the same time?"

Caz Stanley nodded. "The two of them and the Deacon, too. That's when he was doing his time for extortion. And Meeker and DuPree are cousins. I got that from the Houston P.D."

"You have any idea if DuPree is still in town, Sarge?"

The sergeant shook his head. "No idea. But my contact in Houston will be sending me a mug shot of him."

Ron said, "Let me know when it's here. Meanwhile, I better go ask Reverend Thunder if he knows where we can find the man."

"There's one other thing, Chief. Horgan's back in town."

Ron cursed softly. The last thing he needed was the FBI adding to his problems.

"He's outside?"

"Yeah. I told him we had to talk for a few minutes before you could see him. You think he's cooled his heels long enough?"

"Give me a minute to tuck Meeker's and DuPree's sheets away. Then send the SOB in."

The FBI agent entered Ron's office without the two underlings he'd brought previously. He strode up to Ron's desk and gave the chief a cold stare. "You going to ask me to sit down, Ketchum?"

"Have a seat."

Horgan flicked a glance over his shoulder.

"You want to buzz your girl out there, have her close your door?"

"No."

"No?" Horgan knew after the first three seconds he wouldn't be able to stare Ron down, and try as he might he couldn't think of any leverage to use on the chief. The way Horgan's face got tight and red, Ron thought his starched collar might be strangling him. "You're a sonofabitch, you know that, Ketchum?"

"If you have something to say, say it. I'm busy."

"All right," the FBI man went on, "I was trying to make it easy on you. You don't want it that way, fine. We'll let the world in on what I have to say. I talked to Reverend Thunder this morning."

"Regarding?" Ron asked softly.

"Regarding the implicit threat to burn his house down. The one you were so kind to send to me."

"Kindness had nothing to do with it. It was professionalism."

"Right. You realized you had a hot potato you couldn't handle and tossed it to me."

"I recognized a threat that might possibly be serious and connected to a series of interstate crimes. I forwarded it to the appropriate authority. Which complies with the spirit of cooperation Mayor Steadman said you could expect from this department."

Horgan chuckled nastily. "Just can't get under your skin, can I, Ketchum."

"Don't forget I told my sergeant to shoot you, if necessary," Ron said with a straight face. "And by the way, I did have my desk dusted for prints. As soon as I have the time, I'm going to request a copy of yours from the Bureau."

The FBI man blanched, before regaining his bluster.

"Listen, buddy, you're the one who's going to be in trouble. Again. I'm talking to Thunder about the arson threat, and he tells me you're figuring *him* for killing his son. What is it with you Ketchum, your recovery suffering a relapse? You always gotta go after the closest black guy?"

Ron stopped to consider. Not the snide insult, but the substance of what Horgan had just said. "The reverend said I was going after him?"

"He said you were harassing him, all but accusing him of killing his own boy. You better be careful Ketchum. You could have another suit for violating civil rights on your hands."

Ron replied sardonically, "And I bet I could avoid that whole problem if I just turned the investigation over to you Feebs. Oh, pardon me. That's name calling. Maybe you're right about my recovery. But I didn't let you big-foot your way into this murder the first time around, and you're not going to sneak in the back door this time."

The chief keyed his intercom. "You there, Sarge?"

"Yes, sir."

"Agent Horgan will be leaving momentarily. Please be ready to show him out."

"Yes, sir!"

Ron turned back to his antagonist.

"Horgan, you might actually be right for a change. I do consider Jimmy Thunder to be a suspect in the killing of Isaac Cardwell. And right now I like him better for it than I did five minutes ago. Thunder's an ex-jock: he knows there's no defense like a good offense. So any talk about him giving me grief, legal or otherwise, just makes me that much more suspicious. But I am surprised he conned an FBI man into being his messenger boy."

"You sonofabitch!" Horgan hissed.

"Now, you're name calling. But I'll tell you one thing, Horgan.

You aid Thunder in trying to obstruct my investigation, you'll find out real quick just how much clout Mayor Steadman has in Washington."

The FBI man glared at the chief, then stalked out of his office. Sergeant Stanley made sure he followed the most direct route out of the building.

Ron was wondering just how close Clay was to the attorney general and whether he should talk to the mayor about Horgan's recent visit, when Clay Steadman called him.

"Ron, I'm out at my house. There's someone here you need to talk to about the Cardwell case. Can you come right out?"

"On my way, Mr. Mayor. I'll be there directly."

"We'll be around back," Clay told him.

Ron arrived at the Steadman house inside of ten minutes. He left his Explorer in the shade of a mountain alder so it wouldn't be easily visible from the road. The mayor's cars were all tucked into their garage stalls, but a landscaper's truck was parked at the side of the house. The chief skirted the truck and turned the corner at the rear of the house.

Sitting at a wrought iron and glass table next to the tennis court were the mayor and Jimmy Thunder's groundskeeper. That's when it clicked for Ron. The man kept the grounds at both the reverend's estate and the mayor's house. He'd thought something had looked familiar about the man yesterday; he must have seen him, one time or another, working on Clay Steadman's landscaping. If the chief had a more educated eye for such things, he might have noticed some similarities of style. Being a layman, all he'd noticed was that both places had gorgeous, meticulously kept grounds.

The two men stood as Ron joined them.

Clay said, "Ron, meet Art Gilbert. Art, this is our chief of police, Ron Ketchum."

Ron took the hand Gilbert extended. Gilbert had a strong,

calloused hand, but a carefully measured grip. He didn't try to muscle it. The man wore the same blue work clothes as yesterday, but now the baseball cap was gone. He was an inch or two shorter than Ron with thick white hair and a seamed tan face. He was clearly pushing the age where many men might think of retiring, but there was a sense of vigor to him — the kind of energy that drove a man to work on Sundays. It made the chief think Gilbert would work 'til the day he dropped. He wouldn't be surprised if somebody eventually found Art Gilbert slumped over the wheel of his riding mower.

"I saw you yesterday morning at Reverend Thunder's place," Gilbert told Ron. "I didn't think you being there had anything to do with me, but Leroi called me this morning. Said I might want to touch base with you."

"Art does the landscaping and grounds keeping here, too," the mayor said, confirming the chief's hunch. "Apparently, the call he received made him think of something you should know."

The mayor had everyone sit down and poured a glass of ice tea for Ron.

"I appreciate your coming forward, Mr. Gilbert," Ron said. "I intended to call on you. So what do you have to tell me?"

"Well, the first thing I want you to know is what I told Mayor Steadman. I came to him first because I want it clear I have no interest in collecting the reward he's offering."

"Okay." That elevated the man's credibility in Ron's eyes.

"Leroi said you were asking about if anything unusual happened while that young fella who got killed was at the house."

"That's right."

"Well, another visitor was at the house while Reverend Cardwell was there."

"Did you hear a name?"

"Didi DuPree. And I heard a lot more than that."

"What else did you hear?" Ron asked.

"I heard DuPree and the reverend talking on the patio one morning. I was pruning a flowering crabapple. I don't know if they thought I was too far away to hear or if it didn't matter what an old white guy who worked with shears overheard."

"Which was?"

"They were talking about a money-laundering scheme … and DuPree was telling the reverend there was no backing out now. The reverend was in it, like it or not, so he'd better sit back and get used to the idea. Enjoy it. Think of counting all the money he'd be putting into his pocket."

"How did the reverend respond?"

"I don't know because that was when they went inside."

"Mr. Gilbert," Ron said, "How did this talk about a crime make you feel?"

Art Gilbert shrugged. "Once Leroi's call gave me a nudge, it made me feel I better talk to the mayor. Otherwise, I just mind my own business." When the landscaper saw the chief would like to hear more, he went on. "I suppose maybe I'm too tight mouthed for my own damn good sometimes. But in my line of work, I hear enough that if the people saying it knew I was hearing it, it'd shock them good."

That brought a dry chuckle from the mayor.

"Now, if I went around gossiping about everything I heard, I'd probably never have to buy another beer anytime I went into a bar. Except long before that, I wouldn't have any clients left. So what I heard was one fella saying something shady, and then I saw another fella turn his back on the other guy and walk away. I guess it wasn't my first thought to run to the police. As it is, I hope you'll keep it to yourself where you got what I told you."

"Don't worry about that, Art," the mayor said.

Ron accepted the explanation.

"All right, Mr. Gilbert. Can you tell me what this Didi DuPree looks like?"

"He's a black fella, but a real light skinned one, if you know what I mean."

"How light?"

"Lighter than me. At least where I've been exposed to the sun all my life. He's got black hair, more wavy than kinky. I didn't get close enough to really notice the color of his eyes. I'd guess he was a little shorter than me. You might think he was somewhat on the thin side to look at him, but he kind of held himself like he wasn't anyone to be messed with. So maybe he's stronger than you'd think at first glance."

Ron said, "Thank you for your help, Mr. Gilbert." Then he added, "By the way, you do some really fine work."

"Thank you, sir. I've made it my life." Art Gilbert nodded to the mayor and turned to go.

"Oh, Mr. Gilbert," Ron said.

The old man turned around. "Yes?"

"If you overhear anything else while you're working at Reverend Thunder's estate, I'd appreciate hearing about it right away."

Art Gilbert gave the chief a small salute and left.

When Ron was alone with the mayor, he told him, "The FBI is back. Horgan might be looking to cause trouble."

The chief outlined his talk with Horgan: that the FBI agent had talked to Thunder; the reverend's complaint that Ron was harassing him; Horgan hinting that Ron might be facing a civil suit, or worse, for violating, poor Jimmy Thunder's civil rights.

"You're playing everything straight up?" the mayor asked.

"Absolutely. My office contacted Horgan regarding the threat about the church burnings because it felt real to me, and it referred to a string of hate crimes well beyond our jurisdiction. The sonofabitch is using that for cover to try to hijack our investigation. I knew that might happen, but I felt I had to tell him anyway."

The mayor nodded.

Clay said, "Don't let him distract you. I'll start lining up political support. If Agent Horgan wasn't smart enough to take my first warning, he'll learn what it feels like to get hit with the proverbial ton of bricks."

"Leave a couple for me to chuck at him," Ron said.

Clay Steadman laughed briefly.

"I can't stop Jimmy Thunder from counterpunching, though," the mayor said.

"Yeah, I know."

"You really think it could be him?"

"Could be."

"Well, if he takes you to court, try not to let that distract you, either. The town will pay for your lawyers."

"Good." Ron knew that Clay Steadman understood that a lot of mud might be splattered all over his beloved town if Ron had to arrest Jimmy Thunder for the murder of his son. It was inevitable that charges of racism would be lodged against the chief of police and his department. Ron asked, "You sure you still want the bastard who killed Isaac Cardwell?"

Clay nodded. "More than ever."

CHAPTER 26

From the mayor's house, Ron drove over to Texas Jack Telford's place on Timberline Drive. He wanted to hear from someone beyond Jimmy Thunder's inner circle that the reverend was actually at home playing cards on the night Isaac Cardwell was killed. Not that corroborating testimony would remove suspicion from the reverend, but it would give Ron a feel for just how much of what Thunder was handing him was true, and how much was bullshit.

As with many of the residents of Goldstrike, Texas Jack was better than well off, if not actually filthy rich. But unlike many of his economic peers, the five time world poker champ was a character, a maverick. He had a funky old home that he kept adding onto, even though he was the only one who lived there. And he did all the construction himself.

As for landscaping, there was none, other than what nature provided. No immaculate lawns, flower beds or pruned ornamental trees here. Just the idiosyncratic house that Texas Jack built set hard against the wilderness. His home was part of his rough-hewn persona.

When Ron pulled into the driveway, he saw that yet another room was being added on to the house. Studs framing the walls and roof of an area roughly 20 feet square stood adjacent to what Ron thought he remembered to be Jack's home office. Stacks of lumber, sheets of plywood, rolls of insulation, tools, boxes of nails and all sorts of other construction materials lay neatly positioned next to the construction area.

Ron knocked on the back door because Texas Jack liked to have everyone enter his house through the kitchen. He said that way folks could get right down to eating, drinking and lying to one another. Presently, Texas Jack's housekeeper, Maria, came to the door. The poker champion's sense of self-reliance didn't extend to dusting or doing windows.

The chief had been out to Texas Jack's when Clay had taken him around, upon his arrival in town, to introduce him to several of Goldstrike's leading lights. He'd met Maria then, too, and by the look in her eyes as she opened the door, she still remembered him.

"Good day, Chief Ketchum. How may I help you?"

"Texas Jack here, Maria?"

"I'm so sorry, no. He is in Reno for a personal appearance."

"When will he be back?"

"Perhaps later tonight. Certainly by tomorrow."

Maria peered around Ron, looking down the driveway.

"You expecting someone?" the chief asked.

"My husband. He comes to pick me up soon."

Looking at the kitchen clock, Ron saw it was five after five.

"Will you please leave a note for Texas Jack?" Ron inquired. "Tell him I've been here, and ask him to call me at his earliest convenience."

"Of course," Maria responded. She craned her neck again, this time looking out at the trees. Then she turned her face to Ron and confessed, "I don't like being out here all alone."

"Has someone being bothering you?" the chief asked.

"Not someone. Something. Every time I look out a window, I think I see that mountain lion. Even when I know I am imagining things, it still scares me. You're going to catch him soon, aren't you, Chief Ketchum?"

"We're doing our best," Ron replied.

Before returning to headquarters, Ron decided to do an impromptu patrol to get a sense of the town and the surrounding area. The decision made him think that he should have drawn a rifle from the department armory. Not that he could tell one mountain lion from another just by looking at it. If he saw one at all. On the other hand, should he come across the beast they wanted, confronting, attacking, maybe eating someone, he'd want to go after it with more firepower than just his sidearm. He decided to issue an order that all patrol units would carry a rifle from now until the lion was killed.

He should have thought of that sooner.

He laughed to himself. All those years on the LAPD had prepared him for dealing with just about any predator imaginable — except the four-legged kind. Live and learn, he thought.

Ron couldn't help but notice that for a beautiful early evening at the height of summer everything was unusually quiet. There were no hikers about. No cyclists on the roads. Not even any cars pulled over at the scenic overlooks. As he came into the built up areas of town, he saw that there wasn't much vehicular traffic on the streets or pedestrian traffic in the open air malls. At only two cafes did he see patrons sitting at sidewalk tables, and of these there was only one couple snuggling together at the first cafe, and a single man reading a newspaper at the second.

The only thing the chief could think was that Texas Jack's housekeeper wasn't the only one with the mountain lion on her mind. But people wouldn't stand for being held hostage for very long. The pressure on him to kill the beast would mount.

It was no small irony that at that moment the chief wouldn't have minded seeing some of the media horde that had descended upon the town out and about enjoying themselves.

Oliver Gosden followed Isaac Cardwell's trail to the serene setting of St. Mark's Episcopal Church. The building was a tastefully done modern interpretation of a small country church. The predominant building materials were quarried stone and redwood. The deputy chief pulled into the parking area at the side of the church and walked to the front of the building. A display sign there carried the church's name. Since August constituted the doldrums of the liturgical calendar, the only message on the sign was: *Everyone welcome.* Oliver stepped inside to see if anyone was taking advantage of such a democratic invitation.

The electrical lighting inside was dim, and the sun was lowering by now, so it took the deputy chief's eyes a moment to adjust to the relative darkness. At first, he thought he was alone, but then he saw a crown of white hair fringing a pink scalp in the front row of pews. He started that way and was about to speak up when he noticed the old man's head was bowed in prayer. He also saw that the old guy wore a clerical collar. Probably just the man the deputy chief wanted.

Mindful of his manners and good department-community relations, Oliver took a seat across the aisle. He looked up at the altar and the figure of Jesus upon the cross. Helluva way for anybody to go, he thought, whether you're the Son of God or a poor black minister from Oakland.

Offhand, he couldn't remember the last time he was in a church. Probably for some unlucky cop who bought it in the line of duty. No, wait. It was for his cousin's wedding, and that had to be … four years ago. Some cops went to church, of course, but they were usually what Oliver thought of as the hard-on religious. Those militants not only had to believe for themselves, they'd try with all their might to get you to believe, too. The deputy chief had always seen those types as just looking for one more way to establish their authority over someone else.

Lauren was a bit more of a churchgoer than he was, but not too much more. She'd seen a lot of good people die on the operating table. Cops and surgical nurses encountered death too frequently not to wonder if there really was a God. Or if there was, did he really have a Plan — the capital P kind? And if he did have a plan, was it all one big practical joke?

In his darker moments, that was the view Oliver subscribed to: the Lord wasn't mysterious at all; he was just a real kidder.

After all, from a celestial point of view, how could human beings mean more than cartoon characters meant to everybody else?

Still, Lauren had told him that when he'd been shot she had prayed, and prayed hard, that he wouldn't die. She didn't want to be a widow, and she didn't want Danny to grow up without his father. Even after Oliver had been taken to the hospital and been operated on, it had been touch and go for seventy-two hours. Lauren said she'd prayed the whole time.

Some made it and some didn't, but he did. Who was to say that Lauren's prayers hadn't helped? If they had, he certainly was grateful for all the extra time he'd been granted with the two people he loved most in the world.

In that spirit, and with nobody looking, Oliver quickly played the supplicant himself. He asked that the Lord keep his family safe and well. And asked that the Lord give Oliver and his wife a daughter. And if it wasn't asking too much, let him catch the bas — the person or persons responsible for nailing Isaac Cardwell to that lightning-struck tree.

The deputy chief's communion with the Almighty was interrupted when he felt someone looking at him. Which made him open his eyes, surprising him that he'd closed them in the first place.

"I'm sorry. Did I disturb you?"

It was the minister across the way. He'd finished with his own prayers.

"No, no," the deputy chief assured him. "Must have dozed a little, that's all."

"Oh, I thought ... well, never mind. I'm Reverend John Brantley, the pastor of St. Mark's."

"Oliver Gosden, deputy chief of police." Oliver crossed the aisle and shook hands with Brantley. "I'm afraid I'm here on official business. Is there somewhere we could talk?"

"Of course. Let's step outside. Follow me, please."

The pastor led the deputy chief through the sacristy and out the back door of the church.

"What a lovely evening," Brantley said, smiling. "How may I help you?"

Oliver thought the man's expression was almost beatific. He'd just renewed his faith. Then he'd stepped outside into one of nature's better neighborhoods. And now a cop was going to ruin the man's day.

Well, it wasn't as though he had any choice in the matter.

"Pastor Brantley, do you know who Isaac Cardwell was?"

"Yes, of course."

The man's smile disappeared, but there was still a sense of serenity in his eyes.

"Did he ever come to your church?"

"Yes, he did. On three or four occasions. He introduced himself to me on his first visit. He impressed me as a very fine man."

"Did you talk much with him?"

"Usually just for a few minutes. Social protocol, you know. But once I invited him into my parsonage and we spoke for almost an hour."

"What did you talk about, if you don't mind me asking."

"We talked about the challenges we faced in our respective ministries. And … " Brantley paused, plainly trying to decide if he would be breaching a trust to go on.

"Please, Pastor, help me. I'm trying to find the man's killer."

Brantley nodded. "Yes, of course. I'm not sure that it will help you, but he told me he was trying to save a particular soul. And he was in some anguish that he might fail."

"Did he say whose soul?"

The pastor shook his head.

"When was the last time you saw him?" Oliver wanted to know.

"He stopped in to pray the night before he died."

"Do you remember the time?"

"It was shortly before sunset. I lock up the church just after dark."

"Do you know where he went from here?"

"No, I don't."

"Was there anyone else in the church who might have seen where he went?" Oliver had a small lead here and he didn't want to let it peter out.

"There was one other person at the back of the church while Reverend Cardwell and I were up front?"

"Do you know that person's name?"

"I wish I could help you, but I'm afraid this person wasn't much more than a blur. I think it was a white man, but even that would be guesswork. I have cataracts, you see. I'm scheduled for surgery next week."

Now, Oliver noticed there wasn't only a sense of peace in the man's eyes, there was a milky haze symptomatic of his condition.

"I wish I could be of more help," Brantley said. "Reverend Cardwell touched my life only briefly, but I feel I'm the better for having met him. I've heard all the news reports, of course, and I think of what his final moments must have been like quite often. I wonder if at the end …

The old man's voice trailed off.

Oliver said, "Pastor, from everything I heard, if anybody's gone to Jesus, it's Isaac Cardwell."

John Brantley nodded. "Oh, certainly. Of that, I have no doubt. No, I was wondering if at the end Reverend Cardwell asked God to forgive his executioner, just as Jesus did. I rather think that he might have."

The pastor excused himself and found his way back into his church.

That idea had never occurred to the deputy chief: Forgive the guy who nailed you up? Not him. He never took his Bible lessons that seriously.

But when Oliver walked to the parking lot from the rear of the church, he noticed the sun shining off something golden, something under the bushes not ten feet from his patrol unit. He walked over, squatted, and peered at the source of the reflection.

A pair of wire frame glasses.

Isaac Cardwell's glasses were missing and hadn't been found. Until now. Oliver would bet his pension that those glasses had belonged to the slain minister. And he'd never have seen them if he hadn't come out of the church the back way. And if the sun hadn't been shining at just the right angle.

Hadn't he just asked — prayed — for help in finding the killer? And now he'd found the spot where Isaac Cardwell probably got bashed on the head, at least the first time. It was enough to make a man stop and think. But not for too long, at least not right then.

Oliver radioed the chief and Officer Benny Marx, the crime scene specialist.

Under the illumination of a bank of portable high-wattage lights, Officer Marx found blood spatter, too. Not a lot of blood had been spilled, but enough to dot the sidewalk that bordered the parking area and several leaves on the bushes near where the glasses lay. Officer Marx should have no trouble collecting samples to be compared with specimens taken from Cardwell's body.

The gold wire frame glasses were photographed in place and then carefully bagged.

"This is where he got it," Oliver told Ron. "No doubt about it. This white guy at the back of the church followed him in, and then he ambushed him when he came out. Cardwell probably parked his car about where I put my unit, and maybe when he went to open his door, bang. Killer pops him a good one to the back of the head, and Cardwell's glasses go flying. It's almost dark and the perp has his plans to crucify the man so he doesn't take the time to get down on his hands and knees to find the glasses he knocked off."

The deputy chief looked to see how the scenario played out for his boss.

"Pastor Brantley said his vision was pretty bad, didn't he?"

"Yeah. He's got cataracts he's getting fixed next week. What's that got to do with anything?"

"Nothing with what happened out here in the parking lot. I'm with you on that. But what I was thinking, this white man he saw, it might have been a real light-skinned black guy."

Oliver's mouth fell open. "Are you kidding me?"

"No," Ron said, and seeing what was plain on the deputy chief's face, he added, "and I'm not subscribing to the Klan Weekly again, either. Remind me to tell you tomorrow about a guy named Didi DuPree."

"Tomorrow? What about right now?"

The chief held up the plastic evidence bag containing the gold wire-frame glasses.

"It's my turn to talk to Mahalia Cardwell. She should be able to identify these for us."

CHAPTER 27

Ron called Mahalia Cardwell's suite from the lobby of the Hyatt. He invited her down to have a cup of tea with him. He told the old lady that they might have a lead in her grandson's killing, and he needed her help pursuing it.

She agreed to join him, but said it would take her ten minutes to get ready. The chief buttonholed the assistant manager and told him he could use his assistance. Two minutes later, Ron slipped into the hotel restaurant, where he'd meet Mahalia Cardwell, through the kitchen entrance. He stepped directly to a table that had just been screened off by the restaurant staff from the rest of the dining area. This had been accomplished by repositioning several large potted plants.

Ron knew that if people hadn't been out on the town this evening because they were anxious about the mountain lion attacks, they wouldn't be going out tonight, either. That meant the large media contingent lodged at the Hyatt was most likely dining and drinking, rather than sitting in their rooms studying the offerings of the Gideons. He didn't want to be seen talking to Mahalia Cardwell; he certainly didn't want the snoops from the press to see the glasses they'd found.

The chief instinctively felt Isaac Cardwell's killer was still in town, but that certainly didn't mean he couldn't be scared off if the media alerted him that the cops were closing in. He probably should have just talked to the old lady in her suite, but with his reputation he was leery of being alone with Mahalia Cardwell in a private setting. The old lady didn't like him; she'd made that plain. He did want to afford her the opportunity to fling some more mud on him if he made her really angry.

A few minutes later, Mahalia Cardwell appeared, also through the kitchen door. Ron's strategy would have worked neatly except for one thing. The old lady had brought Ben Dexter with her.

The chief stood, careful to conceal the evidence bag with his body.

"Making me come through the kitchen like that," Mahalia Cardwell complained, "I thought I was going to have to start earning my keep."

"I believe the mayor told you that your stay is on him," Ron replied.

"And if it wasn't, I'd be happy to cover it," Dexter said with a smile. "Good evening, Chief Ketchum. I was interviewing Mrs. Cardwell when you called, and she invited me to come along. I didn't know, however, we'd have the pleasure of engaging in your little subterfuge." He gestured at the wall of potted plants. "Is all this to spare you from the prying eyes of my colleagues?"

Dexter was only partially successful in masking the appearance of how vastly amused he was. Ron wanted to pistol-whip the sonofabitch. But he knew some wishes were never to be granted. So he ignored the reporter.

"Mrs. Cardwell, I'm sorry if I've called on you at a bad time. And I meant no offense by asking you to walk through the kitchen. The information I have for you is of a very sensitive nature, and has to be kept confidential. Perhaps you could call me tomorrow when you have the time to speak privately."

Mahalia Cardwell's eyes were shrewd. "You're not going talk to me in front of Mr. Dexter?"

"No, I'm not."

She turned to Dexter, and she was succinct. "Please leave us."

For just that one instant, Ron could have kissed Mahalia Cardwell. The way Dexter's doggy little smirk turned to ashes was a memory that he would cherish for the rest of his life.

"But we have an *agreement*," the reporter asserted.

"Not now." The old lady seated herself, symbolizing her change of allegiance.

That left the two men on their feet, but Dexter didn't have a leg to stand on. He saw the hard expression on Ron's face and knew it would be counterproductive, at a minimum, to continue the debate. He tried killing both the chief and the old lady with a look. When that didn't work, he turned on his heel and stormed off.

A waiter came and took their order for tea and, at Ron's request, summoned the maitre d'. Ron asked that his meeting with Mrs. Cardwell be kept free of eavesdropping from the press, and the kitchen and serving staff should be alerted that reporters and/or photographers might try to eavesdrop. The chief was assured that he'd have complete privacy.

After they were served and the waiter had gone, Ron handed Mahalia Cardwell the evidence bag. He said, "Please don't open the bag, but will you please look at these glasses and tell me if they belonged to your grandson?"

The old lady took the bag wordlessly, and the grief brought by recognition softened her stern features. She turned the glasses to look at them from several angles, as if she were remembering the face on which they'd once rested. Then she handed the bag back and nodded.

"They're my baby's."

She dried the tears that were beginning to well in her eyes. Ron allowed her a moment of silence and she regained her composure — and her usual fierce visage.

"Mrs. Cardwell," Ron said, "it's very important to the success of this investigation that you not mention the specifics of anything I show you or repeat to the press anything we talk about. If you do so, the killer may run."

"Where's Jimmy Thunder going to run to?" she demanded. "Everybody all over this country knows his face."

Ron rubbed his chin as he met Mahalia Cardwell's harsh gaze. "Mrs. Cardwell, I will tell you that I consider Reverend Thunder a suspect in the killing of his son."

"Suspect? He *did* it."

Ron paused to look for the right reply.

"Your heart may tell you that. That might be what you want to see proved. But I have to look for evidence, and follow wherever it may lead. That's the only way I can do my job. That's the only way you'll ever get the justice you want."

"Oh, I'll have my justice, Mr. Chief of Police. Either you'll give it to me or God will."

That turned Ron to the other topic he wanted to discuss.

"Mrs. Cardwell, did you spend anytime outside your suite today? Have you walked around town?"

"I can't go outside without all those people sticking their cameras in my face. I even have my meals sent in. That's why I was talking to Mr Dexter. I recognized him from TV. I figured if I talk to him the others will leave me alone."

"Have you watched the news?"

"Yes."

"Then you know about the two mountain lion attacks?"

"I heard about that."

"Do you know that attempts are being made to link those attacks to what people are calling your curse on the town of Goldstrike?"

"I saw Dexter asking your mayor about it. He said he don't believe it."

"I don't either. But I have reason to think an increasing number of people in town are finding the idea credible."

"Must mean some folks have themselves guilty consciences."

"What it means," Ron said bluntly, "is that your words could be leading to an increasingly dangerous situation. One that could cause trouble in which innocent people might get hurt."

Mahalia Cardwell was unmoved.

"At least you didn't say *my* people. Colored folks. I've seen one or two around here. And don't you talk to me about innocent, either. Never has a child been born that's more innocent than my baby was."

Ron changed directions, but kept the tone in his voice as hard as the old lady's.

"Okay. You're not worried about anyone else, white or black. All you want is your grandson's killer."

"That's just about right. Makes me as mean as anybody else, doesn't it? Were you expecting better?" Mahalia Cardwell jutted her jaw defiantly.

"Maybe I was, from the woman who said she'd raised such a good man." Ron saw his remark cut Mahalia Cardwell deeply, but right then he didn't give a damn. "Here's something for you to think about. I've got a small police department. We already have our hands full. We get any more problems, it's going to be a drag on our efforts to catch Isaac's killer. Maybe your curse will turn around and bite you. You keep that in mind."

But letting his temper get the better of him was a mistake. Mahalia Cardwell got up and left in a bigger huff than Ben Dexter had.

Ron didn't think it would do a whole lot of good to chase after her and ask her to recant her statement calling down the wrath of God on Goldstrike.

She'd probably repeat it, with embellishments, to the delight of the lurking media.

CHAPTER 28

When the chief got back to his office, he found Corrie Knox asleep in his chair. She had her feet up on his desk, and sneakers on her feet. As much as he liked basketball, he wasn't in the mood to play right now.

Not even with her.

He stepped around his desk and was about to jostle her shoulder when he saw the sheet of paper on his desk. It was covered with the writing of a precise feminine hand. When he saw the subject matter, he knew the slumbering Warden Knox was the author.

Safety Tips Regarding Mountain Lions

- Never hike alone.
- Always carry a sturdy branch or walking stick.
- Leave your pets at home.
- Always clean up after cooking outdoors.
- Always store food away from tent.
- Always keep small children close at hand.
- Pick up children immediately if you see a lion.
- Never move toward a lion.
- Never run.
- Hold your position or back off slowly.
- Never turn your back or crouch.
- Make yourself look as big as possible.

- Be threatening: Wave arms, shout, throw sticks and stones.
- If all else fails, fight back with your fists and feet.

Fight back with your fists? Ron had to wonder about that one. He'd have to ask Warden Knox if mountain lions were known for having glass jaws. He looked at her and thought once again what a terrific looking woman she was. Not beautiful or even pretty. She had too much character, too much strength for either of those labels to apply. But she had a face you'd never get tired of looking at. At least, he wouldn't.

Just then her eyes fluttered open.

She held his gaze and said, "I fall asleep in your office, I guess you've got a right to stare. You come to any conclusions?"

"I can't decide if you look twelve or thirteen."

She laughed, a surprisingly deep sound that seem to come from all the way down in her belly. "Oh, no. I'm *real* old. In fact, I've been worried about the birthday I've got coming up."

"Yeah, right."

"Really. Next one's the big three-O." She waggled her feet. "Like the shoes?"

"Too clean. They need to be stepped on some. But I don't have the time right now."

"That's okay. I don't have the energy. Spending all day hunting, and being very, very careful about it, is pretty damn tiring. I barely had the reserves to buy the shoes."

Ron nodded toward her tip sheet. "It's really a good idea to slug a mountain lion?"

Corrie Knox put her feet down on the floor. "Beats yelling, 'Mercy me.' Of course, like any other fight, it helps to get in the first punch. A good shot to the schnozz might actually discourage a cat if it's not too hungry or otherwise has a burr up his ass. A good bash from a stick or a beaning from a rock is better, though. You get less torn up."

She stood up and yawned and stretched.

"Needless to say, Tucker and I didn't find the bastard yet. So,

I thought you might want to distribute these safety tips. They're pretty standard stuff, but the public is woefully ignorant."

Ron considered the suggestion. "Yeah, it's probably a good idea. I'll get the mayor's office busy on it in the morning." In response to another jaw-cracking yawn from Corrie, Ron asked, "You want me to give you a ride back to your room? So you don't fall asleep at the wheel."

"Well, that's another thing I wanted to mention."

"What?"

"I let Tucker Marsden have my room, and I can't stay there with him because … well, we were together once upon a time, and after we weren't any longer, it took us a long while to put a working relationship back together. So I was wondering …"

"Yeah, it's okay. You were right. Last time, I hardly knew you were there."

Corrie Knox smiled sleepily and said, "Oh, I can make my presence known, if you want me to."

Ron dodged the implicit offer with a counterproposal, to take Corrie to dinner. But she said she was too tired; she wouldn't want her face to fall in the mashed potatoes. She suggested they go back to his cabin and just have some munchies on his front porch. The chief followed Warden Knox as she drove her GMC 4x4 back to his place. He stayed alert to her driving, ready to honk his horn if it looked like she'd fallen asleep at the wheel and was about to drift off the road. But they made it without mishap.

After they arrived, Corrie opted for a peanut butter and raspberry preserves sandwich on rye and a glass of skim milk. Ron went with a Foster's lager, a dozen slices of sharp cheddar and a handful of hard pretzels from Hanover, PA.

Like Clay Steadman's place, though on a far more modest scale, Ron's cabin sat on a rise and overlooked the town and the lake. Behind the cabin loomed tree covered slopes that topped out at eight to ten thousand feet above sea level. Above the mountaintops, in a jet black sky, every star in the northern hemisphere tried to outshine all the others.

"Pretty nice place you got here," Corrie said.

"Yeah," Ron agreed. "It's not bad for public housing."

"You don't own it?"

He shook his head. "Town does. I pay a nominal rent, which, if I stay on the job 10 years, can be converted to a down payment and applied to a purchase price that was set when I moved in."

"Pretty sweet deal." Corrie took a bite of her sandwich and washed it down with a slosh of milk. Ron sipped his beer, and for the next several minutes they ate quietly and listened to the sounds of the night.

"I talked to Mahalia Cardwell tonight," Ron said finally. "She's the grandmother of the man who was killed. I told her it would be helpful if she made a public statement saying the mountain lion attacks had nothing to do with her wanting to see her grandson's killer caught."

"Did she agree?"

Ron shook his head. "I don't know if she's just being perverse. Or if she thinks it will make somebody snitch. Or —"

"Wait a minute," Corrie said. "Isn't there already a $100,000 reward? If somebody had knowledge of the crime, wouldn't *that* make him come forward?"

"That's the carrot; Mrs. Cardwell seems to prefer the stick. She also seems to think that causing an uproar will motivate me in some way she'd like to see." Ron turned to look at Corrie in time to see her licking peanut butter off a finger. "Do you think there's any chance this cat might just move on?"

"I don't know. Its behavior is already abnormal. It might move on, or it might stay right here and go back to eating its usual prey. I don't see that second possibility happening, though.""

"Why not?" Ron asked.

Corrie explained her theory that the cat was getting old, losing its ability to run down and kill its usual prey. She went on, "Tucker and I were talking today, wondering if people would stand for anything less than nailing this animal's hide up in your

Muni Complex. Seems to me if this lion just moved on and we don't kill him, people could never rest easy around here."

Ron said, "That's probably true. But I think if that were to happen, people would want Mahalia Cardwell's hide, thinking she brought all this trouble on them in the first place. And because Mahalia Cardwell is black it could spill over into an ugly racial situation."

"I didn't know you had many minorities up here."

"The year round population of the town's about twelve thousand. Perhaps ten percent are minorities. Part time residents and visitors might add another five hundred minorities at any given time. Before last Friday, I wouldn't have thought anybody had any reason to worry about skin color. But then Isaac Cardwell got nailed to a tree, and I got a chance to read some local hate mail. Now, *I'm* worried."

Corrie had finished her sandwich and she got up. "Want another beer?" she asked.

Ron shook his head, just gave her his empty bottle. She went inside and came back a minute later with her feet bare. She pulled her chair closer to Ron's and put her feet up on the porch rail.

"If I fall asleep, just throw a blanket over me, will you?" she asked.

"If that's what you want."

"Well, you could carry me inside. But I have to warn you, I go one fifty."

"I think I can manage."

She gave his upper arm a squeeze and waggled her eyebrows. Then she laughed her deep laugh again but this time it had a nervous edge, and Ron thought if the light were better he'd have seen her blush.

"Okay, back to business," she said. "The best way to battle superstition is with, what else, education. It seems to me your town could use a brief history lesson and a short lecture on wildlife biology."

"You going to provide them?" Ron wanted to know.

"I could write the scripts, but I think a local authority should present them." She grinned at him mischievously. "How about you doing it?"

"How about the mayor? He's got his own daily TV show."

"Okay. He'd be good, too."

"And what would he say?"

"Well, he could say how for most of our history the population in the West was relatively small, and what people we did have were allowed to slaughter the wildlife at will. But we all know how crowded California is now. And in 1990, the people of this state, in their wisdom, passed Prop 117. Which made mountain lions a protected species. You protect a species and — barring environmental degradation — it will flourish.

"So, here we are. More and more people are competing for land with more and more mountain lions. Even with Prop 117, there's no question people will prevail, but the wild beasts will have their moments. More and more of them, in fact."

"So you don't worry about job security much?"

"Hardly at all. Unless something changes, the number of attacks on people will increase."

"This is *good* news?" Ron asked.

"No, but it's the kind of news people can understand. Show them the data, and they'll see the results are perfectly natural and predictable. No hocus-pocus to the situation at all."

"What about the biology?"

"Well, I can jot a few things down about the effects of feline leukemia and other diseases, what might happen if a cat loses an eye or becomes lame, how even predators lose their teeth, and how they adapt to that."

"How do they?" Ron inquired.

"Mostly by going after smaller game, and when even that gets to be too much, by starving to death. What I'm getting at is if you give people the facts then seemingly aberrant behavior becomes more comprehensible. Reasonable precautions can be taken."

"And if people don't want to be reasonable?"

Corrie frowned and thought for a minute. "Then we go one of two ways."

"Yeah?"

"One, we offer anyone who believes in the curse a little mountain lion doll and a pin."

Ron laughed. "Voodoo?"

"Sure. Fight one superstition with another. Or with humor. However they take it."

"And number two?"

"We find the sucker and nail his hide to a wall." Corrie stood up and stretched. "I've got to get to bed. And don't bother carrying me."

"No?"

"No. I wouldn't want you to say you sprained your back or something. Give you another dodge to get out of that basketball game."

Ten minutes later, Corrie was asleep, and Ron had showered and lay in his own bed. He felt better, at least about Ms. Knox. He sensed not only was their attraction mutual but so was their nervousness. It reassured him that she had doubts, too.

He was just about to turn out the light when his phone rang. He picked it up on the first ring and still had time to run through a list of possibilities of who might be calling: Sergeant Stanley, Oliver, Clay Steadman, Leilani . . .

"Hello, Ronny. You there, Son?"

His father. Walter Ketchum. The *unrepentant* bigot.

"Yeah, Dad. I'm here."

Ron and his father had been estranged for more than thirty years, from the time Walter Ketchum had beaten DeWayne Michaels half to death until the time Ron used his unfortunate upbringing to defend himself in the wrongful death suit brought by Marcus Martin on behalf of the family of the late Sharrod Carter.

Ron had agreed when his lawyer, Jack Hobart, suggested using the twist on the disadvantaged youth defense. He knew immediately, of course, that this would be a slap in his father's face, but he didn't care. At that time, he occasionally had trouble even remembering what his father looked like. It bothered Ron only a little when Jack told him they'd have to subpoena his father to corroborate that Walter was, in fact, the cracker sonofabitch they made him out to be.

But what Ron hadn't expected in the least, could never have imagined in a million years, was that the trial would lead to a grudging peace between the two of them, if not an outright reconciliation.

The day Walter Ketchum showed up in court to testify, he didn't avoid looking at his son. He didn't swear at him. He didn't spit at his feet. He strode right up to him, embraced him, and cackled that he hadn't had such a good laugh in years as when he heard what his son's defense strategy was going to be.

"It was goddamn brilliant!" Walter said. "Take the spooks' own favorite lament — Wasn't my fault, Your Honor, I was *deprived* — and turn it right around on them." When Walter had told all his old retired cop buddies of this ploy, he informed his son, two of them had laughed so hard they'd given themselves hernias.

Then Walter took the stand and didn't hesitate in painting himself as the redneck racist his son said he was. He was shameless in laying out his prejudices for the world to see. Ron had a hard time not squirming as he listened to his father testify.

But he knew how effective the old man had been when Marcus Martin said he had no questions for the witness. After finishing his testimony, Ron's father stopped him in the corridor outside the courtroom.

"Ronny, I was happy to get up there for you today," Walter Ketchum said. "I know you've hated me for a long time now, and maybe from your point of view, you've had reason. But this trial of yours brings up an interesting point, one maybe you never thought about. That is: If you *really* got twisted around because you had a racist for an old man … maybe I did, too."

Then his father kissed Ron on the cheek and left.

Four days later he suffered a stroke that almost killed him.

"Your voice sounds better, Dad," Ron said, "like you're getting stronger."

"That's Esther's doing. Makes me do my therapy every goddamn day, whether I want to or not. I get more exercise now than when I was a cop, kicking ass and taking names. You want the truth, I think she just likes to torture me. Get back at whitey every chance she can."

In the background, Ron heard Esther Gadwell, the African American LPN who took care of his father, tell Walter to watch his old fool white trash mouth or she'd show him what it really meant to put a hurt on somebody.

"Esther says hello," his father told Ron.

"Tell Esther I hope she's fine, too. What's up, Dad?"

There was a pause before his father spoke. "Ronny, I'm not trying to stick my nose in here … but how's that case of yours coming?"

"We're working it. Making some headway. But you know how it is. I can't go into details. For all I know, the press or the feds may have my line tapped."

Walter Ketchum snorted. "Press! There was some faggot here today from one of those New York tabloid rags trying to get me to dump some dirt on you. If I still had two good legs under me, I'd have kicked his ass all the way around the block."

Having been ministered to by a black woman the past three years, Walter Ketchum had come to make the reluctant admission that a dark skin wasn't *always* the sign of either a criminal mentality or natural rhythm. But he was completely hopeless when it came to homosexuals. He would never allow a gay person near him, so he'd never get to see gays as human beings.

"Is that what you called about, Dad?" Ron was getting tired.

"No. I called because I have to spend so much time sitting on my ass, and I've used most of it the past few days staring at the picture of that boy nailed to the tree in your town."

"And?"

"And I think it would be a mistake on your part to think this was a racial thing."

Which was just what Ron had told Oliver. But hearing the same thing from his father made him get his back up.

"Why wouldn't it be a racial thing?"

"Why? Because it's too … shit, I've been trying to think of the word … I know! What it is, it's too *artistic*."

"Artistic?"

"Yeah, for a redneck. A kill all the niggers moron is gonna nail a guy to a tree? Make him look like Christ in blackface. It's too precious."

"I hate to sound like an echo, Dad, but precious? Nails?"

"Look, Ronny, I'm telling you. I study this picture in the paper, what I see is a painting. I don't see a redneck murder. Sure, somebody obviously hated this poor joker, but it was for personal reasons."

"Dad, everything we've turned up on Isaac Cardwell says if he'd been any holier he'd have been able to multiply loaves and fishes. Nobody had any personal reason to hate this guy."

Unless it was Jimmy Thunder, but Ron couldn't share that thought with his father.

The old man showed he was still capable of surprising Ron. He backed off. "Okay, so maybe you've got some facts I don't know about or you can't talk about. But just believe me on this one thing: The Klan, Nazi skinheads or any other of those pus-brains, they'd killed this Cardwell, you'd have found him tied to that tree or hanging from it."

"How do you know that?"

"Hey, I'm the expert, remember? That's why you had me testify in court."

Ron couldn't argue with that, so he simply told his father goodnight.

CHAPTER 29

Tuesday

Ron and Oliver got together that morning in the chief's office. They exchanged the information they'd gleaned they day before. They agreed that some facts fit neatly with each other, and they agreed that the "white" man Pastor Brantley thought he saw at the back of St. Mark's almost certainly was their killer, but they debated who that white man might be or even if he was white at all.

"Okay," Ron said, "we're splitting hairs here. We both like the guy at the back of the church. We both agree that he's fair-skinned. So whatever the hell racial category society assigns this bastard is really beside the point. Agreed?"

Oliver nodded.

"So, I'll tell you my idea and you tell me yours. Fair?"

"Fair."

"What Ms. Royce and Ms. Chenier told me was that Jimmy Thunder's got himself a case of the financial shorts."

"You trust them?"

"Not at all. But then Art Gilbert, the landscaper, tells me he overhears this character Didi DuPree talking to Thunder about money laundering. This I believe. Because what reason would Gilbert have to lie about it?"

The deputy chief was stuck for an answer to rebut that one.

"And," Ron continued, "Caz Stanley found out Jimmy Thunder, Didi DuPree and Deacon Meeker were all at Huntsville together. And DuPree and Meeker are cousins."

Oliver started flicking the top of his cigarette lighter. Ron was half-tempted to tell him to give in and go outside for a smoke. But he maintained his focus.

"Now, what would Thunder want with anything as heavy as money-laundering if his own perfectly legit operation was rolling right along raking in bundles of cash? That wouldn't make sense."

"Maybe DuPree came to Thunder instead of the other way around," Oliver suggested. "Told the man I've got a business proposition for you here that you accept or else."

Ron gave the idea a long moment's thought. "That doesn't quite work for me. Thunder went both straight and big-time after getting out of the joint. A lowlife, even one as scary as this DuPree is supposed to be, tries to muscle a citizen with money, he's taking an awful risk. A rich citizen comes to us, saying he fears for his life from some scumbag, he knows he's going to get deluxe service. All the stops will be pulled out to send the scumbag right back to stir, if we don't cool his action permanently. And I think a guy who's got away clean with killing as many people as DuPree supposedly has would be too slick to force his way in where the risks would be so high."

"So you like Thunder inviting the devil in?"

Ron smiled. "Yeah, nice turn of phrase. I think DuPree was brought in through his cousin, the deacon. Let's say Jimmy Thunder's TVQ ratings have slipped for whatever reason, and his take is down. He starts to see the beginning of the end. He'd already lost his place in the high life once, he damn sure doesn't want to lose it again. Hell, he's only lived up here on the top of the mountain for a few years.

"So, he says to the deacon, go ask your cousin Didi if he'd like to have me wash some money for those folks he knows with all that cash on their hands."

"A drug connection?"

"Could be drugs. But, hell, people are making fortunes smuggling immigrants and even goddamn *Freon* into the country these days. So who knows about that? But we know that he got a positive response, from what Art Gilbert told me. And we also know that Thunder got cold feet.

"Now, looking at Didi's sheet, he doesn't strike me as the type who just shrugs off getting jerked around … but he can't kill Thunder. That would defeat his purpose. Without the reverend, there's no way to make the money laundering scheme work. So what's DuPree going to do?

"He kills Thunder's son as an example. He figures losing an estranged kid won't mean that much to Jimmy. But by crucifying Isaac he sends a very specific message to the other man of the cloth: Play ball, or you get nailed to the next tree."

All of that played for Oliver, but he still had a question. "This DuPree is light enough to be mistaken for a white man?"

"Sergeant Stanley came up with his picture. Got it from the Texas prison authorities. I found it on my desk when I walked in this morning." Ron flipped the photo of the man to Oliver. "You tell me if a half blind pastor looking across a dimly lit church couldn't think this guy was white?"

Oliver looked at the picture and nodded. "Yeah, he could pass for white."

"So why do you like this Ring character so much?" the chief asked.

The deputy chief laughed mirthlessly. "Probably shouldn't say so, but one of the reasons I like him is I'd really like to stomp the sucker flat into the ground."

"You know, Oliver, I couldn't get away with saying that about a black guy."

"You could if it was just the two of us, and the black guy was as big an asshole as Ring."

"But you've got other reasons, right?"

"Yeah. The man was right out front that the whole purpose of his book is to destroy Jimmy Thunder. In fact, the fucker was tickled about it. But the stuff he has on Thunder, at least what he told me, it isn't all that bad. Not by today's standards. He beat his wife and ran out on his child. That's shameful, except how many times have we heard it before, and how much sense of moral outrage does anybody have left these days, anyway? The worst thing Ring brought up was when Thunder killed that Braddock kid who played QB for New York. But he did his time for that, and everybody already knows about it.

"So I was asking myself, 'What if Ring has himself a book contract and no book to go with it?' At least no book that's going to sell worth a damn. Seems to me he'd be in some serious shit. But then the last thing he tells me is, wouldn't it be just great for him and his book if Jimmy Thunder did his kid?"

"We all know the answer to that," Ron said.

"Right. So I ask myself, could this prick have given himself the great ending his book needs by doing Isaac Cardwell and hoping we pin it on Jimmy? Even if we don't, he can write that we should have."

The chief nodded. "Yeah, I can see that, just taking your word for the kind of jerk Ring is. But Thunder's still a real possibility. Say that Isaac found out about the deal his father and Didi had cooking and made a threat to his father to expose it. Tell Jimmy Thunder that he was going to tell Ring everything. That made Jimmy hesitant to go forward with the money laundering. Which fits with Art Gilbert overhearing DuPree's threats. Add DuPree's threat to Jimmy deciding he wants to keep living the good life. What's Jimmy's only choice? He tells DuPree to take care of Isaac and save his reputation, and he'll go along with the deal."

"Now, you've got two ways of putting DuPree in the church."

"And you've got one way for Ring," the chief said. "But we know my guy's got a rap sheet, and we don't know if your guy does."

"I'll find out," Oliver said. "My money says he does."

"No bet," Ron replied.

Ron knew that he had to find Didi DuPree soon to keep working his angles on the killing. That was assuming the man was still in town. Ron hadn't served in the army during the Vietnam War, but he'd met plenty of older guys who had. He knew what di-di meant in Vietnamese: *Get outta Dodge.*

Even if the man had left town, though, DuPree's cousin, Deacon Meeker, was still nesting under Jimmy Thunder's roof. Ron might have to have a heart to heart with the deacon. Come to that, maybe he should have another little talk with the good reverend himself. Rattle the man's cage a little harder this time.

Ron drove over to Thunder's estate and pulled up at the entrance. He pushed the button on the intercom.

"Who is it?" came the gruff tones of Deacon Meeker.

"Chief Ketchum. I've come to talk to you. Let me in."

There was a long moment of silence and then, "Just wait right where you are."

Neither Meeker's tone nor his message was at all accommodating, but there was a tone in the man's voice, almost a cockiness, that made Ron think it would be in his own interest to show some patience. He sat and looked out at the grounds, at Art Gilbert's handiwork. The man had more than a green thumb, he had a serious gift.

Ron wondered how much Gilbert would charge to replant his windowboxes.

It took six minutes by the chief's watch before a golf cart pulled up to the other side of the gate. Deacon Meeker was driving. But Ron's focus was on the passenger. He had a hard time not grinding his teeth when he recognized Marcus Martin.

Ron got out of his Explorer as Martin stepped from the cart.

"Do you have a warrant to enter this property?" Martin asked from the other side of the gate, not bothering to address Ron by name or rank.

"No."

"Then you can't come in."

"I don't necessarily want to come in. I'd just like to talk with the deacon there."

Deacon Meeker smirked at the chief.

Marcus Martin said, "As of now, I represent Reverend Thunder and everyone in his employ. I'm authorized to tell you that none of my clients will be speaking to the police. Not unless they are legally compelled to do so, and then only through me."

"Somebody worried about something?" Ron asked.

"With certain people there is always reason to worry."

"You making this about me, Marcus?"

"It's well known you have a certain history."

Ron looked over the lawyer's shoulder and saw two figures step out from behind a stand of trees. Jimmy Thunder and Ben Dexter. Martin followed Ron's gaze, then he looked back at the chief.

"How's it feel to be on the outside looking in, Ketchum?"

"Like I've already got you surrounded, Marcus."

The lawyer didn't like the crack, but Ron was already turning his back on him as he headed back to his unit with a wave of his hand. "Thanks for the advice, Counselor. Next time I come, I'll bring warrants: search, arrest, whatever I need."

"Hey, wiseass," Martin hissed.

Ron stopped and turned. "Now, Marcus, that remark was positively uncivil."

"You think you're something, don't you? You were lucky those other times. Lucky I didn't peel the lily-white skin right off your ass."

The chief looked at his lifelong nemesis for a silent five count. He wouldn't put it past the asshole to be wearing a wire. Just hoping to record something he could use against Ron. So the chief decided on an indirect approach.

"You want to play some ball, Marcus?" Ron asked. "I've got a key to the gym at the rec center. We'll play a little midnight basketball, just you and me. You look like you've pudged up a bit, but maybe you've still got it, huh? We'll play one-on-one to twenty-one — or until whoever's left standing. Whaddya say?"

Hate came off Marcus Martin in waves.

"Come on, Counselor," Ron taunted. "You're letting down your side. After all, you called it, I'm white. You afraid to play basketball with a white guy?"

The lawyer started shaking so hard Deacon Meeker looked worried. Ron himself wondered, in a detached way, if Marcus was going to have a seizure. Fine with him if he did.

It was downright risky for Ron to bait a black man even obliquely, especially if he was wearing a wire. But he hated Marcus Martin, had hated him since the first time they'd met, and he wasn't going to hold back now, whatever the risk.

"Pussy," Ron said with contempt. Then he corrected himself. "Oops, sorry. That was sexist. And besides I just met a woman who could whip your ass on the court. What I should have said was: chickenshit."

Maybe it wasn't smart to be so blunt but, brother, was it satisfying. If he ever had to own up to his words in court, it would be worth it. Of course, now that he thought about it, recording a person without his prior knowledge and consent was a crime in California. That thought gave Ron a wonderful feeling of license about what he'd said.

He turned his back on the lawyer again and had the door of his patrol unit open before Marcus Martin found his voice. "You know why I'm here, you cocksucker?"

"Racial solidarity and a big fee?" Ron opined, looking at Martin once more.

"I'm here because Special Agent Francis Horgan, head of the FBI office in San Francisco, said a prominent member of the local African American community might need his civil rights protected. You be real careful about any warrant you obtain. Ain't just us niggers you got to worry about. Cut just one little corner and the federal government will be breathing down that red neck of yours again."

"Score one for you, Marcus," Ron said, keeping a lid on his temper. "Give me a call at headquarters if you change your mind about playing ball."

CHAPTER 30

Corrie Knox and Tucker Marsden had been out hunting the mountain lion since four a.m. They followed the big cat's tracks through the pine forest above the north end of Lake Adeline. The trail led them to the skull of a fawn.

"Look," Tucker told Corrie. "The fucker's gone back to eating Bambis. All is right with the world again."

Tucker held his rifle at the ready while Corrie knelt for a closer inspection of the young deer's skull. She had a professional's detachment about the demise of the fawn. Deer were the staple of a lion's diet. It was one of their reasons for being. Even so, she felt a sense of foreboding as she looked at the fragment of bone.

"This is one hungry animal," she said, rising. "It's almost as if he knows he won't be able to hunt much longer, so he's gorging while he still can."

She scanned the forest, not forgetting to look up.

Tucker said derisively, "Don't go all mystical on me now. Let's remember we're the professionals here." Then he paused to look around, too. "You know, I think that bastard's not too far away. He could be watching us right now."

"I feel the same way," Corrie said.

"Heeeere, kitty, kitty, kitty," Tucker crooned. "Come on out so we can put a couple rounds between those great big cat eyes of yours."

The two game wardens stood back to back, rifles ready,

straining to see any sign of the cat. The animal was close; they both sensed it. They also knew there was almost no chance they'd get so much as a glimpse of it, much less a clean shot.

"So what's this chief of police you're bunking with like?" Tucker inquired softly.

"We're not bunking."

"No?"

"No."

"So, it's platonic?"

"So far," Corrie responded. If Tucker wanted to be so nosy, she thought, let's see how he responded to that.

"Guy's supposed to be a racist, if you can believe what you read in the paper," Tucker said. He felt Corrie stiffen against his back.

She said, "He's supposed to be in recovery, if you read closely."

Tucker tried another tack. "Must be an older dude, being the chief of police and all."

"Yeah, he's older."

There was a flash of movement through the trees that caused both hunters to bring their rifles to bear. But it wasn't the lion, just a mature doe, perhaps the dead fawn's mother. In the twinkling of an eye, she disappeared. Corrie and Tucker watched to see if the big cat, who they were sure was nearby, took up pursuit. But no chase ensued.

Their adrenaline drained and they slumped against each other.

"Kitty didn't take off after Bambi's mom," Tuck said. "And there's a lot more meat on her bones."

"She's a lot faster and stronger, too. Maybe our cat isn't up to that kind of chase any more."

"Would explain why he's taken a fancy to us puny bipeds. So how *old* is this guy you're not sleeping with?"

"Pretty old."

"Like he could be your father?"

"Not that old."

"Well, tell me he's good looking at least."

"He's good looking … and he can hit a jump shot from the

three-point line."

Tucker laughed. "A cop *and* a jock. How phallic can you get?"

"Yeah. Its' almost as bad a combination as a game warden who's a rock climber — and we know how great that worked out. There is one difference between the two of you, though."

"Yeah, he's old."

"The difference I meant is that Ron's a grownup."

"I'll grow up when I get old."

"I don't want to wait."

"Which was why we broke up."

They let a long silence ensue, before Tucker finally filled it. "I hate to admit this, but if you get something good going with this guy, I'm happy for you."

"Why do I feel there's a kicker coming?" Corrie inquired.

"No kicker. I'm only sorry it couldn't be me."

"What, you got noble when I wasn't looking?"

"Yeah … Makes you hot, doesn't it?"

Corrie gave Tuck an elbow in the ribs, but not a hard one.

"You think your new friend is going to catch his killer?" Tuck asked.

Corrie paused a moment, then answered, "I don't know. But I think he has to be doing at least as well tracking his quarry as we are with ours."

The patrol unit carrying Officers Jack Dennehy and Bert Cardozo pulled up behind the chief's car on Lake Shore Drive just outside of Jimmy Thunder's estate. The two uniformed patrolmen walked over to where the chief sat waiting for them.

They greeted him with salutes, a gesture Ron appreciated after all of the various kinds of shit he'd been taking from people. After his confrontation with Marcus Martin, the chief had backed his unit onto the public thoroughfare and radioed Sergeant Stanley to send him the two senior patrol officers on duty.

"What can we do for you, Chief?" Dennehy asked.

Ron handed him a copy of the photo printout of Didi DuPree,

along with DuPree's rap sheet. Dennehy shared the material with his partner. The chief instructed his two officers, "Wait right here and watch for this guy. He may be on his way in or on his way out. Better for us if you collar him trying to get in. But either way, you make the arrest."

"What's the charge, Chief?" Cardozo wanted to know.

"Suspicion of murder. One look at this guy's sheet, you know he's bad. So be careful."

"How careful, Chief?" Dennehy asked blandly.

"As careful as you have to be. I'll back you whatever you do. But the point of all this is I want to talk with this guy."

"Anything else we should watch out for?" Cardozo inquired.

"There's a lawyer inside the gates name of Marcus Martin. He may try to give you some grief about harassing Jimmy Thunder. He gets in your faces, try to be polite. You're public servants on a public street doing the public's business."

"Tell him to piss in his hat, only politely," Cardozo said.

"Kid gloves all the way?" Dennehy wanted to know.

"As long as the only hassle he gives you is verbal, let it roll off your backs. But if DuPree shows up, don't let Martin stop you from bringing him in."

"Didi Du, straight to you. Gotcha, Chief," Cardozo said.

Dennehy rolled his eyes. "He wants to do stand-up, Chief. Everybody's a comedian but me. I don't have a fucking sense of humor at all. I'll make sure we bring this mope in if he shows."

Ron had considered replacing Cardozo, and Dennehy had seen what he was thinking. The cop interceded for his partner.

"Really, Chief. Bert'll be okay. And he'll do better than me talking to this lawyer, if he comes out. I hate fucking lawyers. Especially since my divorce."

Now the chief wondered if he should replace them both. Maybe have Oliver and Caz Stanley sit out here. But he didn't want to take the time or cause any griping in the ranks. He'd have to trust them.

"Okay. Just remember, don't underestimate DuPree."

The two cops saluted again, and Ron left.

That, he hoped, was one chore taken care of. Now he had to keep his cool when he confronted Special Agent Francis Horgan of the FBI — even though the fed had sicced Marcus Martin on him, trying once again to screw him and hijack the Isaac Cardwell case.

As Ron drove off, he got the first glimmer of an idea that might let him turn things around on Horgan. In fact, he might take things one of two ways, depending on his mood.

Clay Steadman looked at the memo Ron Ketchum had routed to him, and he had the same thought the chief had: *Punch* a mountain lion? Even for an icon of the Hollywood fantasy factory, the notion seemed a reach. But there it was in black and white along with all of the other do's and don'ts of dealing with your local feline carnivores.

The chief wrote to the mayor that Warden Knox thought these safety tips should be publicly disseminated, and he was deferring to her expertise. He suggested that the tips could be posted on the home page of the town's website immediately, a press release could be drafted for the noon news, and the mayor could discuss the tips on his evening TV program.

What Ron Ketchum hadn't mentioned was that publicizing the information would frighten the public more. If ignorance was bliss, a public warning meant something was closing in on you fast. The increased public tension would make both the mayor's job and the chief's job harder. But Clay Steadman didn't believe in keeping people in the dark. Democracy worked best, in his view, when the BS was kept to an absolute minimum. And secrecy generated nothing but BS.

The mayor was pleased that the man he'd hired for his chief of police seemed to feel the same way. His thoughts were interrupted when his secretary buzzed him and announced that the deputy chief of police was in the outer office and requested a moment of the mayor's time.

"Send him in," the mayor said.

Oliver entered the mayor's office and saluted smartly.

The two men had met several times, but didn't really know one another personally. Oliver Gosden was Ron Ketchum's hire, and Clay Steadman's approval of that hiring had been routine.

"That's not necessary," the mayor informed the deputy chief.

"It's not?" Oliver asked, dropping his arm.

"Simple good manners are all I ever expect from anyone. Have a seat, Deputy Chief."

Oliver sat down.

"What can I do for you?"

"I'm trying to get a line on a suspect in the Cardwell killing, Mr. Mayor. This particular suspect is a foreign national. I was sure he'd have a criminal record, but NCIC and Interpol say he's clean."

"But you still think he isn't?"

"What the man does, he writes celebrity biographies. But what he really is, he's a character assassin. Only when I look at him, I think he might've carried the assassination part one step further to help his book along."

Clay Steadman recognized and accepted the necessity of dealing with the mainstream media. But his opinion of paparazzi and attack biographers was that they were bacteria in search of an antibiotic.

"What's this guy's name?"

"Colin Ring."

"He's a Brit?" the mayor asked.

"Yes, sir."

"I know some studio people who do book acquisitions. That's what you were thinking, wasn't it, Deputy Chief? See if this character has done something that hasn't made the police blotter, but still doesn't pass the smell test."

"That's just what I had in mind, Mr. Mayor."

"I'll let you know if I come up with anything."

Oliver stood and almost saluted again, but he caught himself.

"I appreciate your help," he said.

"That's what I'm here for," the mayor replied. "You're married, aren't you, Deputy Chief?"

"Yes, sir."

"After things calm down around here I'd like to have you and Mrs. Gosden out to the house for dinner. So we can all get to know each other a little better."

"I'd like that, too."

If only he could get over the urge to salute the man every ten seconds.

Ron found Francis Horgan where he expected him to be — at the Hilton. It was just the kind of all American place where a fed was bound to stay. Clean, comfortable and more justifiable on the old expense account than the Ritz-Carlton .

The Hilton, like every other hostelry in town, was supposed to be sold out. But law enforcement people knew that every good hotel manager held back at least one suite for his boss, his girlfriend, or the president of the United States: some person of significance who might drop in unexpectedly.

Accordingly, the suite was one of the best the hotel had to offer. And if you were an important minion of the federal government, like Francis "the Feeb" Horgan, why, you got a discount. Good corporate PR. Ron, however, was less than thrilled that Horgan got to live the good life at taxpayer expense while he fucked around with Ron's investigation.

"Would you like me to call up and announce your arrival?" the hotel manager asked the chief.

"No," Ron said. "Let's make it a surprise. Mr. Horgan and I enjoy playing our little tricks on one another."

Knowing his bread was buttered locally, the manager graciously acceded to the chief's wish.

Which let Ron brush right past the junior feeb who opened the door to the suite. The guy didn't have time to do more than shout, "Hey!" before Ron found Horgan enjoying his breakfast on a balcony with a panoramic view of Lake Adeline.

Seeing that the table had been democratically set to include Horgan's lessers — two in number judged by the place settings —

Ron decided the initial part of his play. He seated himself as if he had an engraved invitation in his hand. He took a croissant from a basket and poured himself a cup of coffee. He helped himself to fruit salad and scrambled eggs. Not bothering to look at Horgan, he started to eat his fruit salad.

Maybe ten seconds passed in silence. Ron chewed contentedly, even as he felt the two junior feebs congregate close behind him. Finally, Horgan's burning fuse hit black powder.

"What the fuck do you think you're doing, Ketchum?" the senior fed demanded.

Ron speared another piece of fruit and looked up. Horgan's face was the color of magma.

"Just thought I'd see how the other half lives," Ron said. "You know, feed at Washington's trough just like you feebs."

Horgan grabbed the fork out of Ron's hand, sending a strawberry cascading down the front of his crisp white federal shirt. Half a dozen splotchy red blemishes now marred the garment, as if it had developed a sudden and severe case of acne.

"I don't think those stains are going to come out," Ron said.

While Horgan struggled to connect his vitriol to his vocabulary, the chief looked over his shoulder. As he expected, two junior G-men were there, giving him their best Tommy Lee Jones hard guy stares. But they couldn't quite bring it off. Not enough presence to be truly menacing. They were doomed to careers as bit players.

"Why don't you gentlemen see if you can find some club soda and a sponge for your boss?" Ron suggested. "Maybe you can save the day, after all."

The chief took a bite of croissant as the two young FBI agents looked to their boss for instructions. With a jerk of his head, Horgan exiled his junior auxiliary from the balcony. Ron got up and closed the sliding glass door behind them.

The chief went to the balcony railing and looked out at the lake. He was alone with his prey now. The only question was which way to take him.

"I'm trying to decide what to do about you, Horgan," he said.

"You don't seem to be a man who can accept a polite warning."

"You're not going to do dick about me, Ketchum. I'm the one who's going to ream you."

Ron turned to look at the fed. The shadow of a smile played at the corners of his mouth. He was glad the fed had made the choice for him. And even given him material to work with.

The chief said, "Interesting choice of words there, Horgan. 'Dick … Ream.' But then you work out of San Francisco, don't you?"

The fed's face flushed as he shoved away from the table and got to his feet. "What the hell is that supposed to mean?"

"Come on now, Horgan. You don't have to be coy with me. Oh, wait a minute. You do have to be coy. The military did away with 'don't ask, don't tell, ' but I have to wonder how the bureau feels about gender orientation. Probably still a bit homophobic is my guess. By the way, Horgan, just what is it three feds in a hotel room do at night for fun?"

Ron thought his dad would be proud of him right now.

He thought he had Horgan, too. The fed had balled his fists and he looked like he was about to wade into Ron. Which was exactly what the chief wanted. He couldn't just stomp Horgan, as much as he'd like to, because even Clay Steadman wouldn't be able to fix that. However, if he defended himself from an attack by the fed that would be a whole different matter.

But Horgan didn't bite. He'd never be mistaken for a leading man, either. Or maybe he just saw in Ron's eyes that he'd pitch Horgan right off the balcony and take his chances with the consequences.

The fed unclenched his hands. A shiver ran through him like a man whose fever had just broken. Then Horgan even managed a ghastly smile.

"It's not going to be that easy for you, Ketchum."

"More's the pity," Ron said. "I guess it's on to plan B."

"If that means running and crying to that pri —" Horgan bit the end off the word. Ron had him self-conscious about his language now. "To your goddamn mayor, don't bother. It won't help."

"No?"

"No. The bureau is rock solid into the church arson investigation. Now, even the attorney general's behind me being here."

"To investigate the arson threat."

"To investigate it any way I want."

"So I fucked myself by doing the right thing and relaying that letter to you?"

Horgan only smiled.

"Then I'm probably just asking for more trouble by going to Plan B."

"What the fuck are you talking about, 'Plan B?'" Horgan asked with a sneer.

"Well, Plan B is taking you and — what the hell — the whole FBI to court for slander."

Horgan's jaw dropped momentarily. "You must be nuts, Ketchum. You can't do that."

"I can and I will. Not more than an hour ago, Marcus Martin, Esquire, told me to my face that you said he should come to town and represent Jimmy Thunder because you feared I was about to violate Reverend Thunder's civil rights."

The FBI agent looked like he wanted to rebut Ron's statement, but again he couldn't find the words. His mouth moved and bubbles of saliva formed on his lips, but no coherent language emerged. He looked like he needed a distemper shot.

"What?" Ron asked. "Marcus wasn't supposed to let that tidbit slip? Afraid he did."

Before he could censor himself, Horgan muttered, "That nigger."

"Naughty, naughty," Ron said with a smile. "Anyway, what you said to Marcus is totally without foundation. It could cause me grave personal and professional damage. So, I'm going to do what any red-blooded American would do: I'm going to sue your ass. And since there's a lot of press in town, it ought to make the national news. Who knows, between all the depositions you'll have to give, and all the news interviews you'll have to do defending yourself, maybe you won't find time to fuck with my investigation anymore."

Ron started to leave, but Horgan grabbed his arm.

The chief leaned his face in close enough to smell the FBI man's fear. "Or if you like we could go back to Plan A right now."

The door to the balcony slid open and the two junior feebs looked ready to jump to their boss's aid. But Horgan dropped Ron's arm.

"There's also a Plan C," Ron said. "You run your church arson angle legitimately. You don't even think of crossing me again. And maybe, just maybe, I won't blow up your career right in front of your eyes."

Horgan dropped his eyes and a moment later he nodded.

Ron plucked a grape from the fruit salad and left.

CHAPTER 31

The chief returned to headquarters feeling only marginally better. True, he'd neutralized Horgan for the time being, had even shamed him in front of his toadies, but eventually the man would delude himself that he hadn't turned tail, that he'd simply given himself room to maneuver. Guys like Horgan were masters at kidding themselves, and their bile had a longer shelf life than nuclear waste.

So, the trick was to solve the Isaac Cardwell case while Horgan was still licking his wounds.

The file he'd found on his desk upon his return contained the lab results on the blood found outside St. Mark's church. The blood was Cardwell's. Along with finding Isaac's glasses outside the church, it confirmed the fact that St. Mark's was almost certainly where Isaac Cardwell was first attacked. The physical evidence made it imperative for Ron to find the "white" man who had been seen at the back of the church by Pastor Brantley.

Ron had to get his hands on Didi DuPree.

He buzzed Dinah, his secretary, and asked her to have Sergeant Stanley sent in immediately. The sarge kept him waiting less than a minute

"I was just on my way to see you, Chief."

"Okay, but let's take care of what I have first."

The sergeant nodded deferentially and Ron told him he wanted to make finding Didi DuPree a priority. Every patrol officer should be given a picture of the man and be instructed to be on a constant lookout for him. The sergeant was to emphasize that DuPree should be considered armed and dangerous. All appropriate precautions should be taken. Additionally, the officers stationed outside of Jimmy Thunder's estate were to be rotated every four hours. Backup for those officers was to be close at hand at all times.

Ron nodded to Sergeant Stanley. "Your turn."

"Chief, I heard through a friend in the media that you're going to be on the TV news sometime soon."

"Yeah?"

"Jimmy Thunder's doing a heart to heart with Ben Dexter about how you suspect him of his son's murder. About how he's being persecuted in his time of mourning. About how you … well, you know what they're going to say about you."

"I can imagine," Ron replied dryly.

"I just thought you ought to know in advance. Maybe you want to have a response prepared for Annie Stratton to release."

Ron considered. "Yeah. Have Annie tell anyone who asks that this department will follow its investigation wherever it may lead and will not be deflected by any outside pressure."

The sergeant gave a tight grin of approval.

"You got anything else for me, Sarge?"

"A couple things. Foot patrols report that those safety tips about the lion that we posted on the Internet are already being talked about. We've had people stop officers and ask if they should keep their guns loaded."

It was just as Ron had thought, the warning only made people more frightened.

"Load their guns, huh? Our response to such questions is that everyone has the same rights and responsibilities they've always had. But, at a time like this, when people are nervous, it's more important than ever to remember gun safety rules. We don't want little kids picking up loaded weapons. We don't want people drilling their neighbors or even their neighbors' pets. We will not cut anyone any slack for the illegal discharge of a weapon."

Sergeant Stanley nodded.

"What else you got, Sarge?"

"Just one thing. A citizen wants to see you personally. About the Cardwell case."

Sergeant Stanley opened Ron's door and gestured to someone waiting outside. A big young guy in his early twenties stepped into the chief's office. He had long dishwater blonde hair that was held back in a ponytail. He wore a work shirt that said Chevron over one pocket and Buster over the other. He had on blue jeans and black work boots.

Buster looked distinctly nervous. His eyes darted about Ron's office.

"Buster Lurie, Chief," the sarge said by way of introduction. "He works at the Chevron station at Lake Shore and Route 99."

Sergeant Stanley withdrew and closed the door behind him.

"Have a seat, Mr. Lurie," Ron said, gesturing his visitor into a guest chair. "What can I do for you?"

"Just listen to what I have to say, I guess. I've got a tip about that black guy that got killed. But every time I try calling the reward number the goddamn line is always busy. So, I figured I finally better come in and see you."

Buster Lurie looked over his shoulder as if he expected someone to bust in on them. Possibly with guns blazing.

"Something got you spooked, Mr. Lurie?" Ron asked.

"It's what I saw. What I have to tell you."

"In that case, why don't you just tell me? Then you won't have to worry about it anymore."

"This'll still count toward me getting the reward, won't it?" Lurie asked with concern. "I mean, you don't have to phone it in, do you? 'Cause I must've tried fifty times."

"If your information is helpful, I'm sure the mayor won't mind that you brought it in directly."

"Good, " Lurie said. He rubbed his hands together nervously. "But you'll still keep it quiet that I was the one who told you?"

"During the investigation, yes. If your tip leads to an arrest and a trial, you might have to testify in court as to what you're about to tell me." Ron saw the trepidation in the young man's eyes. "The reward is for the arrest and conviction of Isaac Cardwell's killer," the chief explained.

"Okay, okay." Now Lurie rubbed his palms against his thighs. "Then here's how it went. I work at my uncle's service station, and that tight SOB won't ever let me work on my own car during business hours, which are from six a.m. to midnight! That means if I want to put my car up on a lift I got to work on it when nobody's awake but me 'n' the goddamn owls."

Ron thought he was going to have to prompt this guy if he didn't get to the point soon.

"Anyway, about half past three on the morning you found that Cardwell guy stuck to that tree, I was working on my car at the station. I was minding my own business, had my Mustang up on the lift, draining the oil out of my crankcase when I hear this goddamn big screech of tires behind me. It was so loud it lifted me off of my feet and spun me around. I was lucky I didn't brain myself on the bottom of my car. That or piss my pants. And when I looked outside, you know what I saw?"

"What, Mr. Lurie?" Ron asked with rapidly thinning patience.

"There's this beautiful black Lamborghini. It's stopped smack in the middle of the intersection. Like the driver saw the stop sign only way too late."

"And the driver was?"

"Jimmy Thunder."

With those two words, Buster Lurie richly rewarded Ron's forbearance.

"You recognized the driver of the car that night as the Reverend Jimmy Thunder?"

"That's what I just said. It wasn't raining right then, and I recognized him from TV. And I saw the plate on the Lambo, too. It was: T-H-U-N-D-E-R. I could even see the look on the guy's face: it was like something awful had just happened. Then the Lambo screeched again, and was gone quick as a wink."

"And you're sure of the time you saw Jimmy Thunder?"

"There's a clock on the wall in the service area. Right after the Lambo split, I looked at it to see how much time I had left to work on my car and catch a little sleep before I opened the station at six."

So Jimmy Thunder had lied to him about being home all night, Ron thought. He was out near the scene of the crime very close to Isaac Cardwell's time of death, as estimated by Dr. Ryman. If that sonofabitch Marcus Martin hadn't come to town, Ron could have yanked Thunder in and grilled him. As it was, he wondered if he had enough to get a search warrant to go over Thunder's estate with a fine-tooth comb in hopes of finding the murder weapon.

"So, what do you think?" Buster Lurie asked, interrupting the chief's reverie. "Is this good stuff or what? Because I sure could use that reward. Open my own station and work on my car whenever I goddamn well please."

The chief replied, "It's useful information, Mr. Lurie. No question about that. Whether it leads to anything, we'll have to wait and see. But tell me something. You look scared about something. Maybe about talking with me. Why is that?"

"Are you kidding? A guy who owns a Lambo and lives in a mansion on the lake, he's got plenty to lose. I know what can happen to someone who squeals on a guy with money."

Ron would bet Lurie's sense of peril was inspired by a lifetime of TV viewing ... but with Didi DuPree wandering around unaccounted for, and his role in Jimmy Thunder's life not entirely defined, the young man's instincts might not be far wrong.

"You may have a point," the chief responded. "So we'd both do well to keep our little talk confidential."

"Bet your ass," Buster Lurie said. Then he added, "No offense."

"None taken. Tell me, Mr. Lurie, when you saw Reverend Thunder, do you think he might have noticed you?"

Buster gave it all of two seconds thought before he shook his head.

"Tell you the truth, the way he looked to me, I think the station could've been on fire, with the gas tanks exploding, and he wouldn't have noticed."

After Buster Lurie had left, Ron had Dinah bring him the Goldstrike Hotel and Motel Directory. Leafing through it, he counted forty-two different entries. Lodgings in town ranged from five star to fifty-five dollars per night with a free breakfast. Then there were the campgrounds where you could park your own motorized bed and breakfast.

But Ron didn't see Didi DuPree as the RV type.

He also didn't see any mid level hotel that cried out as the sure bet for the former houseguest and jailbird friend of Jimmy Thunder. After staying at a posh lakeside estate, it was reasonable to assume DuPree would want to maintain a certain level of creature comfort, so Ron would start looking at the upscale places first. But he didn't know the state of DuPree's finances, so he'd have to work his way down the amenities scale if his hunch didn't pay off.

This wasn't going to be nearly as easy as pegging the feds to stay at the Hilton. But then legwork was the basic exercise of any police investigation. Ron considered sharing his burden with Oliver, but decided against it. The deputy chief was still hot on his Colin Ring angle, and Ron didn't want to pull him away from that. Who knew? He could be right.

The chief got up from his desk and told himself it would just be a long day behind the wheel, that's all. He informed Sergeant Stanley what he'd be doing, and told the sarge to call him if anything important came up.

Ron considered having the sarge ride along with him for backup, but the man was indispensable at headquarters. What the hell, he thought, he'd dealt with plenty of bad guys in L.A. and he wasn't too proud to call for help.

The only thing that really bothered Ron was the idea that he might log a lot of hours and come up empty. Didi DuPree easily could have lived up to his name and blown town.

Then the chief would have to swallow a ton of pride and ask that shit Horgan for help in finding DuPree.

CHAPTER 32

Didi DuPree was still in town, but not in a hotel, and certainly not in a Winnebago.

He woke up at mid morning in a private residence. Nothing so grand as the Thunder estate, but the place still went for upwards of a couple million bucks and had a view of the lake. Before he ever opened his eyes, Didi knew that he was alone in the bed. But nearby he could hear and smell the woman who'd taken him in.

He lazily spread his eyelids revealing orbs as cool, gray and uncaring as stones in a fast-moving stream. He had hair the color of anthracite that swept back in waves from a high forehead. His nose was long and broad, his mouth was full and wide. He wore a new goatee, grown in just enough to look respectable.

In repose, as he was now, he looked almost slight. But when Didi moved, and he could put it in overdrive while most folks were still fumbling for the ignition switch, all sorts of long, ropy muscles popped out.

He got to his feet in one fluid motion and eased silently over to where the woman sat naked, clickety-clacking away at her computer. The words just flew up there on that little TV screen like magic. Rat-a-tat-tat. Just blasting out the story from her head. Didi appreciated her speed, if not her dialogue:

BRETT

The world's not big enough for you to hide from me, Colonel.

If that was the case, Didi thought, the colonel ought to cut off ol' Brett's johnson right then and there and gag him with it. But, no, he had to tell the hero how big his hard-on was. And then in the final scene the colonel would get his ass handed to him. That was the kind of thing that had made Didi stop going to the movies. Real bad guys *never* gave anybody a second chance.

But Didi didn't care about Brett or the colonel. He just want to make sure that ol' — he had to look at those surgically crafted tits before her name came back to him — Gayle Shipton hadn't been writing about any of the stories he'd been telling her the past few days. Not that she could *never* use them. He wasn't a tease. He'd just said she had to wait until he said it was okay.

They'd met last Friday when Didi had been sitting in one of the sidewalk cafes this town seemed to have no end of. She'd strolled right over to him, given him a long look and said, "I bet you're dangerous. I need a dangerous man right now."

What Didi had needed was a place to stay, so he let her sit down.

She said she was a screenwriter. She'd come to her "getaway" house to do a complete rewrite of a dogshit excuse for a script that was holding up a sixty million dollar production. She had ten days to do the job. And she needed only one more thing before she sat down and got started: a man. Someone with a real edge to him. She was sure he was that man.

She told Didi he could have her any time she wasn't working, and he could have all the coke he could snort. That was her offer. Take it or leave it. Then she gave him a little flash up her red miniskirt to show him just what he'd be leaving if he said no.

Didi told her he didn't do drugs. Gayle Shipton's knees slapped together audibly and she almost walked away. But then she remembered the other half of her offer. What about that, she asked.

"I always was partial to anything shiny and pink," Didi allowed.

Gayle Shipton was so happy with his response she not only took him home, she offered him the possibility of doing an uncredited punch-up of any scene in which she bogged down. And since she was getting five hundred thousand dollars for her rewrite, she was prepared to be generous.

But the woman, running on coke and speed the past four days, hadn't bogged down anywhere, in bed or at her rat-a-tat-tat computer.

Besides, Didi had his own project in mind. One that involved serious money.

The woman didn't miss a keystroke when he put his hands on her shoulders, so he gave her right nipple a little twist. Just living up to his billing. She was the one who'd said he was dangerous.

"I gotta go out," Didi told her when she looked up, startled.

It took Gayle Shipton a minute to remember who *he* was. Then she smiled. "I've been meaning to ask, will you drive me down to Betty Ford when I finish this fucker? I've got a room reserved. We'll put you up somewhere nice in the Springs."

"Keep treating me right, we'll see."

That was close enough. Gayle went back to beating the hell out of her keyboard. Didi watched for a moment, one professional admiring another. If the movie went by as fast as she typed it, he might give it a chance after all.

Didi showered and got dressed. He donned a midnight blue silk suit, sunglasses, and a broad brimmed hat whose color was almost as cool a gray as his eyes. He left his Beretta in his suitcase. He'd warned Gayle not to mess with his case. But the way the woman was cranking on her movie script he doubted she'd get up to pee before he got back.

Didi borrowed Gayle's little froggy black Porsche 911. He let the sport car's engine rev for a moment, savoring the muted growl of another fast, tight, and if necessary, lethal machine. Then he sped out of Gayle's garage and went looking for the Englishman that Jimmy's boy, Junior Cardwell, had mentioned last week.

Didi fished in the still waters of his mind for the Englishman's name.

Ring, he recalled. Colin Ring.

***

"Colin Ring," the librarian said, handing three books to Deputy Chief Gosden with a look of disdain on her face.

"What?" Oliver asked. "You've read them, and they're no good?'

"I haven't read them, and all three were purchased by my predecessor."

The deputy chief didn't want to hear anybody else's gripes. He also didn't want to go back to his office where he'd likely be distracted. The library was part of the Muni Complex just like police headquarters. If somebody just *had* to see him, they only had to walk down the hall. He thanked the librarian for her help and took the books to a carrel in a quiet corner.

It didn't take long before Oliver decided that pissing all over people's reputations was what Colin Ring liked to do best. He wasn't a great writer, but he conveyed a sense of venom in his work that was powerful. Repugnant, too. The deputy chief understood now why the librarian had turned up her nose.

Ring's first book, the only one Oliver dimly remembered hearing of, bludgeoned a famous singer. It exposed her as a drug abuser who battered the two children she'd so publicly adopted. Ring also detailed the fact that the woman had been abused as a child herself: Mom had set her hair on fire one day when an audition hadn't gone well. The singer's scalp had been scarred and hair regrowth had been incomplete. Thus the reason she always wore such ludicrous wigs, and had a hard time keeping a husband, Ring asserted. None of the singer's own suffering was offered as mitigation for the battery Ring claimed she inflicted on her own children. Rather, it was cause for alarm, a warning that the authorities ought to take her kids away from her.

As Oliver thought he recalled, that warning had been heeded. He also seemed to remember the singer had been confined to a mental hospital after attempting suicide.

Ring had also destroyed the career of a leading man by revealing that he was both a homosexual and a pedophile. The biographer waxed nauseatingly righteous in this effort, claiming that he was saving innocent young boys from a predatory monster. He may even have been right. But his target, even at the height of his career, had been strictly a B-list actor, who had been reduced to doing infomercials by the time Ring got around to knifing him. The library book was dusty, telling the deputy chief it wasn't borrowed frequently. Oliver couldn't imagine it had sold well either.

The last hatchet job was a bio on a movie studio head who was found guilty of income tax evasion after Ring detailed that the man wrote off the cost of hookers and drugs as a miscellaneous business expenses. That might have tickled or terrified Hollywood insiders, Oliver thought, but it had to make most of America yawn.

If you didn't eviscerate somebody who spent a lot of time in *front* of the camera, somebody the public really knew and considered a personal acquaintance, or better yet really knew and already hated, you were nothing in the character assassination business.

So Colin Ring had blown three people out of the water, but, in a business sense, only his first target had been worth shooting in the first place. The deputy chief checked the copyright dates of all three books and saw that the most recent one had been published ten years ago.

He wondered if Ring had picked the wrong target again in Jimmy Thunder.

Oliver knew that a lot of conspiracy-minded African Americans thought whitey was out to get any black man who made more than minimum wage. But he'd never bought that. Black people had character flaws, bad luck and the right to fail like anyone else. And who would really give a rat's ass if Jimmy Thunder dropped off America's cable TV channels tomorrow? Or stayed there for the next forty years.

But … but if Jimmy Thunder could be convicted for — or even just plausibly accused of — crucifying his saintly son to keep his fame and fortune, why, people would buy that book by the truckload. Colin Ring would be back in the big time.

More than ever, the deputy chief liked the Englishman as his doer.

CHAPTER 33

By lunchtime, Ron had worked his way through the five-star hotels and was halfway through the four-star tier. Nobody had a Didi DuPree registered, or recognized the photo of the man that the chief had shown them. But the concierge at the Renaissance, an astute middle-aged redhead whose nametag read Marjorie Fitzroy, gave the picture of Didi a prolonged examination.

Ron waited patiently while she sorted out her thoughts.

"I may have seen this man, but not looking like this," she said.

"What do you mean?" Ron wanted to know.

"Well … look at the shape of his head. It's basically narrow and rectangular but his jaw forms a fairly sharp V. Then there are the high, prominent cheekbones. I saw a man who shared those characteristics, but he wasn't clean-shaven. He had a goatee. I couldn't see his eyes because he wore sunglasses. I couldn't tell about the forehead or the hair because he had a hat on. But I could give you at least a maybe."

"You're very perceptive," Ron complimented.

"Thank you. I worked my way through college as a life-drawing model. While all the students were busy looking at me, I had nothing to do except look back. I got really good at studying faces. I've found it pays to keep up that skill in this job, too."

Ron asked for a description of the hat and sunglasses. Gray hat with a broad brim over elliptical silver frames with black lenses, Marjorie Fitzroy told him.

The chief thanked the concierge for her help. She told him anytime.

He used the lobby phone to call Sergeant Stanley. He relayed the description of the man the concierge had seen and asked the sarge to have Didi Dupree's image digitally modified on the department's suspect ID software. He was to be disappointed, at least temporarily.

"System's down, Chief. There's a ghost in the machine. Computer techs are working on it right now."

"If it lasts more than a couple of hours, do it the old-fashioned way. See if you can find a sketch artist."

"What? You mean someone who can actually draw by hand?"

"I thought you knew everyone in town, Sarge."

"Yeah, but this one's a reach."

The chief gave Sergeant Stanley Marjorie Fitzroy's name. "I bet *she* knows somebody who could do it."

"Yes, sir," the sarge said, his nose slightly out of joint.

"You might enjoy talking with her, anyway," the chief mollified. "One knowledgeable pro sharing information with another."

"Yes, sir."

"Don't sulk, Sarge. She's very nice. Very sharp. Good-looking, too."

"Sure, but will Mom like her?" Sergeant Stanley asked deadpan.

Ron laughed. "Touché, Sarge. But if the computer doesn't come back up soon, give her a call. Work something out. And there's one more thing I'd like you to do. The next time you rotate the car outside Jimmy Thunder's estate, have the officers watch for Deacon Meeker. If he comes out, have the watchers radio for a unit to tail him. He might just lead us to cousin Didi."

"Will do, Chief."

Ron hung up and considered what to do next.

The growl in his stomach told him that it better be lunch. He was going to need something to eat before he could continue his rounds. He drove over to What the Hell, a burger place that thumbed its nose at the nutritionally correct, served king-size charcoal grilled patties on jumbo sesame seed buns, and piled on the extras until the customer said stop. Ron had told the owner, Sherm Mason, that if he ever decided to franchise the place, Ron would invest all of his pension fund for a piece of the action.

Sherm, a genial black man, responded that he liked living in Goldstrike too much to be distracted by taking his business elsewhere. But he was thinking he might someday open a rib joint locally with a similar approach to dining. Call the place No Bones About It. He said if he did, he might let the chief buy a small interest.

Ron finished his burger with a smack of his lips. He knew he'd have to do an extra half hour in the gym that night to work off his indulgence. A price well worth paying, to his mind.

On impulse, he decided to take a break from looking for Didi DuPree.

He'd go and see if he could find Texas Jack Telford at home today.

Ron not only found Texas Jack at home, he found him atop it. Jack was up on the roof of the new addition to his house nailing a sheet of plywood to the frame. With all his hammering, Jack didn't hear Ron drive up. Nor did he hear the chief approach on foot. In fact, Ron had to call out to the five time poker champ before the man knew he had company.

And then the presence of someone so unexpectedly close startled Texas Jack. He sent a box of nails flying. Ron had to duck as a torrent of pointed steel missiles flew at him.

"Jesus, who was that?" Jack yelled from his perch. "Are you all right?"

Ron lowered the forearm he'd raised to shield his eyes. It was polka-dotted with a dozen beads of blood, but none of the wounds felt more than superficial.

"It's me, Jack. Ron Ketchum. Sorry I took you by surprise like that."

"I'll be right down, Ron. Hope to hell you didn't get hurt."

"No, I'm all right."

The chief bent to pick up the nails that had scattered all over the ground near him. He'd gathered a handful when he experienced the shock of recognition. These were exactly the same kind of nail that had been taken out of Isaac Cardwell. He looked over his shoulder and saw Texas Jack had his back to him as he made his way down the ladder from the roof.

Ron pocketed one of the nails.

He couldn't conceive of any reason why Jack would have wanted to kill Isaac Cardwell. But the man had been Jimmy Thunder's alibi. He was supposed to have been at Thunder's estate on the night of the murder. Who knew what kind of relationship the poker champ had with the televangelist? Ron certainly didn't. But he was going to bring his purloined nail into the lab and compare it with the ones taken from the crime scene. Just to make sure he wasn't imagining things.

"Good Lord, look at your arm!" Texas Jack said, hurrying toward the chief.

Jack was in his early sixties, but he was as whipcord lean as any cowboy from his namesake state. A multi-millionaire from his winnings and his books on how to play poker, he looked completely at home in his work worn jeans and denim shirt. He had steel gray hair worn short enough that he didn't have to mess with it, and deep blue eyes that missed absolutely nothing that went on at a card table.

But his poker face was almost comically distorted as he gawked at Ron's arm. The blood from each of the puncture wounds had run down Ron's forearm and combined with the flow from the others. The chief looked like he'd been slashed from wrist to elbow.

"It's not nearly as bad as it seems," Ron said. "If you've got a paper towel, I can just blot up the blood."

But Texas Jack insisted Ron come inside. When Maria, the housekeeper, saw the chief's arm, she exclaimed and fussed over him, too. Ron washed off his arm with cold water in the kitchen sink, dried himself off with paper towels, and applied the antiseptic spray he was given.

He declined Jack's offer of a shot of whiskey, but took Maria up on an iced tea.

When the two of them were sure Ron was all right, Maria disappeared, and Jack seated Ron at his kitchen table. That was fine with the chief; it was time they got down to business.

"Jack, I'm investigating the murder of Reverend Isaac Cardwell, and the reason I'm here is that your name has come up."

Now, the cardplayer's face and voice were perfectly neutral. "It has?"

"Yeah. Jimmy Thunder told me he was playing cards with you last Thursday night."

"Oh, okay. I see now. Well, that's right. We were playing cards. We play once, sometimes twice a month. Usually at his place. But every once in a great while he'll come out here."

Ron told Texas Jack that Thunder had claimed the game had gone on all night.

"That's what usually happens when we play. And I don't own a wristwatch so I can't tell you exactly what time I left his place. But I can tell you it wasn't dawn or even close to it. Let's just say it was several hands and several grand earlier than normal."

Which inclined Texas Jack's story closer to that of Buster Lurie, the gas station attendant, than the one Jimmy Thunder told.

"What was the reverend's mood that night?"

"Well, that was a little off, too. I mean he's not a bad player for an amateur, and he knows to keep a straight face when he plays his cards. But there was something about his eyes, I remember, like he was a little edgy. And I didn't think it had to do with the game."

"Does the reverend set himself a limit for what he can lose?"

Texas Jack's face remained as impassive as ever, but he took an unusually long time to answer. In fact, Ron had to prompt him.

"Is this too personal a question?"

"No. It's … well, you may have heard I have a hard time getting any kind of a game in town these days. There are only two, maybe three fellas in town who'll play me. Jimmy's one of them. So it isn't so much they decide how much they can lose. It's more like I decide how much I'll take on any given night. I make it enough so they don't think I'm coddling them, but not so much they stop playing."

Ron nodded.

"I hear you still like to play basketball," Jack said.

"That's right."

"Well, imagine how you'd feel if nobody'd ever let you touch a ball again."

"Awful," Ron said sincerely. Thwarted, desperate and depressed, too.

"So that's why I called it an early night. As I say, Jimmy looked spooked about something and I felt I better go easy."

"He didn't mention what was bothering him, did he?"

"No, he didn't."

Ron thanked Texas Jack for his time and the iced tea.

Jack said he was welcome. Then he asked Ron if he could hitch a ride with him. Jack's car had conked out on the way back from Nevada yesterday, and he wanted to pick it up at the garage.

"Sure. My pleasure," Ron said.

On the drive into town, the chief picked up on something that had niggled at his mind the past few minutes.

"The mayor must be one of those two or three guys who'll play cards with you."

"Why do you say that?" Texas Jack asked.

"He's the only source I can think of for how you know I play basketball."

Texas Jack gave Ron a crooked grin.

"You're not going to go out and arrest your boss if I admit it, are you?" he asked

Ron laughed at the idea and shook his head.

"Well, then, I'll admit that when Clay Steadman is in town he writes me a check every few weeks that makes my remaining years more secure."

Jack's reference to a means of payment sparked a synapse for Ron. It made him think about the idea that Jimmy Thunder might be going into the money-laundering business. Which brought up another question.

"Does Reverend Thunder pay by check, too? Or does he use cash?"

Texas Jack chose to remain silent again.

"I'm afraid that's more than idle curiosity, Jack. It could have a bearing on my investigation." Not that the chief wanted to tell Texas Jack, but if there was dirty money already in Thunder's pipeline, and he used any of it to pay his gambling debts, Ron might have to impound Jack's winnings. Assuming the poker champ still had the cash on hand.

"Is this a private conversation we're having here?" Texas Jack wanted to know.

"Nobody in the car but you and me."

"Well, like I told you, I don't like to win too much at any one time. But the problem with Jimmy is, he's run up quite a tab with me. He owes me close to two hundred thousand dollars. That was another reason I went home early that night. What's the point of building up a pile of markers?"

"You don't think Jimmy Thunder will repay you?"

"I've got my doubts," Texas Jack admitted. "At least for the short term. I think the man has himself a serious cash flow problem."

Just what Ashanti Royce and DaChelle Chenier had told Ron.

Jack's assessment lent further credibility to the idea that Jimmy Thunder might be desperate enough to get into some big time crime with Didi DuPree. But would Thunder have been desperate enough to have his own son killed?

The more Ron thought about it, the more he wanted to talk with DuPree. He also wanted to renew his conversation with Ms. Royce and Ms. Chenier. They may have been providing sexual favors to Jimmy Thunder, but it made more sense to the chief that their primary purpose had been to further the money-laundering scheme — rather than to help Thunder with his ministry, as they had claimed. It was just too much of a coincidence that the two women and DuPree should all leave Thunder's mansion within days of each other.

To Ron, it was a case of three very slick rats abandoning a ship that if not actually sinking had at least sprung a serious leak.

Ashanti and DaChelle had indicated they were going to L.A. Ron still had friends in the LAPD. He'd call and ask if the department had a professional acquaintance with the ladies. Ask his pals to be on the lookout for DuPree, too, in case he showed up down there.

Driving on autopilot, Ron braked for an intersection with a four way stop. A pickup truck stopped across the intersection in the on-coming lane and honked its horn. The noise jarred Ron's consciousness back into the here and now. There was no cross-traffic, so the chief didn't know what the pickup driver was honking about.

Then Ron saw that the pickup driver was Art Gilbert.

Gilbert drove across the intersection and stopped even with Ron's window.

"Glad I saw you," the landscaper said. "I thought of something else you maybe should know."

"What's that?" Ron asked.

Gilbert noticed that there was someone with Ron. He scrunched down to see who it was. Texas Jack looked back at him.

"You want me to tell you now?" Gilbert asked.

Ron thought about it. He looked at Texas Jack. Jack was still looking at Art Gilbert.

"You'll keep anything you hear to yourself, won't you, Jack?" Ron asked.

Texas Jack nodded, finally putting his eyes on Ron. "Sure thing."

"Okay, Mr. Gilbert. Go ahead."

"Well, last week, there was this British fella. He tried to bribe his way onto my crew so he could gain access to Reverend

Thunder's estate."

Colin Ring, Ron thought immediately. "What did you tell him?"

"Turned him down flat. He got kinda mouthy about it until I picked up an electric hedge trimmer. Then he went on his way."

"This was before Isaac Cardwell was killed?"

"The day before. I don't know if it means anything. I thought you could sort it out."

"I'll do my best. Thank you, Mr. Gilbert."

Art Gilbert nodded and drove off. Ron put his patrol unit in motion.

"I know that guy from somewhere," Texas Jack told the chief.

"Who? Art Gilbert?"

"Yeah. I've met him before. Or at least seen him."

"He keeps the grounds for both Jimmy Thunder and the mayor. Maybe you saw him at one or both of their places."

Texas Jack shook his head. "That's not it."

But Jack couldn't recall where he'd met Art Gilbert. Not before Ron dropped him off.

CHAPTER 34

After reading as much of the collected works of Colin Ring as he could stomach, Oliver Gosden went to see Alta County District Attorney Bob Heath. The deputy chief explained to the DA his suspicions concerning Ring. Oliver asked if there was any way they could persuade a judge to issue a subpoena for Ring's notes on his biography of Jimmy Thunder.

The deputy chief said he might find something incriminating in them.

But the district attorney only laughed. "Subpoena a writer's notes based on nothing more than a cop's hunch? Try that and you'll have the wrath of every scribbler in the country descend on you. You'll be on shit lists from the supermarket tabloids to the Harvard Law Review."

"What are they going to do me?" Oliver asked. "Send hit men?"

"Worse. They'll send lawyers. They'll fill your life with misery."

"Hey, didn't they subpoena that screenwriter's stuff at the O.J. trial? You know, all those notes or whatever that proved Mark Fuhrman said, 'Nigger, nigger, nigger.'"

"The defense team did that. Not us minions of the state."

"So what's sauce for the goose ain't sauce for us? Is that what you're telling me? What about talking to some of the eggheads over at the CCL?"

The CCL was the Center for Constitutional Law, a think tank established in town by Clay Steadman as a counterpart to the

American Civil Liberties Union. The ACLU's charter was to protect the individual from a society that might deny him his constitutional rights. The CCL's raison d'etre was to formulate constitutionally valid laws to protect society from individuals who refused to recognize anybody's rights to be secure in their life, liberty or property.

The mayor said in creating the CCL he was in no way diminishing the vital work of the ACLU. Rather he was trying to establish a balance of interests that previously had not existed. But the ACLU had been so pissed at Clay Steadman they refused to accept any further donations from him. On the other hand, cops all across the nation applauded the fact that they finally had some legal heavyweights working their corner of the ring.

Hence Oliver Gosdens suggestion to Bob Heath.

"I'll do that for you, Deputy Chief. And maybe they'll surprise me and come up with some angle to help you. But you know what I think they'll say?"

"What?" Oliver asked dryly.

"I think they'll say that if nothing else you won't be able to get this man's notes because all he'll have to do is invoke his Fifth Amendment right against self-incrimination. Because, at heart, you're looking to hang him with his own words."

"Shit," Oliver lamented. Heath was right. Short of stealing Ring's notes, he wasn't going to get them.

"Sorry, Deputy Chief. If this guy is your killer, you're going to have to do some more police work to get him."

So, that was just what Oliver decided to do. He was going to stick as close to Ring as the man's own shadow. He was going to dog his steps, make him sweat and scoop him up when he cracked. Problem was, Oliver couldn't find the bastard.

He wasn't at his hotel, and when the deputy chief started checking all of the writer's local haunts, as squeezed out of his old friend the Swiss hotel manager, he was always one step behind. Ring had already come and gone. Or he didn't show up at the same time every day. All the bartenders, waiters, waitresses, hostesses, customers and barflies that Oliver talked to knew Ring. They liked him, too. He was described as gregarious, quick to buy the next round, an amusing storyteller and a good tipper. And, man oh man, did he ever listen when you had any dirt to dish.

But after several hours of hard effort, Oliver hadn't been able to find his man.

He had heard something interesting at his last stop, though. A bartender told Oliver, "Yeah, Colin was here about an hour and a half ago. Had a pint, saw there was no crowd to speak of and took off."

No, the bartender told the deputy chief, Ring hadn't said where he was heading.

"But here's something," the barman informed Oliver. "There was another guy looking for him, too."

"Who was that?" the deputy chief inquired.

"Don't know the gent, and he didn't give a name."

"What'd he look like?"

"Gray hat, shades and a goatee."

"But you weren't able to help him, either, right?"

"No," the bartender said. "But he came in just fifteen minutes after Colin split. So maybe he had better luck finding him."

Ron's manhunt for Didi DuPree failed to yield results by five that afternoon. With a dozen lower end motels still to check, Ron decided to turn his energies elsewhere for the remainder of the day. He returned to police headquarters and his office.

Dinah, his secretary, had gone home for the day, so he picked up his phone and called Sergeant Stanley's extension himself. He asked the Sarge to bring in the evidence bag that contained the nails taken from the body of Isaac Cardwell. Sergeant Stanley appeared in his doorway within minutes.

"Come on in, Sarge, and close the door," Ron said.

The sergeant followed orders and took a seat facing the chief across his desk. Sergeant Stanley laid the evidence bag containing the nails in front of Ron. The chief examined the nails through the transparent plastic of the evidence bag. Each of them was stained with blood from being driven through Isaac Cardwell's body and being removed from the same. In addition to the bloodstains, there were smudges of black on the nails from penetrating the charred exterior of the lightning-struck incense cedar tree.

But for all their discoloration they were exactly the same kind of nails as the one Ron now took from his pocket. Sergeant Stanley's eyes went wide when he saw the match.

"Jesus," Caz Stanley whispered. "Where'd you get that nail?"

"Texas Jack Telford's house," the chief replied.

"You're kidding?"

Ron shook his head. "It seems Reverend Thunder owes Jack almost two hundred thousand dollars in gambling debts."

The sarge processed all the new information quickly.

"Chief, that might be a lot of coin to you or me, but it's gotta be lunch money for Texas Jack."

"He seemed to consider it a substantial sum when he mentioned it to me."

Both men looked at the unblemished nail on the chief's desk. Then the sarge asked, "Jack doesn't know you have that, does he?"

Ron shook his head.

"It'd have to be a matter of principle more than money," Sergeant Stanley insisted.

The chief gave that idea some consideration. Texas Jack had told him the he was careful about not winning too much from the handful of men who'd still sit down at a card table with him. So money *wasn't* his primary consideration. Love of the game was. But if one his opponents refused to pay what Jack had won, that would remove any sense of legitimacy to the game. Reduce it to a charade. Implicitly make a mockery of Jack.

That might piss him off, all right, but enough to crucify a man?

The intuitive sergeant seemed to understand Ron's silence almost completely.

"If Texas Jack killed Isaac Cardwell like that, it could have been as a warning. Pay up or you're next."

That paralleled Ron's idea that Didi DuPree might have killed

Isaac as a warning to his father. Ron was not happy that his suspect list was expanding when he wanted it narrowed.

"When we're done here, run Texas Jack's name with NCIC. Let's see if his past isn't more colorful than everybody already thinks."

"Yes, sir."

"Any movement at the Thunder estate?" Ron asked.

"No. Nobody in or out all day. They're hunkered down."

"Any word out of Mahalia Cardwell?"

Sergeant Stanley shook his head.

"Any feedback on the lion situation?"

"A day goes by without any more bad news, people start to lighten up. Not that there are many runners or hikers out on the woodland trails. But in town the pedestrian traffic is back to normal and the cafés are full."

"How about the media? Are they behaving themselves?"

"I think they're getting bored. Annie Stratton is encouraging the notion there are greener fields elsewhere for them. They might start buying into the idea soon. Even Ben Dexter hasn't come out yet with that story accusing you of harassing Reverend Thunder."

"That's the best news I've heard all day. Okay, Sarge, let's keep this information about Texas Jack strictly between you and me. We'll look at it some more after you do the background check on him."

"Yes, sir."

As Sergeant Stanley picked up the evidence bag, the chief handed him the nail he'd stolen from Texas Jack's house.

"Sarge, find out every place in town where they sell this kind of nail."

"Sure thing, Chief."

Thinking ahead to tomorrow, Ron had one final question.

"By the way, did you ever get in touch with the concierge at the Renaissance about finding a sketch artist for that likeness of Didi DuPree?"

"Yes, sir," Sergeant Stanley said, seeming uncharacteristically sheepish. "I'm meeting Marjor — I'm meeting Ms. Fitzroy at the hotel in an hour. She seemed to think she could be of help herself. I should have something on your desk in the morning."

"Very good, Sergeant." Ron kept a straight face as Dan Stanley left. But he found the idea that he might have played the inadvertent matchmaker for his dedicated bachelor sergeant both amusing and gratifying.

With things at least temporarily quiet, Ron thought it would be a good time to go shoot some hoops.

CHAPTER 35

Corrie Knox took a swig of water from the canteen that Tucker Marsden had offered her. She made sure she'd left him a last gulp and handed it back. He finished it off. It had been a long day and they were both tired.

The sun was lowering and the temperature was dropping. The sweat that had flowed through the heat of the day was starting to dry on their bodies. Tuck pulled his shirt away from his chest.

They had to be especially vigilant now. Their physical resources were nearing depletion. Their senses were dulled. And mountain lions hunted at twilight. All day, they had tracked the animal, expending as much energy on watching, listening, and maintaining field position — placing yourself for a clear shot if your prey broke from cover — as they had hiking up and down the mountain.

"The fucker's still out there," Tucker said softly. "He's been leading us around in circles all day."

"Damn, I wish we had a dog," Corrie lamented quietly.

"I'd want three. Give us three good dogs and a guy who knows how to handle them and we could have bagged this bastard in time to have lunch by the pool."

"Whine, whine, whine," Corrie retorted. But she said it with a smile, and Tucker smiled back.

"What do you think, we have another half hour before it gets too dark to see?"

"Too dark for us to see," Corrie replied.

"Whaddya say we try to get this cat to follow us for a change?"

"Yeah, as long it's in the direction of our truck."

The two game wardens moved carefully through the forest of alpine evergreens. The shadows of the trees lengthened. Each pool of darkness had to be approached with the utmost caution. Their rifles were lethal, but only if you had the time to get off a good shot. There was no question that with the coming of night the odds were quickly shifting in favor of the lion.

With the light about to fall past the point where a clean shot would be possible, they headed directly for the highway. It was time to get out of the woods. Time to get out in the open where the cat wouldn't have any cover.

As they set foot on the pavement, knots of tension in their necks and shoulders began to unwind. Their truck was parked at a scenic overlook about a quarter mile downhill from where they stood. Five minutes and they'd be on their way into town.

"Well, hell, boys and girls, that was certainly a fun day," Tucker said.

"Let's do it again real soon," Corrie agreed wearily.

"I know. We'll come back tomorrow."

They'd walked only twenty yards down the road when they heard an animal grunt. The sound had an almost mocking, derisive quality to it.

Tucker frowned. "That sonofabitch is just right inside those trees there laughing at us. Why don't we see if we can have the last laugh?" He headed back up the road, trying to pinpoint the animal. Then he veered toward the trees.

Corrie yelled, "Tucker, stop! It's too dark. You'll never see him."

She was greatly relieved when he heeded her warning.

Then he cupped a hand to his mouth and shouted at the trees. "Think you're so smart? Well, we're going to dinner. What the hell are you going to do?"

He turned his back on the woods and started down the road toward Corrie.

"Thanks," Tucker said. "You were right. False pride will get you killed every ti—"

The mountain lion struck from the trees like a bolt. It leaped and hit Tucker Marsden from behind, high on his back and shoulders. The impact sent the big game warden tumbling down the slope of the road head over heels, the cat scrambling right along with him.

By instinct, Corrie jumped out of the way, up against the face of the mountain. Then she shouldered her rifle, but the two moving bodies were already several yards downhill of her. By now, Tuck was purposely continuing to roll, trying to keep the cat from getting a purchase on him, trying to keep those ghastly fangs from crushing his neck. Corrie had no way to take a shot at the cat without risking that she'd kill Tucker.

But she had to do something. The cat was pummeling her partner with its paws, and pretty soon one of its swipes would bring him to a stop. That or its razor sharp claws would sever a major blood vessel. In the dark gray wash of the day's last light, shooting downhill, Corrie snapped off three quick shots from her Winchester 94.

She didn't want to hit anything. Rather, her intent was to fire scant inches above the tumbling, scrambling bodies. Close enough for the cat to feel the passage of the rounds, hear flat, echoing cracks of the rifle shots to know it was in danger.

Her aim must have been off though, because she heard a feral howl of rage and pain — and was reasonably sure it hadn't come from Tuck. Her heart leaped with joy at the thought she might have gotten lucky and nailed the cat. But then she saw the lion escape into the trees, moving somewhat unsteadily, but not as if it had been shot.

Corrie ran down the road to where Tucker lay curled on his side. She knelt next to him, her rifle pointed at the trees in case the cat made another try. But there was no sign that the animal was coming back.

"Jesus," Tucker gasped in pain. "I feel like I've been through a threshing machine."

Corrie dropped her eyes to him for just a second.

He was a mass of abrasions from the road surface and lacerations from the cat's claws. A flap of his scalp hung loose. He shirt and pants were in bloody tatters.

"I think I broke my right leg," Tuck groaned.

"I'll get you out of here," Corrie promised. She kept her eyes on the trees. "I thought I might have hit him, but I don't know."

"You didn't. Those shots were damn close, though." Tuck had to grind his teeth to master a wave of pain. "You *were* just trying to scare the fucker away, right?"

"Of course."

"Good. I'd hate to think you were willing to sacrifice me."

"Unh-uh. You've got a real future ahead of you when you decide to grow up."

Corrie used all her strength to help Tuck up to his good leg. She managed to do it while making him cry out only once. Tuck put his arm around Corrie's shoulders and they began a halting, three-legged walk to their truck.

Corrie held her rifle at the ready in her right hand.

"So, my shots did scare the lion off then?"

"Sorry, Annie Oakley. But it was more of a guy thing."

"What do you mean?"

"In all that tumbling and rolling and swiping and scrambling …"

"Yeah?"

Tuck smiled through his pain. "Right at the last second there, with the only good leg I had left …"

"What, Tucker?" Corrie asked with exasperation as they reached the truck.

"I kicked the fucker square in his nuts."

CHAPTER 36

Didi DuPree stood before the bathroom mirror in Gayle Shipton's house and shaved off his goatee. Too bad. He hadn't had it long, but he'd already come to like it. The beard had made him look … what was the word he was looking for?

Jazzy. That was it. Like he could be blowing clarinet in some smoky little place back home in the Big Easy.

But he'd heard from a bartender at a place he'd doubled back to in his search for Colin Ring that the deputy chief of police had been there looking for the man, too. The barman had even been straight enough with him — and with the tips Didi had been leaving he'd better be — to say that he'd mentioned Didi to the cop.

Didi was pissed but he didn't let it show. Best way to keep things cool was to be cool. He told the bartender it was no problem. He just asked what this cop looked like and what his name was so he could say hello if he happened to bump into him.

Oliver Gosden, he was told, and the barkeep gave him the description of a medium tall, muscular, dark-skinned nigger.

Didi thought he might see if this cop was dumb enough to have his address listed in the phone book. Small town cops sometimes were. Maybe he'd go burn down the cop's house for him. Give him something else to think about while Didi was out tending to business.

After Didi had given himself a clean shave, he grabbed a tube of goop he'd bought at a drug store. Bronzing cream the label said.

He was going to bronze himself up good. Get so dark they wouldn't serve him lunch at a soda fountain in Mobile.

Didi knew he was part spade. How big a part he wasn't exactly sure. He didn't really care, either. He knew he had an African nose and mouth, and pale skin and fair eyes. He was white *and* black, and you couldn't get any cooler than that.

Wave of the future, that's what Didi was.

But right now he was going to explore his dark-skinned heritage. That thought gave him another idea. Made him smile. He found a pair of scissors and clipped his hair close to the bone. Then he took his razor and started shaving his scalp. He'd bronze up his melon, too.

Gayle came in while he was shaving his head. She'd put on some silver silk lingerie since he'd last seen her. "What are you doing?" she asked, her eyes wide.

"Creating the new me, baby. I ain't just dangerous. I'm a man of mystery."

Didi wiped off his head and bent over for her. "Feel that."

She ran her fingers over his smooth pate.

"Imagine grabbing on to that mother while I'm licking your lollipop."

"God!" Gayle Shipton exclaimed. "I've just got to have you do some dialogue for me,"

Didi grinned and started applying the bronzing cream to his scalp. "You done enough work you can go out to dinner with me?"

"Yes ... but you know what you need?"

"What?"

"Wait here. I'll be right back." She returned quickly with a gold earring. It was a small, understated, elegant hoop. "I'll have to pierce your ear," Gayle said.

Didi laughed. "You go right ahead."

Let's see the cops or anyone else recognize him now, Didi thought.

Maybe he'd get lucky and find Colin Ring tonight. Show ol' Gayle just how dangerous he really was. See if she could handle it. If not, he hoped she was done with her script. Wouldn't be any rewrites if she got squeamish. But even if he didn't spot his prey tonight, it'd be all right. Didi was learning the man's habits, picking up his rhythms.

Ol' Colin Ring would be buying his last round any time now.

Ron's BlackBerry chimed while he was on the basketball court. Made him miss free throw number one twenty-three in a row. Right when he'd been thinking that a visionary league like the NBA might be ready to accept his suggestion for a designated free throw shooter. Somebody the coach could call on maybe only twice a quarter, once in any overtime period. Somebody who'd replace that useless twelfth man who sat on the end of the bench. Say some steely-nerved white guy who'd stayed cool when he'd been shot at, and would laugh at any chump fans trying to distract him as he calmly swished his two shots. Him, for instance.

Ron looked at the text message on his phone and called Corrie Knox. She answered on the first ring and did her best to sound calm.

"Can you get right over to Community Hospital?" she asked.

"Be there in five minutes."

He didn't need to ask why she was there.

"I'll be in the emergency room," she told him.

Ron pulled his uniform and his gun out of his gym locker, threw them in the back of his patrol unit, and drove to the hospital as fast as he could without using his lights and siren. No point fraying people's nerves any more than they already were.

"Who was it, and how bad is it?" the chief asked when he saw Corrie at the hospital. He had his badge pinned to the waistband of his gym shorts, and his holstered gun in his hand. A cop didn't leave either of those items in his car. Not even in an affluent place like Goldstrike.

"It was my partner, Tucker Marsden," Corrie explained. "He's going to be okay, but he's got a compound fracture of his right leg and multiple lacerations and puncture wounds."

They walked over to an empty waiting area. Ron asked how the attack occurred and Corrie told him.

"You're all right, though?"

"Only my pride is bruised, Chief. Only my pride."

"I don't see what you could have done that you didn't do."

"I don't either," Corrie admitted. "But I'm sure something will come to me."

"Maybe next time you should carry a knife," Ron suggested. "You can't get a clean shot, just grab your blade and wade right in."

For just a second Ron thought he'd pissed her off, that she might wade right into him. But then the image he'd conjured caught up with her and she laughed her deep laugh.

"Thanks for the jab," she said. "I'm not usually prone to self-pity."

"Sure. You've never let your partner get eaten by a lion before."

"Okay, okay. I'm over it." Then Corrie finally noticed the gym clothes Ron was wearing. "Interrupted your game, huh?'

He shrugged. "Just shooting free throws and spinning some middle-aged fantasies."

"Fantasies, huh?"

"Yeah … about how I could find a place in the NBA."

Corrie laughed again "Wow! You do have a rich imagination."

"Hey," Ron objected. "I want you to know I could have beat you at HORSE the other night."

"Oh, yeah? How?"

"By dunking the ball."

Corrie repressed more laughter. "You really expect me to believe that?"

"Want to put some money on it?" Ron asked evenly.

She looked him over, paying particularly close attention to his legs.

"How tall are you?"

"Six-two."

"Palm the ball?"

"With either hand."

She had one more question: "And how old are you?"

Ron had never been shy about his age, but now he had to force himself not to hesitate before answering. "Forty-eight."

Corrie looked him over again, this time from the bottom up. She studied his face. She calculated. She came to her decision.

"Tell you what," she said. "You show me you can dunk … and I'll indulge any other fantasy you may have for, say, a period of twenty-four hours."

"Oh, yeah?"

"Excluding any third parties, yeah. If you show me you can dunk."

"And if I can't?"

"I'll still be nice to you. Buy you a cane and a shawl. Visit you at the old folk's home once a month."

Ron started to laugh, but he cut it off as an ER doctor approached. He nodded to Ron and spoke to Corrie. "Warden Marsden is ready to be taken to his room. We've set his leg, debrided his wounds and sutured his scalp back in place. He's sedated now, and tomorrow we'll be transferring him, at his request, to a hospital near his home."

The chief asked, "Doctor, how many people are aware of this attack?"

The physician tallied the number in his head. "Six ER staffers that I know of. Two have gone on break, and I wouldn't be surprised if they've started talking about it with others."

"I wouldn't either," Ron said. "Did you notify the mayor?"

"No."

Corrie shook her head when Ron asked her if she'd spoken to anyone outside the hospital about the attack. He rubbed his face and cupped his chin.

"This is not something I want to keep secret, believe me. I just want to pass the word in the way that will do the most good and cause the least amount of fear."

"I'll talk to my people," the doctor said. "We'll do our best to keep it in-house, at least for tonight."

"Thank you," Ron said. "I'll go see the mayor. I'm sure he'll have some idea of how to proceed." Ron was about to leave for Clay Steadman's house when Corrie asked if he could wait for her for just a second. She wanted to say goodbye to Tucker.

He said he'd meet her in the parking lot.

Two minutes later, she joined him at his patrol unit.

"I was wondering if you have someone you could spare, someone to go after the cat with me. I think I can track it, but I'm not ashamed to admit I'd like someone to cover my back now that Tucker's out of the picture."

"There's no one else the state can send you?"

"Sure. But Fish and Game is a bureaucracy like any other part of government. It might take two days, three, or who knows how long. I want to go out tomorrow morning. You don't want to wait, do you?"

"No," Ron admitted, "I don't. Look, I'd go with you myself, but there's no way, politically, that I can afford to take time away from the Cardwell investigation."

"I appreciate that. I didn't mean you specifically."

"Shit. I feel like I should do it, though."

"Look, all I need is someone dependable. Someone who won't lose his nerve in a tight spot."

Oliver Gosden, Ron thought immediately.

Right behind the name came the idea that, in light of Mahalia Cardwell's *curse,* maybe it would do the town some good to see a black man help bag this frigging beast.

"I've got just the guy you need," Ron said. "He'll meet you at police headquarters."

"We'll need to head out first thing," Corrie informed him.

"He'll be there."

Assuming the deputy chief didn't quit after he pulled him off his Colin Ring investigation and made him go play Dan'l Boone, Ron thought.

CHAPTER 37

Wednesday

Ron was halfway out the door of his cabin with Corrie Knox the next morning when Clay Steadman called. He asked Ron to come over to his house immediately. The chief wanted to ask if he could postpone the meeting for thirty minutes, but his gut told him Clay had something serious to discuss. As of last night's deliberation about the latest attack by the lion, Clay hadn't decided what to do.

Apparently, now he had.

The problem was, Ron had called Oliver last night and told him to report in to headquarters at five a.m. that morning, but he hadn't told him the reason why. Now, Ron wouldn't be there to explain.

He informed Corrie of the situation. She took it in stride.

"Your deputy chief is the guy you say he is, he won't let either of us down."

Warden Knox drove off in her GMC 4x4 to collect her new hunting partner. Ron, still filled with misgivings, went to see the mayor.

Terry Castlewood was up early, moving quietly about the kitchen of his home while his parents still slept. He ate two bananas and washed them down with a pint of orange juice: potassium, magnesium, calcium, Vitamin C, and fructose. Everything he'd need for his morning run. He made a quick pit stop to empty his bladder, then stepped out to his backyard to stretch.

He knew his parents wouldn't like him going out for a run all alone, what with that mountain lion scaring the bejesus out of everyone. But, hell, it'd been a couple days now since the big cat had picked off that pooch. It was probably long gone by now. And, anyway, it was time to begin training for football.

Terry was the starting tight end on the Goldstrike High School football team. He'd made all-state last year, and, as a senior this coming year, he'd be a team captain. He had to be in shape when the squad got together for its first practice.

He had three scholarship offers already and expected at least a dozen more by the time his final high school season was over. Two years from now he intended to be an all-American. By that time the pro scouts would be saying he caught the ball like Kellen Winslow and was as tough as Mike Ditka — in Terry's opinion the two best tight ends ever to play the game.

At six-four and two-forty, the boy figured he was the perfect hybrid of his two idols.

And with plans like his, he was not going to let anything interfere with his training program. Including the police warning people not to run alone until the mountain lion was caught. To hell with that. He had to run, and it had to be uphill. That was how you built up leg strength.

Just to be on the safe side, though, Terry slipped back into the kitchen and helped himself to his mom's carving knife. The thing had a blade on it that was a good six inches long. He fastened it to the outside of his left forearm with two rubber bands.

At first light, Terry slipped out of his backyard and bounded along the street toward Highway 38, heading up into the mountains.

The August sun was brightening the day, but at 6,000 feet elevation, there was the first hint of autumnal coolness in the air. It wouldn't last long, but the brisk air charged Terry up. Made him glad he woke up early and got a jump on the rest of the world. He loped along the mountain road with the fluid ease only strong young muscles can provide. He was on the brink of greatness; he could feel it.

As he strode along, climbing the slope of the mountain, Terry looked at the forest on either side of the road. From what he'd heard, that mountain lion couldn't go much more than a hundred and sixty pounds. A guy that size, Terry would eat him alive. He'd almost *like* to have the damn thing come after him.

Yeah, he could see it now. He'd do in the beast, and its head would be mounted at the Muni Complex. There would be a plaque with his story on it: *Terry Castlewood killed this lion with his bare hands.* Okay, maybe not barehanded. He slipped the carving knife off his forearm and held it in his right hand.

But even if he did the big cat in with a knife, the reputation he'd have going into college would be awesome. What defensive lineman or linebacker would ever think he could scare Terry after he'd killed a lion? And the coaches, they'd —

Terry was so lost in fantasy he never felt the mountain lion stalking him, never heard its charge, never saw it pounce on his back.

He was slammed to the road surface like he'd been gang-tackled. The skin on his back felt like it was being ripped off in sheets. He knew then that the lion had him, and he'd made a terrible mistake. In savage confirmation of this judgment, he felt the lions fangs sink into the flesh around his neck.

But here the lion *was* overmatched. Terry had a twenty inch neck of which he was inordinately proud. He'd gone to great lengths to strengthen his neck to take on 300-pound linemen without getting it snapped. The big cat had to extend its jaws so wide, around so much dense muscle, that it couldn't bring enough pressure to bear to sever the boy's spine.

The bite was more than sufficient, however, to make every muscle in Terry Castlewood's powerful upper body spasm. The force of the sudden, unexpected contractions threw the lion off

Terry and flipped the boy onto his back.

Now, he could see the lion — and the big cat was coming back for him. It was with more than a little surprise, but not much comfort, that he realized he still had the carving knife in his hand. Years of being trained never to fumble the ball had instinctively made him keep his grip on the knife. But it seemed a pitiful defense against the horrifying array of dagger sharp teeth advancing upon him.

Still, he extended the blade. He didn't feel much like Tarzan now. Nothing like the hero he'd imagined himself to be only moments ago.

The big cat stopped and snarled as it saw the steel blade glinting in the sun. The animal recognized that its prey was putting up a defense. The lion darted to its left, hoping to circle the knife, but Terry kept the point of the blade between him and the predator. It's shriek of frustration made Terry's bowels turn liquid.

The mountain lion feinted the other way, but Terry grimly kept the cat at bay with the knife. Then the boy saw the lion gather the muscles of its rear legs. He started to shake, fearing the animal was about to attempt to leap over the knife and fall on him from above. He might be able to get the knife up in time to impale the cat, but it would still come down on him, and who knew if there'd be anything left by the time it was done with him.

He had to stop the big cat from pouncing, so he scrambled to his knees and thrust the knife at it as far as his arm could extend. He didn't even come close. The mountain lion backed off with a casual speed that mocked Terry's attempt. But then it made a mistake. Trying to remove the last obstacle between itself and its meal, the cat swiped a paw at the knife. The knife did go flying from Terry's hand. But the animal's footpad hit the knife's blade, and Mom kept her cutlery sharp. Blood poured from the cut.

The mountain lion roared with pain. It held its wounded paw off the ground.

Some deep-seated instinct for survival made Terry bounce to his feet. The lion snarled at the boy as he got up but it made no move to attack him. Terry thought the beast must be reluctant to put any weight on its injured, bleeding foot.

"Go on," he shouted, his voice ragged with fear. "Go on, you motherfucker, get the hell out of here!"

But the cat didn't run off. Instead, it lowered its wounded foot and advanced one tentative, limping step at a time on him. Terry backed up. He tried not to stumble, but he thought giddily if he'd had a cliff edge nearby he might prefer to jump than to let the lion have him.

His eyes darted to the verge of the road. He saw several loose rocks there. Without taking his eyes off the animal, he bent to scoop one up. Injured or not, the mountain lion was gathering itself for another run at him.

Terry's hand closed on a rock. He rose to full height, and fired it at the cat. The chunk of stone the size of a baseball caught the animal on the shoulder above its wounded foot. It's howl froze Terry to his bone marrow. But when he saw the beast recline on its haunches to relieve the pain in its front leg and paw, the spell was broken.

The boy ran down the mountain road faster than he'd ever run before. Roars and bellows followed him as the predator saw its prey disappearing. The soundtrack of many a future nightmare drove Terry to even greater speed.

He knew if the big cat caught up to him it would find a way to kill him.

But it didn't catch him. With his heart about to burst and his lungs on fire, Terry pushed through the gate of his backyard. He barely had time to register the horrified face of his father in the kitchen doorway before he collapsed.

Oliver Gosden, early to work, didn't know why he hadn't thought of the idea yesterday. Mahalia Cardwell was still in town. She was Colin Ring's only known source of venom against Jimmy Thunder. So if he wanted to find Ring, why didn't he just ask Mrs. Cardwell to call the Brit and invite him to her suite.

And if the old woman wouldn't help him out, he could muscle the people at her hotel to fake a call to Ring, saying Mahalia Cardwell wanted to see him, and draw him out. Then Oliver could have another talk with the sleazebag, and dog his steps from there.

There was no more need to go chasing after the sonofabitch. He'd tell Ron that was just what he was going to do . . . but where the hell was the chief after he'd dragged Oliver out of bed so early.

The deputy chief started flicking his cigarette lighter open and shut.

He was just about to go get a cup of coffee when Warden Knox poked her head in his office. Not a bad looking woman, Oliver thought. He wondered if the whispers going around the department about her and Ron were true. She seemed pretty young for the chief to him.

"Good morning, Deputy Chief," she said. "May I come in?"

Oliver nodded. He was surprised, however, when she closed the door behind her. She took a seat in a guest chair and looked right at him.

"The chief hasn't called you in the past few minutes, has he?"

"No, but I expect him any minute now."

"I'm afraid he won't be coming. Not right away."

Oliver wondered how she knew that, but he wasn't about to ask. Crossing the threshold into your boss's private life was always an iffy proposition. And not one to his liking at all.

"In that case, I have some matters to attend to, Warden Knox." Oliver started to rise.

"If you'll just give me a minute, Deputy Chief. The chief asked me to talk to you."

"He did?"

"Well, actually I said I'd do it because the mayor called the chief to his house."

"What's this all about?"

"It's about backing me up." Corrie told Oliver what had happened to Tucker Marsden the previous night.

"And Ron Ketchum said *I'd* back you up?"

Oliver couldn't help it, he flashed on all the old jungle movies from his boyhood. It was never the great white hunter who got eaten by the lion. It was always the poor black Stepin Fetchit helper who called the boss, "Bwana."

Corrie saw the trepidation on Oliver Gosden's face. "The chief said you wouldn't lose your nerve in a tight spot. He said you could look the devil in the eye and not blink."

"The devil doesn't scare me. He's a city boy like me. But going out in the woods, looking for a —"

There was a knock at Oliver's door.

"Excuse me, sir," Sergeant Stanley said, opening the door. "I thought I saw Warden Knox step in here." He looked at Corrie. "There's been another attack. A boy named Castlewood out on Highway 38 not twenty minutes ago. He's being taken to Community Hospital right now."

Corrie looked at Oliver. "I'm going to talk to that boy. Then I'm going after that cat. I'd like to have some backup, but if necessary, I'll go alone."

The look on Corrie Knox's face left no doubt she was serious.

"Well, shit," Oliver said.

But he got up and went with her.

After telling Sergeant Stanley to call his wife and tell her to keep their son at home and indoors that day.

"The first thing we have to do," Clay Steadman told Ron Ketchum, "is inform the town of what happened last night to Warden Marsden. I'll speak to the media again this morning."

Ron nodded. He had expected nothing less. Still, it grieved him that the media circus that might have been about to fold its tents and move on would now extend its stay indefinitely.

"The next thing we have to do is involve the community in a positive way, and I've already taken some steps in that direction."

"What do you mean?" Ron asked, feeling uneasy. He looked at the mayor across a coffee table positioned between the two men in Clay Steadman's living room.

"I mean that we've got to give people the sense that they're defending themselves."

"Isn't that my job? The job of my department?" Ron felt his forehead grow hot, and he knew he'd have to watch himself here. He and the mayor had never really butted heads, but this might be the first time.

Clay saw the anger in Ron's face, and almost rose to meet it. But the situation was more important than either of their egos. So he picked up the cup of coffee sitting on the table in front of him, leaned back and took a sip.

"With Warden Marsden gone," Clay asked, "what are we doing about this mountain lion? Let Warden Knox go after it alone or wait for the state to send a replacement?"

"She's going out after it this morning with Deputy Chief Gosden." At least, Ron hoped Oliver had agreed to accompany Corrie Knox.

"The deputy chief has experience at this kind of thing, does he?"

Ron frowned. "He's a solid man in any situation."

"But he's never been in this one before, has he?" the mayor said, making his point. Then he put his coffee cup down and leaned forward, leading with his chin if Ron wanted to take a poke at him. "I talked to Caz Stanley last night and asked him if anyone in your department had the skills to help Warden Knox."

"You didn't come to me before talking to one of my men?" Ron was having a really tough time now controlling his temper.

Clay Steadman just shrugged.

"Caz and I go back a long way. We're friends. If I want to talk to him, I talk to him. He knows I'm not trying to undermine your authority over your department, and I hope you can see that, too. But if you want, we can go out back, beat on our chests, and screech at each other."

There was no point in that, Ron thought. Everybody knew who the eight hundred pound gorilla in Goldstrike was. He chose to remain silent.

"Anyway," Clay continued, "Caz told me that you already asked him if you have any hunters in your department, and he told you no."

"That's right."

"But there are several hunters in town, and I know a lot of them. I've called a number of the most dependable of them this morning. To a man, they've agreed to help."

Ron's eyes narrowed. "Who are these men, and what are they going to help with?"

"That's where I want your input. Yours and Warden Knox's when she's available. Do we send them out into the woods with her — and the deputy chief, if you want to keep him there — or do we have them work with your officers as a sort of mountain lion SWAT team you can call on?"

"Who are these guys?" Ron repeated.

The mayor told him: two doctors, two lawyers, a business executive and an actor.

"The actor would be you?"

Clay Steadman nodded. "All of us have hunting experience."

Knowing the mayor was in his ride to the rescue mode at least made the reason behind the idea clear to Ron. It also told him that there was no way he was going to change Clay Steadman's mind. The thing that bothered him most, though, was that as much as he disliked the idea — and he hated it — he couldn't think of a better one.

So presented with lemons, he attempted to make lemonade.

"We'll have to get Warden Knox's input," Ron said, "but what I'd see would be three two-man patrols. You guys could watch the outskirts of town, be a defense against the animal jumping into somebody's backyard again. I think that was the incident that scared people most."

Clay nodded, accepting the suggestion.

"You'll need police radios to advise my department of your location and any situation that may arise," the chief said. "And unless it's a matter of life or death —"

"Or letting the lion get away," Clay added.

"Or that," Ron conceded. "You and your men will not fire a shot in this town unless I give you permission."

"Agreed."

"Sergeant Stanley will coordinate your patrol schedules."

"We'll work things out with him," Clay agreed.

"And this will be the one and only civilian *supplement* to the police force. Or you can find yourself a new chief."

Ron and Clay stared at each other and it might have gone on a long time, had the phone not rung. The mayor looked away and picked it up. He listened to the caller and said, "Right away."

Then he told Ron about the attack on Terry Castlewood, and they were on their way out the door. But Clay Steadman stopped Ron and told him not go to the hospital. Warden Knox and Deputy Chief Gosden were already on their way. Having Clay there, too, would be enough official representation.

The mayor told the chief to go find Isaac Cardwell's killer.

CHAPTER 38

"You're not being straight with me, Jimmy," Marcus Martin said. "You've got to tell me the truth. I'm your lawyer. Nobody can make me repeat a word that passes between us."

The attorney sat with Jimmy Thunder in the sunroom of his mansion. A spread of breakfast rolls and fresh fruit lay on the table between them. The lawyer was looking at his client, but the televangelist stared unheeding into the distance. Martin wasn't sure if the man had heard a word he'd said the past fifteen minutes.

Deacon Meeker stood at the entrance to the room with his arms folded across his chest, making sure there were no disturbances. Making sure he heard every word, as well.

"Jimmy, look at me," Martin said. When his words produced no result, he leaned across the table and grabbed Jimmy Thunder's wrist — and got a far nastier reaction than he'd ever expected. Jimmy pulled his arm free, and jumped to his feet. His eyes were wild and his mouth curled in a snarl. He looked like he was going to jump right over the breakfast table at Martin and rip his throat out. He might have done just that, except Deacon Meeker got to him in a hurry and wrapped both arms around the TV preacher.

"Be cool," Meeker urged softly. "Be cool now, Jimmy."

Then the deacon whispered something in his ear that Marcus Martin couldn't hear. Whatever he said, it calmed Thunder down. The moment of almost tender intimacy between the two men reminded the lawyer that they'd been in prison together. Being very careful to keep his face blank, Martin wondered just what experiences they'd shared in that den of Darwinian terrors. He honestly didn't think there had been a sexual relationship between the men, but they had to share some kind of bond, and he didn't want to know what is was.

Deacon Meeker got Jimmy Thunder back in his chair, whispered something more to him, and returned to his post at the door.

"All you've got to know is I didn't kill my boy," Jimmy told his attorney.

Marcus Martin nodded. "I do know that … but me knowing it is not enough. We've got to make sure *everybody* knows it. Make sure everybody *believes* it."

That fucking redneck Ron Ketchum had turned the tables on Martin again. Making that crack about having them surrounded, and then posting a cop car outside Jimmy's gates. Sure enough, he'd created a bunker mentality inside the Thunder estate. Nobody went out, not even for groceries. Anything they needed, they had it delivered. Anything that was delivered, Marcus Martin checked through it to make sure the cops hadn't planted a bug.

Jimmy's busloads of believers wouldn't be coming in anytime soon, either. The reverend's TV show, *The Sound of Thunder*, was in reruns for the foreseeable future. That could be plausibly explained as a consequence of a father mourning the loss of his son. But there was so much media in town — all of them demanding interviews, with only Ben Dexter being accommodated — that they were sure to notice that Jimmy had gone into a shell.

Denied the ability to fill their air-time and news-holes, the press would pick up on the cops parked outside and start speculating. Was an arrest imminent? Did the police have evidence against Reverend Thunder? Were they about to uncover something damning? *Could he really have killed his son?* Media masturbation like that could ruin Jimmy Thunder.

Marcus Martin tried to think of a legal means to force Ketchum to remove his cops from the street in front of Jimmy Thunder's estate. Parking that damn patrol car there twenty-four hours a day was like pinning a scarlet letter on Jimmy. Except in this case the letter was K for killer. But even if Martin found an effective legal argument to make the cops leave, he was leery that Ketchum might turn that victory around on him and transform it into a public relations debacle.

He could almost hear the questions that would be raised, among the public, if not in court. If Reverend Thunder's done nothing wrong, why should it bother him to have a police car around? What was he afraid of? What was he *hiding*?

That was just what Marcus Martin had been trying to find out when Jimmy blew up at him. Well, he wasn't going to make that mistake again. But he was going to try to get the man to stand up for himself.

"Jimmy ... Reverend Thunder, you can't let this man, this Ron Ketchum, make you cower. He is your enemy, not me. You have to go out and confront him publicly. I know you did that once, but with a man like this trying to beat you down, you have to stand up to him again and again and again, if necessary. He's not going to give up, and neither can you. You have to fight 'til you win. I can help you. Ben Dexter can help you. But in the end you have to stand up to him."

Jimmy Thunder looked at his attorney and confessed, "I'm afraid."

"Of Ron Ketchum?" Marcus Martin asked in disbelief.

The reverend shook his head.

"Then what? Tell me, and I'll help you."

"I don't know if there is any help for me."

"Let me be the —" Martin began, but Jimmy Thunder stood up and started walking away. "Where are you going?"

Considering the reverend's station in life, his answer shouldn't have surprised Marcus Martin, but it did. Even Deacon Meeker looked mildly astonished .

Jimmy Thunder said, "I'm going to pray for my son's soul."

When Ron arrived at police headquarters, he checked with

Sergeant Stanley to get the lay of the land. The deputy chief, he was told, had left with Warden Knox, but Ron already knew that from Clay Steadman. He asked the Sarge what kind of mood Oliver had been in when he left.

"Hurried, concerned … and pissed at you, Chief."

"Great," Ron muttered. "How'd your meeting with Marjorie Fitzroy go?"

Sergeant Stanley had a fine time with the concierge from the Renaissance Hotel. He had, in fact, made a date with her for Saturday night, providing there was no emergency to keep him on the job. But the chief didn't have to know all that, the sergeant felt.

"Quite productive," he said. "Ms. Fitzroy is something of a sketch artist herself. I offered to have the department pay for her services, but she declined. There's a likeness of the man she saw on your desk."

The sergeant had more to say, but he paused to look for the right words.

"What is it, Caz?" Ron asked.

"We got a response to our queries on Texas Jack. The computer turned up a hit."

Meaning Texas Jack had a criminal record, which made the Sarge unhappy. Jack Telford was well liked locally.

"That's on your desk, too, Chief. I'm still working on compiling a list of all the places in town that sell the kind of nail you asked about."

Ron commended the sergeant for his good work, and went to his office.

The drawing Marjorie Fitzroy had made was placed on Ron's desk side by side with the photo that the Texas prison authorities had provided of Didi DuPree. Even a quick glance revealed that the man Marjorie Fitzroy had seen, and then sketched, was almost certainly DuPree. Ron would have the drawing duplicated and have officers take copies and re-canvass the hotels he'd checked yesterday. He'd bring the original along with him to the places he'd visit today.

Maybe they were getting closer to the elusive Mr. DuPree.

But after the chief checked out Texas Jack he wondered if he was getting any closer to Isaac Cardwell's killer. Or simply enlarging the suspect pool.

At the age of eighteen, John Ralston Telford had been convicted of petty theft in Houston, having made off with twenty-seven dollars from a bake sale at a Baptist church. He'd been sentenced to ninety days in the Harris County Jail.

But on the third day of his incarceration, Texas Jack had been remanded to the prison wing of the county hospital and his sentence was suspended upon his hospital discharge ten days later.

The ever efficient Sergeant Stanley apparently had investigated this curious turn of events, because there was a name and a Texas phone number for Ron to call for the details of what had transpired. He picked up his phone and punched in the number.

After six rings, the call was answered by a gruff but not unfriendly voice with a deep Texas twang. "Gusek residence."

"Good morning. This is Chief of Police Ron Ketchum of Goldstrike, California calling. Am I speaking to Deputy Gus Gusek?"

"*Retired Deputy* Gusek. You got your man, Chief. Your sergeant told me I could expect your call."

"Did he mention the reason?"

"Yes, sir. He told me you wanted to hear about when Texas Jack Telford was a guest of Harris County, while I was working at the jail. That was some years ago, but given who that particular inmate turned out to be, I doubt anybody who heard that story forgot it."

Gusek told the tale to Ron.

Texas Jack was just getting started on his card playing career, and he'd found a game with a bunch of boys who worked at an oil refinery. Jack was sure he could make a pile in this game, but he lacked a stake. He asked his girlfriend, JoEllen Joslin, if he could *borrow* the proceeds of the bake sale that had just been held at her daddy's church. When Jack told JoEllen the reason he needed the money, she adamantly refused. He took it, anyway, when she wasn't looking. Jack won a hundred and seventy-nine dollars playing poker with the Baptist bake sale money. He was sneaking into the Jenkins' house through JoEllen's bedroom window after the game when he was caught by Pastor Henry Joslin. The pastor immediately suspected Jack of attempting an unspeakable sexual assault on his fair young daughter.

Denying that idea vehemently, Jack was forced to admit the real reason for his presence in JoEllen's bedroom. He naively thought neither Pastor Joslin nor JoEllen would mind his little transgression since he told them it was his intent to return not just the twenty-seven dollars he'd taken, but fifty-four dollars as a sign of his gratitude.

The moral outrage of hard rock Baptists, however, was not to be alleviated by a petty bribe. The Joslins squealed on Jack, pressed charges, and off to the hoosegow he went.

"What happened to him there?" Ron wanted to know.

"I'm getting' to that," Deputy Gusek responded.

The sad truth was, Jack got himself corn-holed. The big old boy who got put in Jack's cell on the second night of the young man's sentence did it. That kind of thing was just a fact of life behind bars. It could happen in almost any lockup. Most of the people who committed crimes knew it was one of the risks they took. The ones who didn't know, should have.

Texas Jack hadn't known, and when he learned the hard way, he refused to play along. He ignored the code of inmate etiquette that said you didn't rat on your fellow con no matter what he did to you. While Jack was getting raped, he started screaming at the top of his voice. He kept right on screaming until the guards knew they'd have to go in there and fetch him out before the prisoner who was trying to make Jack his punk killed him.

"You were the one who saved Jack, weren't you?" Ron asked Gusek.

"Yeah, I guess I was. I had a kid brother back then. Just a couple years younger than Jack. He was always gettin' in trouble, being arrested. I heard Jack screamin', and I just had to go help him out. Once I did, I took sort of an interest in him. Enough to find out what his story was anyway."

Even when they got Jack to the hospital, he still refused to keep quiet about what had happened. All his bellowing started to upset the doctors and nurses, and pretty soon respectable people took to whispering the dread word of reform. The authorities decided they didn't need all that hooraw, a bunch of do-gooders coming in and telling them how to do their jobs, so they cut Jack a deal. Close his trap and his sentence would be suspended as soon as he got better. Keep bellyaching and he'd go right back to the pokey to serve out his time — if he lived that long.

Jack took the deal.

Ron asked, "Just so I understand the situation, was the man who raped Jack Telford black?"

"As midnight in a coal mine," retired Deputy Gusek confirmed.

CHAPTER 39

Ron headed out in his patrol unit to continue his pursuit of Didi DuPree. But his search wasn't as single-minded as it had been the day before. What he'd just learned about Texas Jack Telford was preying on his mind, distracting him.

How deeply had it scarred Jack's soul to be raped as an eighteen year old by a black convict? Enough to kill an innocent man a lifetime later simply because he shared the same skin color? That seemed beyond belief — unless you'd worked as a homicide dick. Then you knew the motives, means and opportunities for the taking of a human life were endless.

Ron remembered being a rookie on the LAPD and hearing from an old-timer about a murder that had been committed in Encino in 1968. A man in his seventies had been gunned down as he was raking leaves off his front lawn. The killer turned out to be from the Irish Republican Army. The reason for the killing: the victim had betrayed the Easter Uprising in 1917.

Don't get angry, get even. No matter how long it takes.

No matter if the reason for evening the score doesn't exist outside of the killer's own sorry imagination. Maybe Isaac Cardwell had been killed not because he was black but because he'd borne an unfortunate resemblance to the man who'd raped Texas Jack. Or maybe it was that *plus* the fact that Isaac's father, Jimmy Thunder, was stiffing Jack for a lot of cash. Exactly what affront might have been committed against the poker champ was impossible to say.

In fact, Ron was far from sure that Texas Jack had killed Isaac Cardwell — but he knew that Jack had possessed reasons to commit murder equal to many of those that lay behind the one hundred and ninety-three other homicide cases he had worked.

The chief had just pulled into the motor court of the Crestline Motel when he received a call. He was requested to call headquarters immediately by landline. With all the reporters in town, and all the uproar going on, it was a given that police frequencies were being monitored by the media.

Ron called from a phone outside the motel's registration office.

Sergeant Stanley told him, "Chief we just got a call from Charmaine Cardwell, Isaac's widow. She'd like you to call her at home."

The sergeant gave the chief an Oakland number. Ron's call was answered on the first ring.

"Hello." The woman's voice was soft and tentative.

"Mrs. Charmaine Cardwell?"

"Yes."

"This is Chief Ronald Ketchum, calling from Goldstrike. I was given a message that you wanted to talk with me."

"Yes. Thank you for calling. I would have gotten in touch with you sooner but … we buried Isaac yesterday. I've been very busy."

"I'm truly sorry for your loss, Mrs. Cardwell. My condolences to you and everyone in your family." There was a pause, and in the silence Ron could hear the question she wanted to ask. "We're doing our best to find your husband's killer, Mrs. Cardwell. It would be wrong of me to make any promises, but I am hopeful that we'll succeed."

"Thank you, Chief Ketchum. I'm not vengeful. I wouldn't dishonor my husband's memory that way … but I do hope there will be justice. I'm very fearful of not having any means to comfort my son as he gets older. I don't want to see Japhet grow up bitter or angry."

"We will do our best, Mrs. Cardwell. All of us up here. I can promise you that."

"There's something I have to tell you, Chief Ketchum: I received a letter from my husband. A letter sent from your town. This morning was the first chance I had to read it."

A jolt of adrenaline made the hair on the chief's neck stand on end. He tried to keep his hopes from getting too high, and the excitement from his voice. "What does it say?"

"Most of it is personal. But near the end of the letter, Isaac says that he's worried for his father's safety."

Cardwell, the man who'd been killed, had been worried about Thunder, the man who was hiding behind his wrought iron gates and his lawyer?

"Do you think your husband might have meant that in, say, a metaphysical sense? The well-being of Reverend Thunder's soul?"

"No. Isaac wrote very clearly and precisely. Here, I'll read to you what his letter says: 'I think my father could be in real jeopardy. There's someone close to him, someone unlikely to arouse his suspicions, who may mean to do him harm or even kill him. I cannot imagine that it is only coincidence that has brought this man so close to my father. I need to confirm my suspicions before I act. To make a false accusation would be unforgivable. Perhaps the local library will have the resources I need. If it doesn't, I will call you from a public phone and ask you to see what you can find in a library in Oakland or Berkeley.'"

"Your husband never made that call, did he, Mrs. Cardwell?"

"No."

"Do you have any idea of the person he was referring to?"

"I'm sorry, no."

Ron sighed. "Mrs. Cardwell, would you please send me a copy of that letter?"

"The whole thing?"

"Yes, please." Ron heard the woman start to cry. "Mrs. Cardwell?"

"I'm sorry." She paused to compose herself. "I was just concerned that people might see that Isaac wrote how much he loved me. But after the whole world has seen the horrible way he died, why should that bother me?"

Ron couldn't answer her.

Lauren Gosden hadn't been able to follow her husband's instructions and keep their son, Danny, at home. She had to go to work. When you were a surgical nurse and you were scheduled to assist on a bowel resection for a colitis patient, you just didn't call in and tell the patient and the surgeon to cool their heels until you could make it. Mountain lion or not, they wouldn't understand.

Neither would Lauren if she were in their place. Still, she couldn't get angry with Oliver. He was just being a loving father and husband. His first thought was to protect the people he loved most, and Lauren loved him for that. Even so, she and Danny left the house, looking both ways before stepping outside, and made it safely to Community Hospital.

Lauren's first stop was the hospital's day care center, the Sunshine Ward. The facility provided a safe, clean, home-like environment; the staff was well trained and entirely dedicated. Nobody who worked at the hospital ever had a concern about leaving her kids in the Sunshine Ward.

But when Lauren walked in with Danny that morning there was an unfamiliar feeling, an almost frightening chill in the air. At first, Lauren noticed nothing outwardly wrong, and then she recognized, to her great dismay, what had disturbed her. The kids had been divided — segregated — into two clusters: white and others.

The white kids made up the far larger group simply because most of the people who lived in town and worked at the hospital were white. The four black, two Latino and two Asian children were tightly bunched around Allison Page, the Sunshine Ward's director. Five year old Patrice Williamson was crying her heart out to Allison.

Lauren's heart almost burst with pride when Danny instinctively walked right up to the distraught little girl and protectively put his arm around her shoulders.

Allison turned and saw Lauren and the concerned expression

on her face. The day care director said, “Give me a minute and we’ll talk.”

Lauren backed off and looked at the other group. Three other staff members were talking to the white kids in hushed tones. A number of the children in this group were shaking their heads in response to what they were being told. But Shane Watrous, a six year old friend of Danny’s, whom Lauren had reassured by being present at his tonsillectomy, saw her and waved happily.

Lauren waved back. Then Allison Page touched her arm and gestured her over to a quiet corner.

“What in the world is going on?” Lauren asked the day care director.

“A problem has come up. A serious one, I’m afraid. A number of the white children have been told by their parents not to play with the black children.”

“What?” Lauren couldn’t believe what she’d just heard.

“Have you heard about the attack this morning?”

“Just that my husband called and told me to keep Danny home.”

Allison gave Lauren the details of the Castlewood attack, and told her there had been another the previous night.

“I didn’t know about that. This is getting really scary.”

“In more ways than one,” Allison said. “The ER staff who treated Warden Marsden started talking about what happened last night. Pretty soon it was all over the hospital … and more than a few people, I’ve heard, started speaking harshly about Mahalia Cardwell. Asking who was she to put a curse on them and the town. They hadn’t killed her grandson. They hadn’t hurt black people. They weren’t bigots.”

“But by this morning all those open-minded folks had already told their kids not to play with the black children,” Lauren said, understanding the situation now.

“Not all, but far too many. Then the kids started talking. And when Jenny Wright told Patrice she couldn’t be her friend any more because she’s black, it broke Patrice’s heart.”

"Goddamnit," Lauren said.

"Exactly." Allison sighed.

Lauren felt two small arms go around her leg. Looking down, she saw Shane Watrous give her a gap-toothed grin. She ruffled his hair … just before her son stormed up and shoved the white boy away from his mother, knocking him down.

"Daniel Gosden!" Lauren scolded fiercely. She'd never in his young life struck her son, but she was sorely tempted right now.

"He's white," Daniel accused.

"So are your grandparents," his mother reminded him sternly.

Allison had knelt next to Shane to comfort him, but when the boy saw Danny Gosden continuing to glare down at him, he broke into tears.

That did it. Lauren took her son by his ear, the one she intended to fill with a lecture he'd never forget. She told Allison, "I'll take care of this one. You and Shane can expect a heartfelt apology very shortly."

The day care director looked up at Lauren.

"I'm trying to figure out a time when as many parents as possible can attend an emergency meeting. We can't allow this to continue."

"No, we certainly can't," Lauren agreed.

CHAPTER 40

Media creatures of every size, shape and job description were still pouring into Civic Auditorium as Clay stood at the lectern waiting to address them. Finally, the doors at the rear of the room closed, everybody got settled and Annie Stratton cued the cameraman who would provide the live television feed to the town. The red light came on.

"Thank you all for coming on such short notice," Clay began. "I have some serious matters to discuss with everyone this morning. It is my duty to tell you that there have been two more mountain lion attacks, one yesterday evening and another this morning."

The mayor provided the details of each incident as the throng of reporters penned their notes and held their recorders high to capture every word. Clay thought he saw relief in the faces of most of the audience that there had been no fatalities, but here and there in the crowd he saw expressions that came close to disappointment.

Clay continued, "The state has assured me that additional game wardens will be sent to join in the hunt as soon as possible. Also, efforts are being made to locate and contract with a qualified houndsman to aid the hunters. Until such time as outside help arrives, Deputy Chief of Police Oliver Gosden will assist Warden Cordelia Knox in hunting this animal.

"Additionally, I will be joining with five volunteers from the community, all of whom have a great deal of hunting experience, to supplement the patrols of our police department to prevent this animal from entering the built-up areas of town. If anyone, in any part of town or the surrounding areas, sees a mountain lion close to any place of human habitation, please call 911 immediately.

"It is, of course, every citizen's right to protect himself, his family and his home, but I must urge everyone to make the use of firearms an absolute last resort. We must avoid any tragic accident that would result from an over anxious homeowner with a gun making a rash decision to use his firearm.

"For the time being, the police department will pick up anyone jogging on the state roads within ten miles of Goldstrike and return them to a place of safety. Sightseers who stop at scenic overlooks will be escorted back to their cars and sent on their way."

Up 'til this point, Clay's delivery had been one of calm, measured tones, intended to reassure those who heard him. Now, his voice dropped slightly in volume, but became titanium hard. The wattage of the light in his eyes seemed to double. Even if a person had never seen a Clay Steadman movie, he'd know that this was not a man to trifle with, not now.

"Anyone who refuses to comply with the police in maintaining good social order will be arrested. And I can promise that each person who is arrested will be prosecuted. We are faced with something of a crisis here. This is not the time for ornery individualism. This is the time for everyone to pull together. I sincerely trust that I will have everyone's cooperation in this matter.

"I understand that you all have questions you want answered and opinions you'd like to offer. That is why I'm calling a town meeting for seven p.m. tonight. Anyone who wants to attend can start lining up now. When the line reaches the capacity of this auditorium as determined by the fire marshal, notice will be given. Everyone else will have to watch from home. Phone lines and computer links to this auditorium will be made available for those citizens who can't find a seat right here. People will not be allowed to congregate on the grounds of the Muni Complex. As of now, and until further notice, there will be a dusk to dawn curfew.

Anyone whose job doesn't require him to be outside, must be off the streets between those times."

The mayor then said he would take questions, but had time for only a few.

Annie Stratton did the honors of selecting the mayor's interrogators.

"Mr. Mayor, will you be allowing press coverage of the town meeting?"

"There will be a camera to televise the proceedings over the government access cable channel. You're certainly welcome to watch that." Clay looked at Annie for a second and interpreted the look she gave him. "Ms. Stratton seems to think it would be a good idea to allow a few of you to be present to provide pool coverage. So you can work that out with her, but I have to tell you that the overwhelming majority of seats will be reserved for the people of this town."

"Mr. Mayor, do you still believe that Mahalia Cardwell's curse has nothing to do with these mountain lion attacks?"

"I still cling to a rational turn of mind," Clay said. "That's a lot less fun, I know, but when I want make believe, I either go to the movies or make one. I'd suggest you think along similar lines."

Annie called on another reporter, but Ben Dexter, sitting next to the man, put a hand on the other reporter's shoulder and preempted him.

"In light of the fact that everybody else seems to have forgotten this little item, Mr. Mayor, is your chief of police making any progress in finding the killer of Isaac Cardwell?"

"The investigation is proceeding, Mr. Dexter." Clay paused, as if to make a decision. He nodded almost to himself and went on. "Perhaps you can tell us what's on the Reverend Thunder's mind concerning that matter, as you're the only one he's talking to these days."

There were those in the media mob who'd heard rumors that Dexter had gained exclusive access to Jimmy Thunder, but what Clay had just done was to make that fact common knowledge.

In doing so, he set the press to chasing its own tail. Now, Dexter would get a taste of the media grilling he usually helped to dole out to others.

But Clay wasn't done with the man.

"I've also heard talk, Mr. Dexter, that in preparing your story on the death of Isaac Cardwell, you're going to emphasize the role our chief of police is playing in the investigation. My advice to you on that point is to provide a fair accounting. I think highly of Ron Ketchum." The only SOB Clay had met whom he couldn't stare down. "If he were to be slandered in any way, I'm sure the town council would vote to provide the resources for him to defend his good name in court."

Clay gathered his notes and left the lectern. He knew Annie Stratton would tell him that he'd done fine in setting the media to cannibalize Dexter, but she'd tell him he would be criticized for throwing that last dart at Dexter as attempting to chill the free press.

The mayor didn't care. Some of the press, to his mind, needed to be chilled. Ben Dexter, he'd like to flash-freeze.

Before Clay could get off the stage, the line for the town meeting that night was already a dozen people long.

CHAPTER 41

Colin Ring sat on the balcony of his hotel room, making notes of his visit that morning with Mahalia Cardwell. He'd found her as delightfully vicious as ever. The Englishman paused in his writing and looked out at the glorious aspect of Lake Adeline and the crown of Sierra peaks that surrounded it. He thought he might move to Goldstrike.

The town's name was proving to be bloody well prophetic. He was striking gold on a regular basis. In his scavenging among the nightspots of the rich and indiscreet, he'd already come up with possibilities for three more books. Killer ideas all of them.

He had it on reliable information — credible enough for him at any rate — that one of the pashas of the fabled Silicon Valley, and a major philanthropist in the local theater scene, was also a leading purveyor of child pornography on the Internet. This target excited Ring greatly because he hated sods who buggered kids, and he'd never gone after a high tech titan before.

Then there was that berk named Edward Derby. Same arsehole whose son was nearly lost to that bleeding lion that had everyone up in arms. Derby's game was a stock fraud called "pumping." Ring had never heard of it, but his source, whom he'd lubricated with single malt scotch to the point of amnesia, had explained it to him. A bunch of snotty nosed touts in their brokerage offices conspired to drive up the price of an essentially worthless stock. Then they got on their phones and flogged it to an unsuspecting public. The price roared up even further. Whereupon the touts scarpered with their profits, and the bottom promptly fell out. A touch complicated that one, but with half of bloody America owning stock these days, it had relevance. Besides which, he'd also tell his readers about the mistresses, drugs and foreign real estate these young thieves secretly bought with the money they stole.

It occurred to Ring that these two ideas veered perilously close toward investigative journalism. Of a sensational sort, to be sure. Still, there was a measure of respectability, of redeeming social purpose, in exposing these walking canker sores. Ah, well, it couldn't be helped.

But his last book idea involved his true love: the complete destruction of a heretofore lionized public persona. Even better, from Ring's point of view, the man had once been a member of the British aristocracy. The class that had turned its back on him after he'd risked his life for crown and country for fifteen bloody years. This particular over privileged bastard had married an American heiress because his family money was long gone. Then he'd shocked his bride by renouncing his title and standing for Parliament as a member of the Labour party! Equally shocking, in the teeth of the Thatcher onslaught, he'd won. A single term, anyway. After that, he further reduced his station in life by moving to his wife's native California and becoming an American. Once a citizen, he decided it would be to his advantage to have his wife's money without the burden of her company. He didn't resort to anything as crude as murder, but he did poison his wife with some very clever drugs that drove her mad. He now visited her at a private hospital quarterly. An apt financial interval, Ring thought.

God, but Ring was having a grand time in Goldstrike. The place was bloody gorgeous, the pickings were immense, and he heard that the social whirl really picked up when ski season began.

He'd also heard that he was already gaining a measure of fame among the legions of the resentful, the envious and the spurned who simply ached to betray those who'd once been closest to them.

Ring had been told there was a bloke making the rounds

actively seeking him out.

He couldn't wait to find out what this chap had in store for him.

Corrie Knox and Oliver Gosden were out hunting the lion.

They'd gotten to see Terry Castlewood for just a minute before he'd been taken into surgery. The lion's bite at the back of his neck hadn't severed his spine as the animal had intended, but tests showed two cervical vertebrae had been compressed. The doctors were at a loss to explain how Terry had made it all the way back home before collapsing, and were concerned that there might be permanent damage, even paralysis.

The boy told Corrie and Oliver all the details of the attack as closely as he could remember them. There was only one point on which he embellished on reality. He said he'd slashed the lion's paw deliberately.

"That fucker swung his paw at me, and I let him have it with my knife," Terry claimed.

Neither Corrie nor Oliver believed this heroic rendering of events, but they didn't dispute the claim publicly. Considering what Terry Castlewood had been through, and the uncertain future he faced, it was a boast for him to hold on to, one he'd undoubtedly come to believe himself.

As they'd left the hospital, Terry's teammates, coaches, fellow students, and team boosters had already arrived to await the outcome of the young man's surgery.

The two hunters found the blood trail on the highway where Terry Castlewood had told them he'd last seen the animal. Corrie Knox's concern was heightened. The amount of blood on the pavement indicated a serious wound. The lion had to be in considerable pain.

"Here it is," Oliver said. He'd found the carving knife that the boy had used to defend himself. He gently put a thumb to it. "Sharp blade. Probably made a deep cut."

The thought made the deputy chief's face brighten. "This

bastard has to walk around on a wound like that, maybe it's already infected, just a matter of time before it gets infected, he keels right over and dies."

"It's possible," Corrie conceded. "But more likely he's holed up somewhere cleaning the wound with his tongue. That's what cats do."

"Never did like stinkin' cats," Oliver muttered.

Before they'd gone to the site of the Castlewood attack, Corrie had taken Oliver home to change clothes. He didn't like to be out of uniform, but she told him with all the police gear he wore on his uniform belt, he clanked and jingled as he walked. That wouldn't do when hunting in the woods. Stealth, that's what they wanted. Clothes with soft, smooth finishes; shoes with soft soles. She told him he'd have to keep his footsteps close to the ground, and his feet pointed straight ahead; splayed feet snapped more twigs.

Now, as they were about to enter the trees, Corrie brought up one last point. "You're sure you don't want a rifle? I've got another Winchester in my truck."

"What, a little toy cowboy rifle like yours?"

"In 1901, Teddy Roosevelt killed *fourteen* mountain lions in one hunt with a little toy cowboy rifle like this. The ammo's 190-grain Silvertips I hand load. Believe me, the combination will get the job done."

The deputy chief was not persuaded. "I take range practice twice a week with my handgun. I don't know from rifles. Only cops who do are the SWAT boys."

"Okay, well, now's the time to draw your weapon. What we'll do is follow the blood trail and the lion's tracks. I'll lead; you follow. When we get into the trees, move as quietly as you can and keep looking all around you. Don't forget to look up. You ready?"

Oliver nodded, his face grim.

They stepped off the highway.

The deputy chief told himself this wasn't any worse than going after an armed gang-banger in a South Central alley. Certainly not as bad as a high speed pursuit down the Santa Monica Freeway in heavy traffic. He made a hundred other comparisons to the dangers of being an L.A. cop.

The problem was, he didn't believe any of them.

CHAPTER 42

Ron Ketchum wasn't the only one who thought What the Hell would make a great restaurant franchise concept. Sherm Mason's daughter, Carolyn, a business administration major at UC-Davis felt the same way. She'd been working in her daddy's restaurants ever since she was a little girl. The first one had been in San Bernadino where she had been born.

Carolyn Mason had learned to do arithmetic by making change for her father's customers. She'd learned about inventory control. She'd learned about profit margins. She'd learned that greeting people with a smile didn't add a penny to your overhead, and it kept the cash register ringing all day long.

When she was seven, Carolyn started to develop asthma from the exhaust pipe air quality of San Bernadino. The doctor told her parents that moving to a place with clean air would be of great benefit to Carolyn. Sherm Mason asked the doctor what kind of air he was talking about. Like up at Arrowhead or Big Bear? The physician said that would be good, but he vacationed in a little town in the Sierra. He'd never breathed cleaner air than up there.

Within a month, Sherm had sold the restaurant it had taken him years to save for, and more years to turn into a thriving local institution. When it came to the health and welfare of Sherm and Geneva Mason's little girl, every other priority got bumped down a notch or off their list entirely.

Because both residential and commercial real estate in

Goldstrike sold at a considerable premium above that of San Bernadino, the Masons had to move into a much more humble house, and the first What the Hell site had previously been a two chair barber shop.

But they'd kept smiling and serving the best, biggest, juiciest burgers anybody could wrap their hands around, and now they had a considerably nicer house and a restaurant on Pinnacle Drive that seated forty and served take-out to a small army of regulars.

Given her lifetime of practical experience, Carolyn was an honors student. She kept her father's books via computer when she was away at college. During summer vacation, she worked out of a small office at the back of the restaurant, keeping the books each day before Daddy opened for business. She'd finished her spreadsheet work an hour ago, pleased that, as ever, What the Hell continued to be a small gold mine.

What occupied Carolyn's thoughts at the moment was how she could duplicate that gold mine back in Davis. She wanted to follow in her father's footsteps. She had already found the location she wanted. She knew she could find investors among her father's customers. She knew the nuts and bolts of the business.

Her only concern was whether she had her father's *joie de vivre,* and his ability to find employees with similarly sunny dispositions. She was certain that these would be absolutely essential elements to her success. Along with getting Daddy's permission to use his restaurant's name as her own. She felt there was magic in those three insouciant words: What the Hell.

She also felt hopeful Daddy would go along with her once she laid out her plans for him. He'd never denied her anything she'd really wanted and showed a willingness to work for. A happy smile had just settled on Carolyn Mason's lips when she heard a tremendous crash of shattering glass.

Horrified, she realized that someone had just smashed the restaurant's front window. Her fear grew exponentially when she threw open the office door and saw that What the Hell had become an inferno akin to its name. Just the other side of the wall of flames,

Carolyn saw the indistinct figure of a man on the sidewalk out front.

He must have seen her, too, because he shouted: "That's for Terry Castlewood!"

Carolyn had no idea what he meant, but she darted back into the office for the fire extinguisher that was kept there.

She wasn't going to let her father's restaurant burn down without a fight.

Ron had just finished another futile interview in his hunt for Didi DuPree, this one with the manager of the Log Cabin Lodge, when his BlackBerry chimed. He answered the call and Sergeant Stanley told him What the Hell had been firebombed.

The chief was rolling with his lights and siren on within seconds. His arrival, however, was not as swift as he would have liked. Pinnacle Drive was blocked for half a block by media vehicles. Two fire trucks and an ambulance had gotten through, but he couldn't. Not until he got on his loudspeaker and announced that any vehicle blocking the thoroughfare would be towed and impounded. That got some action: The newsies quickly moved their cars onto the sidewalk.

When he reached the burger joint, the fire was out. But he arrived in time to see someone being loaded into the back of an ambulance. That person was burned and moaning. Ron's heart sank when he thought who the burn victim must be. The doors of the ambulance slammed shut and it roared off down the street the chief had just cleared.

Clay Steadman was already on the scene, standing just behind the group of firefighters who were making sure the blaze had no chance to rekindle itself. It was clear that the reporters wanted to talk to the mayor and the firefighters about the blaze, but the look on Clay's face was so deadly than none of them dared to approach him.

Ron knew just how he felt.

"Was that Carolyn Mason they just took away?" the chief asked.

The mayor nodded.

"Sherm and Geneva know yet?"

"No. They're on their way here. I'll take them to the hospital and stay with them as long as they'll have me."

"It was definitely arson?"

Clay informed Ron that Carolyn had been able to tell him what she'd seen and heard — how she'd tried to save her father's business.

"Sonofabitch," the chief whispered.

"Find this guy, Ron. Right away." Then the mayor nodded at something behind the chief.

Ron turned and saw Special Agent Horgan arrive with his two minions. Well, there was no question that this was a hate crime. That gave the feds all the opportunity they'd ever need to stick their noses back into things.

What was ironic, Ron wouldn't have minded some help at this point — if Horgan had been an actual human being.

"I'll get right on it," the chief said.

"Do that, but do one other thing for me first."

"What's that?"

"Go to the Hyatt and get Mahalia Cardwell. Tell her that she'll be a guest in my house for the remainder of her stay in town."

Ron knew Clay was concerned for the old woman's safety.

Still he thought: Better your house than mine.

Mahalia Cardwell kept Ron waiting thirty minutes while she completed her packing, all the while complaining about how she was being inconvenienced. Ron was entirely lacking in sympathy and didn't keep it from showing on his face. The old lady made him carry her bag to his car.

Once they got underway, Mahalia Cardwell turned to the chief and said, "You don't like me, Mr. Chief of Police, do you?"

Ron took his eyes off the road long enough to answer. "Not a bit."

Mahalia nodded as if she'd not only expected the answer but

also derived satisfaction from it. Maybe it confirmed her opinion that he was a cracker. But Ron couldn't worry about that.

He had some questions for the woman. "Mrs. Cardwell, did your grandson do anything between the time Colin Ring first visited you and the day he left with Ring to come to Goldstrike?"

"Do anything like what?"

"Like maybe try to learn about who his father was from an objective source."

"I told Isaac everything he needed to know about that Jimmy Leverette."

From the way the old woman sneered at the mere mention of her former son-in-law, Ron thought Mahalia Cardwell was going to spit in his car. But she restrained herself.

"I'm sure you did. But did he talk to anyone else?"

"He went to the library."

"In Oakland?"

"Berkeley. Went to read up on what a famous man his daddy is."

"Do you know if Isaac made any notes on his research?" Ron inquired.

"I didn't see any. Would've torn them up if I had." She put a hand on Ron's arm and he was surprised by the strength of her grip. He stopped for a red light and looked at her until she removed the hand. "I told your boy, and I'll tell you, too. It was Jimmy Thunder who killed my baby, and nobody else."

The light changed and Ron stepped on the gas.

"You know that, do you?" he asked.

"I surely do. I also know a rich black man is the hardest man in America to bring to justice these days. He gets himself some fancy lawyers and a black jury, he could probably nail the governor of California to a tree and not lose any sleep. Tell me you don't think that's true."

Ron had strong feelings about jury nullification and other miscarriages of justice, but he wasn't going to get into all that with Mahalia Cardwell. "I think pretty much everybody gets what's coming to them, one way or another."

"I do, too. I truly do." The old woman regarded Ron with a smile that was anything but warm. Like she knew some secret about him that he didn't know himself.

The chief thought this lady was fast approaching Marcus Martin status in the select company of black people he really disliked. Not that he could admit it. That would never do for a recovering bigot.

By the time they arrived at the Steadman house, the mayor had returned home. He met Mrs. Cardwell and the chief at the front door. Clay's houseman took the old lady's bag to her room, and the mayor escorted his guests to the living room.

When they were all seated, the mayor spoke bluntly. "Mrs. Cardwell, there was another attack by the lion this morning. A teenage boy was seriously hurt."

"And so was a young woman when her father's restaurant was firebombed by a moron who believes in your curse," Ron added, feeling a sudden rush of anger at what had happened to Carolyn Mason. "Who do you think that girl's mother and father should curse, Mrs. Cardwell?"

The old woman regarded Ron with cold eyes and a stony silence. She didn't like him muddying up the purity of her desire for vengeance. Not that she was about to take responsibility for causing harm to an innocent person. You can't feel guilty and be self-righteous at the same time.

The mayor cleared his throat and gave the chief a look: This wasn't a good cop, bad cop scene. This was a star turn. Indignant second bananas were not required.

Ron got the message. He went and looked out a window at the front grounds of Clay Steadman's house.

He saw Art Gilbert lovingly pruning a flowering plum tree.

Over his shoulder he heard the mayor tell the old woman, "I'm not superstitious, but apparently a lot of people around here are starting to take your words seriously. Worse than that, they're taking them as license to commit crimes. You've made things very difficult for everyone.

"You could make them a lot better by issuing another statement that you'd spoken in anger, and that your feelings had been misinterpreted. I never had the good fortune to meet your grandson, but I think that any clergyman who truly believes in his calling would prefer forgiveness to vengeance. I think that's what Isaac would have wanted."

Mahalia rebutted, "You tell me this, Mr. Steadman. You think my baby wanted to get killed the way he did? No, sir! He did not! Things get bad enough around here, somebody's gonna tell what they know about Jimmy Thunder. How he murdered my Isaac. That happens, you can arrest him and your town will be right with the Lord again. This is His curse, not mine. Or do you think on old woman can make wild creatures do her bidding?"

A silence followed, and Ron thought — hoped — that Clay would drop the kid gloves and tell Mahalia Cardwell to hit the road. But he showed a greater forbearance than Ron would have and simply had his houseman show his new guest to her room.

The mayor came to join the chief and look out the window.

Clay said, "The only thing I can say for her is that in her place I'd probably be just as bloody minded."

Ron didn't dare get started on the subject of Mahalia Cardwell. He didn't want to say anything unfortunate. Instead, he inclined his head in the direction of Art Gilbert.

"Man does beautiful work, doesn't he?"

Clay nodded. "If Art loved film the way he loves plant life, he'd make a great director. He has an instinctive sense of visual composition."

"How long has he worked for you?" Ron wanted to know.

"Two and a half years. Got his name from Pat Sims, down the road."

"Beautiful," the chief repeated.

Then he said he had to go catch an arsonist.

CHAPTER 43

Terry Castlewood was out of surgery when Ron got back to Community Hospital. His prognosis was guarded. Maybe he'd walk again, maybe he wouldn't. There were a lot of people in the hospital chapel saying prayers for him. Others congregated in the lounge outside the recovery area and talked in hushed tones. It was these people the chief wanted to see. He wanted to know who among them would react so violently — dementedly — to the lion attack on the young football star.

Ron was sure the firebombing at What the Hell had as much to do with sports as it did with race. Most of the outrage people felt was focused on the fact that Terry Castlewood had been a local hero, one who showed the potential to be a big league jock. Hell, even Ron, who didn't follow any team except the Los Angeles Lakers, had remembered seeing the boy's picture on the sports page of the *Goldstrike Prospector.* So it stood to reason that Terry's fans would be the ones who could point the finger at the most twisted among their number.

The problem was, Ron had been anticipated. By the feds and the media.

He saw Horgan and his minions talking to a distraught middle aged couple — Terry Castlewood's parents, the chief would guess — in a glass walled office behind the nurse's station at the entrance to the intensive care unit. Reporters buttonholed people right and left. Ron was amazed the FBI men were allowing the newsies to conduct their interviews without hindrance. Maybe the feds hoped to get their leads from the nightly news or the morning paper.

Or they figured he'd show up and play the heavy. He could give the media the bum's rush. He could suffer their noisy wrath when he did. Ron was about to run that risk when his BlackBerry chimed again.

Sergeant Stanley was calling once more, this time with good news.

"Somebody dropped a dime on the firebombing," the sergeant said.

Ron looked around. Nobody had noticed him yet.

"Does it sound legit?" he asked.

"Woman says she's the perp's mother."

"Was she broken up about calling in?"

"Oh, yeah. Tears, sobs, the whole nine yards."

Regret was always a good indicator of a snitch's sincerity, especially when it was a parent turning in a child.

"What'd she say?"

"She overheard sonny-boy bragging on the phone in his bedroom about what he'd done: 'Charbroiled a nigger.' He went on about how it was tough to know when they were done cooking, though, since they're black to begin with. Mom didn't appreciate his comedy routine. She said she hadn't raised him that way."

"Is this moron a kid, still at Goldstrike High?"

"He's thirty-four, unemployed, lives with Mom. Dad's dead. Junior is supposed to be a former jock himself. Now he's a booster. He's taking a nap after his busy morning."

"You've got cars at the house already?"

"Front and back, Chief. I just called to see if you wanted to be in on the arrest."

Ron looked around again. This time Horgan was staring at him. Ben Dexter, too. Both doubtlessly wondering who the chief was talking to.

Ron told the Sarge, "No, go get him right now. Bring him in quietly. Call the mayor, Annie Stratton and the DA. Let them figure out how they want to handle everything."

"Will do, Chief."

Ron hung up. He walked past Horgan who'd come out of the room where he'd been conducting his interview. He walked past Ben Dexter who'd been talking to a high school kid. He acknowledged neither of them.

He stopped a nurse and asked if Carolyn Mason was in the intensive care unit. He wanted to find out how she was doing. He wanted to see Sherm and Geneva, and tell them the man who had hurt their daughter and burned down their restaurant had been arrested. They had the right to be the first to know. But he doubted the news would give either of them much comfort.

It certainly seemed poor compensation to him.

After she'd sucked him dry and laid twenty grand cash on him, straight out of a floor safe in her bedroom, Didi DuPree had finally agreed to help Gayle Shipton with the dialogue for her screenplay. Of course, he didn't know spelling and he certainly didn't know typing. So he had to dictate to Gayle what all the characters should say to each other.

Didi had made it only to the eighth grade before he found his life's work, but he noticed a few things about rewriting a screenplay right off. Like they started with a scene he knew she'd already finished a couple days back. So ol' Gayle was not only rewriting somebody else's dog poop dialogue, she was also rewriting her own. Worse than that, she was rewriting him, changing what he had to say right as it came out of his mouth.

He'd give her lines that were funny and sharp. But she'd type them out her own way. Change a word here or there. Do just enough to fuck up the rhythm, take out all the sly fun.

If he hadn't needed a place to lay low, he'd have slapped the shit out of her.

Wasn't right to hire someone with talent to do a job and then fuck with him. It was no wonder movies sucked the way they did. You ran beef through a grinder you got hamburger not sirloin.

Gayle looked up at Didi when he stopped talking.

"What's next?" she wanted to know.

Didi put his artistic ire aside and swiveled her chair around. He slipped his hands under her arms, and lifted her to her feet. She'd been amazed how easily he'd picked her up the first time he'd done it. Told him she'd never have believed how strong he was. It made her hot just thinking about it.

Didi had said she didn't know the half of it.

"What," Gayle asked, "you want more? Now? Can't you get enough? We're working here."

"Don't frown, baby. You'll sprain your face-lift."

"God, you're such a natural," Gayle enthused, taking no offense. "I think we can use that line in act two somewhere."

Didi sat down on Gayle's chair and pulled her onto his lap. He felt almost paternal toward her now. Maybe he should have kids someday, he thought. He'd be good with them. Teach them to deal with the world on their own terms.

"Listen to me now," Didi said gently, stroking Gayle's bare inner thigh. "The show's gonna go on. I'm gonna hunt and peck around this computer, and write some stuff that'd make you pee your pants, if you ever wore any. But right now, I got a favor to ask."

"What's that?"

Didi heard the uncertainty in her voice, so he hugged her a little closer and licked her spine at the base of her neck. Goose bumps popped up all over her shoulders and back, and a tremor ran through her. He had her now. No doubt about it.

"It's nothing *illegal,* is it?" Gayle wanted to know.

"Of course not, baby. I'll do all the law breaking around here."

Gayle quickly squirmed around so she was straddling Didi; he wasn't wearing any pants, either. "You keep talking like that, I'm going to fall in love with you."

"Mmm, mmm, mmm," he said as he felt her warmth surround him. "I believe you already have."

Didi knew enough to keep quiet then, except for some pro forma sound effects, until they finished. When Gayle slumped in his arms, she asked him what he wanted her to do.

"There's a man I want to meet. An Englishman. Name of Colin Ring. Big red-faced guy is what I hear. The way I got it worked out, he's going to be at one of three places tonight between ten and midnight. All I want you to do is find him for me. You smile at him real nice, and invite him back here. Tell him there's somebody he's just got to meet. Can you do all that?"

Gayle Shipton said she could and she would.

Just as long as Didi kept writing and let her take the credit for it.

As the late afternoon sun slouched toward evening, Corrie Knox decided to call it quits. She remembered all too clearly what had happened the day before when she and Tuck had pushed their hunt too far into the twilight. Oliver Gosden was truly a brave man, she had decided, one who didn't let his obvious fear keep him from doing an important job. But when it came to being an outdoorsman, he was never going to remind anyone of Lewis and Clark.

Martin and Lewis, maybe.

No, that was uncharitable. After several hours in the woods, he no longer made all the noise of a marching band. Even so, there wasn't a creature in the forest that wasn't going to hear the deputy chief coming from a long way off; at one point, before she suggested he stop it, he'd even been clicking a cigarette lighter open and shut. The only way they were going to spot the mountain lion they wanted was if it got pissed at Oliver for interrupting its sleep.

They had seen signs of the animal, though. They'd followed his tracks, his blood and his dung. They'd chased the tracks right through the bed of a crystal clear mountain stream. The icy water must have helped the cat's wounded paw to stop bleeding, because there was no more blood to be found on the other side of the stream. Then the footprints disappeared as the mountain lion moved onto a patch of rocky terrain. From there, the only way the hunters could try to follow the animal was on pure instinct. Corrie's not Oliver's.

Still, there were times when Corrie thought all she had to do was look up and there it would be, perched on a tree limb like the Cheshire cat from *Alice in Wonderland.* But no such luck. Not even a ghostly, mocking feline smile to shoot at.

Most likely, the animal had ultimately done just what she predicted hours ago: found a hidey-hole in which to lick its wounds.

"Let's head for home, Deputy Chief," Corrie said.

Oliver, who was one big raw nerve by that time, didn't argue. Instead, he asked, "You think the state will have someone here to help you tomorrow?"

"Let's hope," she answered.

They made it back to Corrie's 4x4 without incident. When they were underway, Oliver turned to Corrie and said, "You know it was out there with us today, don't you?"

"Most of the day, anyway. Right up 'til the end. But then where else would it be?"

"I mean, it was watching us."

There was no question, Corrie knew, that people could feel when they were being stalked. The awareness came without the aid of conscious sensory input. You didn't see, you didn't hear, you didn't smell the predator … but just like a lobster at a seafood restaurant, you were aware that something was sizing you up for dinner.

Corrie told Oliver a story.

"There was this trapper name of Caleb Marsh who lived in Idaho a little over a hundred years ago. Guy was something of a local legend. He routinely shot grizzlies and wolves, and thought nothing of it. Then one day he felt he was being followed, and he spotted this mountain lion."

Corrie glanced over to see if Oliver was paying attention. His eyes were as big as kid's, one listening to a ghost story. "This isn't bullshit, is it?"

The game warden shook her head, put her eyes back on the road, and continued.

"Anyway, this went on for almost two years, the lion stalking this guy. The really strange part was, the lion seemed to be teasing him, giving old Caleb Marsh little glimpses of himself. Because, normally, if a mountain lion doesn't want you to see it, you don't."

Corrie interrupted her narrative to negotiate a sharp curve in the road.

Once that was taken care of, Oliver demanded to know, "So what happened? Marsh shot the lion?"

"That's not the general conclusion. Caleb Marsh disappeared. The only way anyone ever learned of his story was from a journal that was found in his abandoned cabin."

Oliver waited until Corrie braked for a stop sign and then he said, "I hate that story, but it fits right in with a theory I've got about this animal."

"What's that?"

"I think it's gotten personal with him. I think he'll keep right on going after people."

Corrie believed that there were always sound, scientific reasons to explain animal behavior … but she'd come to the same conclusion.

"I do, too," she said.

Oliver stopped into Ron's office before he went home. He dropped like a sack of cement into a guest chair, and regarded the chief bleakly. "I can't begin to tell you how much I enjoyed my day," he said.

"Didn't get the cat, huh?"

Oliver shook his head. "We managed a draw, though. He didn't get us either."

"Just so you know, I'd have gone out there myself if it were politically possible."

Oliver understood. He even believed the chief.

"Wasn't a great day here in civilization, either," Ron said. He told Oliver about the attack on What the Hell.

"How's the girl?" the deputy chief wanted to know.

"Alive but suffering. Clay had her flown out this afternoon to a burn specialist in San Francisco. Her parents went with her."

"You get the asshole who did it?"

Ron told him the story of the idiot's mother dropping the dime on him.

"Good for her. The DA going for attempted murder?"

The chief shook his head. "Not immediately, anyway. The mayor turned the perp over to the feds. They're going to prosecute him for hate crimes and civil rights violations. If he gets less than fifty years, then the state will prosecute. This way, we get Horgan out of our hair. Maybe for good, but at least for a little while."

"Is he going to try to claim credit for the arrest?"

"Can't. Clay already talked to the media mob. Told it straight. A tip was called in; an arrest was made. The credit goes to Shirlee Fansler for doing the right thing instead of protecting her mutant offspring."

"Too bad we don't have somebody's mama who knows what happened with Isaac Cardwell," Oliver said.

"Yeah, that is a shame. But we did get some news on that front." Ron told Oliver about the call from Charmaine Cardwell. And what Mahalia told him about her grandson visiting the Berkeley library.

The deputy chief picked right up on the salient point. "If Isaac knew somebody represented a threat to his father, and that person found out Isaac knew —"

"Isaac gets nailed to a tree," Ron finished. "I talked to the librarian down in Berkeley. She remembers Isaac coming in, said he was reading in the magazine stacks for the most part. But he didn't borrow any materials."

"I don't supposed, just this once, he had a moment of weakness and left the magazines he was reading out for somebody else to put back on the shelf. Somebody who might remember what they were."

Ron shook his head. "No. He stayed right in his saintly character and tidied up after himself. But I did ask the librarian to cull any mention of Jimmy Thunder or Jimmy Leverette that appears in their collection, copy it and fax it to us. She said we should have the material sometime tomorrow or possibly the next day."

"Better than nothing," Oliver opined.

"The mayor left something for you," Ron said, handing Oliver a manila folder. "He left it with me when he saw you weren't back. I took the liberty of reading it."

Which is just what Oliver quickly did.

"Colin Ring was an SAS commando."

"Elite soldiers," Ron said. "Like our Special Forces people."

Oliver continued reading. "He was separated from the service less than honorably after the *accidental* training death of a recruit under his command."

"Clay said even his people couldn't get the details on that, but the fact that whatever happened has been hushed up tells you something, doesn't it?"

Oliver replied, "Tells us Ring screwed up, maybe got a little too reckless or brutal. Some poor kid dies, the brass cover their asses. But Ring, he gets booted out of his pretty uniform. That gives him a permanent hard-on against the establishment, and he decides to become a character assassin."

Ron nodded "And, as you pointed out, maybe a real killer, too. Clay said that his publishing contact told him Ring has to be desperate for his book on Jimmy Thunder to succeed. He's been down so long that if this one doesn't go big time, he's finished. I think we should have another chat with our British friend real soon."

That point raised a question in Oliver's mind. "You ever find Didi DuPree?"

"No. The man is not staying in any public lodging in this town. Maybe he rented some private digs, so tomorrow I'm going to have Sergeant Stanley start calling real estate offices. But, on the chance he's left town, I had to ask the feds to look for him, too."

"Outside of town, you mean."

Ron nodded again.

"So, are we going to look for Ring now?" Oliver wanted to

know.

"Not immediately. The mayor's called a town meeting for to-night. My presence is required."

"Me, too?"

"No, but Lauren would like to see you. She called this after-noon. There was a little fracas with Danny at the Sunshine Ward today."

Oliver's heart turned to ice at the idea that *anything* bad had happened involving his son. "Nothing serious?"

"No bleeding. Some bruised feelings and a lesson or two that needed to be learned, that's what it sounded like to me."

"I'm going home then."

"Okay," the chief agreed, "but be sure to tune in the town meeting."

CHAPTER 44

Clay Steadman stood at the lectern on the stage of the Civic Auditorium that evening sipping from his customary glass of water. He looked calm as he waited for everyone to enter the room and settle down. The audience that was filling the seats and had been lined up since that morning to hear the mayor speak, and to tell him what was on their minds, was considerably more agitated. The mayor's staff people on the auditorium floor tested the microphones that would be used to take questions from the audience.

On the stage, seated behind the mayor, were Ron Ketchum, Corrie Knox, Annie Stratton, Bob Heath, the district attorney and Francis Horgan of the FBI. Off to one side, were a pair of technicians, one to handle phone calls, the other for Internet questions.

The working press had been limited to ten front row seats in the section to the mayor's left. They'd been told that they would have a chance to ask questions like anyone else — but they would also be subject to questioning if any of the citizens of Goldstrike so desired.

In due course, the last seat was filled. Ron looked around to make sure the ten cops he'd assigned to the meeting were in place. Annie cued the pool TV camera. The town meeting began.

"Good evening," the mayor began. "My thanks to all of you here for waiting so patiently to attend this town meeting. A number of serious issues bring us together tonight. I'll bring them up point by point, and then we'll discuss them. Anyone among you here, or those watching at home, may question any one of us. The person who has the floor at any given time will be heard out. Any attempts to heckle or shout down a speaker will meet with forcible ejection, courtesy of the police officers you see at various points around the room.

"Anyone who objects to another speaker's point of view with a punch, kick, or other hostile physical response will be arrested and prosecuted. I trust, however, that this will not be necessary."

The look Clay directed at all corners of the audience said it had damn well better not be. He then introduced the others who shared the stage with him. Just as he finished, the phone rang.

The mayor gave the phone tech a mild glare and the ringing stopped abruptly.

The audience reacted with laughter.

"Please give me a chance to speak first," Clay said dryly. "Everyone will get a turn. We'll be here as long as it takes."

The mayor looked down, took a sip of water, and began to talk to his town.

"There are three very serious subjects that need to be addressed here tonight. The death of Reverend Isaac Cardwell, the recurrent attacks by a mountain lion, and the response of our community to the first two situations."

Clay paused to look closely at his audience, taking long enough that it almost seemed as if he was weighing the character of every person seated in front of him.

"When I first saw Isaac Cardwell nailed to a tree, I was appalled. I was sickened that such a thing could still happen in our country. I almost refused to believe my eyes that a murder so heinous could happen in Goldstrike.

"Despite my revulsion, I took comfort in certain facts. I knew then, and know now, that we have a chief of police, a deputy chief, and a police department staffed with men and women who have the ability and experience to make sure this outrage is brought to a just resolution. Beyond that, I was certain that the people of our town are far too decent to let a killer find shelter among them. It is on this second point, however, that I've experienced a measure of disappointment, and to some extent have had my eyes opened.

"As the investigation into the killing of Isaac Cardwell began, Chief of Police Ronald Ketchum was given a stack of hate mail received by the Reverend Jimmy Thunder, Isaac Cardwell's father. More than a dozen pieces of this filth-spewing mail were postmarked locally. Needless to say, none of the cowards who sent this garbage backed up his twisted convictions with a return address.

"I never would have thought such lowlife scum could be found in our beautiful town. I also never thought of myself as naive, but in this case I was very badly mistaken. Perhaps a lot of you are, too, if you think Goldstrike doesn't have the same problems as every other town in this country. Take a look around you now. See if you can tell which of your neighbors is a hater."

Clay let them have the time to follow his suggestion. Some did, some didn't.

"There used to be a saying during the Vietnam War years: America, love it or leave it. This was the admonition offered by the proponents of a certain political point of view to those who didn't agree with them. I always thought the Love It or Leave It people didn't get it. Our country was founded as a democracy, a form of government that is a *contest* of opposing views. It is only by pitting ideas, policies and programs against one another that we can find out which work and which don't. But some people think that their way is the only way. There's a name for that kind of thinking: totalitarianism.

"The malignancy espoused by the writers of the mail I saw goes even farther. It condemns people not for the views that they hold as adults, but for the very color of the skin with which they are born. We all know the name for that kind of thinking."

Clay paused for a sip of water and moment of reflection.

"As long as I am the mayor of Goldstrike, this will be a very uncomfortable place for racists. At the next meeting of the town council, I will propose a series of educational forums for residents of all ages. These forums will look at issues of race as frankly as possible. They will look at where we've been, where we are and discuss where we ought to go. But more than that, we'll look at why so many of us, of all colors and backgrounds, feel the need to look down on *somebody.*

"That's the first part of my plan — the love-it part, if you will. Unlike the simple-minded, bumper sticker thinkers of the past, however, we will not have a leave-it clause to our plan. Rather, we will issue a defend-it challenge to bigots of all stripes and hues.

"If you think a white skin or a black, brown, red or yellow one, makes you better than everybody else, well, step right up to the microphone. We'll give you a public opportunity to tell us why. But be prepared to defend whatever you have to say. Because we'll also muster the best minds on the opposite side of the argument to debate every point you make. Which shouldn't really worry anyone who knows he's cut from better cloth. So if you're not just some weasel whose idea of courage is a sneak attack, this is your big chance: Tell us why you're right and everybody else is wrong. Interested parties may call my office and I'll pay the toll charges, if necessary."

Clay stared directly at the audience — and into the camera — for a long moment to leave no doubt this offer was just what he described it to be: a challenge. Then he shuffled his notes and moved along.

"The next matter before us tonight is the series of attacks by a mountain lion. In and of themselves, these attacks are frightening. Two runners have been mauled and a small child was placed in jeopardy in the confines of his own backyard. Fortunately, nobody has been killed.

"Actually, there's a bit of good news to report. Just before I took the stage tonight, I spoke with Terry Castlewood's doctors. They report his surgery went very well, and the swelling around his spine is going down at a remarkable rate. They're much more hopeful than they were just this morning that there will be no permanent physical impairment."

Applause and cheers issued from the audience.

"We're doing everything we can to track and kill this mountain lion. Warden Cordelia Knox and Deputy Chief of Police Oliver Gosden were out hunting it today, unfortunately without success. I've made a personal request to the governor to have more game wardens sent here to help us as soon as possible. He explained to me that state personnel are stretched thin, and that all available game wardens are meeting the needs of other communities, but he assures me that we will have additional help within forty-eight hours. I've also been in touch with a houndsman — a professional tracker — from Louisiana. As soon as his credentials can be verified, the town will offer him a contract. If all goes well, we can expect him to be here in two days also."

This, too, brought applause.

"It is my responsibility to do everything I can to safeguard the well-being of the people of this town. That is why I must tell you now: There is no such thing as a curse on this town. If anything, Goldstrike has received more than its fair share of blessings. But recently an elderly woman who was wounded to the depths of her soul spoke out in anger. Her words were publicized, and in light of the coincidence — the *coincidence* — of the attacks by the mountain lion, this so-called curse has been given credence by too many people who should know better. If you think our town is cursed, be ashamed of yourself.

"And if you think an elderly woman's anger gives you license to hate black people, to strike out at them, you should not only be ashamed, you also had better find yourself a damn good lawyer. Because we are going to come after you, we are going to find you and we are going to lock you up."

Clay's anger was plainly visible now. A tic started at the corner of his left eye. He took a deep breath and another drink of water before continuing.

"This is exactly what we did to a … a man who made the grievous mistake of firebombing the What the Hell restaurant on Pinnacle Drive. Carolyn Mason, the owner's daughter, was inside at the time. She tried her best to save the place where her father earned his livelihood. As a result, she was burned over fifty percent of her body. I spoke to Carolyn's doctors, too, before I came out here tonight. They're watching her closely for infection, but they expect that she will live. Her recovery, however, is expected to be prolonged and painful. I hope all of you will join me in sending out your prayers to Carolyn, Sherm and Geneva Mason. Our town will be far the poorer should they decide to leave us.

"Someone who *will* be leaving us tomorrow morning is Reggie Fansler. He's the man who threw the firebomb … the man who said he was getting even for Terry Castlewood. Terry's parents have told me that one of their son's two greatest athletic heroes is Kellen Winslow — a black man. They also said that Terry liked nothing better after winning a football game than going out to celebrate at What the Hell. Reginald Fansler didn't act on Terry Castlewood's behalf. He acted out of the sickness of his own tortured soul.

"And if I make only one point tonight for any of you to remember, let it be this: Heaven help anyone else who raises his hand against *any* of his neighbors in this town."

Clay gave everyone several beats to absorb his warning. Then he nodded his head to Annie Stratton who rose and stepped forward.

"The floor is now open for questions and comments," she said.

The town meeting commanded TV ratings in Goldstrike that would have levitated network executives to Nirvana, or its multimillion dollar stock option equivalent. But as always there remained an uninterested minority who wouldn't have tuned in to the Second Coming. First among them was Colin Ring.

He had a pint of beer in his fist at a bar called the New York Shock Exchange, and he couldn't believe that wizened old cowboy and cop actor who ran the town was on every one of the twelve bleeding tellies in the bar. The man blathered on endlessly in some noxious amalgam of a brimstone sermon and a schoolboy civics lessons.

Ring would have rather watched anything else. Bloody baseball even.

He looked around and was disgusted by how everyone else present was riveted to every word. Could all these wankers be so star-struck? Or, worse, were they really interested? If it were the latter, he'd have to reconsider his plans to take up residence.

The only interest Colin Ring had in Clay Steadman was if somebody handed him some dirt on the old sod. Now *that* would make a corking good book. But not one that would come easily. He'd already tried everything he could think of to find any gossip about the mayor and come up empty.

He was just about to drain his pint and toddle over to the Mermaid's Slipper when the woman came in. Blonde. Either a natural or someone who frequented a *very* expensive salon. A pearl gray silk mini-dress with a thin silver belt defining a deliciously narrow waist. The breasts were so perfect they had to be implants, but the legs were long and shapely and there was no faking that. As she walked past, though, Ring thought her face bore an unfortunate resemblance to a mackerel. No real problem there, however. He wasn't a face man.

Still, he had noticed the intriguing way she'd smiled at him.

He gave it a five count and turned around. She was seated alone at a table for two, and she smiled at him again. Cor! She wasn't wearing any knickers and she just flashed her fanny at him. Her bush had been pruned to a narrow strip.

Mrs. Ring's little boy Colin hadn't grown up shy. He got over to the woman's table two steps ahead of the waitress, sat down and ordered a pint, just as if he belonged there.

Then he turned to the woman and asked, "What'll you be having, darlin'?"

"Whatever's right to start a friendship," Gayle Shipton answered.

She immediately wished Didi had been there to whisper a better line to her.

But it seemed to work for Colin Ring.

Annie Stratton made a point of starting with the townspeople and ignoring the reporters. She'd get to the newsies later. They could stew for a while. She gestured to a woman near the back of the central section of the auditorium. An assistant with a microphone made his way back to her.

"My name is Lucy Blaine," she said. The woman looked to be in her early forties, had long strawberry blonde hair and the air of a slightly wilted flower child about her. "I understand, Mayor Steadman, that you support a rationalist view of natural phenomena. But there are many of us, including Native American peoples, who take a more spiritual point of view. We believe a spark of the divine exists in all things. We believe that there are larger powers than ourselves, and they can be influenced to act on our behalf or against us. I personally believe that such a spirit exists in the mountain lion you're trying to kill. I don't think you'll succeed no matter how many hunters and trackers you bring in. But even if you do, what's to say the spirit of another wild animal might not be turned against us? Or some other type of natural disaster might be visited on us. Before *any* further life is taken, I suggest we, as a town, approach Mrs. Cardwell and see if we can't heal the hurt in her heart. I think that's our only chance to get things back to normal around here."

Scattered applause rippled around the room. Annie picked out a man seated in the front row of the right hand section. He was a husky white guy dressed in casual clothes who looked to be in his mid-thirties. He seized the microphone instead of letting the staffer hold it for him.

"My name is James FitzHugh, and the first thing I want to say is I am not a racist. I was raised to be a good Catholic, and the nuns beat it into my head that we're *all* God's children. I also learned, when I was studying my family tree, that one of my great-grandpas was an indentured servant back in the Old Country *after* Lincoln freed the slaves here. So, I'm not a fan of human bondage. That said, I also have to say it really frosts me every time I hear a black person say that whatever is bad in his life is my fault. Mine or some other white guy's. What is that if not racism? Nothing bad that happens to black people in America is the fault of the person who looks back at them in the mirror each morning. I get the impression a lot of blacks in this country think everything would be just peachy if only the white folks disappeared. My answer to that is look at how things are over in Africa — or Detroit, for that matter — and tell me how things are when blacks don't have whites to use for scapegoats. I don't know if animals have spirits like that lady just said, but I agree with her that Mrs. Cardwell was pissed off when she laid into our town. Call it a curse or not, she knew she was directing her anger at white people."

FitzHugh handed the microphone back, and received significantly louder applause than the first speaker. Annie consciously chose a black man seated at the left of the room as the next up.

He was of medium height and a slim build. He had a receding hairline. He wore gold wire-frame glasses and a sports coat, giving him a professorial appearance.

"My name Christian Banneker. One of my forebears, Benjamin Banneker, helped design Washington, D.C. Almost every male member of my family has been a college graduate for the past one hundred years. Almost every female member of my family has been a college graduate for the past seventy-five years. My relatives have become ministers, educators, doctors, and officers in the military. Following in Benjamin Banneker's footsteps, I am an architect. I am also the heir to two very fortunate traditions. The first is being a member of a family that insists on rectitude and education as the pillars of a good life. The second is to be a citizen of a country that recognizes that human nature is both flawed and perfectible. I don't blame white people for my shortcomings; I only ask them not to overlook their own. We all have work to do on that person we see in the mirror each morning. Lastly, I would like to express my heartfelt sympathies to the Cardwells, the Castlewoods and the Masons."

Banneker's comments received the best reception yet. When the applause died down, Annie called on a man in the dead center of the audience.

He was tall and rawboned, wore khaki slacks and a plaid shirt, and looked to be in his fifties. "I'm Ezra Tilden, and I guess I'm kinda like the chief of police up there. I was raised to think that some people were better than others because of their skin color or their religion or their accent or whatever the hell else my parents thought up. And I believed what I was taught for a good long time. But finally I got out in the world enough and grew enough brains to figure out that what I was taught as a child was both right and wrong. Some people are better than others. But there are no hard and fast rules as to why. Skin color surely isn't a sign. You know how I figured that out? I met a *blind* racist. This man had been born blind, but he told me blacks were no damn good. I asked him how he knew what the hell color a person was when he couldn't see anybody. Then just to mess with his head, I asked how he even knew everyone wasn't playing a big joke on him and *he* was black."

That got a laugh from the crowd. Even the mayor smiled.

Tilden continued, "I agree with Clay Steadman that our town isn't cursed. If God wanted to kick some ass around here, He wouldn't be working on such a piss-ant scale. *One* mountain lion? If that's the best God can do, he's gettin' old."

People started to laugh again, but Tilden held up his hands.

"Please. I don't mean to make fun of what happened to the folks who did get attacked, and that poor young Mason girl. Or Reverend Cardwell, either. I'm glad that Fansler punk is in jail, and I hope his pain will be prolonged, too. As for whoever killed the reverend, I wouldn't mind seeing *that* sonofabitch nailed to a tree — as long as it was a dead tree. Wouldn't want to hurt any innocent plant life."

Tilden looked over his shoulder at the first speaker, Lucy Blaine, momentarily. "Ma'am, I'm not qualified to say whether we've all got a divine spark in us, but I figure if that's so, maybe people have got a little more of it than mountain lions. I say we trust our police department to catch the people who are dangerous to us, but the state of California has to trust us to protect ourselves from animals that are dangerous to us. A bunch of do-gooders in Los Angeles and San Francisco pass a proposition saying you can't hunt man-eating predators? Well, to hell with that! It'd be like us passing a proposition protecting drive-by shooters. Wouldn't those city folks scream then?"

Amid a flurry of favorable outcries, Ezra Tilden turned his gaze directly toward Clay Steadman.

"Mr. Mayor, I've got to tell you, if I see any mountain lion around my house, I won't stop to ask if it's our local marauder. My policy will be to shoot on sight. If that's civil disobedience, so be it. If you want to prosecute me, I'll take my chances with a jury of my peers. That's all I've got to say."

Clay met the man's eyes and spoke softly. "I'm afraid we'd have to accommodate you with that prosecution, Mr. Tilden. You or anyone else of a similar mind."

Annie Stratton decided it was time to let the working press have its turn.

Gayle Shipton, who'd spent years in pitch meetings with the *sleaze de la sleaze* of Hollywood, figured she could put up with just about any man for an hour or two. But this limey letch was almost more than she could take. He'd ordered stout for *her,* vile-looking black stuff that looked like it had passed through a barnyard animal with a urinary infection.

That, and he had his hand up her skirt before she even got a chance to see if he had clean fingernails. Well, okay, she'd flashed him a little of the old beav, but he didn't have to be so rough about it — and so obvious. They were seated at a small table, and if anyone ever took their eyes off the damn televisions, they'd get quite a show.

When Colin Ring tried to stick one of his fat fingers inside her, she pinched the back of the offending hand sharply enough to draw blood. He quickly — thankfully — withdrew it, and she tugged her dress down. But when the Englishman spotted corpuscles flowing freely from the rip in his flesh, he saw red in more ways than one. For one head-spinning moment, Gayle thought he was going to bash her right there.

She saved herself by saying in a husky snarl, "You play rough, I play rough. You play nice, I'll play nice."

Not a bad line, Gayle thought. Of course, maybe she was just remembering it from some old Lauren Bacall movie. Still, it seemed to be working. The brows over Colin Ring's piggy little eyes unfurled themselves and a grin appeared at the corners of his lipless mouth.

"Too bloody right!" the Englishman roared with laughter. He slapped the table hard enough to produce a credible impression of a gunshot. For the first time, all the eyes in the bar turned away from the televisions and looked at them.

Gayle quickly lowered her head. She didn't want to be remembered being seen with this creep. If people couldn't see her face, all they'd recall would be her hair and her tits. In this town, that wouldn't narrow things down much.

When she thought it was safe, she looked up.

Colin Ring was regarding her with a devilish grin.

"Very well, my dear," he said. "Where shall we go to play nice? Your place or mine?"

Damn! He was right, she thought. Her stupid line implied an invitation. That was the problem with spoken dialogue: you couldn't rewrite it.

What was she supposed to do now? She hadn't played things the way Didi had told her — to tell Ring there was someone he had to meet. She'd revised Didi's scenario so she could play the *femme fatale.* What a dipshit mistake that had been. Now, if she told this pickled porker there was someone who wanted to see him, he'd be sure to smell a rat.

Well, one thing was for certain, his place was out.

"My place," Gayle said with a smile she hoped wasn't too transparently phony.

As they rose to leave, she hoped to God that Didi had a way out of this for her.

A reporter from *The New York Times* asked the first question. "Mayor Steadman, with the exception of a few people like Mr. Tilden, many people respond to questions concerning matters of race, religion or other sensitive subjects by saying what they think is publicly acceptable, while they privately hold views that are just the opposite. How do you know a majority of the people in your town don't, in fact, believe that Mahalia Cardwell has cursed it, and resent her and other African Americans for what she's done?"

Clay studied the man, looking at him as if he were a specimen best examined under a microscope.

The mayor began with a question of his own: "How do you know Mr. Tilden isn't a hypocrite and a liar, too?"

With his words, Clay did what many would have thought impossible: He made a reporter blush.

"He … he simply struck me as credible," the reporter said defensively.

"But other people don't? Mr. FitzHugh was quite blunt about his resentment. He doesn't like to be blamed for other people's problems, and I don't know of anyone who does. Mr. Banneker is proud of himself and his family and doesn't want people to stereotype him because of his skin color, and that's perfectly natural. Ms. Blaine expresses a reverence for life greater than mine and perhaps your own. In fact, all of the people who have spoken here tonight have struck me as both sincere and vitally concerned about their town.

"Still, your question is *how* do I know when people are not being honest. I'll tell you how: I can *smell* deceit. It stinks. It has just about the same rank odor that cynicism has. But let's put my nose to the test." The mayor looked over to the phone monitor. "Do we have a call you can put on the speaker?"

With the click of a button, a woman's disembodied voice sounded in the room. She sounded middle-aged with no discernible accent. "Hello? Hello, am I talking to the town meeting?"

"Yes, ma'am, you are," the mayor said.

"My na —"

"Please, if you don't mind," the mayor interrupted, "would you withhold your name? We'd like you to remain anonymous so there will be no reason for you not to give bluntly honest answers to a few questions. Would that be all right with you?"

"Oh … well, okay. Sure. I have something to tell you, but what do you want to know?"

The audience listened with fascination to the drama Clay had constructed.

The mayor said, "Let's start at the beginning: How did you feel when you learned of Reverend Isaac Cardwell's death?"

"Awful. Just terrible … I wept." The woman's voice filled with emotion. "I looked at the picture of that poor man in the paper and I asked myself, 'How could anyone do such a thing?'"

"Did it matter to you that Reverend Cardwell was black?"

"No!" There was a pause for reconsideration that nobody in the audience missed. "Well, yes it did. That image reminded me of pictures I've seen in books. History books, you know. Where blacks had been lynched or burned. I felt a deep sense of shame that something like that could happen in my town. I felt *angry*, too. It felt like the anger my husband describes to me when he hears about a man attacking a woman. He takes it personally when one of his own kind does something like that. I felt the same way."

"So you think the killer is white?" the mayor asked.

"Yes."

"For what reason?"

"Like I said, it's happened a lot before. I just didn't think it would happen here."

"How do you feel about Mahalia Cardwell and her so-called curse?"

"I feel sorry for her. I know if I'm angry, she has every right to be in a rage … but she had no business saying what she said. If it's not a curse, it's at least very clear she hopes something bad will happen to Goldstrike, and that's not fair. We didn't want Reverend Cardwell to die. I believe most people in town would give anything we could to undo what's happened. No, what she said wasn't right."

"Do you think people lie to reporters?"

"Well … I have to admit I think that's true. At least some of the time. But mostly I think that's because reporters don't respect anybody's privacy. Having somebody stick a camera and a microphone in your face and put you on television, it's like having the whole country drop in when the house isn't picked up. You just get rid of them as fast as you can."

The audience laughed at the analogy.

"But it's not always funny," the caller cautioned. "I mean, look at what happened here. This poor man dies a terrible death, nailed to a tree, and instead of trying to show his family some respect or compassion, a pack of those people rush right up to them and want to know how they *feel.* They feel like hell! Any *idiot* would know that. The way I'd feel, I'd want to bean as many of those reporters with my frying pan as I could!"

The unnamed caller received a rousing ovation.

The mayor addressed the Times reporter. "To me, sir, that smells like truth."

"Of course, it's the truth," the caller responded. "But, Mr. Mayor, there really is something I have to tell you."

"Go right ahead. You've been very patient."

"Well, it's about the killing. Reverend Cardwell's, I mean. At least, I think so."

"What is it?" Clay wanted to know.

"Well, just a little while ago, in the trees behind my house, my son found a hammer. It has blood all over it. I thought you should know."

CHAPTER 45

The lousy Brit groped Gayle almost all the way home. He kept up the rough stuff, too. He was one of those creeps who thought women enjoyed being hurt. That or he just enjoyed doing the hurting. One time he squeezed so hard, Gayle feared he'd ruptured her right implant. The sonofabitch! Gayle thought what she ought to do was get him home, get him hard, and do a Lorena Bobbitt on him. If she could find the nerve. As it was, the only way she could finally defend herself from the driver's seat was to nearly let the car run off the road a couple times. The second time she did that it calmed him down for the duration.

When Gayle pulled the Porsche into the garage beneath her house, she bolted from the car like Secretariat leaving the starting gate. Even so, she felt the breeze from a grab that just missed.

"The game's afoot," Ring said with a laugh.

Gayle's heart turned to ice. She immediately abandoned any thought of dealing with this bastard on her own. If Didi was anywhere but right inside waiting for her, she was going to wet herself.

She ran up the stairs to the first floor, and she heard heavy footsteps pounding along behind her. Oh, God, she thought, he was *chasing* her. She cried out, "Didi … Didi!"

Gayle skidded on the polished hardwood floor of the foyer and stumbled into the living room, snapping a three inch Ferragamo heel. She lurched, twisted, and was about to do a header into the fireplace when two strong hands plucked her deftly out of the air.

She looked over her left shoulder and there behind her, holding her close and smiling, was Didi.

"Baby, you gotta call Arthur Murray," he said. "Or you can forget about goin' to the prom with me."

Gayle fell in love with Didi that very moment.

"Who the bloody hell are you, mate?" Colin Ring demanded.

He stood in the entrance to the room breathing heavily from his dash up the stairs. His face was crimson with anger. His fists were bunched, and the forward tilt of his body said he meant to use them.

Didi didn't answer immediately. He took Gayle's earlobe, gently, between his teeth and pulled on it, all the while looking defiantly at Colin Ring. Gayle, feeling safe once again, couldn't help but smile maliciously at her former tormentor.

Ring's face tightened. He realized by now that he'd been set up in some way, but he really didn't mind. He'd come here with the bint for a good hard shag, and that's just what he meant to have. If he had to break some little wog's neck to get it, well, that would just be the bloody foreplay, wouldn't it? He uttered a martial sounding grunt and slid into a much practiced karate stance.

Didi opened his jaws and whispered in Gayle's ear, "You remember ol' Brett and the Colonel from your movie? Watch how it's really done."

Ring had just started his charge when Didi picked Gayle up and threw her at the Brit. High and hard. Shrieking all the way. Give the man credit, Didi thought, he didn't try to catch Gayle or otherwise cushion her fall. He just batted her aside with an efficient little forearm sweep

Then he kept right on coming. Only by this time Didi had a silenced gun in his hand, and he shot Colin Ring squarely in his belly.

"Karate chop that, motherfucker," Didi said.

The slug knocked the Englishman off his feet and sent him skidding backwards across the hardwood floor. He came to rest in a seated position against a built-in bookcase. Ring wasn't dead, however. His eyes were open, and he looked madder than ever.

Didi stepped over to Gayle and helped her up. "Nothin' personal, baby," he said. "But a man's gotta do what a man's gotta do."

Gayle looked like she didn't know whether to scream or jump out a window, but she still managed to tell Didi, "That's the first time I ever heard you use a cliché."

Didi laughed. No doubt about it, the woman was single-minded. "I'll try to do better. Now, I know you're upset. You might get a whole lot more upset. And I know you got two questions to ask me. So why don't you tell me those questions?"

Gayle couldn't find her voice. But she managed to glance fearfully over at Colin Ring.

"Don't worry about him," Didi said. "He ain't goin nowhere. This real life: the gutshot don't foxtrot."

Didi smiled at Gayle. "See, I still got my stuff. You liked that one, didn't you?"

Gayle asked the first question Didi wanted to hear. "Are you going to kill him?"

"Yes," Didi said.

Gayle proceeded immediately to the second question. "Are you going to kill me?"

"Not if you're a good girl," he said.

Didi didn't have the time to instruct her in the details of polite behavior because Colin Ring parted with a groan that said he wouldn't be keeping them company much longer.

"I got to talk to this man," he said, taking Gayle's hand to bring her with him. She tried to hold her ground. Rather than simply yank her along, Didi explained patiently but quickly, "Look, I know you're a little shaky, this being your first time and all, but this is your big chance. I mean, all sorts of writers do ride-alongs with cops. But how many get to do a shoot-along with a stone killer?"

Despite the terror that was devouring her every vital organ, the question had resonance for Gayle. If she got out of this alive, she'd be able to sell her story for millions. Better yet, she'd be able to write and *direct* the project. She let Didi lead her forward.

"Look at the man's eyes," Didi told Gayle, nodding at Ring. "Still got some fire in them. He's not ready to check out just yet. We got a little time here." He turned to Ring and answered the man's original question. "My name is Didier DuPree. You are Colin Ring, I hope."

"Bugger you, you wog bastard."

Didi said, "Now, I ain't even a lawyer, but I still know that's non-responsive."

He shot Ring in his right foot. The Brit cried out, but his diaphragm wasn't up to producing much in the way of volume anymore. There was still hatred in his eyes for Didi, but those fires had been banked a little, too.

"Okay," Didi allowed, "you're sure not American, and you look just like Junior Cardwell described, so we'll take it on faith who you are. That means all you really gotta tell me is your room number at the hotel where you're staying."

Then Didi thought of something else.

"Oh, yeah. If you write on one a them laptops, you better give me any password I might need."

The look on Ring's face, while still pain-wracked, turned incredulous. "This is about my bloody *work?*"

"Oh, yeah. See, I know all about your book on Jimmy Thunder. I just happened to be in the right place at the right time and overheard Junior Cardwell tell him all about it. I was so tickled, I decided I had to be the first one — and the only one — to read it. You want to look at it this way, I'm your biggest fan."

"Sod all," Ring lamented

"Yeah, I can sympathize. Sometimes the price of fame comes awful high. And it's about to go right on up, if you don't tell me what I want to know."

Didi aimed his gun at Colin Ring's crotch.

"Funny thing, ain't it, baby?" Didi asked the mesmerized Gayle. "Man knows he's dyin' … but he wants to go with his johnson still on him. Never can tell. Might be some pussy on the other side."

Ring concurred. He told Didi his room number and his

computer password

Didi had watched closely for any sign that the Englishman was lying. When he was sure he hadn't seen one, he finished Colin Ring off neatly with a shot in the forehead.

Gayle gasped. Didi slipped an arm around her waist and said, "That's how you do it in real life, baby."

He walked her over to a sofa and sat down with her to explain a few things.

"The important thing for you to remember here is you are my accomplice. You brought the man here into your house. You're as guilty as I am … and that's where I get my peace of mind about lettin' you live."

"But … but I … I didn't know …" Gayle ran out of gas when she heard how lame her explanation sounded. Even if it was the truth, she'd have to rewrite it, and she didn't think Didi would help her with the phrasing.

"See, baby, it sounds bad even to you. So, here are a few other facts you best remember. Nobody in the whole wide world knows I've been here. And that dead body over there, and a shitload of physical evidence in your house, it's all on you."

For the first time, Gayle noticed that Didi was wearing surgical gloves. She'd done enough rewrites on thrillers to know what that meant. Didi hadn't left any fingerprints on the murder weapon, and there'd be no gunpowder residue on his hands.

Didi added, "Could also be some sharp-eyed sonofabitch even noticed you picking up that poor fellow."

And though she'd ducked her head at the bar, Gayle knew the waitress who brought that goddamn stout to their table must have seen her with Ring. She was trapped, and she knew it.

"What do you want me to do?" she asked quietly.

"Just play along, baby. You 'n' me, we've had some good times. No reason why we can't part friends."

"You're really not going to kill me?"

"Not unless you lose your head and start screaming to the first cop you see. Hell, maybe not even then. Because I believe you really understand you're in too deep to ever get out clean."

Gayle nodded involuntarily. Fatalistically.

Didi smiled and instructed her, "Now, go on over there and take the man's wallet out of his coat. Find the card key to his hotel room. Leave as many fingerprints on it as you can."

She did as she was told, too stunned by how her life was completely under Didi's control. Colin Ring's eyes were still open as she bent over him, trembling. He seemed to watch her with lethal disapproval. If she'd written this scene, he'd jump up and crush the life out of her just as she took his wallet. But she lifted it from the inside pocket of his coat without any trouble, other than struggling to keep her stomach down.

But when she turned around and saw Didi closing all the windows, that scared her as much as Ring coming back from the dead would have.

"Why are you doing that?" she asked in a plaintive squeak.

"Shit draws flies, baby, and you got a two hundred pound sack of it just layin' there."

A wave of relief passed through Gayle that left her weak. He wasn't going to kill her — yet. But what Didi had said made her ask. "You mean we're going to leave him here? In my house?"

"Can't think of a better place," he said, stepping over and taking her arm. "Just one more reason for you not to talk to any cops. And for me not to ace you. Come on now, you got to break into the man's hotel room. And then we'll go see Reverend Thunder, maybe ask him to pray God forgives us our wicked ways."

He led Gayle down to her car and soon they were on the road.

Didi had no intention of letting Gayle live, of course. But, as a business practice, he'd come to believe in just-in-time dying. That was, never kill your mark a before he had exhausted every last ounce of usefulness.

He'd gotten the idea from the time he'd been given the job of taking out a big shot from the auto business. The guy had thought he was so famous he could hump and dump the daughter of a Mob wise guy and get away with it. Well, that old boy had learned better.

But before he had, Didi'd been obliged to sit and listen to his target talk to a group of his colleagues at a convention. The man had about bored Didi to death. But then he let loose with this one little nugget about the just-in-time delivery of auto parts. Said it saved the modern businessman all sorts of grief. Didi had embraced the idea and made it his own.

Paid to keep your ears open.

So, ol' Gayle's number wasn't up just yet, but the countdown had definitely commenced.

CHAPTER 46

The bloody hammer lay beneath the thick branches of a Douglas fir, right where the caller had said it would be.

The tip at the Civic Auditorium hadn't been more than a second old before Ron had popped up and told the caller he'd get right back to her. Then he quickly stepped over to the phone monitor's desk and broke the connection. He knew from experience that the phone numbers of all incoming calls at town meetings were noted and recorded by caller ID. The reporters present who'd already leaped to their feet and tried to shout out questions to the caller had bellowed complaints at Ron. This drew a partisan response from the crowd, catcalls instructing the media to let the police do their job without taking a lot of crap from them.

The mayor had to restore order with the deadliest whispered, "That's enough," Ron had ever heard. The way he did that, above the tumult, making himself heard and obeyed, impressed the chief that the mayor was both one fine actor and a genuine force of nature.

Then there'd been the problem of Special Agent Horgan trying to horn into the investigation. Clay had dispatched him quickly, too. He'd been told that thanks to the Goldstrike PD, Horgan had been given a tip on church burnings and a defendant in a hate crime. If that wasn't good enough for him — if he didn't include himself out once and for all — the mayor had some markers with someone even higher than the attorney general of the United

States. He'd call one of those markers in and make sure Horgan's career ended before he could drive down out of the Sierra.

After that display of raw power and ruthlessness freed Ron from the FBI's shadow, he got back to the caller, asked for her address, told her to sit tight and not talk to anyone else about the hammer. He called Oliver and Benny Marx, the department's crime scene specialist, and now the three cops looked at the hammer.

"You see that?" Benny asked, shining his flashlight on the striking end of the claw hammer. "That's more than just blood."

All of them squatted for a better look. They saw strands of hair — kinky black hair — caught in the dried blood. "At a guess," Benny offered, "we've found our murder weapon. We're awfully damn lucky the tree kept the rain from washing away the tissue residue."

"Yeah," Oliver commented. "Unless that hammer was used in another, more recent killing. Say, somebody else is avenging Terry Castlewood. Leaving us a body we don't know about yet."

Officer Marx looked aghast at the speculation.

"Don't even think like that," Ron told Oliver. "Benny, I'm going to send two units out here. You stay with them, and secure the area until it's light enough for you to do a proper job."

"You mean watch the area from *inside* the patrol units, right, Chief?"

Ron nodded. He wasn't going to expose any of his people to the possibility of a lion attack in the dark. It was a danger of which the tipster, Gwyn Reese, had also been aware. She said she'd gone out with her son, Kieran, to walk their dog, Barkley. Kieran Reese had the dog on a leash, and his mother watched over son and pet with a flashlight and a .45. Kieran had called out when he saw the hammer, and he'd later told Ron that Barkley had sniffed at it, but otherwise it had remained undisturbed. Now, Ron and the others had to leave the area before their clomping around obliterated any evidence.

Benny waited for his backup in Oliver's unit while the chief and his second in command talked in Ron's Explorer.

"I don't see the Reese family as being our perps, do you?" the chief asked.

"Unh-uh."

"So we ask ourselves, if this hammer did kill Isaac Cardwell, how did it get there?"

"And we both know we're not all that far from a certain service station where that informant — what was his name again?"

"Buster Lurie."

"Yeah, Buster. The fella who was changing his oil and saw Jimmy Thunder on the night of the killing. We're not too far from there, are we? Jimmy might've just stopped at the side of the road right where we are now and flung that hammer clean over the Reese house. How's anybody gonna connect it to him then?"

"Fingerprints?"

"We can always hope."

"But we're not forgetting about Colin Ring, either," Ron said, "not after what we learned about him. Or even Texas Jack, for that matter."

"Yeah," Oliver replied, dryly. "Just maybe it was a white guy who did it."

Ron snorted. "How'd the situation with Danny work out?"

"He's not ready to join the Black Muslims, but it put his nose seriously out of joint anyone would look down on him or his friends because of their color."

"His first time?"

Oliver regarded Ron coolly. "Yeah."

"Glad he's got parents like you and Lauren to see him through." Ron moved on to another subject. "You feel like maybe taking an hour, seeing if we can put our hands on Mr. Ring?"

"Can't. I gotta get home. Gotta be up early and go lion hunting."

"The state might come through with someone to relieve you tomorrow."

Oliver shook his head.

"If you'd told me that a couple hours ago, I'd have said, 'Amen.'

But after watching that town meeting, hearing that old guy, Ezra Tilden, talking about shooting mountain lions on sight, I changed my mind. That man's attitude made me think of the bad old days. You know: just keep plugging niggers 'til you get the right one."

"I didn't think it was that bad."

"Then you don't know."

Oliver went back to his unit and sent Benny Marx to wait with Ron.

The chief considered debating Oliver's point with him further, but a call came in from the car stationed outside Jimmy Thunder's estate. Two unfamiliar subjects, a blonde female and a black male, had just entered the property in a black Porsche. The cops on duty were passing the word along in case the chief was interested.

He was. He asked Officer Marx to presume on the hospitality of the Reese family for a few minutes until the relief units came. Then he drove off to see what was happening at Jimmy Thunder's.

The two cops on duty, the ones who'd called Ron, were Santo Alighieri and Divine Babson. The same pair who'd found Isaac Cardwell's abandoned car in the supermarket parking lot. They were beginning to impress the chief as especially alert cops.

He pulled in behind their unit, and the two patrol officers got out of their 4x4 to meet him, and to stretch their legs. Working a stakeout, Ron remembered, could leave you with stiff legs and a very tired ass.

"What've we got?" he asked the two patrol cops.

They repeated the description of the subjects and started to elaborate.

"The woman was driving. The dude was riding shotgun," Alighieri said.

"The woman saw us parked out here, and looked like we made her nervous," Babson added. "But I also got the feeling she was just about tempted to call out to us for help."

"Yeah, me too. But she didn't call, so we didn't help. We didn't want to step in a pile of shit, cause anybody any hassle."

"But we thought you ought to know."

Ron asked, "Did this guy look anything like your flyer of Didi DuPree?"

Both cops shook their heads.

"Darker skin," Babson said.

"Shaved head," Alighieri added.

Babson said, "He looked over and saw us, too. Gave us a big shit-eating grin. We were tempted to go over there and talk to him just for that."

"It sounds like they didn't drive right in," Ron said.

"They didn't," Alighieri responded. "There was some discussion over the intercom before the gates opened, but we were too far away to hear it."

"Got the license plate on the Porsche, though," Babson said. "S-C-R-P-L-A-Y. Registered to a Gayle Shipton. Addresses in L.A. and right here in town on Wildcat Lane." Then with a grin, Officer Babson commented, "Santo even says he knows her."

Ron looked at the other cop. Alighieri was clearly embarrassed.

"I don't know her, Chief. I said I know *of* her. She wrote *Deadly Nightshade.* I thought it was a pretty fair movie."

"Awful dialogue," Divine Babson interjected, drawing a look from her partner.

"Anyway, I like to do a little writing myself. So when a guy I know pointed her out to me one time, I just thought I'd keep her in mind. If I ever had a script that was ready to show, you know."

"Santo writes much better dialogue, Chief."

Ron sighed inwardly as Officer Alighieri stared daggers at his partner. He estimated, at a minimum, eighty percent of his cops, even the better ones, were star-struck by Goldstrike's celebrity residents. Well, at least this one didn't want to be an *actor.*

He wondered if Gayle Shipton's appearance at the Thunder estate was Marcus Martin's doing. Maybe Martin had it in mind to make Jimmy Thunder a movie star. Tell his life story — right up to the point where the racist chief of police makes Reverend Thunder's life a living hell.

Officer Alighieri curbed Ron's wandering attention. "Chief, I didn't like this guy Ms. Shipton was with. He looked wrong in every way."

Ron looked at Officer Babson. She nodded her agreement.

"Of course, maybe he was just her agent," she offered, repressing a laugh.

"But he didn't look like Didi DuPree?" Ron repeated.

Again, both cops said no.

"But I think if he comes back out soon, we ought to follow him," Alighieri said. "Have another unit take our place here."

Ron respected a good street cop's instincts … but he wondered how much this one's hunch was being influenced by a sense of melodrama. Did he imagine the woman was in trouble when she wasn't? Did he imagine himself riding to her rescue … and having her launch his Hollywood career?

Then there was the question of throwing Sergeant Stanley's orderly manpower assignments out of whack. Ron was sure he'd already created some dislocation by stationing two units outside the Reese house. Doing any more juggling might not be wise.

He shook his head.

"No. You two stay right here." Then a thought occurred to him. "Do you have a camera in your unit?"

"Yes, sir," Officer Babson said.

Ron looked at the gated entrance to the estate. A floodlight stood sentry at either side of the driveway. Plenty of candlepower to get a nice clear picture. The chief turned back to his cops.

"Whoever is the better photographer, do a paparazzi ambush of the Porsche if it comes back out. Get me a picture of this wrong dude. I want to have a look at him for myself."

Didi DuPree vanishing and this new guy showing up was just too much of a coincidence for the chief to abide.

CHAPTER 47

When Ron pulled into his driveway, he saw Corrie Knox's 4x4 parked there. The warden herself was sitting on his front porch. He didn't overlook the fact that she had her hunting rifle leaning against the porch railing within easy reach.

Ron got out of his unit and sat in the chair next to her.

"Didn't know if I'd find you here," he said. "With your friend from the state not needing the motel room any more, I thought you might be back there."

Corrie said deadpan. "Water pressure's better here. I can get all the shampoo out of my hair."

"That's certainly important. You wouldn't want to get dandruff."

"No way."

They sat in silence for several minutes just unwinding from the day, looking up at the stars and the moon, glad to have each other's company.

Then Ron asked, "You think you might need that rifle sitting here?"

Corrie looked at him. "In a word, yeah."

"I thought you said mountain lions hunt at dawn and dusk."

"Normal mountain lions. This one, I'm not making any bets what he's going to do next." She sensed Ron's uneasiness at her remark, and laughed. "Relax. I'm not getting flaky on you. It's just that this animal is into some extremely idiosyncratic behavior."

"Maybe we should send a shrink out with you," Ron offered.

"Ha-ha."

"I didn't get to ask earlier, how was Oliver?"

"Stalwart but not stealthy. Kept flicking his cigarette lighter."

"Cops don't get much ninja training. He wants to get right back at it tomorrow, though."

That surprised Corrie. Ron explained Oliver's reasoning.

"That's kind of ironic," she said. "I thought he might have felt the other way. I know old Ezra "Shoot on Sight" Tilden gave me some mixed feelings."

"What do you mean?" Ron wanted to know.

"Well, given my job and my education, I think the indiscriminate slaughter of wildlife is both abominably stupid and environmentally unsound."

"But?"

"But I think Mr. Tilden raised quite a good point: Who are the people in big cities to determine what's right for the people in the mountains? I thought maybe the deputy chief might feel something like that. You know, who are the white folks to determine what's right for the black folks?"

"If you carry that logic all the way out, who is anyone to determine what's right for anyone else? That line of thinking makes society impossible and anarchy inevitable."

"Whew!" Corrie smiled. "The thinking man's cop."

"Didn't go to college for twelve years at night for nothing," Ron said with a tired grin.

"You think we'll be as content to follow the rules, Mr. Philosopher, when us white folks aren't the majority any more? That's the way all the population experts say things are going."

Ron was quiet for a moment. Then he said, "I know what the projections are, but I don't think they'll hold water."

"Why not?"

"Because I don't know of any country anywhere, at any point in time, where the majority population simply allowed itself to lose its dominant status."

"So what do you think will happen? White folks will make

some last ditch stand, guns blazing?" Corrie asked her question in a joking tone, but Ron answered seriously.

"I think we're seeing some of that already. White supremacists camps like Elohim City, Oklahoma; those jokers who tried to set up the Republic of Texas a couple years back. People with simple minds and a lot of firepower are trying to reconstitute the country, or at least their piece of it, the way they see fit. Most of those folks don't exactly embrace the idea of the brotherhood of man, either."

"But you don't condone those groups," Corrie said.

"No. I just try to understand them. A lot of people think they're just angry white trash, but fear of the outsider — the old tribal mindset — is pretty universal. Cuts right across racial and ethnic lines."

"You mean in this country?"

"Around the world."

Corrie gave the idea a moment's rumination, then asked, "What about South Africa? The black people there were brutalized by apartheid for decades, but the black government has formulated policies of forgiveness and reconciliation."

"That's true," Ron agreed. "It was also Nelson Mandela's doing. He's been both noble and smart. Along with the U.S., South Africa is about the only multiracial country in the world that places a premium on civil rights for all of its citizens."

"Why do I feel there's a 'but' coming?"

"There is," Ron answered, rubbing tired eyes. "The 'but' is that South Africa has such an overwhelming black majority it has room to be noble. But how do you think the government and the black majority of that beautiful, sunny, resource rich country would feel if, say, millions of white people fleeing dead-end futures in Central and Eastern Europe started pouring across their borders? How do you think they'd feel if their population experts told them they'd be a minority in the foreseeable future? How do you think they'd feel if their social institutions were threatened by all sorts of strange foreign languages and cultural influences? You think they'd accept that complacently?"

Corrie said, "You put it like that, no. I can't see anybody standing by passively. So what does it mean? Pretty soon we'll all be right-wing, racist crazies?"

"Insofar as mankind is still a tribal species, we're all racists already. I'm just one of the few who's been publicly exposed. I'm the subtext of what we're talking about here, right? Or am I thinking a little too highly of myself?"

There was a moment of embarrassed silence as Corrie marshaled her thoughts.

"No, you've got it right. I want to know more about you, and I thought I could be subtle about it. Apparently, I'm pretty lead-footed in my interrogation techniques."

Ron laughed. "You as an interrogator, Oliver in the woods. Apparently, we all have our weaknesses. But even Emily Post might get stuck for the right way to ask someone if he's a racist."

Now, it was Corrie's turn to laugh. "When Tucker asked me if you were, I said you were in recovery. You are, aren't you? In recovery?"

Ron sighed deeply. "Most of the time. I think."

He told her the story about his father and DeWayne Michales.

Then he continued, "Now, you'd think a guy who'd seen his father almost beat his best friend to death because of his skin color would have learned a lifelong lesson. Something to the effect: if somebody's a good person, what does his skin color matter? If somebody's a bad person, what does his skin color matter? In short, what the hell does skin color matter?"

Ron chewed the insides of his cheeks for a moment, as if reluctant to speak, to confess, what was on his mind. Corrie recognized they were in sensitive territory here. She wanted to tell him he didn't have to bare his soul to her, but before she could, he told her what he'd never told anyone else.

"There are some black people — certain individuals — who if I don't hate outright, I come pretty damn close. I tell myself it's because of what they've done, not what they look like. And I believe that. Believe it completely. After all, there are a number of white people I include in that same category. But with the black people, because they're not *my* color, I wonder if I wasn't just a little quicker to feel animosity, and there are times when I ask myself if I don't feel that dislike just a bit more intensely.

"I'm very aware of these feelings. I watch them very closely. I can honestly say I've never let them affect the way I do my job. I'd quit if I ever did." Ron laughed harshly. "Of course, there'd be people waiting to shove me out, too. So there I am. Do you think I'm in recovery?"

"Yeah. And probably more honest with yourself than most people, including me, have the courage to be."

"Yeah, well. We all evolve as fast as we can." Ron got up, yawned, and stretched. "Come on, let's go to bed."

Corrie was silent for a beat, and then she laughed her deep laugh. This time with a ribald note to it.

"You know what I meant," Ron said. "Hell, as tired as I am, it wouldn't matter if we did sleep in the same bed."

"Must be terrible getting old," Corrie teased, standing and picking up her rifle.

There was more than enough moonlight for him to see the mischievous, challenging look on her face. He reminded himself that she wasn't as young as she looked. That she'd told him of one lover, and doubtless there must have been others. He wasn't *really* robbing the cradle, even if he still felt like it.

He took her hand and led her inside.

Marcus Martin hadn't wanted to let Didi DuPree and the white woman inside at all. He explained that it was not in Reverend Thunder's interest for them to enter the estate. In fact, with the police sitting right outside watching everything, it would be best if they just backed out and drove away. Immediately. But Deacon Meeker had pushed Martin aside.

"Come on in, Didi," he'd said into the intercom, opening the gates.

Now Didi, Meeker, Martin, Gayle, and Jimmy Thunder sat in

the mansion's massive living room. Martin and Jimmy sat on one sofa, Didi and Meeker, with Gayle between them, sat on a facing sofa. Gayle was as waxen as if she'd been stolen from Madame Tussaud's. Didi stroked her thigh idly, as one might pet a cat.

On Didi's lap was the computer Gayle had taken from Colin Ring's hotel room.

"Man had a lot of nasty things to say about you, Jimmy," Didi said, scrolling through the text on the computer screen. He stopped, read a notation, and grinned. "That old lady, Cardwell, went upside your head with a frying pan. That for real?"

Jimmy didn't answer. He appeared slightly less lifelike than Gayle. Marcus Martin, on the other hand, looked like he was about to burst a blood vessel. But the casual way in which Deacon Meeker had moved Martin's two hundred and twenty pounds aside let the lawyer know that keeping quiet would be, by far, the most prudent thing to do.

"Yeah, this man, Ring, he runs your character down all the way to China. Says you beat your wife while she was pregnant, ran out on her and Junior, never gave your boy a dime, or even owned up to him after you got rich." Didi leaned forward. "And Mr. Ring, he never even got to talk to me about your prison years. But, you know, I been helping ol' Gayle here with her writing. I bet I could fill in some blanks in this here book, too. Make 'em look just like ol' Colin Ring wrote those prison stories himself."

For the first time, Jimmy showed a flash of anger. His muscles gathered themselves for movement. But acting on Jimmy's behalf, Marcus Martin wisely put a restraining hand on the reverend's arm.

"How'd it look," Didi went on, "if everybody found out Deacon 'n' me had to protect you from becoming some of those big bucks' punk? The ones that wanted to prove a football player isn't so tough. How'd it look if folks read the deacon went out and got you your own punk to keep the nights from gettin' too lonely? You think all those fine Christian folks you got coming here on buses would part with their money for some fudge-packin' man?"

Not daring to show the least sign that she was listening, Gayle Shipton thought this was incredible stuff. Somehow or other, she had to get out of this alive. She had to write this story. Using as much of Didi's language as possible.

Didi continued in his quietly menacing voice. "Of course, once you got out of the joint, you went right back to pussy like any real man would. Thing was, you were hardly ever content to have just one in bed with you at a time. Ashanti and DaChelle can testify to that. They'll be back by-'n'-by, too, in case you're wondering. Then we got your drugs to talk about, too. How you like your blow and your ecstasy. But you know what your biggest problem is, Jimmy? The man who wrote all these awful things about you, he just got himself killed. Now, if somebody should ever discover this book at some later date, who's it gonna look like did the man? You could deny it all you want. But everybody knows you already killed one man. So why not another?"

"Mighta been one time, Jimmy, you were nobody's nigger." Didi snapped the laptop computer shut and stared hard at the reverend. "But you're my nigger now."

It was at that point that Marcus Martin decided he would have to do something he'd never have believed possible. Something that would gall him the rest of his days.

He'd have to call Ron Ketchum and ask for his help.

As Didi and Gayle drove back to the screenwriter's house, he was pleased with the way things had gone. Jimmy would fall in line. There was nothing like being revealed as a prison-cell faggot to empty a preacher's collection plate. Nothing like the threat of going back to the joint, maybe even Death Row, to terrify an ex-con. And as bad as Jimmy might be feeling about Junior's death right now, there was no point in the man losing everything he had. No future in it at all. Didi was sure that Jimmy knew all the black-mail threats were just window dressing. What lay behind them was the certainty that Didi would kill him if he didn't go along.

But it was best not to say that right out loud. Not to someone you might be doing business with for years to come. And this scam he'd cooked up for the Reverend Thunder's ministry had been the sweetest idea of his life.

It'd all started when his cousin, Deacon Meeker, had called him and asked if Didi might find something for him to do real soon. His gig with Jimmy was going south; the faithful were getting tight with a dollar. Everybody's standard of living would start to suffer real soon.

Up 'til then, Didi had only talked to his cousin, Deacon, maybe once a year. And he hadn't given Jimmy Thunder any serious thought in a long time. But right when Deacon called, Didi was a little strapped for cash himself. He decided it would be a shame to let a money machine like the Reverend Thunder's fall by the wayside. If it could no longer do what it was originally built for, maybe it could be turned to another good purpose. Say, washing some serious amounts of dirty money.

While working out the plan in his mind, Didi had been introduced to these two whip-smart colored gals out of L.A., Ashanti Royce and DaChelle Chenier. Stone foxes both of them. Best of all, they were flexible in their thinking about what was right and wrong. Once he'd met the ladies, Didi's plan fell into place.

What he'd do was become a money-laundering broker. Not work for any one outfit. But offer his services to anyone who had some sizable funds they needed to have cleaned and pressed. When a customer came along, DaChelle with her background in criminology, and computers, could hack into the right data bases and find out if there was too much heat on a potential customer. And from all her dealing with cops, she'd be sure to smell an undercover pig a mile away. Ashanti, the demographer, knew the U.S. census reports like the back of her hand. She could generate endless *contributions* to Jimmy Thunder's ministry from folks who'd be astounded to learn that they'd made them. Not that they ever would.

Jimmy, he'd get a healthy cut, attention from the ladies, and Deacon Meeker would be on hand to keep an eye on things for

Didi. Everything had been working out without a hitch — until Junior Cardwell had popped up out of the blue. That boy had started to put a serious crimp in things.

Didi had never actually seen anyone saved from himself before. Certainly not anyone as avaricious as Jimmy Thunder. But Junior was actually starting to turn his old man around. Made the reverend truly think about giving up all the good things he'd worked so hard to con out of the suckers. Got him to think about doing what was *right*.

But then ol' Junior got himself nailed to a tree. Which just went to show, Didi thought, that no good deed goes unpunished.

Oops. He'd let another cliché slip by, even if he didn't say it out loud.

Didi looked over at Gayle. Sure enough, he decided, her time was just about up. She'd gotten all of Colin Ring's notes and his computer out of the Englishman's hotel room for Didi. And try as he might, he couldn't think of another thing she could do for him.

Not even one last bump 'n' grind. He knew from experience that when you got a gal down for one last ride and she knew what was coming — and somehow they all did — why, it just wasn't fun for anybody. So, he'd spare Gayle that much.

He'd just take her inside, do her quick, and leave her there with ol' Colin Ring.

Nobody knew he'd been staying at Gayle's house. He'd leave nothing behind to connect him to either killing. That smartass cop who'd popped up and taken his picture on the way out of Jimmy's place might have thought he had something. But what he had was the way Didi *didn't* look.

That dark guy with the gleaming bald head and the earring might get blamed for stealing Gayle's car, but Didi would bet they wouldn't have the Porsche on the stolen auto wire before he could drive it down to Reno. Once he got there, he'd just leave the keys in the car and the door unlocked. It'd be gone in two minutes.

Wouldn't take him a whole lot longer to catch the first plane out to anywhere far away. Then he'd make a connection to New

Orleans. He'd let his hair grow out and his skin color fade. Before you knew it, the guy who'd been photographed with ol' Gayle, he'd be gone for good.

Jimmy's lawyer, Marcus Martin, would have to make a permanent departure in the near future, too. But killing him would take a little planning. Couldn't just do the man inside of the Reverend Thunder's house. What Didi had to figure out was how to get Martin back to L.A. alive and then ice him in some untraceable way. He didn't know how to accomplish that yet, but he was confident something would come to him.

It always did.

They were pulling up to Gayle's house when Didi stopped her from pressing the garage door opener. "Leave it outside, baby. I got another little errand to run."

Gayle looked at Didi without saying a word. But somehow she knew that this irregularity — not driving into the garage as usual — meant it was all over for her. Didi was going to kill her now. She was as certain of it as she'd ever been of anything. Worse still, she was sure Didi knew she knew.

As Gayle brought the car to a stop in front of her garage door, her hands froze on the steering wheel. Her whole body started to shake. Her shoulders hunched as if she were a leaf blown from a tree, curling in on itself. She wanted to scream, but could make only small mewing sounds. Tears slipped from her eyes and scalded her cheeks.

Didi reached over, turned off the engine and took the key. He got out of the car, walked around to her side and opened the door for her. He waited a moment in silence. When she didn't come out, he spoke softly.

"Come on, baby. I promise: It'll be easier than going to the dentist."

Christ, she thought, the bastard even had to come up with a great exit line. But was a knack for dialogue really a basis for a relationship? Was it enough reason to *die* for a man?

"Come on now," he repeated, his voice a little harder this time.

To her great shame, she obeyed him. What the hell was wrong with her? He was going to kill her whatever she did. Shouldn't she at least make it *hard* for him?

Getting to her feet, wobbling on one three inch heel and one sheared-off flat, she looked Didi in the eye and said, "I hope your dick falls off, you trip on it, and fall into a tree chipper."

Feeling compassionate, Didi replied, "Sure, baby. That's just what'll happen."

But it wasn't.

From the woods at the edge of Gayle's property came a growl. Two luminous feral eyes appeared. Didi and Gayle reached the same conclusion at the same time: mountain lion.

But Gayle's thinking leaped one step ahead. She knew what Didi would try to do here. Exactly what he'd done to her with Colin Ring. He'd try to throw her at the lion. Only this time she wasn't going to let him.

Before Didi could grab her, Gayle raised the foot wearing the remaining spiked heel. As he grasped her shoulders, she raked the heel down his shin and directly into his instep. Didi bellowed in pain, releasing her and bouncing up and down on his good leg. Gayle ran out of her shoes and around the Porsche. She dived into the passenger seat, and before Didi could get his bearings, she pulled both doors shut and locked them.

Didi looked at the lion. It had edged forward, but only a little. So, the killer peered into the car at Gayle. His face wasn't contorted with rage, as she'd expected. It registered only disappointment, mild disapproval. Didi reached around to the small of his back, and brought out his gun.

He took one more look behind him — and now the lion was nowhere to be seen.

"You want to come on out, baby?" he asked.

Gayle shook her head. If he wanted to kill her, he would have to do it the hard way. The killer shrugged. He held up the car key, let her look at it, and inserted it into the lock. But with Gayle's finger holding the button down, he couldn't get the door to open.

Now, Didi looked angry. He'd run out of patience. He turned to face the car squarely and raised his gun to shoot Gayle.

Which was when the lion leaped off the roof of Gayle's house and took Didi. Slammed his face smack up against the driver's side window, which, thank God, didn't shatter. Gayle heard the growl of the beast, the scream of the man, and the snapping of Didi's spine. A jet of bright red blood shot out of Didi's neck as an artery was severed. It splattered the Porsche.

Gayle didn't recoil. She watched in rapt fascination, trying hard to remember every detail of sight and sound, whispering fiercely, "Kill him, kill him, *kill him!*"

The lion needed no encouragement. It finished the job quickly. Then with its face painted in Didi's blood it stood on its hind legs and looked in at Gayle. It pushed the Porsche with its front paws, as if to tip it over. But the sports car was too heavy, too well balanced. The big cat gave Gayle a grunt. Not really angry, just disappointed in her the way Didi had been.

But the mountain lion didn't know how to fire a gun, so it took Didi DuPree's mangled neck in its mouth, flipped his body on its back, and carried the killer into the woods to eat.

Gayle told the departing predator, "If you need an antacid, pal, it's on me."

Hey, she thought, that was a pretty good exit line, too.

CHAPTER 48

Thursday

Ron and Corrie were a tangle of interlocked arms and legs when the phone rang. Their eyelids snapped open in unison, as if they'd been choreographed. Extracting circulation-deprived limbs from the jumble, however, was managed with far less artistry. Both of them saw that the morning sun had peeked over the horizon. The day was still young, but they were already late to meet it.

The phone rang again.

"Oh, God!" Corrie exclaimed. "That has to be the deputy chief wondering where the hell I am. Quick, pick up the phone," she instructed Ron. "Tell him I'm on my way."

Ron watched her scurry nude into the bathroom. Then he answered the phone.

It was Oliver, all right, but he wanted to talk to the chief, not the game warden.

"Found Colin Ring," he said without preamble.

"Where?" Ron asked.

"Dead in a lady screenwriter's house."

Gayle Shipton. The name clicked into Ron's head from last night.

"Is she dead, too?"

That was when Oliver threw him a curve.

"No, she's just fine. But she says that DuPree character you wanted is dead."

Ron was stunned. "She killed him?"

"Nope. It was the mountain lion. Finally nailed somebody."

"Jesus!" Ron got Gayle Shipton's address from Oliver.

Then he ran into the bathroom and jumped into the shower with Corrie.

But it was purely a matter of hygiene.

Ron raced to Gayle Shipton's house with Corrie right behind him in her 4x4. Officers Santo Alighieri and Divine Babson had been reached just before they ended their shift, and they were at the Shipton house when Ron and Corrie arrived. Oliver was there with Dr. George Ryman, the town's volunteer medical examiner, and two more patrol officers.

The lot of them met with Gayle Shipton on the balcony outside her living room. Alighieri and Babson identified her as the woman they'd seen last night at the Thunder estate. They also confirmed that the Porsche outside was the car they'd seen. Ron thanked the officers and dismissed them. He told the other patrol officers to wait outside and hold at bay any media types who showed up.

Dr. Ryman did the obvious and pronounced Colin Ring dead. Then he, too, went outside to wait for Officer Benny Marx to wrap up his work behind the Reese house where the bloody hammer had been found. The crime scene specialist hoped to make it to the Shipton place within the hour.

Gayle Shipton admitted picking up Didi DuPree in a cafe. She said she'd been interested in some recreational sex. But once she got him home, he'd pulled a gun and told her she was his *slave*. If she didn't do exactly what he wanted, he would kill her.

In response to Ron's question, Gayle said, yes, Didi had shaved his head and darkened his skin. He was the man with her last night. They'd gone to the Thunder estate right after Didi had killed Colin Ring. He'd forced her to lure the Englishman to her house so he could have her gain access to the key to his hotel room, and steal all of Ring's material on the book he was writing about Jimmy

Thunder.

Gayle detailed the blackmail plan against Jimmy Thunder she'd heard at the reverend's estate last night — but, no, she hadn't heard what it was Didi had wanted from the man.

Finally, she described how Didi had planned to kill her when they returned to her house last night. But the mountain lion had intervened.

Corrie spoke up. "I know you must have been terrified, but did you notice if the animal had any distinctive markings?"

Gayle recalled without difficulty that the lion had a scar over its left eye.

She'd written down everything she'd seen and heard as soon as she'd run into her house.

She'd also copied to a flash drive everything that had been on the hard disk of Colin Ring's laptop computer, and photocopied all of his handwritten notes on her office copier. Then she'd mailed the works to her agent in L.A. She'd phoned him, told him what had happened, and he promised that he'd have an auction set up for the rights to her story by lunchtime.

But Gayle didn't mention any of this to the police. She simply told them that all the material Didi had forced her to take from Ring's hotel room was down in her car. They were welcome to it.

She further said she had a project to finish with a crushing deadline. If they didn't mind, she was going to complete it down in Palm Springs. She didn't say specifically at the Betty Ford Clinic. But since she had felt it best to flush all the drugs she'd had on hand before she called the cops, she thought she might as well check in now.

Gayle gave Ron her attorney's name and number in case they needed to reach her. She was pleased the chief was sophisticated enough to accept that. It made her think maybe she should have a cop around to give her technical advice on her new project.

But someone younger.

Ron, Oliver and Corrie regrouped outside of the Shipton

house. The two cops glanced up to make sure Gayle wasn't eavesdropping from her balcony. She wasn't. But out of professional paranoia, they spoke quietly anyway.

"So," Oliver asked Ron, "knowing the woman makes up bullshit for a living, how much of that story do you think we ought to believe?"

"The general outline. She admitted she picked DuPree up for sex. That was supposed to make us think she was being honest, had nothing to hide."

"She kept referring to the man as Didi," Corrie offered. "Doesn't sound like she was much of a slave to me."

Oliver barked out a short laugh. "Maybe he hadn't gotten around to having her pick any cotton."

Ron smiled thinly. "Okay, let's look at what we have here. Ring's dead upstairs, and who knows how much of DuPree is left out in the woods. Just because they're both dead, though, does that mean we like either of them any less as Isaac Cardwell's killer?"

"I want to read Ring's notes and manuscript before I tell you how I feel about him," Oliver said. "But I like DuPree better right now. Isaac Cardwell was about to wreck DuPree's scam, and we all saw upstairs the man liked to exercise his right to bear arms."

Corrie gave a bemused shake of her head.

"What?" Ron asked.

"I was just thinking how ironic it would be," she said. "DuPree turns out to be your killer, and he gets eaten by the mountain lion? Nobody will ever believe it wasn't divine retribution. Maybe not even me."

Ron and Oliver looked at each other. Cops were professional cynics. They'd never admit to sharing such a belief. But they both knew if it worked out the way Corrie had said, Goldstrike would be stuck with its very own legend.

The chief wanted to offer one more possibility, however.

"Part of the blackmail angle DuPree had on Jimmy Thunder, maybe the biggest part for some people, was he'd had homosexual relations in prison. In Ms. Shipton's word, the good reverend had a *punk*. How do you think Texas Jack might feel about that, if he'd heard about it somehow? Jack was raped in a jail cell as a young man by a black inmate. Then Jimmy Thunder stiffs him for two hundred thousand dollars in poker debts. Then, maybe, Texas Jack finds out the reverend had brutalized a young man the way he'd been assaulted himself. You think that just might set him off?"

Oliver nodded. "Only thing is, if it did, I'd see Jack nailing *Jimmy* to that tree."

"Unless he knew it would hurt him more to lose his son," Corrie suggested.

The deputy chief knew deeply it would grieve him to lose his son.

"Could be — if he knew that."

Ron said, "I'm going to push Sergeant Stanley on finding out where that nail I took from Jack's place is sold in town. Maybe that will lead to something."

Just then Officer Benny Marx pulled up, having finished his work at the Reese house. He walked over to his superiors. He told them he hadn't found any footprints in the area of the hammer, other than those of the tipsters: mother, son and canine. What he had found were marks indicating that the hammer had, in fact, been thrown to its final resting place. The tool was now on its way to the state police lab in Sacramento for analysis.

Benny Marx looked up grimly at the Shipton house. "I used to think I'd never get a chance to practice all the evidence gathering skills I learned. Now, I get nightmares."

The comment raised a thought in Ron's mind.

He asked Corrie, "Will you need Officer Marx's help when you find DuPree's remains?"

Benny blanched at the thought of going out into the woods. Corrie blanched at the thought of taking him. The deputy chief was enough of a tenderfoot for her.

"Why don't we just bag the cat first?" she suggested. "The other stuff can wait."

"Yeah," Benny agreed fervently.

"You ready, Deputy Chief?" she asked.

"Yes, Mem'sahib," Oliver replied. But they both grinned as they headed off to Corrie's 4x4. Officer Marx hurried inside Gayle Shipton's house in pursuit of nightmares that fell within acceptable limits.

Ron decided it was time to return to the scene of the crime.

The original one.

CHAPTER 49

Didi DuPree. Colin Ring. Jimmy Thunder. Texas Jack Telford.

Those were the names of the men among whom Ron expected to find the killer of Isaac Cardwell. If he was overlooking someone, he'd have to give himself a kick in the ass to think who it could be. Which in a manner of speaking was just what he intended to do.

He was going to look again at the tree to which Isaac Cardwell had been nailed. Look at it, not in the hope of finding new evidence, but simply to review the setting. To see if it would suggest which of his suspects had committed the crime. To see if he could imagine which of those men had driven the nails through Isaac Cardwell's flesh and into the lightning-struck tree.

To get to the tree from the Shipton house, Ron had to take Highway 99, the road that would lead him across the Tightrope. Ron didn't have the same dread about the Tightrope that Oliver did, but he maintained a healthy respect about crossing the narrow, guard rail free length of blacktop.

You wanted to make sure your tires, brakes and suspension were in good working order before you ventured out upon this particular stretch of road. A mechanical failure here would be more than costly. A twitch in an arm or leg muscle wouldn't be a real good idea, either. And forget about sneezing.

Of course, you could manage your end of things just fine, and a sudden stiff crosswind might still send you sailing. But Ron figured that would be a case of your number being up, and if that happened you could be at home in bed and you were still going to check out.

The chief's philosophical detachment was put to the Tightrope's most severe test when, just after he'd begun his crossing, a semi-tractor rig appeared around the curve in the oncoming lane. The huge truck took up every bit of its own side of the road, and the overhang of its trailer intruded into Ron's lane. Not much. But on the Tightrope you didn't want to yield a millimeter of ground.

The two vehicles *crept* toward each other. Tectonic plates moved faster. Ron saw the trucker staring fixedly at an imaginary point in the center of his lane. Guiding his vehicle as if it were on a rail. Beads of sweat stood out on the man's forehead. The truck driver knew he had to take it slow, but a high-profile rig like his provided a much bigger target for a gust of wind than a car.

Small comfort for Ron. If a strong wind caught the far side of the truck while it was passing his car, they would both go over the edge.

Several moments — and lifetimes — later the front bumper of each vehicle broke the same plane. Now they were creeping past each other. As the trailer of the rig approached, Ron thought for sure he was going to lose his left sideview mirror. He was perfectly prepared to let it go. There wasn't a hair's-breadth of roadway to his right.

But when he came abreast of the trailer, the mirror wasn't snapped off — only its finish was removed. In a long screeching banshee wail that seemed to go on forever, the mirror's housing was abraded by the aluminum body of the trailer. Oliver would have had a heart attack.

By the time an eternity passed and the vehicles finally cleared one another, Ron's nerves weren't exactly rock-steady, either.

The chief eased his patrol unit toward the center of the road to give himself some breathing room. Then, looking to his left at the staggering vista of mountains and lake he was now able to appreciate, he was struck by a sudden insight. He immediately moved his unit to the dead center of the pavement and came to a complete stop. Checking his rear view mirror to make sure the semi had cleared the Tightrope, and no other vehicles had moved onto it, he turned on his emergency lights.

Even from this position of relative safety, he exited his vehicle carefully. He stepped as close to the town side drop-off as he dared and looked down. Far, far below were the pointed tops of countless evergreens. Not far beyond the stands of trees were houses and a road. Diamond Bay Road. Where the Reeses lived. Where the bloody hammer had been found.

Now Ron understood that the killer had nailed Isaac Cardwell to the tree, driven up to the Tightrope and flung the hammer over the side. He had every right to expect it would never be found. If he'd thought to throw it over the wilderness side dropoff, he'd undoubtedly have been right. But in the dark, when the killing had occurred, and presumably somewhat agitated by having committed murder, the perp must have failed to make the distinction.

Ron got back in his patrol unit, switched off the lights, and made his way off the Tightrope before any other vehicle came along.

It was a small lead, to be sure. But the discovery made Ron feel lucky. Like the breaks would be coming his way now. One around each bend in the road.

As Ron came around the bend in the road where he and Oliver Gosden had discovered the body of Isaac Cardwell, he saw something so outrageous he felt like he'd just been hit in the gut by a heavyweight left hook.

Four teenage boys, all of them white, but one in blackface, were re-enacting the murder. The boy in blackface was being "crucified" by the other three. Everyone involved, including the "victim," was laughing uproariously. They thought the whole thing was hilarious.

Ron was infuriated.

He pulled up on the wrong side of the road in a screech of tortured rubber. He flicked on his lights and sirens, and was out of the car with his riot gun in hand.

The boys froze for a second when they realized what was happening. Then they started to scatter. Except for the kid in blackface, who was tied to the tree.

Ron fired a round into the air and roared, "Police! Stop and drop!"

There was no arguing with that voice of command, not punctuated as it was with gunfire. The three boys immediately fell to their faces with their hands stretched out. The kid tied to the tree raised his hands, but he wouldn't meet Ron's eyes.

"Stay right where you are," Ron ordered. "God help you if any of you moves a muscle."

Without taking his eyes off them, the chief made his way back to his car. He called for a back-up unit, and told the dispatcher to advise the responding officers to make sure they had four pairs of handcuffs. And for Sergeant Stanley to be prepared to book four juvenile offenders.

His instructions were spoken loudly enough to produce moans and sobbing among the boys.

Ron looked at the yellow crime scene tape that had been knocked down. Now, even if he wanted to, he wouldn't be able to look for any further evidence. The area had been tainted. It had never occurred to him that he'd need to post officers to protect the integrity of the site.

He was angry at himself for that oversight. But right now his wrath was focused outward.

In a hard, chilling voice he said, "I'm going to charge the four of you with trespassing on a crime scene. If the DA will go along with it, we'll look into obstruction of justice charges. I don't know if the FBI would consider this a hate crime, but I'll check with them, too."

All four teenagers were sobbing now.

"If any of you has a criminal record, you're going to be looking at jail time. If you don't, you'll probably get probation, but you'll have established a criminal record for yourself. And, without a doubt, you and your parents will have a very unpleasant meeting with Mayor Steadman. Don't be surprised if he comes up with some punishment for you that would make jail seem like a pleasant alternative."

Ron wondered if Clay would go along with the idea of having these four cretins pilloried. He had to repress a laugh. Of course, he would. He'd probably make them build their own stocks.

A patrol unit arrived within minutes. Nobody got a response time like the chief of police. It was one of the perks of the job. The four teenagers were cuffed and packed into the caged back seat of the patrol car. Ron gave orders for them to be booked and their parents to be called. But they were not to be released until he got back to headquarters.

When he was alone again, he tried to calm his mind, douse his emotions. He looked at the dead tree. Now it was the site of two crucifixions: one real, one symbolic. Both profane. Both carried out on that ugly-as-sin stalagmite of decomposing wood, standing there in malignant contrast to all the vibrant, fragrant evergreens around it.

Damn thing ought to be cut down.

Unable to clear the stark image of the burlesque crucifixion from his mind, Ron got back in his unit and drove off. What he'd just seen made him think how graphically gruesome the real thing must have been: Isaac Cardwell, a living man, being nailed to a dead tree.

The epiphany that came from that thought hit Ron so hard he almost ran his car into the side of the mountain: a brand new idea of who the killer could be.

Who the killer *had* to be.

Someone who had been right in front of him the whole time.

Doing his subtle best to mislead Ron.

But the charred tree itself was the most compelling evidence.

CHAPTER 50

The chief called Sergeant Stanley into his office as soon as he returned to headquarters.

"What do you have for me on that nail I asked you to track down?" Ron asked.

"Five retail outlets in town sell that kind of nail, Chief. Two hardware stores, two home improvement centers, and a lumber yard." Stanley gave Ron the names and addresses of all five businesses. "Locating the stores was the easy part … and, I'm sorry to say, if you still think Texas Jack is your man, a guy at the lumber yard remembers him buying building materials, including nails, two weeks ago."

Ron saw the look of dismay on Caz Stanley's face. The sergeant didn't want to believe Texas Jack could be the killer.

"Do all the stores have surveillance cameras?" the chief asked.

"Three out of five," the sergeant replied. "I thought of that, too. I asked the stores not to erase anything. But I haven't picked up any DVDs from their security systems yet."

"Have somebody do it right away, Sarge. And one more thing: tell Benny Marx to finish any evidence gathering work he has to do on Colin Ring's computer and notebooks first thing. I want to read everything the man wrote about Jimmy Thunder."

Sergeant Stanley saluted and was about to leave when he remembered something. He took a small envelope out of his shirt pocket.

"I almost forgot, Chief," he said, handing the envelope over. "This came express mail this morning for you."

It was from Charmaine Cardwell. The copy of the letter she'd received from her dead husband.

"Thanks, Sarge. That'll be all for now."

Sergeant Stanley closed the chief's door on his way out.

Ron opened the envelope. There was no note to him enclosed, only a photocopy of the letter he'd discussed with Isaac Cardwell's widow yesterday. Out of necessity, but with more than a little regret, he read the whole thing. It was, as Charmaine Cardwell had said, very personal and deeply moving, the heartfelt words of a man who had loved his wife and child.

Reading Isaac Cardwell's letter made Ron feel both deeply sad and profoundly angry that such a good man had been taken so brutally from his family. This couple should have been allowed to grow old together, to raise their son and any other child they might have had, to see their grandchildren being born and their posterity secured.

Ron moved on to the passage that was most relevant to him now:

I think my father could be in real jeopardy. There's someone close to him, someone unlikely to arouse his suspicions, who may mean to do him harm or even kill him. I cannot imagine that it is only coincidence that has brought this man so close to my father.

Hearing those words yesterday only made Ron wonder whom Isaac had been writing about; seeing them today made him more certain than ever he knew who the killer was.

Now, he had to find out *why* the killer had struck, why he'd chosen Isaac Cardwell for his victim. He was about to go out looking for answers when his secretary buzzed him.

"Yes, Dinah?"

"Chief, there's a Marcus Martin here. He'd like to know if you could see him."

Corrie Knox and Oliver Gosden followed the mountain lion's

tracks for a mile into the forest. Over the last hundred yards of that distance, the animal had dragged the body of its victim, leading Corrie to wonder if the animal had grown tired of carrying its burden. That would be consistent with her idea that they were dealing with an older cat.

The mountain lion had cached the mortal remains of Didi DuPree between a sugar pine and a large boulder. Corrie carefully removed the soil, leaves and branches with which the animal had covered its leftovers. Didi was not a pretty sight.

Both arms were gone, as was the left leg. Didi had been eviscerated, and the cat had packed his chest cavity with dirt to preserve the meat. Didi's head was still aligned with his shoulders but was separated from them by twelve inches, and his face had been torn off.

The intermediate scavengers such as coyotes and crows had yet to sup, but legions of bugs were having their turn at the killer turned coldcut.

Corrie rose and kept her rifle levelled. Oliver had his handgun extended. The safeties of both weapons were off. They both sensed the mountain lion was nearby. A big predator didn't stray far from the prey it had taken until *all* the food it could consume was gone.

The game warden and the deputy chief looked carefully in every direction — including up — to make sure they were not the next entrees on the menu at the Fang 'n' Claw Cafe.

They listened to the sounds of the forest as closely as their hearing would permit.

As for their sense of smell, they tried their best to ignore it.

"I do believe Mr. DuPree's getting a bit ripe," Oliver said. "Must've forgotten his deodorant or something. I think we'd better get his sorry ass tagged and bagged."

The deputy chief used his portable radio to summon help to remove the body. The overworked, overanxious Benny Marx showed up thirty minutes later with two other cops, Dr. Ryman, and two attendants from the morgue at Community Hospital. Benny photographed the scene. Dr. Ryman declared the life and times of Didi DuPree to be at an end. The attendants loaded Didi's available parts into a bag and carried it away. Soon, Corrie and Oliver were left to resume their hunt.

The deputy chief took his cigarette lighter out of his pocket. He was about to start flicking the top open and shut when he saw Corrie looking at him. He put it back in his pocket.

"The sonofabitch beat it for a while when the crowd was here," the deputy chief said of the mountain lion. "You feel that?"

"Yeah."

"But now he's back."

"Unh-huh," Corrie agreed.

"I hate this shit."

"Hasn't been my favorite hunt, either."

Then they moved off carefully through the trees, following the lion's tracks. Not that they entertained any great hope of killing the animal that day. Or even sighting it. But simply waiting in place for the lion to show itself was too frustrating. Too damn scary, too.

Guns and all, standing still made them feel like a pair of sacrificial lambs.

Ron figured Marcus Martin had to want something from him. He thought it was too damn bad the sonofabitch didn't wear a hat. He'd have loved to see Marcus come through his door with one in his hand.

He knew Marcus hadn't come to threaten or bluster. If that had been the case, the lawyer would have *demanded* to see the chief. No, he was here to ask a favor. It was always sweet to see your enemies humbled, Ron thought, but right now he didn't have time.

So, as soon as the lawyer sat down in a guest chair, the chief asked in a neutral tone, "What do you want?"

"Reverend Thunder is in danger," Martin said, being equally blunt.

"From whom?"

"A criminal named Didi DuPree, and one of the reverend's

own associates, Deacon Meeker."

The chief was pleased to hear that the news of DuPree's horrific demise had yet to become common knowledge.

"Why is Reverend Thunder associating with a criminal?" Ron wanted to know.

"I can't answer that."

"You mean you *won't* answer," Ron countered. The two men stared at each other. Martin looked away first. The chief moved on. "Why can't he simply dismiss the deacon?"

"He's in fear for his life."

"Have you heard any direct threat to that effect? You know, something that would stand up in court."

Marcus Martin knew he was being mocked. He'd expected as much. But he'd come to achieve a goal and he meant to do it.

"I've heard threats of blackmail. Attempts to coerce the reverend to participate in a criminal enterprise," the lawyer explained.

Which was just what Gayle Shipton had told Ron earlier that day.

"Blackmail's painful, but usually not lethal," the chief said. "And, by the way, did Jimmy go along with the plan?"

"He did not."

"That's when you heard the death threat?"

"It was implicit," Martin hissed.

Ron nodded. "I believe you. But proving it could be tricky. You know how defense lawyers are."

"Are you going to help or not?" Marcus Martin demanded.

Ron watched his lifelong nemesis practically quiver in righteous indignation.

"Cops are handy people to have around when you need them, aren't they, Marcus? Even me." Ron got up. He'd spent too much time already jerking the lawyer's chain. "Come on. Let's go see the reverend. There's something I want to ask him anyway."

"What?" Martin asked defensively.

"You gonna play lawyer games at the same time you're pleading for help, Marcus?"

Marcus Martin insisted on knowing what Ron wanted to ask Jimmy Thunder.

When Ron told him, the lawyer couldn't find a single reason to object.

Except that he couldn't figure out what Ron was up to.

On the way to Ron's car, the chief and Marcus Martin ran into Lauren and Daniel Gosden. Greetings were exchanged. Ron was even civil enough to introduce Marcus Martin.

"Oliver's not here," Ron explained to Lauren. "He's out on duty."

"I know," Lauren said in a tone of mock disapproval. "You sent him out into the woods with a young blonde."

"It's okay," the chief replied. "She only has eyes for me."

"Why, Ron Ketchum. You dog."

Marcus Martin cleared his throat. He wanted to get going.

Lauren turned and gave him a look that guaranteed no interruptions from him for at least the next five minutes. But she got down to business.

"I wanted to talk to you, anyway, Ron. You heard about Daniel's problem yesterday?"

"Yes."

"Well, we got that all worked out. And since Oliver told me how much you liked my last button, Daniel wanted to give you my new one."

Lauren looked down at her son, who was still laboring under the weight of lessons recently learned. He raised his eyes to Ron and extended his arms to be picked up. Ron obliged.

"This is it," Daniel said, showing the button to the chief. If featured a picture of Lauren as a toddler, taking her first steps, with her older, and white, brother and sister each holding one of her hands. All three children were beaming. Beneath the image were the words: *Mitigate Your Hate.* Daniel asked, "Where should I put it, Uncle Ron?"

"Right here. Straight across from my badge." Ron helped the

boy pin the button to his shirt. Then Daniel gave him a kiss on the cheek.

"Would you like one, Mr. Martin?" Lauren asked. She had a plastic bag filled with buttons.

"Of course," he said. He pinned the button to the lapel of his suit.

He was far too shrewd to do anything else.

Lauren said she planned to distribute the buttons at Community Hospital, and she asked Ron if it would be all right if his officers wore them, too. He said sure. Have Sergeant Stanley make them available to anybody who wanted one.

Then he put Danny down, said goodbye, and he and Marcus Martin went to his patrol unit.

Ron looked at their matching buttons and said, "Looks like we're finally members of the same team, huh Marcus?"

The lawyer took his button off and put it in his pocket.

CHAPTER 5

Sergeant Stanley had his button on when he dropped into Clay Steadman's office.

The mayor noticed. "Nice button, Caz. Where'd you get it?"

The sergeant told him, and offered his to the mayor, telling him he could get another one. The mayor accepted and pinned it to his sport coat. Then he listened as Sergeant Stanley told him that the mountain lion had finally claimed a life — fortunately, not a life that would be greatly missed. He filled Clay in on the saga of Didi DuPree, Colin Ring, and Gayle Shipton.

Clay laughed mirthlessly.

"What's funny?" the sergeant asked.

"I was just thinking nature plays fairer than the movie business. In Hollywood, the writer would have been eaten alive and the heavies would have survived."

"If you say so, Mr. Mayor." Casimir Stanley was one of the few Goldstrike cops who didn't aspire to celebrity.

"But I don't suppose we can count on the lion being so discriminating in the future. I don't think the townspeople will take much comfort in the fact that it was a *bad* guy who got eaten. This news is going to crank up the panic and the anger."

"You have to announce it?"

Clay gave his old friend a look, telling him he should know better.

"Yeah. Fortunately, I'll also be able to announce I hired that houndsman from Louisiana. He'll be landing in Reno tonight. Ready to go tomorrow. And the governor promised we'll have more help from the state for Warden Knox by the morning, too."

"That's good."

"It's an improvement," the mayor conceded. "But I'm going to impose a dusk to dawn curfew starting tonight. It'll stay in effect until we kill this animal. Have the chief come by when he gets back in and we'll work out the details."

The sergeant stood up and saluted.

"Send Annie Stratton in, too, will you, Caz?" the mayor asked. Then he paused and sighed. "You know, all this stuff is beginning to wear on me. If I didn't have a reputation as a macho sonofabitch to uphold, I'd let Annie make some of these announcements."

Ron thought Jimmy Thunder looked like he was on the brink of a breakdown: mental, emotional, physical. Take your pick. In just the few days since Ron had seen him last, his deterioration was stunning. His skin looked lifeless and gray. His body slumped as if he'd lost the will and the wherewithal to stand upright. His eyes had sunk deeply into his face, and the light behind them was so dim it made the chief wonder if the man was functionally aware of his surroundings.

But the reverend had enough presence of mind to enrage his lawyer.

Jimmy Thunder told Ron that Marcus Martin must have misunderstood his conversation with Didi DuPree. Nothing criminal was either mentioned or implied.

Deacon Meeker, whose brow had suddenly beaded with sweat at Ron's appearance with Marcus Martin, now smiled. He was sure he had the situation sized up. One con didn't rat on another, not even years after both of them got out of the joint.

Meeker's cocksure attitude crumbled and turned surly, however, when Jimmy Thunder informed him his services would no longer be needed. Jimmy told the deacon he thought he would be more at home in the secular world. The reverend's one-time acolyte looked like he might have argued the point with his fists, had Ron not been there. As it was, he merely confirmed the reverend's opinion of him by removing the little gold cross from his collar and grinding it under his heel before he stomped out.

Jimmy Thunder watched the deacon's departure for a moment and then turned to Ron. "Have you found the man who killed my son?" he asked.

"Mahalia Cardwell is sure you did it," the chief said impassively.

For just a second, anger flared in Thunder's tired eyes, but it quickly faded.

"I've given that woman every reason in the world to hate me."

"That's her opinion, too. But there's another little matter."

"What's that?" the reverend inquired, though he sounded past caring.

"You were seen driving your car on the night your son was murdered. Not far from where he was murdered. When you said you were here playing cards with Texas Jack Telford."

Marcus Martin stepped forward and took Jimmy Thunder's arm.

"Don't say another word to this man, Reverend."

But Jimmy did. He nodded at Ron and said, "That's a beautiful button you have there. Wouldn't it be something if we could all get along like that?"

"Yeah," Ron replied. "It would."

He took off his button and handed it to Jimmy Thunder.

Then he asked the reverend the question that had brought him to the man's house and he got an answer that didn't surprise him at all.

The information the chief got from Jimmy Thunder led him to the estate next door to Thunder's own acreage. A discussion with the neighbor was the first link in a chain of six brief interviews Ron conducted that morning at some of the more lavish properties in town. At the final stop, he was given a long-distance telephone number.

But when he returned to his office and called it, the houseman who answered the phone told him the party he was trying to reach was abroad for the summer and wouldn't be returning for another two weeks.

Stymied from that angle, the chief called the librarian in Berkeley he'd talked to yesterday — the one who remembered Isaac Cardwell stopping in before he'd come to Goldstrike with Colin Ring. She answered, but in a state of high agitation.

A radical protester shouting about the over-representation of white male writers in the library's collection had just tried to set the contemporary fiction section on fire. But the can of lighter fluid the protestor had been using as the accelerant for her home-made flame thrower had blown up in her face. It was just terrible. The protester was horribly burned. The emergency sprinklers had put out the fire, but had also soaked thousands of books. And the library's acquisition committee had scheduled an emergency meeting to heighten the sensitivity level of its purchasing policies.

The librarian was courteous enough to take the name Ron gave her and promised to see if there was any reference to it in the library's magazine collection, but she couldn't promise to call him back immediately.

He said as soon as she could find the time would be fine.

As Ron tried to think of another approach to his problem, Sergeant Stanley knocked on his door and entered his office with a stack of DVDs in his hand.

He said, "Here you go, Chief. All the surveillance video from the two home centers and the lumber yard. The two hardware stores are your no-tech, mom and pop places, but the owners both promised to do their best if you want to bring a picture in to show them."

The sergeant put down the discs and rolled out Ron's TV stand.

"We've got discs going back two weeks at the home centers, and a month at the lumberyard. Where would you like to start?"

Ron sighed at the prospect that lay before him. He looked at the ten DVDs Sergeant Stanley had secured for him. There was no way of guessing which, if any, of them showed the face he wanted. Still, he knew he had to look.

"Start with the lumberyard," he said.

Sergeant Stanley powered up the TV and the DVD player and inserted the first disc to play. He handed Ron the remote control and said, "I'll be right back with a cup of coffee, Chief."

Ron said thanks.

Then he settled in to watch the first of the low-resolution black and white videos that retail management used to see who was stealing more from them on any given day — their customers or their employees.

Ron got lucky.

He didn't have to play all the discs before he found the face he wanted. He'd had to slog through barely more than half of them. With judicious use of fast-forwarding, that had taken him only two hours.

He viewed the transaction three times. By his watch, it had taken only thirty seconds for the killer to plunk the item down on the counter, tender his cash, receive his change and walk away with his purchase. But there was no mistaking the man's face. And there was no doubt he'd just purchased a box of the same kind of nails used in the crucifixion of Isaac Cardwell.

The chief stopped the video at the point where the buy occurred and ejected the disc from the player. The date and time stamp on the video's jewel box indicated it had been shot a week ago, last Thursday afternoon. Just hours before the murder.

Ron was pinning down the details of the crime piece by piece, but the one element that still eluded him was motive. Why had the crime been committed? And why had Isaac Cardwell been the victim? None of the old standby reasons — money, sex, and vengeance — seemed to fit.

Insanity was another reason, of course, and nailing somebody to a tree was certainly a sign of a disordered mind. But Ron would bet courtside tickets to the NBA Finals that the killer had never hurt another person in his life. In fact, when he called Sergeant Stanley in and gave him the man's name, and told him to run it through the state and federal databases for criminal histories, the Sarge said, "You've got to be kidding."

Ron said he wasn't.

He also asked Caz Stanley to have a sandwich and a soda sent in. He was getting hungry.

The last thing he reminded Caz to bring him was Colin Ring's writings.

Maybe he'd find his answer there.

CHAPTER 52

There were still two hours until sunset, but Corrie Knox decided to call it quits for the day. When she and Oliver had paused to have granola bars for lunch, the deputy chief had called in to headquarters, and Sergeant Stanley had given him the good news about the imminent arrival of the houndsman and the additional officers from the Department of Fish and Game. He also mentioned the curfew the mayor was imposing. In light of those developments, Corrie decided there was no point in pushing their luck.

Especially since for the last hour both hunters had felt the sensation that they were being stalked had increased dramatically.

So much so they could practically imagine the mountain lion salivating.

But they never saw so much as its shadow.

"One clean shot," Oliver said in response to Corrie's calling off the hunt. "Come on, you will-o'-the-wisp sonofabitch, give me one clean shot."

"They prefer sneak attacks," Corrie reminded him.

"The bastard's so close, been doggin' us so long, it's gotten very personal for me."

"Him, too, I think." Corrie never would have thought she'd say something like that — but at that moment, she believed it. "Listen, tomorrow we can dog him with real dogs. You can come along if you want."

Oliver kept scanning the trees. "I just might do that."

Then, being very careful, they walked out of the forest and back to the highway. Even there, they felt they were being watched from the trees. It was only when they got into Corrie's 4x4 and drove off toward town that they could tell themselves they were no longer being stalked — but even then an ominous tingle played at the muscles of their shoulders and necks.

"I want to thank you for your help," Corrie told Oliver as she drove. "I know the past couple of days weren't easy for you."

"You're welcome — and they weren't."

"We'll get him tomorrow."

"Then let's hope everybody obeys the curfew," Oliver replied. "Let's hope everybody's *real* careful tonight."

The deputy chief called headquarters from Corrie's 4x4 and spoke with Sergeant Stanley. Both men knew the conversation was likely being monitored, and took care to speak elliptically. Oliver recognized the irony of the situation. Cops bugged the bad guys' conversations, making them speak in code. Reporters eavesdropped on cops, making them use circumlocutions.

"Progress?" Oliver asked, regarding the Cardwell case.

"Chief's busy with his new reading."

Colin Ring's material, Oliver surmised. Didi DuPree hadn't needed a court order to get that stuff, now had he? But then Didi had wound up as cat chow, and they'd inherited it. Life as it should be, the deputy chief felt.

He'd dearly like to read Ring's notes and manuscript, too. But after a day of having the mountain lion size him up for kibble, all Oliver wanted now was a warm bath and to see Lauren and Danny. He'd catch up on his reading later.

"Same cast of characters?" Oliver asked, meaning suspects.

"Might be a surprise guest appearance."

A new suspect? That got Oliver's attention.

"The chief want me to come in?"

"Hasn't said so, Deputy Chief."

"Let him know I want in." If there was to be an arrest.

"Will do."

"Meanwhile, I'll be at home."

"Ten-four."

When Oliver broke the connection, Corrie asked him, "Ron's making progress in the Cardwell case?"

"Maybe. He might have found a joker in the deck."

"Wouldn't surprise me the way things are going around here. Nothing ever turns out quite the way you'd expect."

"Ain't that the truth?" Oliver agreed.

Then he closed his eyes for the rest of the ride home.

The sun was setting as Ron returned to reading Colin Ring's manuscript, "Hollow Thunder." He'd just spoken with Sergeant Stanley about enforcing Clay Steadman's curfew edict. All pedestrians were to be off the street before dark. Vehicular traffic was to be limited to those going to work, returning home from work or leaving town. The fatal attack last night at Gayle Shipton's house had been on the fringe of the built-up area of town, as had been the backyard invasion of the Derby house, but there was nothing to say the mountain lion might not venture deeper into residential or commercial areas. The police didn't want any innocent bystanders in the way if a patrol unit spotted the animal and officers responded with gunfire.

Picking up where he'd left off, Ron was glad that he'd made his breakthrough — found the man he knew in his gut had killed Isaac Cardwell — before he had begun reading. If Ring had things right, Jimmy Thunder had more enemies that he'd have ever imagined. There were other televangelists, both black and white, whom Thunder had demeaned. There were officials of charitable organizations to whom Thunder had promised large donations and then failed to make them. There were former teammates from his pro football days whom Jimmy had publicly humiliated by revealing their personal failings and holding them up to his flock as examples of how people should not behave.

Wading through all those suspects could have muddied the

water for years.

But one thing Ring had made eminently clear was the visceral hatred Mahalia Cardwell felt for her former son-in-law towered above the animus anyone else bore him. She blamed Jimmy Thunder for the death of her daughter. And now her grandson.

Even with what Ron had learned, however, he still hadn't found a motive for why his suspect had killed Isaac Cardwell. It was all that stopped him from going out and arresting the man right now. A hand knocked softly at his door. He looked up and saw Corrie.

"I went back to your place and cleaned up," she said. "Hope you don't mind."

It was the first time they had a chance to talk privately, without distractions, since last night. He still thought she looked awfully young — but he no longer worried about it.

Ron said, "I don't mind. You clean up real nice."

Corrie smiled, somewhat ruefully.

"Glad I'm good at something. I certainly haven't been able to find that lion."

"You'll get him tomorrow, when you have the dogs to help."

"That's what I told the deputy chief. He went home."

"There's a man who knows his priorities."

"How about yours? They include taking a break for dinner?"

Ron had been sitting at his desk long enough to feel stiff. He was starting to get hungry again, too. And he knew if you pressed too hard at detail work, you just might overlook the one fact you needed most. Sometimes a break was just what the doctor ordered.

Especially when the doc looked like Warden Knox.

Ron stood up, and was slightly dismayed by all the cracks, pops, and creaks he made doing so. He saw Corrie was grinning at him.

"It's okay," she said. "I'll rub some liniment into those tired old bones tonight."

Ron stepped around his desk to join her and said quietly, "We'll see who rubs what into whom."

The moment they drove out of the police parking lot they were both aware how the town was not itself that night. Under the lavender sky of dusk, the curfew had swept the streets clean of strollers, shoppers, and moviegoers. Restaurants were closed. Sidewalk cafes were deserted. All of this on a night when the temperature held steady at its daytime high.

Normally, the temperature in Goldstrike fell appreciably at night. At an elevation of six thousand feet, the heat of the day dissipated quickly. Even in August, the mercury could get down to the fifties shortly after dark. But not tonight. If anything, the temperature seemed to be rising.

"Warm front must be moving in," Ron said.

Above the mountains to the north of town, heat lightning flashed from fat black clouds stalled over the peaks.

"Rain?" Corrie asked.

Ron sniffed the air. "Don't think so. Just a hot, sticky night with a few special effects thrown in for atmosphere."

"Good night to hunker down, anyway," Corrie said, looking out at the empty streets.

"Yeah. People won't complain if it's just one night at home." Ron concurred. Then he nodded toward the ghost town view ahead of them and said, "It looks pretty eerie, doesn't it? Wouldn't surprise me if that mountain lion out there felt the difference and decided to come into town to look things over."

"The way I felt out in the woods today, it wouldn't surprise me if we find him under your desk when we get back to your office."

"That bad, huh?"

"I keep telling myself that I'm a scientist, a trained professional, an outdoorswoman of considerable experience — and the longer this thing goes on, the less I can relate it to anything I've experienced before. I grit my teeth when I think I'm becoming superstitious, but I'm starting to believe not every mystery is susceptible to rational analysis."

Ron looked at her. "In other words, you're spooked."

"You bet."

He said, "The hotel restaurants have to be open to serve their guests, but that's not what I had in mind."

"Me neither."

"You want to see if we can get a cup of coffee somewhere. Then we'll drive around, see if we can spot the lion asking for directions to my desk."

"Sure," Corrie smiled. "If we see him, I'll line up the shot and you can steady my rifle"

"As long as I have one hand free to hide my eyes," Ron responded.

They found coffee but not the mountain lion. An hour later, they'd just stepped into Ron's office when the phone rang. Ron took his seat and answered on the second ring. Corrie listened in from a guest chair.

"Chief Ketchum."

"Hello, Ron. This is Jack Telford. I'd like to report a theft."

A *theft?* Why had the call been put through to him, Ron wondered.

"Jack, you may have noticed we're a little busy around here right now. Did you lose anything valuable?"

"A nail," Texas Jack replied.

Ron didn't say a word.

"Not worth a penny, in and of itself," the poker champ continued. "But maybe it's come to mean a great deal more to some folks."

"You got something to say, Jack, say it."

After a brief pause of his own, Texas Jack did. "I was thinking I might have given you the wrong impression the other day. Talking about how Jimmy Thunder owed me all that money, and how I didn't expect to get it back. What with Jimmy's poor son being killed so recently, it seemed, upon reflection, I might've pointed a finger at myself. What with policemen being naturally suspicious people, anyway."

Ron responded, "We get a lot more suspicious when we learn a person has a rap sheet. And an unfortunate history."

Jack's silence was considerably longer this time.

Finally, he went on, "What I did, Ron, was think about those nails I dropped that day you came by my place. I guess I must have a suspicious nature myself. And I didn't get to be the card player I am without being good at details. So I counted those nails. The ones I picked up and the ones I'd already put in my roof. I searched all over to make sure I hadn't missed any, and I came to the conclusion that one was taken. You wouldn't know what happened to it, would you?"

"I've got it, Jack."

"Glad to see I haven't lost my touch."

"Tell me something," Ron said. "Whatever happened to the guy who attacked you in the Harris County Jail?"

"That old boy? He got out. But not long after that he had the misfortune to get drunk and pass out on some railroad tracks — shortly before a fast freight train happened to come rumbling through. Kind of ironic, I thought, that boy pulling a train. So to speak."

"Poetic justice," Ron agreed.

"How much thought have you given that it was me nailed that Cardwell boy to that tree?" Jack asked.

"Enough to check you out."

"You checked hard enough, you know I had a complaint against one man — not a whole race of people — and my score's been settled."

"Yeah, so you tell me."

"So I don't have to worry about you visiting me in any official capacity?"

"You've got no worries from me, Jack."

"Then I've got something for you."

"What's that?"

"You remember I told you about knowing the fella in that garden truck the other day?"

"Unh-huh," Ron grunted.

"I recalled where I saw him. It was at a funeral. Only reason I was there was to keep a friend company. I didn't know the family, and they didn't know me. But the old boy I was with played the horses like nobody you ever saw. Then he'd turn around and lose most of his money to me — just to keep his edge at the track. My friend brought me to the funeral because he was a friend of the family whose boy was being buried that day."

"And who was that?" Ron wanted to know.

"Quite a fine young athlete by the name of Roger Braddock, played quarterback for New York. If you pay attention to such things, you'll remember he was the boy Jimmy Thunder killed."

"Sonofabitch," Ron whispered.

Now he had the motive.

"And that fella in the truck," Jack went on. "My horse-playing friend, who I just got off the phone with, tells me his full name is Arthur Gilbert Braddock. Former groundskeeper at the track in Maryland my friend favored. And, of course, the dead boy's daddy."

"A son for a son," Ron murmured. "After all these years."

"That's why I'm telling you all this, Ron Ketchum. I'm a man who believes in squaring accounts. And if Braddock had killed Jimmy Thunder for what he'd done to his boy, I'd never have let on about him. But that boy, Isaac Cardwell, he had no more business being killed than Roger Braddock."

"No, he certainly hadn't," Ron agreed.

CHAPTER 53

Well after darkness had fallen, the mountain lion slipped out of the wilderness. It left behind the shelter of the endless pines and the cover of the brush and boulders. Using great stealth, it crept forward onto the hard manmade surface and passed the boundary of the town limit. The trees were sparse here; there was hardly any of the natural shelter on which it depended when hunting.

But the supply of game in this place was boundless.

The big cat's gut burned with hunger. It rarely got enough to eat these days; it was almost always ravenous. Bringing down an adult deer on which to gorge was beyond it now. It had to subsist on rabbits and squirrels and fawns. But not long ago it had found another source of food: the two-legged creatures. Their senses were dull and they were slow afoot.

They should have been easy prey for the big cat, and sometimes they were. But at other times they had proved dangerous. They surprised the cat with defenses beyond its instincts and experience. But it was learning.

The cat slunk through the shadows where the streetlights didn't reach, amidst the orderly rows of lairs in which its new prey lived. Sniffing the air, the scent of quarry came from every direction. The animal could hear the sounds of their calls and the noises they made moving about, though these were muted by the enclosures of their lairs.

The lion pressed itself into the deep shadow at the mouth of an alley as a car approached. It watched from concealment as two members of its newly favored food group rolled past. The cat understood instinctively that the two-legged creatures were beyond its reach in these moving lairs. No, it had to pounce on them as they walked upright. Unprotected.

Then the big cat's head whipped around as it caught a scent. It was not alone in the alley. With a grace and strength it had not completely lost, it turned silently and sinuously around and moving low to the ground crept deeper into the alley.

A pair of eyes appeared in front of it. Terrified eyes. The lion caught the sour scent of its prey's fear. The big cat moved carefully, taking no chance to allow its cornered victim any avenue to escape. As it closed in, a deep, low growl rumbled deep in the lion's chest.

Just before it could pounce, the prey bolted.

But as the alley cat tried to leap over its savage cousin, the lion batted it out of the air with one fierce swipe of a paw. The domestic feline hit the base of a brick wall and lay still, stunned, when the lion pounced upon it, the weight from its one hundred and forty pound body snapping the little cat's neck.

The meat from the prize was barely worth the lion's effort. It was an appetizer, nothing more. The big cat's hunger was only further whetted. It needed to eat more. It needed to eat now.

The big cat moved back to the mouth of the alley.

It saw no two-legged prey. The hard surfaces all around it were empty. The cat moved out of the alley, further into the town. Game was everywhere, but none of it was within reach. All the two-legged creatures were in their lairs. The cat's hunger almost drove it mad.

Then out of the endless array of olfactory impressions available to its keen nose, the cat found a familiar scent: one of the two-legged creatures it had been stalking the past two days. This one had spent much of its time outside. If the cat could find it now, at a place in which it was vulnerable …

The mountain lion stalked with a new sense of purpose. A sense of direction. It was closing in on one of the scents that had filled its mind for the past two days. This was a creature of significant size.

This was meat worth the taking.

Oliver and Lauren Gosden had put Danny to bed and turned in early themselves. Lauren had told her husband of passing out her new buttons at the hospital and to the Goldstrike PD. She said she thought she'd made some progress at reconciling the hard feeling that had arisen in the Sunshine Ward — among both the adults and the children. Oliver told Lauren of his day in the woods with Corrie Knox. How they'd found the ghastly remains of Didi DuPree, and how'd they'd felt the cat had been watching them all day, stalking them, just waiting for them to drop their guard. But they hadn't, and Oliver had to give credit to Warden Knox. She was right out there keeping up her end, moving a whole lot better through the woods than him, and not letting her fear get the better of her.

Lauren told her husband that the chief had all but admitted to her that he and Ms. Knox were an item.

"Dirty old man," Oliver commented.

"You're not envious, are you?" Lauren asked.

Oliver Gosden gave his wife the definitive non-verbal answer.

Now, Lauren lay asleep, the ghost of a smile playing at her lips. Oliver was starting to unwind and drift off himself, sleepy enough to ignore the light sheen of sweat on his forehead from the warmth of the night. He had the sensation he was falling, leaflike, through a medium slightly denser than air when the phone rang.

He jerked upright and answered groggily, "Gosden."

"Oliver, it's Ron. Were you sleeping?"

"Just about." Lauren still was.

"Sorry. But we've got Isaac Cardwell's killer. Sergeant Stanley told me you wanted to be in on the arrest."

Oliver Gosden sure as hell did.

"Be there in ten—"

The deputy chief heard a ripping sound at the back of his

house — a door or window screen being slashed open. This was followed by a low growl. A chill ran the length of Oliver's spine that tightened both his scalp and sphincter muscles.

The mountain lion was in his house. He knew it with absolute certainty.

"It's here!" Oliver whispered urgently, his throat suddenly so dry he had to fight to get the words out. "The mountain lion is in my house!"

That was all the time he could spare for the phone, but he had the presence of mind not to hang up. He laid the receiver on the nightstand so the line stayed open. Then he shook his wife once, firmly. When her eyes popped open and she recognized who he was, he covered her mouth with his palm.

"The mountain lion is in our house. I'm going to get it. Lock the bedroom door behind me, and don't open it until I tell you."

Oliver didn't have time to dispel the horror that appeared in Lauren's eyes. He grabbed his service weapon, and on instinct his Zippo lighter, from the nightstand.

Then he ran into the darkened hallway outside his bedroom.

Praying he got to Danny's open bedroom doorway before the big cat did.

Ron shouted at Sergeant Stanley to man line one on his phone, to maintain the connection to Deputy Chief Gosden's house at all costs. Then he and Corrie Knox sprinted to her 4x4. Ron drove, and Corrie grabbed her Winchester 94 from its bracket. Her fingers danced nervously on the stock and barrel as she held it. With the streets deserted, Ron raced toward Oliver's house without using his emergency lights or siren.

Neither he nor Corrie said a word.

Oliver was less than three feet from his son's room when the mountain lion appeared around the far corner of the hallway. The cat stopped and fixed Oliver with a feral stare. Its eyes glowed hypnotically. Its jaw dropped open and the lion gave a shrill, keening yowl that froze Oliver's soul.

But not his gunhand.

He raised his weapon to fire and —

"Daddy, daddy!" Daniel cried. "There's something bad outside my room! Come quick!"

The deputy chief took his eyes off the cat for only a split-second to look toward his son's room, and he knew instantly he'd made a terrible mistake. He felt as much as heard the cat leaping at him. There'd be no chance to get off a shot now. Maybe no chance to save himself at all.

Out of pure reflex, he dove for the opening of Danny's doorway, trying to hit it as low and fast as he could. He felt a blast of hot, fetid breath on his face. Out of the corner of his eye, he caught the blur of the mountain lion going by *above* him.

Time seemed to slow to a viscous crawl. Oliver floated through the air as lazily as if he were swimming just beneath the surface of a sunlit sea. The lion, having anticipated a stationary, upright target, drifted past high overhead, no more threatening than a fanciful balloon. All Oliver had to do to enter his son's room would be to simply twist a few muscles, bend a few joints, and let the breeze carry him along.

Suddenly, joltingly, painfully, the world rushed back to full speed with a bang. With a swipe so stunning it felt like his hand had been broken, the cat knocked Oliver's gun from his grasp. Next, he felt a flash of pain as scalpel-sharp claws raked his left calf muscle. Finally, he slammed shoulder-first into the doorjamb of Danny's room.

But he was too charged with fear and adrenaline to let any of these traumas incapacitate him — especially when the mountain lion's momentum carried it skidding along the polished hardwood floor affording him the opportunity to escape.

Oliver scrambled on his hands and knees into Danny's room and kicked the door shut.

Just before the cat slammed into it, shook the door in its frame, and howled in rage.

Ron pulled up at the Gosden house. Both he and Corrie heard the savage cry of the animal within the structure. But the lights in the house were extinguished and they couldn't tell who was where. They exchanged a tense look.

"Any other situation," Ron said, "I want as much backup as I can get."

Corrie shook her head.

"Cops aren't trained for this. Too many guns, too many frayed nerves, and we're more likely to shoot the Gosdens, each other, or some neighbor in her nightgown."

And lights in the neighboring houses were coming on in response to the lion's continued uproar.

"We've got to go in now," Corrie said, "before we draw a crowd."

"Or a neighbor opens up with *his* gun." Ron gave Corrie a quick description of the layout of the Gosden house. "Okay, I'll take the front door, you take the back. But we have to do one more thing first."

Ron radioed Sergeant Stanley, told him to advise whomever he could raise on the Gosden's phone line of their movements. He didn't want Oliver to blow away either of his would-be rescuers.

Oliver leaned his weight against the door to his son's room as the big cat slammed into it with another thunderous crash. The deputy chief didn't give way, but the hinges on the doorjamb were starting to yield. If the hardware went, keeping the beast out might be more than he could manage.

Fucking thing had to be getting a running start from the bathroom across the hall, the deputy chief figured. Then he just threw himself at the door with everything he had. That, and bellowed and snarled for all he was worth.

Oliver was past fear and in a rage himself. He wanted that motherfucker *now.* He was half-tempted to throw the door open, half-sure he could strangle the sonofabitch with his bare hands. The lion hit the door and howled again. Oliver roared right back at it.

"Daddy, make it *stop!*" Daniel pleaded through a veil of tears. "Shoot it, shoot it!"

If Oliver'd had his gun, he would have. Right through the door. Now, however, he had to think of something else. He wasn't quite berserk enough to go the barehanded route. And he wasn't going to open the door at all until Danny was out of harm's way.

There was a momentary lull. The cat had backed off and was quiet. Danny was sobbing softly. Oliver had a moment to look around and think. He saw a broom in the corner. His son had been earning his quarter a day keeping his room neat. At the same time, Oliver realized he still had his Zippo held tight in his left fist.

"Danny," he whispered. "Hand me that broom, son. Go on bring it to me."

The little boy looked bewildered, but he wasn't going to question his father at a time like this. He brought him the broom. Then he stepped back and instructed Oliver quietly, "Daddy, you can't hurt a lion with a broom."

Despite everything, Oliver had to smile.

"Danny," he said in a soft, soothing voice, "I want you to go into your closet now. Close the door and don't open it for anything, unless Mom or I come to get you. Can you do that?"

"I'll be scared."

"The lion won't be able to get you in there, son."

"I'll be scared for you."

"Danny, we're all going to be fine. And what I'm going to do to that cat, I don't want you to see. Now, go on, son. Right away." Oliver took a step away from the door to urge Danny on his way with a gentle pat on his bottom.

He watched as his son ran into the closet and pulled the door shut tight behind him.

Then he knew just what he had to do.

But before he could do a thing there was a knock on the wall between the two bedrooms. Lauren told him Ron Ketchum and Corrie Knox were about to enter the house with weapons drawn.

That changed everything. What he had to do now, Oliver

decided, was sit tight.

That plan lasted only the second it took for Danny's bedroom door to explode open, smack the deputy chief square in the face, and knock him on his ass.

But once again the momentum of the mountain lion's charge made it overshoot its prey. When it turned, however, Oliver was still down and trying to clear the cobwebs from his head. A stunned victim. An easy kill. In the split-second before the predator could pounce, however, Daniel Gosden, having heard the commotion, and sensing the big cat was near, screamed in fear from the refuge of his closet. Then Lauren Gosden shrieked from the next bedroom, voicing the horror a mother knows when her child is threatened. The two outbursts confused the cat.

There was more prey nearby, but the lion couldn't see it.

But the cat heard the click-slam of a door being thrown open and footsteps racing toward it. Then there was another two-legged creature in the doorway of the room, joining the one that was just picking itself up.

"Oliver, where's Danny?" Lauren shouted, her eyes scanning the room and not finding her son.

"Here I am, Mommy," the boy called from the closet, not two feet from the cat. He started to open the door to run to his mother.

The mountain lion immediately knew which of these creatures it would take first.

But that was when the deputy chief flicked his Zippo lighter and turned the broom's bristles into a blazing torch.

Ron could wait no longer. He threw his shoulder into the Gosden's front door with all his strength. The deadbolt held and so did the hinges, but the hollow-core door split right down the middle. The chief fell to his knees as it gave way. He quickly looked up to see if the big cat was bearing down on him. It wasn't. He was safe for the moment.

But there was an ungodly racket of screams, shouts, and snarls coming from the bedroom wing of the house.

Corrie got there first, having slipped easily through the slash made by the cat in the screen door at the rear of the house. She saw Deputy Chief Gosden holding a flaming broom, backing the cat into a corner as it snarled and snapped at him, trying to bat the broom from his hand.

But the deputy chief held tight, and suddenly a little boy burst from a closet in the opposite corner and ran screaming to his mother. The cat made a lunge for him and got its face singed for its trouble. The child made it to his mother's arms, but the flames on the broom had almost consumed their fuel and the fire was dwindling, ready to expire.

"Deputy Chief!" Corrie yelled. "Stand clear, give me a shot!"

But before the fire went out completely, Oliver Gosden roared and charged the cat, intending to drive the broom handle right down the animal's throat.

The cat may have been old, but it was still far too quick to be taken by such a clumsy attack — and it, too, was enraged. It coiled itself into a compact ball and sprang from its rear legs. The big cat cleared the burning end of the broom … and there was Oliver's throat right in front of it. The mountain lion opened its jaws and turned its head to rip away its prey's soft exposed flesh in one savage bite.

Ron skidded into the doorway of the bedroom just as Corrie Knox fired her Winchester. He saw the top of the lion's skull cleave off as the round caught the animal in mid-air. It was, without question, a killing shot. But the slug didn't have the stopping power to knock the big cat aside. The lion's momentum carried it straight into the deputy chief and slammed him backwards to the floor.

Even in death, the cat's jaws still closed around Oliver's face.

Daniel Gosden screamed, but the three adults in the room raced forward to aid the fallen man. Ron and Corrie levered the mountain lion's jaws open, and Lauren by herself dragged her husband, who outweighed her by eighty pounds, from beneath the cat's carcass.

At that moment, everyone finally heard the sirens of the

emergency vehicles that were just then pulling up out front. The neighbors hadn't opened fire, but they hadn't sat by idly, either.

Ron looked at Oliver, the dead mountain lion, and then at Corrie.

"We ever need a SWAT officer around here, I know who I'm calling," he said.

Corrie Knox's shot had deflected the mountain lion's head just enough. Oliver Gosden suffered puncture wounds to his right cheek and the tissue just inside his lower jaw. Getting slammed to the floor had produced a moderate concussion. The lacerations to his calf were cleaned and bandaged on site. It wasn't until the following day, when the deputy chief regained his senses, that anyone realized two of the metacarpals in his right hand had been fractured as well.

Corrie Knox insisted she was fine. She sat down in an easy chair in the living room and let a paramedic take her pulse and check her heartbeat, but she insisted nothing was wrong. She even tossed back a shot of scotch Lauren brought her, though she said she didn't usually drink hard liquor.

But there was a twitch at the corner of her left eye that wouldn't stop. Corrie wasn't even aware of it, denied having it until one of the paramedics held up a mirror in front of her.

The paramedics insisted on taking her to the hospital for observation.

Ron added, "Wouldn't want it to ruin your jump shot. Not when we've got that one on one game coming up."

The game warden rode in the same ambulance with the deputy chief, Lauren and Danny following immediately behind in the Gosden family car. While the cat's body was being bagged, Ron called Clay Steadman. He told the mayor of the mountain lion's demise.

He also told him who had killed Isaac Cardwell, and when the mayor wanted to be in on the arrest, the chief of police told him no.

"This is my job," Ron said. "We're going to do it my way."

Ron's way was to be as careful as he could. He had units block off all the streets approaching Art Gilbert's house. Gilbert's three closest neighbors were contacted by phone. Over the course of ninety minutes, at irregular intervals, they quietly got in their cars and drove away. Ron gave his people their orders, and at exactly midnight he drove onto Art Gilbert's property.

Ron's patrol unit set off motion detectors. Floodlights came on, making the vehicle a perfect target.

The house wasn't as grand as any of the estates or mansions at which Gilbert had toiled, but it was a cozy, well-maintained home nonetheless. A wood frame structure painted a pearl gray with a charcoal roof and trim, it was bounded on two sides by screened-in porches. The grounds weren't large, but they were as impeccably landscaped as any property in town.

Uneasy but undaunted, Ron got out of his patrol unit and walked toward the house. As he did, he tripped another motion detector. Another light came on. It pinned the chief like a bug on a board. Ron's hand went to his handgun, but he didn't pull it from his holster.

"What can I do for you, Chief?" Art Gilbert called from the darkness of the near porch.

Ron could barely make him out. Gilbert was little more than a denser inkblot in the blackness of the porch.

"Step outside where I can see you. That'll do for a start, Mr. Braddock."

For a moment there was no response to Ron's use of the man's real name. The timer where Ron parked his patrol unit clicked off the first floodlight. Ron knew if he stood still he'd soon be in darkness himself.

He said, "I know you killed Isaac Cardwell, Mr. Braddock. My deputy chief knows, too. So does Mayor Steadman — and so do all the police officers who have your house surrounded right now. If you come with me now, peacefully, things will work out as well as they possibly can. When we get to the station, I'll let you call a lawyer, or make your statement, before I put you in a cell."

"How did you find out?"

The timer shut off the second light, leaving both men to continue their dialogue in the dark.

Ron hadn't really articulated his thought process for himself before that moment. He had to work it out before he could answer Gilbert. Braddock. He wasn't even sure what he should call the killer.

"The first thing that struck me," Ron began, "was an inconsistency. I couldn't reconcile how a guy who looked like you — a seemingly upright, maybe even uptight, guy — could keep working at Jimmy Thunder's place after he'd heard about something as heavy as money-laundering going on. It didn't seem to fit. You remember how I asked you about that? But then it just wasn't a flinty live and let live attitude, or loyalty to a client, was it?"

"It was loyalty to my son," Braddock said flatly.

"I was glad to have your help at first, pointing the finger at Didi DuPree and, later on, at Colin Ring. I couldn't believe my luck having someone close to Jimmy Thunder who could feed me information. It seemed too good to be true, and it was. Your little tidbits were meant to distract me from thinking about you. And for a while there, it worked."

"You still haven't told me how you found out."

"Your work had a lot to do with it. You're so damn good. Everything you touch, you make beautiful. Lawns, shrubs, flowers, trees. Every *living* thing."

The chief thought his man might respond to his last comment, but he didn't.

Ron continued, "Then people kept making these comments to me, or at least in my presence. Taken separately, they didn't mean much. But at some subconscious level they meshed, and when they did it came at just the right place and just the right time. And I knew it had to be you.

"The first thing I heard was from my father, of all people. He told me that Isaac Cardwell's death wasn't the work of your run of the mill, shit-for-brains racists. He said the picture he saw of the crucifixion was too *artistic.*

"Then Ezra Tilden spoke out at our town meeting. He said he thought the killer should also be crucified, but it should be to a *dead* tree, so no living thing would be hurt."

That drew a grunt from the porch.

"Finally, Clay Steadman told me you'd have made a great film director because you have a natural sense of visual composition. And the last time I saw the tree where you nailed Isaac Cardwell, there were four boys there staging a mock crucifixion, and I got to see just what a powerful image it was. A living person being nailed to a *dead* tree. It was only a few minutes later that everything clicked for me."

Ron paused to let Braddock respond, but the man remained silent.

"You killed a wonderful man in Isaac Cardwell but you couldn't bring yourself to drive nails into a healthy tree. Or maybe it was just that instinct you have for making a visual statement. Either way, it put me on your trail.

"I found out you arrived in town after Jimmy Thunder did. You followed him here. I talked to Thunder's next-door neighbor. You solicited their business, then let Jimmy see the wonders you worked for them. So he came to you. That was a very nice touch. The murder weapon you threw off the Tightrope is in a crime lab in Sacramento right now. It won't surprise me at all to hear it has your fingerprints and tissue samples from Isaac Cardwell's head on it. You never thought anyone would find it. Today I found a videotape of you buying the kind of nails used in the crime. Finally, tonight, I received a phone call from someone who identified you as Roger Braddock's father."

Now, Ron heard a sob come from the darkened house.

"I think you better come out now, Mr. Braddock," the chief said.

Arthur Gilbert Braddock didn't come out, though. He started

shooting. He missed Ron, but he got him moving. That tripped the motion detectors and turned on the floodlights. The chief was an easy target now, even as he dove for cover behind a neatly clipped row of hedges.

Ron wasn't the only one whose position was exposed. The beams from half a dozen police searchlights inundated the Gilbert house in a glaring wash of light. The white haired man stood revealed, tears running down a face twisted in despair and agony. He continued to fire a semi-automatic handgun until he ran out of rounds — but every shot was directed into the floor of the porch on which he stood.

The officers of the Goldstrike PD held their fire. Their orders were to shoot only if they were taking fire or an officer went down. Seeing that their chief was unhurt, they showed flawless restraint, not firing a round.

There wasn't an officer among them who could have fired on Art Gilbert.

None of them believed in assisted suicide.

When his gun was empty, Gilbert ducked back into the house.

Ron ran after him. He wanted to take the man alive. Sergeant Stanley and several more officers were on the chief's heels. Every cop had his weapon drawn. They crossed the porch and entered the house through the kitchen.

A light went on in a room just ahead. There was a scramble of grunting bodies as the cops pressed themselves against walls and ducked behind kitchen cabinets and appliances. There was no telling when somebody who wanted to end it all might change his mind, get mad, and decide to take someone else with him. But no shots were fired. Respiration and heart rates slowly fell back into normal ranges. Sweat cooled and trigger fingers relaxed marginally.

Ron poked his head around the corner.

Gilbert sat in a wing chair next to a fireplace. He had a gun in his lap. Not the semi-auto he'd had on the porch, but a revolver. Presumably loaded. Ron gestured to his people to stay back, and then walked into the room. He took a seat opposite Gilbert.

Arthur Gilbert Braddock pointed his weapon directly at Ron's head.

Ron had his own weapon in his hand, but didn't respond — and he prayed that nobody would open fire from the kitchen.

"You're just not going to shoot me, are you?" Art Gilbert asked.

Ron shook his head and said, "I've already killed one man. I hope to God there won't be a second."

Gilbert nodded, and pointed his gun at his own head.

"Have to do it myself, then."

Ron made no move to stop him, but for his own peace of mind he asked, "Why did you kill Isaac Cardwell instead of Jimmy Thunder?"

Gilbert blinked several times. Tears fell from his eyes, which he brushed away with the back of his gun hand. He let the hand fall to his lap. Ron didn't take this as a weakening of suicidal resolve. The man could still shoot himself or Ron, for that matter, in a heartbeat.

"That was my original intention," Gilbert said. "From the very moment I heard what happened to Roger, I had it in mind to kill Jimmy Leverette. Jimmy Thunder. To kill the bastard who murdered my beautiful boy. I never said a word about what I wanted to do. Never went to Thunder's trial. Never spoke to the press. Didn't even say a word to my wife … but she knew. Eventually, it cost me my marriage.

"When Thunder was in prison, I made one allowance in my thinking. If someone else killed him in there, I'd be satisfied. Every day he was behind bars I prayed that somebody would knife him. But I guess there are some prayers God just won't answer.

"I left home when we got the word that he was getting out. My wife begged me not to go, and when I did, that was the end for us. She was the one who put together that tape of how wonderful Roger had been. She thought if she could bring shame and public condemnation down on our boy's killer that would be enough for me.

"What it did, though, was open all my old wounds, break my heart all over again, make me hate that bastard worse than ever. The other thing it did, of course, was to *create* Jimmy Thunder. The reaction to my boy's death was to make his killer rich and famous. There was no way I was going to let that go unavenged. Not if it took me 'til my dying day to get even.

"But it's a lot harder to get close to a man who's rich and famous. There's always a pack of hangers-on around him. And to do it in a way where you have any chance of … of not going to prison yourself, that's more trouble still. But I had faith. God might have let me down, but I wasn't going to let Roger down. I knew somehow or other I'd get close to Reverend Thunder, and it took me the better part of five years to work everything out, but I did it."

"Then why didn't you kill him instead of his son?" Ron wanted to know.

"That's the funny part," Gilbert answered. "See, after I got close enough to the man to start making serious plans, I saw just how pathetic he was. What he called his *ministry* was just a sham. A *scam*, as you cops like to call it. And folks were starting to catch on. There weren't as many buses coming to his TV studio as there once were. Him and that Deacon character, I heard them talking more than once about losing everything.

"Then that other fella showed up, and I heard him talking to Thunder about money-laundering. So I knew the man I hated was about to go broke or go crooked. If it was crooked, I figured I'd hear something soon enough to pass on to the police, and I could be the one to send him back to prison. Either way, broke or back behind bars, the bastard would be ruined and, to my great surprise, I decided that was enough for me. Then I could go home and try to make peace with my wife."

A pained, almost wistful look flitted through Gilbert's eyes, as he thought of what might have been. But it was soon replaced with an expression of renewed hatred and deep anger.

"Then that Isaac Cardwell had to show up out of the blue," Gilbert said harshly. "I hadn't even known Thunder had a son. But there he was, talking to his daddy in the garden I designed, and his boy was starting to convince Thunder that he had a true gift, a real calling, what could be the beginning of an *honest* ministry. All he had to do was give up the big house, the whores, and the scammed money. Do that, Cardwell said, and Thunder could save his own soul and a lot of others.

"Of course, that idea didn't go down easy. The boy was asking a tiger to change his stripes, giving up all his high living. Then there was that money-laundering fella to think about, too. He didn't seem the sort to take kindly to somebody backing out of a deal with him. But Cardwell kept after his daddy right up to the night he kicked him out of his house."

Art Gilbert fell silent and his eyes went to the gun he held in his lap.

"But you knew Isaac Cardwell would ultimately succeed, didn't you?" Ron asked.

Gilbert nodded. "Felt it in my bones. Knew it before the reverend did. That boy was going to banish Jimmy Thunder and redeem Jimmy Leverette. And that was the one thing I just could not allow to happen. There could be no redemption for my Roger's killer. There could be only pain and misery. Just like mine.

"That was when the idea hit me. A son for a son. Let Thunder know just how I've felt all these years. What could be better? So the night Thunder threw his boy out, I followed him to St. Mark's. I watched him a while from the back of the church, and when he came out I waylaid him."

Gilbert gave a short, dry laugh and shook his head.

"You were right about instinct. I never *thought* about nailing him to a dead tree. It's just that I'd seen the thing so many times driving past it, it must have stuck in my mind. Suggested itself as just the place for what I wanted to do."

"But why *crucify* Cardwell?" Ron wanted to know.

This time Gilbert's laughter was bitter.

"He wanted to redeem his father? *That's* how you die to take away people's sins."

Ron nodded. Then he asked, "Who's going to forgive yours?"

The look on Gilbert's face showed he'd considered the question himself — and hadn't arrived at an answer.

The chief continued, "You want to kill yourself, go ahead. But you'll be closing the book on your own story. And what you've done to Isaac Cardwell will probably eclipse what Jimmy Thunder did to your son. Maybe it'll even let Thunder have the last word on the matter. On the other hand, if you stick around, you get to tell your side to the public. Torment Jimmy Thunder for years. And as screwed up as our courts are, who knows what your ultimate sentence will be?"

Arthur Gilbert Braddock needed less than a minute to consider his alternatives. A grim smile formed on his face. He carefully handed his gun to Ron.

Gilbert was informed of his Miranda rights and taken to police headquarters. He was placed in a cell with a suicide watch, in case he had second thoughts about what he wanted to do with the remainder of his life. The Alta County D.A.'s office was informed of the arrest. They were pleased to hear about the arrest, but concerned that Ron had let Gilbert spill his guts *before* he'd been Mirandized. Ron pointed out that Gilbert hadn't been placed under arrest at the time he'd confessed ... but sorting out the legalities was up to the lawyers now.

Ron, meanwhile, had a call to make. He picked up his phone and tapped out Jimmy Thunder's number. The man answered the call himself. Ron told him, "We have your son's killer. Why don't you come talk to me ... and leave Marcus Martin at home."

The reverend arrived fifteen minutes later, looking even worse than the last time the chief had seen him. But he took his seat and came straight to the point.

"Who killed my son?"

"Art Gilbert." When Ron saw the look of complete bafflement — Thunder really hadn't known who he'd let inside his gate these past two years — he elaborated. "Arthur Gilbert Braddock."

Recognition was immediate. The circle was closed. What Jimmy Leverette had begun in a hotel bar in Dallas had ended on a mountainside in California. The man seemed to wither in his chair. Tears formed at the corners of Jimmy Thunder's reddened eyes, and for a moment it seemed to Ron as if he were crying blood.

The reverend hung his head. In a voice almost too soft for Ron to hear, he confessed, "I saw Isaac nailed to that tree. I must have been the first one to see him. After I kicked him out, after I called off my card game early, I went out looking for him. I wanted to ask him to forgive me. To tell him he was right, and I was wrong. To tell him I wasn't strong enough to do what he wanted of me. To say I was sorry for sending him away.

"When I found him on that tree, I knew God was punishing me. I got out of my car and fell down to my knees and wept. I begged for God's forgiveness … but I was sure even Jesus couldn't forgive me. I got back in my car and drove away as fast as I could, as if I could run from my sins."

"Why didn't you call the police?" Ron wanted to know.

Jimmy Thunder looked up. "I was afraid. Afraid that I'd be blamed for killing Isaac. I knew that Mahalia Cardwell would make sure of that."

Ron couldn't argue with that assessment.

"And … I thought if I was blamed the real killer would get away. I didn't want that." Jimmy Thunder raised his hands in front of him and formed them into fists. "I wanted vengeance. I wanted to lay my hands on my son's killer and choke the life out of him. My son had come to save me. To warn me about Colin Ring, who thought Isaac would spy for him. But he didn't. He tried to show me the way to salvation. He persuaded me to abandon the idea of profaning my ministry by using it as a shell for Didi DuPree's schemes. He did this even though he knew I'd beaten his mother and abandoned him as an infant."

"He believed in his calling," Ron replied quietly.

Thunder nodded, tears sliding off his chin.

"That's just what I have to do now. Follow the path my boy

marked out for me. Be the man Isaac urged me to be, prayed for me to be. I'm going to start a new ministry. One that renounces the tithings of Caesar and offers praise to God."

Meaning Art Gilbert helped to bring about just what he'd feared most, Ron thought. The salvation of Jimmy Thunder.

Then Thunder surprised Ron and made it indelibly clear that the reverend was sincere in his new mission.

Jimmy Thunder told him, "And to honor the spirit of forgiveness and love that Isaac showed me, I'm going to start my ministry by pleading for clemency for his killer. Art Gilbert. The man whose life I ruined."

CHAPTER 54

Friday

The next morning, Ron drove out to Clay Steadman's house to pick up Mahalia Cardwell and take her to the bus depot for the trip back to Oakland. The mayor had already bid the old woman farewell, and he had left for Los Angeles to begin pre-production on his next movie. When Ron arrived at the house, Clay's houseman escorted the chief to the bedroom where Mahalia Cardwell was finishing her packing.

Despite the arrest of her grandson's killer, she was not in the same forgiving mood her former son-in-law had been. On the contrary, she was more angry and bitter than ever.

"Mountain lion's dead, Mrs. Cardwell," Ron told her. "You think that means God knows we got the right man for Isaac's murder?"

"I'm not talking to you," the old woman said.

That was okay with the chief. He didn't want her to talk, only listen.

"I read Colin Ring's manuscript and notes. That let me know just how consumed by hatred you really are. You wanted Jimmy Thunder to be the killer so badly it must be eating you up inside. For what you thought he did to Isaac, and what you know he did to your daughter. And when you told me you thought I was the right man for the job, you were just hoping that a white bigot like me would simply kill him somehow, if I couldn't get him any other way."

"That's exactly right, Mr. Chief of Police," the old woman said acidly. "You're a real disappointment to me."

Ron gently elbowed Mahalia Cardwell away from her packing, and started poking through her belongings.

The old woman shrieked, "Hey, you stop that! You can't take my things!"

"Just helping lighten your load, Mrs. Cardwell."

The chief pulled a semi-automatic handgun from the case. He looked at the pistol's make. "A Webley," he said. "British. Now, where would you get something like this?"

Mahalia Cardwell had nothing to say.

"Ring's notes say he bestowed a 'measure of protection' on you before Mayor Steadman took you into his home. Just in case someone confronted you personally about the *curse* you laid on the town. Of course, you could have used this gun, too, if you felt a certain rich black man was beyond the reach of justice. My deputy chief thought Ring was looking for a big ending to his book, and he was right. Having you kill Jimmy Thunder certainly would have filled the bill. But Colin Ring is dead now, Mrs. Cardwell. And all of Jimmy Thunder's dirty laundry has been hung out in public. He's using his son's memory to try to become a better person. Why don't you see if you can put your hurt behind you, and try to do the same?"

As before, Mahalia Cardwell had nothing to say to Ron Ketchum.

The media mob filed their stories about the arrest of Arthur Gilbert Braddock and the shooting of the lion. Braddock and his relentless quest for vengeance, and now Jimmy Thunder's amazing plea for leniency for him became the focus of the lead story. Warden Cordelia Knox's heroic shooting of the mountain lion became the focus of the other story.

Chief of Police Ronald Ketchum was mentioned in both stories, but he was given no particular credit for the happy outcomes in either case.

Rumor had it that Ben Dexter was planning a special on FBI

Special Agent Francis Horgan's relentless pursuit of racist church arsonists.

And a manila envelope arrived from the Berkeley Library. The harried librarian, in the conscientious fashion of her profession, had come through for Ron. Included among the material she'd sent was a photocopy of an article from *Sports Illustrated* on the death of Roger Braddock. Included in the story was a photo of the graveside service. Captured in the photo — and named in the caption — was the victim's father, Arthur Gilbert Braddock.

The man had gone to great lengths to avoid the media, but they'd nailed him anyway. And Isaac Cardwell had seen his picture seventeen years later.

The horde of reporters cleared out shortly before the Labor Day tourist crowds arrived.

Corrie Knox finally caught up with Ron in the gym at the rec center. He'd just drilled his ninety-fifth free throw in a row when she walked in. She wasn't wearing her new gym shoes.

"Just wanted to see you before I have to go," she told Ron.

"You have to leave right away?"

"Have to get that mountain lion to the lab for the necropsy. See if there was any biological reason for why it acted the way it did. I thought we might have had time for a bite to eat, but I had to keep answering questions for the media."

"Goddamn reporters."

"Hey, I'll be back. I think I'd like to spend a couple weeks here during ski season."

"I never learned to ski," Ron said.

"Then I'll have to teach you," Corrie replied with a smile. She stepped up to Ron, put her hands on his shoulders and gave him a kiss to keep him until she returned. Then a mischievous look entered her eyes. "Hey, you know what?"

"What?"

"Now would be a great time to show me how you can dunk the ball. That way you could spend the time until I get back thinking about the fantasies you want me to fulfill."

"You already did that."

Corrie snorted. "You ain't seen nothing yet. Of course, maybe you were just talking before. I mean, you're in good shape, but you are pretty *old* to dunk a basketball."

Ron knew she was exactly right. Every time he managed the feat, he always wondered if it would be his last time … and he'd already done it once today. And that was the maximum he tried for on any given visit to a gym. He thought any more than that might make him guilty of the sin of hubris. Might blow a knee, too.

"What's the matter?" Corrie asked wickedly. "Performance anxiety?"

"You know it," Ron agreed.

Then he sucked it up and stepped to the top of the key. He looked at the rim of the basket twenty feet away and put everything else in the world out of his mind. First, he steadied his breathing and then he deliberately built up the volume and speed of his respiration. As he launched into his first stride, he may even have shouted. But he couldn't be sure the sound came from him.

All he knew is that his body moved with a strength and ease he couldn't remember feeling for years. He dribbled the ball once as he always did. It came back to him perfectly, and he took off from the dotted line. That was when everything changed.

Normally he didn't let the rim out of his sight for a second, and he extended his arm until he felt the muscles in his shoulders scream but now … now he felt himself twisting in the air even as he continued to rise. He had the ball in both hands and was holding it at waist level. How the hell was he going to dunk with the ball there? *Jump* through the hoop?

No. He brought the ball up with both hands over his head and the rim was right there behind him, and a good foot below the ball. He stuffed it through to complete the reverse jam.

The first one he'd ever done in his life.

Not that he showed the surprise — the delight — he felt. He

just hung coolly from the rim for a second, looking at Corrie, before he dropped lightly to the floor.

"Boy, oh boy," she said with a broad smile, "are we going to have fun."

CHAPTER 55

Friday, the first week of September

Deputy Chief Oliver Gosden was back on patrol with Ron Ketchum. Oliver was behind the wheel. He drove carefully but without visible signs of nervousness across the Tightrope.

Since the episode with the mountain lion, Oliver had become a fatalist. He now firmly believed that when your time was up, you'd go. But not a minute earlier.

The Gosdens had been back in L.A. the past week on R&R.

"I almost decided to stay," he told Ron. "I thought I might see if I could get my rank back with the LAPD."

"And?"

"Lauren and Danny wouldn't hear of it. They like it here. Danny wants to bring all his cousins up and show them his room. Where Daddy and Warden Knox killed the mountain lion."

"That's better than him having nightmares."

"Lauren said she's a mountain woman now."

Ron nodded.

"My parents are thinking of moving up here, too."

"Good for them."

"They say things down in L.A. are getting to be too much to bear."

"There's something everywhere you go," Ron cautioned.

"We still got all those drunks outside that new bar?"

"Now that you mention it, yeah. And the burglary calls are still creeping up. And we still haven't found that floating poker game, either."

"Maybe Texas Jack could help us with that."

"Maybe he could."

Chief Ketchum and Deputy Chief Gosden of the Goldstrike Police Department talked about crime and race, and completed their morning rounds.

ABOUT THE AUTHOR

Joseph Flynn has been published both traditionally — Signet Books, Bantam Books and Variance Publishing — and through his own imprint, Stray Dog Press, Inc. Both major media reviews and reader reviews have praised his work. Booklist said, "Flynn is an excellent storyteller." The *Chicago Tribune* said, "Flynn [is] a master of high-octane plotting." The most repeated reader comment is: "Write faster, we want more."

The Jim McGill Series
The President's Henchman, A Jim McGill Novel, #1
The Hangman's Companion, A Jim McGill Novel, #2
The K Street Killer, A Jim McGill Novel, #3
Part 1: The Last Ballot Cast, A Jim McGill Novel, #4
Part 2: The Last Ballot Cast, A Jim McGill Novel, #4
The Devil on the Doorstep, A Jim McGill Novel, #5
Short Cases 1-3, Three Jim McGill Short Stories

The Ron Ketchum Mystery Series
Nailed, A Ron Ketchum Mystery, #1
Defiled, A Ron Ketchum Mystery, 2

The John Tall Wolf Series
Tall Man in Ray-Bans, A John Tall Wolf Novel, #1

Other novels *[continued on next page]*

Round Robin, A Love Story of Epic Proportions
One False Step
Blood Street Punx
Still Coming
Still Coming Expanded Edition
Farewell Performance
Hot Type
Gasoline, Texas
The Next President
Digger
The Concrete Inquisition

If you would like to contact Joe, or read free excerpts of his books, please visit www.josephflynn.com.

www.ingramcontent.com/pod-product-compliance
Lightning Source LLC
LaVergne TN
LVHW020519100826
845148LV00010B/1285

* 9 7 8 0 9 8 3 7 9 7 5 1 7 *